Acclaim for Kathleen Fuller

"Sparks fly between a forthright heroine and a practical joker with a protective streak . . . but they're not the kind of sparks Charity Raber longs for after embarking on a courtship plan. The two can't agree on anything except that they definitely don't belong together. Does God have a different plan? Kathleen Fuller will keep you guessing with her endearing characters, compelling writing, and unexpected plot twists. A heartwarming and humorous read."

—RACHEL J. GOOD, *USA TODAY* BESTSELLING AUTHOR OF
THE SURPRISED BY LOVE SERIES, ON *THE COURTSHIP PLAN*

"Kathleen Fuller is a gifted storyteller! Her latest, *The Courtship Plan*, made me laugh through the hilarity of Charity Raber—but also cry as Charity deals with trauma in a believable way. Endearing characters and precious life lessons make this novel another heartfelt winner!"

—LESLIE GOULD, BESTSELLING AUTHOR OF
PIECING IT ALL TOGETHER

"Return to Birch Creek for another delightful Amish Mail-Order Bride Novel by Kathleen Fuller. *Love in Plain* Sight combines Fuller's engaging style with a strong plot and compelling characters who will steal your heart. Don't miss this 'must read' story that's sure to remain a lifetime favorite."

—DEBBY GIUSTI, *USA TODAY* AND *PUBLISHERS WEEKLY*
BESTSELLING AUTHOR OF *SMUGGLERS IN AMISH COUNTRY*

"Kathleen Fuller's emotional and evocative writing draws readers into her complex stories and keeps them cheering for her endearing characters even after the final page."

—PATRICIA DAVIDS, *USA TODAY* BESTSELLING AUTHOR

"Katharine Miller has everything she ever wants, until she realizes what she's gotten. *Love in Plain Sight* is Kathleen Fuller at her best. She shines the spotlight on an unlikely heroine who runs away to find herself . . . and discovers what true love looks like."

—SUZANNE WOODS FISHER, BESTSELLING
AUTHOR OF MENDING FENCES

"Fuller continues her Amish Mail-Order Brides of Birch Creek series (following A Double Dose of Love) with the pleasing story of Margaret, the youngest of four sisters who visits Birch Creek, Ohio, to stay with her aunt and uncle to avoid the temptations of Englischer life . . . This charming outing, filled as it is with forgiveness, redemption, and new beginnings, will delight Fuller's fans."

—PUBLISHERS WEEKLY ON MATCHED AND MARRIED

"This is a cute story of two sets of twins learning to grow up and be adults on their own terms and finding love along the way. It is another start of a great series."

—PARKERSBURG NEWS AND SENTINEL ON A DOUBLE DOSE OF LOVE

"Fuller (The Innkeeper's Bride) launches her Amish Mail-Order Brides series with the sweet story of love blooming between two pairs of twins . . . Faith and forgiveness form the backbone of this story, and the vulnerable sibling relationships are sure to tug at readers' heartstrings. This innocent romance is a treat."

—PUBLISHERS WEEKLY ON A DOUBLE DOSE OF LOVE

"Fuller cements her reputation [as] a top practitioner of Amish fiction with this moving, perceptive collection."

—PUBLISHERS WEEKLY ON
AMISH GENERATIONS

"Fuller brings us compelling characters who stay in our hearts long after we've read the book. It's always a treat to dive into one of her novels."

—BETH WISEMAN, BESTSELLING AUTHOR OF HEARTS
IN HARMONY, ON THE INNKEEPER'S BRIDE

"A beautiful Amish romance with plenty of twists and turns and a completely satisfying, happy ending. Kathleen Fuller is a gifted storyteller."

—JENNIFER BECKSTRAND, AUTHOR OF *HOME ON HUCKLEBERRY HILL*, ON *THE INNKEEPER'S BRIDE*

"I always enjoy a Kathleen Fuller book, especially her Amish stories. *The Innkeeper's Bride* did not disappoint! From the moment Selah and Levi meet each other to the last scene in the book, this was a story that tugged at my emotions. The story deals with several heavy issues such as mental illness and family conflicts, while still maintaining humor and couples falling in love, both old and new. When Selah finds work at the inn Levi is starting up with his family, they clash on everything but realize they have feelings for each other. My heart hurt for Selah as she held her secrets close and pushed everyone away. But in the end, God's grace and love, along with some misguided Birch Creek matchmakers stirring up mischief, brings them together. Weddings at a beautiful country inn? What's not to love? Readers of Amish fiction will enjoy this winter-time story of redemption and hope set against the backdrop of a beautiful inn that brings people together."

—LENORA WORTH, AUTHOR OF *THEIR AMISH REUNION*

"A warm romance that will tug at the hearts of readers, this is a new favorite."

—*THE PARKERSBURG NEWS AND SENTINEL* ON *THE TEACHER'S BRIDE*

"Fuller's appealing Amish romance deals with some serious issues, including depression, yet it also offers funny and endearing moments."

—*BOOKLIST* ON *THE TEACHER'S BRIDE*

"Kathleen Fuller's *The Teacher's Bride* is a heartwarming story of unexpected romance woven with fun and engaging characters who come to life on every page. Once you open the book, you won't put it down until you've reached the end."

—AMY CLIPSTON, BESTSELLING AUTHOR OF *A SEAT BY THE HEARTH*

"Kathleen Fuller's characters leap off the page with subtle power as she uses both wit and wisdom to entertain! Refreshingly honest and charming, Kathy's writing reflects a master's touch when it comes to intricate plotting and a satisfying and inspirational ending full of good cheer!"

—KELLY LONG, NATIONAL BESTSELLING
AUTHOR, ON *THE TEACHER'S BRIDE*

"Kathleen Fuller is a master storyteller, and fans will absolutely fall in love with Ruby and Christian in *The Teacher's Bride*."

—RUTH REID, BESTSELLING AUTHOR OF *A MIRACLE OF HOPE*

"*The Teacher's Bride* features characters who know what it's like to be different, to not fit in. What they don't know is that's what makes them so loveable. Kathleen Fuller has written a sweet, oftentimes humorous, romance that reminds readers that the perfect match might be right in front of their noses. She handles the difficult topic of depression with a deft touch. Readers of Amish fiction won't want to miss this delightful story."

—KELLY IRVIN, BESTSELLING AUTHOR OF
THE EVERY AMISH SEASON SERIES

"Kathleen Fuller is a talented and gifted author, and she doesn't disappoint in *The Teacher's Bride*. The story will captivate you from the first page to the last with Ruby, Christian, and other engaging characters. You'll laugh, gasp, and wonder what will happen next. You won't want to miss reading this heartwarming Amish story of mishaps, faith, love, forgiveness, and friendship."

—MOLLY JEBBER, SPEAKER AND AWARD-WINNING AUTHOR OF *GRACE'S FORGIVENESS* AND THE AMISH KEEPSAKE POCKET QUILT SERIES

"Enthusiasts of Fuller's sweet Amish romances will savor this new anthology."

—*LIBRARY JOURNAL* ON *AN AMISH FAMILY*

"These four sweet stories are full of hope and promise along with misunderstandings and reconciliation. True love does prevail, but not without prayer, introspection, and humility. A must-read for fans of Amish romance."

—RT BOOK REVIEWS, 4 STARS, ON AN AMISH FAMILY

"The incredibly engaging Amish Letters series continues with a third story of perseverance and devotion, making it difficult to put down . . . Fuller skillfully knits together the lives within a changing, faithful community that has suffered its share of challenges."

—RT BOOK REVIEWS, 4½ STARS, ON WORDS FROM THE HEART

"Fuller's inspirational tale portrays complex characters facing real-world problems and finding love where they least expected or wanted it to be."

—BOOKLIST, STARRED REVIEW, ON A RELUCTANT BRIDE

"Fuller has an amazing capacity for creating damaged characters and giving insights into their brokenness. One of the better voices in the Amish fiction genre."

—CBA RETAILERS + RESOURCES ON A RELUCTANT BRIDE

"This promising series debut from Fuller is edgier than most Amish novels, dealing with difficult and dark issues and featuring well-drawn characters who are tougher than the usual gentle souls found in this genre. Recommended for Amish fiction fans who might like a different flavor."

—LIBRARY JOURNAL ON A RELUCTANT BRIDE

"Sadie and Aden's love is both sweet and hard-won, and Aden's patience is touching as he wrestles not only with Sadie's dilemma, but his own abusive past. Birch Creek is weighed down by the Troyer family's dark secrets, and readers will be interested to see how secondary characters' lives unfold as the series continues."

—RT BOOK REVIEWS, 4 STARS, ON A RELUCTANT BRIDE

"Kathleen Fuller's A Reluctant Bride tells the story of two Amish families whose lives have collided through tragedy. Sadie Schrock's stoic resolve will touch and inspire Fuller's fans, as will the story's concluding triumph of redemption."

—SUZANNE WOODS FISHER, BESTSELLING
AUTHOR OF *MENDING FENCES*

"Kathleen Fuller's *A Reluctant Bride* is a beautiful story of faith, hope, and second chances. Her characters and descriptions are captivating, bringing the story to life with the turn of every page."

—AMY CLIPSTON, BESTSELLING AUTHOR OF
A SEAT BY THE HEARTH

"The latest offering in the Middlefield Family series is a sweet love story with perfectly crafted characters. Fuller's Amish novels are written with the utmost respect for their way of living. Readers are given a glimpse of what it is like to live the simple life."

—*RT BOOK REVIEWS*, 4 STARS, ON *LETTERS TO KATIE*

"Fuller's second Amish series entry is a sweet romance with a strong sense of place that will attract readers of Wanda Brunstetter and Cindy Woodsmall."

—*LIBRARY JOURNAL* ON *FAITHFUL TO LAURA*

"Well-drawn characters and a homespun feel will make this Amish romance a sure bet for fans of Beverly Lewis and Jerry S. Eicher."

—*LIBRARY JOURNAL* ON *TREASURING EMMA*

"*Treasuring Emma* is a heartwarming story filled with real-life situations and well-developed characters. I rooted for Emma and Adam until the very last page. Fans of Amish fiction and those seeking an endearing romance will enjoy this love story. Highly recommended."

—BETH WISEMAN, BESTSELLING AUTHOR OF *HEARTS IN HARMONY*

"*Treasuring Emma* is a charming, emotionally layered story of the value of friendship in love and discovering the truth of the heart. A true treasure of a read!"

—KELLY LONG, NATIONAL BESTSELLING AUTHOR

THE COURTSHIP PLAN

Other Books by Kathleen Fuller

THE AMISH MAIL-ORDER BRIDE NOVELS
A Double Dose of Love
Matched and Married
Love in Plain Sight

THE AMISH BRIDES OF BIRCH CREEK NOVELS
The Teacher's Bride
The Farmer's Bride
The Innkeeper's Bride

THE AMISH LETTERS NOVELS
Written in Love
The Promise of a Letter
Words from the Heart

THE AMISH OF BIRCH CREEK NOVELS
A Reluctant Bride
An Unbroken Heart
A Love Made New

THE MIDDLEFIELD AMISH NOVELS
A Faith of Her Own

THE MIDDLEFIELD FAMILY NOVELS
Treasuring Emma
Faithful to Laura
Letters to Katie

The
COURTSHIP
PLAN

An Amish of Marigold Novel

KATHLEEN FULLER

 ZONDERVAN®

ZONDERVAN

The Courtship Plan

Copyright © 2023 by Kathleen Fuller

Requests for information should be addressed to:
Zondervan, *3900 Sparks Dr. SE, Grand Rapids, Michigan 49546*

Library of Congress Cataloging-in-Publication Data

Names: Fuller, Kathleen, author.
Title: The courtship plan: an Amish of Marigold novel / Kathleen Fuller.
Description: Grand Rapids, Michigan: Zondervan, [2023] | Series: Amish of
Marigold; 1 | Summary: "When confirmed Amish bachelor Jesse Bontrager
is set up with a woman determined to stay unmarried, sparks ignite as
they seek harmless revenge on his prankster brother"—Provided by
publisher.
Identifiers: LCCN 2022032902 (print) | LCCN 2022032903 (ebook) | ISBN
9780840712745 (paperback) | ISBN 9780840712769 (epub)
Subjects: BISAC: FICTION / Small Town & Rural | FICTION / Amish & Mennonite
| LCGFT: Romance fiction. | Christian fiction. | Novels.
Classification: LCC PS3606.U553 C68 2023 (print) | LCC PS3606.U553
(ebook) | DDC 813/.6—dc23/eng/20220715
LC record available at https://lccn.loc.gov/2022032902
LC ebook record available at https://lccn.loc.gov/2022032903

Zondervan titles may be purchased in bulk for educational, business, fundraising, or
sales promotional use. For information, please email SpecialMarkets@Zondervan.com.

Printed in the United States of America

23 24 25 26 27 LSC 10 9 8 7 6 5 4 3 2 1

To James. I love you.

Glossary

ab im kopp: crazy in the head

ach: oh

boppli: baby

bruder: brother

bu: boy

daed: dad

danki: thank you

Deitsch: Amish language

dumm: dumb

familye: family

frau: wife

geh: go

grossmammi: grandmother

grossvatter: grandfather

gut: good

Gute morgen: good morning

haus: house

hochmut: pride

kapp: white hat worn by Amish women

kinner: children

maedel/maed: young woman/young women

mamm: mom

mann: man

mei: my

mutter: mother

nee: no

nix: nothing

Ordnung: written and unwritten rules in an Amish district

schee: pretty/handsome

sehr: very

seltsam: weird

sohn: son

vatter: father

ya: yes

yer: your

Prologue

Where is he?

Charity Raber checked the clock on the wall of Diener's Diner and huffed. Ten minutes late. *He's going to stand me up. I just know it.*

She closed her eyes and drew in a deep breath. Now wasn't the time to panic. Just because she'd been stood up before—more than once, by more than one guy—didn't mean she would be today.

Be positive! Be confident! She'd repeated those two phrases this morning as she chose her most positive and confident outfit—a light-green short-sleeved dress that matched her eyes and a pristine white *kapp* reserved for church service only. Not only was she dressed for success, she was ready for it.

After a second or two, she opened her eyes and stared at the empty seat opposite her. She didn't feel positive. Or confident. Not even close.

Desperate to distract her doubt-filled mind, she straightened the silverware on her right. Moved the menu in front of her an inch to the left. Wiped off the drop of condensation sliding down the side of

1

her iced tea glass. All the while she tried to ignore the blend of Amish and English voices surrounding her, hoping no one would notice how long she'd been sitting alone at the booth.

She fought the urge to glance at the clock again. Folding her hands together, she stared straight ahead at the front door while warm, mid-May sunshine beamed through the window beside her.

Staring. Straight . . . ahead . . .

Her gaze flicked to the clock again. Only two minutes had passed? *Phooey.*

"Ready to order?"

She glanced up at Norene Yoder, one of three Amish waitresses working the lunch shift. Charity had interviewed for a waitress job at Diener's a month ago. By then she'd lived in Birch Creek for nearly a year, and her savings were almost depleted. She wasn't hired here or at the other two jobs she'd applied for—counter help at Yoder's Bakery and a clerk at the fabric store in Barton. "I'm sorry," each employer said after the interview. "I don't think you'd be a good fit." What did that even mean?

Norene was hired less than a week after she'd moved to Birch Creek in April. Charity was still looking for employment. *Double phooey.* Life was so easy for some people.

"Did you hear me?" Norene asked.

"I heard you," Charity muttered, her gaze aimed at the front door. "And no, I'm not ready to order yet." No reason to elaborate further. Her business wasn't Norene's business.

"Still waiting on *yer* friend?"

"I'm waiting on my *date.*"

Norene arched a pale-blond, perfectly shaped eyebrow, her silver eyes alight with curiosity. "You have a date? We live across the hall from each other and you never said a word."

Norene was one of the prettiest women Charity had ever seen, and she'd seen plenty since her arrival in Birch Creek. The town ebbed and flowed with single women from all over the country who had answered the same newspaper advertisement stating that Birch Creek was jam-packed with eligible bachelors. She couldn't recall the exact wording, but it was clear from the text that single men in this community were yearning for single women . . . and Charity was yearning for a husband.

Soon after she stepped off the bus from Cherry Springs, she realized the ad was misleading, in her case anyway. There were plenty of single men in the community, mostly from the same family. But—a big *but*—very few were ready for or even wanted marriage. Regardless, a few marriages had occurred, so Charity still held out hope that one day she would find the man of her dreams.

And then Norene showed up. Charity couldn't get a man to look at her twice, but every available man in the community noticed Norene.

"Who is he?" Norene pressed.

Charity frowned. Talk about nosy. Then again, Norene would get her answer anyway when he showed up. *If he showed up.* Perishing the thought, she smiled. "My date," she said with a touch of triumph, "is Jesse Bontrager."

Norene snickered. "*Nee.*"

"*Ya.*" Charity emphasized with a terse nod.

"Jesse's going out with *you?*"

She pressed her lips together and glanced down at the white laminate tabletop. Although she wanted to, she couldn't blame Norene's skepticism. When Nelson had pulled her aside after church last Sunday and told her Jesse wanted to meet her for a lunch date, she almost keeled over from shock.

Next to Ezra, Jesse was the most handsome of the eleven Bontrager brothers. Actually, there were only three to compare, since the older ones were married, and other than Ezra, who was already taken, Nelson was the only age-appropriate Bontrager. Nevertheless, tall, wiry, curly-headed Jesse was cute, even if she'd only seen him from afar. But lately the men in Birch Creek seemed to run in the opposite direction whenever she showed up, so she found it hard to believe anyone, including Jesse, was suddenly interested in her.

But when she asked Nelson to repeat himself, he said the *D* word again. *Date.* "He's too shy to ask," Nelson said. "So I'm asking for him."

Jesse had never struck her as shy. Then again she'd been so enamored with Ezra—and once he was unavailable, she'd set her sights on Nelson—that she hadn't paid much attention to Jesse. She'd even hoped that Nelson was going to ask her out, making Jesse's invitation more astonishing.

She wasn't disappointed, though. A date was a date. She'd never had one before. And the prospect of a date was what her dwindling hope and diminishing morale needed.

One date and she could prove herself. One date and she could show everyone she was worthy.

She lifted her chin. "*Ya.* I have a date with Jesse. And he'll be here any second, so we'll order after he arrives."

Norene's laughter faded. "You're joking, *ya*?"

"You don't believe me?"

She shook her head. "*Nee* one has been able to convince Jesse to date. Believe me, I've tried."

"I guess you're not his type then."

The last sliver of humor disappeared from Norene's eyes. "You think you are?"

"He's meeting *me* here. Not you."

Norene glanced around the diner. "I don't see him, and you've been waiting for almost twenty minutes."

"He'll be here. You'll see." *Everyone will.*

She rolled her eyes. "Let me know when you want some food. We're busy and you're taking up a table." She spun around and walked away.

Phooey. Charity slumped. Ever since Norene had arrived in Birch Creek and moved into the room across the hall from her at Stoll's Inn, life had been miserable. Okay, her life had been miserable before Norene moved in, but it was simpler to pin her disappointment and aggravation on someone else, and Norene made it easy.

Why was she interested in Jesse anyway? It wasn't as if she were lacking male attention, including Nelson's. Right before he'd talked to her about Jesse, Charity noticed Nelson couldn't keep his eyes off Norene. And why had she noticed? Because *she* couldn't keep her eyes off *him.*

Nelson was what, the third—or was it fourth?—Bontrager she'd tried to pursue, some more fervently than others. There was Ezra, who was now with Katharine Miller. Before him was Owen, although he never seemed to get the message and ended up marrying someone else. When Ezra had rejected her, she planned to move on to Nelson. And that didn't even count the four men she'd targeted as prospects who weren't Bontragers. Three of them were considerate when they declined her interest, but one wasn't. He'd called her weird and a pest. He wasn't the first one to throw those awful adjectives at her.

That honor was reserved for her mother.

She'd been the one to give her the ad in the first place, practically shoving Charity on a bus to Birch Creek the next day. At first Charity was glad for the chance to prove she wasn't *seltsam.* But after living in Birch Creek for almost a year, she was wondering if *Mamm* was right, that she was a square peg in a round hole that wouldn't fit in anywhere or with anyone.

Her throat burned. *Don't let anyone see you cry.*

Mamm had imparted that nugget of wisdom. *More like hit me over the head with it. Mamm* wasn't even her biological mother, but her stepmother who insisted Charity call her *mamm* since she and her father had married when Charity was eight years old, after her grandmother passed away. Grandmother had never called her *seltsam*.

She crossed her arms and looked at the clock again. Almost twenty-five minutes late. There was no reason to be this tardy for a date . . . except one. She caught Norene smirking at her from behind the front counter.

The ice in her tea was melting, her stomach was turning sour, and Norene was right. Jesse wasn't coming. Either Nelson had gotten his signals crossed with his brother, or he was playing a joke on her. It didn't matter which. Both thoughts made her chest squeeze.

She pulled her wallet out of her purse to leave a five-dollar bill on the table. More than the price of the tea, but she couldn't stomach facing Norene right now. As her fingertips touched the money, the bell above the diner door rang. She didn't bother to look up. Why should she? It wasn't like Jesse would appear for their date at this point. *Or ever.*

Despite the reality check, she lifted her eyes. Her whole body stilled, her hand halfway in the air and gripping a ten-dollar bill because it turned out that was the only amount she had with her. *Jesse.* He came after all.

He walked a few steps farther into the diner, his gaze darting back and forth as if searching for someone. She stuffed the ten back into her wallet, tossed it into her purse, and put her hands in her lap.

Then he turned to her . . . and the world stopped. The clock. Her heartbeat. The frustration always lingering around the edges of her emotions. All she could see and comprehend was the handsome man looking straight at her.

Or was it straight through her?

He shifted his gaze, did another search of the dining room, then shrugged and opened the glass door.

Oh *nee*! He was leaving! "Over here, Jesse!" she screeched.

The entire diner went silent. All eyes were on her, including Jesse's. She squirmed. She hadn't meant to sound that loud. Or that shrill.

His black brows knit above vibrant blue eyes as he met her gaze. Slowly he pointed to himself.

"*Ya*!" She shot from her seat and waved him over again, her hand flapping like a baby bird struggling to fly. "I saved you a seat!" The pitch in her tone jumped an octave. *Nope, not weird at all.*

His frown deepened, and for a second she feared he might leave for good this time. Thankfully he walked toward her.

She sat back down and tried to settle herself. *Be cool. Calm. Confident!* But when he stopped in front of the booth, she blurted, "Hi, hi, hi!"

"Uh, hi." He wasn't frowning as much now, but he still looked confused.

"You can sit here." She wagged her hand toward the seat across the table. "Sit right there."

Jesse glanced over his shoulder, then looked at her again. "Sorry, Charity. I'm supposed to meet Nelson for lunch."

"Oh *nee, nee, nee*." Why was she sounding like a terrified chipmunk? "You're meeting me!" She pointed to her chest with her thumb. "For lunch. Food. Lunch. With me."

He gaped at her.

"We're having a lunch date," she clarified since he didn't seem to comprehend words. "You. Me. Lunch. Foo—"

"Food. Got it." He frowned.

"Hi, Jesse." Norene appeared at his side, standing close to him. Too close.

"We're not ready to order," Charity said quickly. "So, shoo."

Both Norene and Jesse stared at her.

"Shoo?" Norene said, her silver irises turning stormy.

"*Geh.* Leave." The last thing she needed was an interloper, especially since Norene had spilled the beans about being interested in Jesse. "Did you understand *that*?"

From the way Norene glared at Charity, she certainly did.

Yikes, I need to apologize. And she would—later. Right now she didn't want Norene working her charms on Jesse. Why hadn't he sat down? If he would just sit down, then she could calm down.

"Hey, Norene." He turned to her and smiled.

Charity froze again. She'd never seen his smile up close before. Oh, she'd seen him grin when he hung out with his friends and brothers after church, but that was always from a distance. *If only he was smiling at me.*

"I don't want to interrupt your *date*, Jesse," Norene said, inserting herself between him and Charity. "But I wondered if you wouldn't mind dropping by the inn later, if you have time."

Charity's fists clenched. How much *hochmut* and nerve did this woman have to literally ask Jesse out in front of her? Dropping by the inn wasn't necessarily an official date, but Charity had lived there for months. When a single man showed up at the inn, they were there to see one of the single girls staying there. *Except me.*

"Can't today," he said, his smile dimming. He was a tall man, and Norene didn't block him completely from Charity's view. "I've been pretty busy lately. Lot's of plowing and planting on the farm this time of year."

"But you can't work all day and night," Charity blabbed. She slid lower in her seat. Why had she said that? Why was she *helping* Norene? *Dear Lord, please shut my mouth!* At this rate she'd end up planning their wedding.

Norene glanced at her with a satisfied smile, then turned back to Jesse. "I won't take up much of your time. I promise. I'm thinking about buying a horse, and I need some advice." She lowered her eyes, then glanced up at him through her long, light-brown lashes. "I heard you're really *gut* with horses."

"You should probably talk to *mei bruders* about that. They're the experts." Jesse sidestepped her and sat down in the booth.

Charity unfolded her arms and sneered at Norene, but there was very little satisfaction behind it. The date was a disaster already, and that wasn't all Norene's fault, even though she was trying to steal Jesse from under her nose. "We need a few minutes to decide what we want," she snapped. "I'll let you know when we're ready for you to *serve* us."

Norene's mouth tightened. She turned on her heel and headed to the front of the diner.

"Finally, she's gone."

Jesse rubbed the back of his neck. "What?"

Oops. She hadn't meant to say that out loud. Pushing her rudeness and Norene to the side, she attempted the sweetest smile she could and gazed at Jesse. *Sigh.* She had no idea he was so dreamy up close. His blue short-sleeved shirt matched his eyes so perfectly that she barely noticed what appeared to be fresh mud spots on it, or that his hat was frayed around the brim. The most amazing thing about him was his hair. She'd seen Amish men with curly hair before, but Jesse's was on another level. He had corkscrew curls, and she wondered if they would spring back in place if she gently tugged on one.

She gripped her hands together. "Nice day for a date, *ya?*"

His work boot thumped against the floor as he stared out the diner window. He didn't speak for a long time. Long enough for dread to circle her stomach.

Finally, he turned to her, his blue eyes tense at the corners. "This isn't a date, Charity. It's a mistake."

.ᦉৡᦉ.

Jesse's molars ground together. Bad enough his frazzled nerves hadn't settled down since this morning when he chased after a runaway horse. The mare ran straight past Zeb and Zeke's horse farm. Jesse called out to her several times, praying she wouldn't take off for the open field on the opposite side of the road. Eventually she slowed down so he could catch up to her, and after several minutes of some of the stickiest sweet talk he'd ever uttered, she trusted him enough to guide her back to the farm.

On the way back to the corral, she stepped in a puddle and kicked some mud on him, probably out of sheer spite. Zeb had taken over from there, leaving Jesse free to help Zeke patch the fence she'd broken through. His twin brothers specialized in rehabbing abused horses, and the ironically named Miss Peach was one of their worst cases.

Only when Zeke had mentioned his wife, Darla, was making bacon cheeseburgers and waffle fries for lunch did Jesse remember he was supposed to meet Nelson. There was no time to change his dirty shirt so he wet a washcloth and dabbed the spots with water before hurrying to Diener's. He ended up tardy by almost thirty minutes, and when he didn't see Nelson, he thought his brother had given up on him.

Then Charity screeched at him from the other side of the diner, and now here he was sitting across from her, trying to comprehend why she thought they were supposed to have lunch together.

Wait. Had Nelson set him up with her? That was the only logical explanation.

In the background he could hear Charity and Norene's voices, but he was unable to process their chatter. He stared out the window. Why would his brother do this? Jesse had played many a prank on his siblings over the years, and he'd been on the receiving end of a few. But this one took the pie and the cake. Charity Raber was the strangest and, from the way she talked to Norene, rudest woman in Birch Creek—if she was even old enough to be considered a woman. He was only eighteen but she looked like a child. Stick thin with carrot-colored hair and more freckles than he could count in a lifetime, she wasn't just boyish looking. She was homely.

"Nice day for a date, *ya*?"

Her sunny tone dug into him and he continued looking out the window. What was he supposed to say? No way he was going through with Nelson's stunt. Even if he was interested in dating—and he'd made it clear to everyone he knew that he wasn't—Charity Raber was the last person he would ask out. It wasn't that long ago she was bugging Ezra to spend time with her. What did that make him? Second helpings—maybe even third? No thanks.

Honesty was the best policy, although he'd made a farce of that saying more than once in his life. He turned to her and said, "This isn't a date, Charity. It's a mistake."

Her fair skin turned the color of ripe rhubarb, transforming her freckles into a solid, rosy mass. "What do you mean a *mistake*?"

His right foot tapped faster. "A misunderstanding—"

"You said mistake." She pursed her lips together.

He winced. *Nelson is going to regret this.* "I thought I was meeting *mei bruder* here for lunch. Not you. That's the misunderstanding."

A pause. "You're not shy, are you?"

Odd question, but he shook his head anyway. "The opposite, actually."

"So Nelson didn't ask me out on your behalf?"

"*Nee.*" Is that what he'd told her?

"This isn't a date." The words came out in a barely intelligible mumble.

"It's not."

She glanced at the tabletop, and from her lack of response he thought he might be in the clear. If she still wanted to have lunch, he'd join her. He was close to famished now and Diener's had a reputation for good burgers. To make amends, he'd pay for her meal too. But he'd get the money back from Nelson later.

"It could be a date," she said, her small voice disrupting his thoughts. "Couldn't it?"

Yikes. "*Nee.* It can't."

"Why not?"

"Because I don't like you that way." He glanced out the window again.

"Why not?"

He met her gaze, surprised at her sincere expression. She wasn't trying to make him uncomfortable. She really wanted an answer. "You're not *mei* type."

"What's your type?"

Her inquisition was turning out worse than a date. Or so he guessed. He'd never been on one, but surely they weren't this harrowing. Her question prompted a question of his own. *What is* mei *type?* He'd never thought about it before. All he could say was, "Not you."

Her eyes filled. "You could at least be nice about it."

He frowned. "I thought I was. You wanted me to be honest, *ya?*"

Two tears, one from each eye, dripped down her cheek. She rubbed them away with both hands. "*Ya.* This is *mei* fault, of course."

"Charity, I—"

"I'm *so* sorry I'm not your type." She scrambled out of the seat.

Grimacing, he watched her dash out the diner door. Her questions hadn't just thrown him for a loop, but almost off a cliff. Did she want him to lie to her? To pretend they were on a date and that he liked her?

"Where did your *date* run off to?"

Norene's snide voice twanged his last nerve. Charity might be desperate and *seltsam*, but Norene was full of herself.

He turned to the window again, frowning. Charity had disappeared. Maybe he should have agreed with the so-called date, and afterward made it clear he wasn't interested in her. But that wouldn't have been right either.

Norene slid onto the seat across from him, her smile unnerving. "I'm on break, and I haven't had lunch yet."

He looked around the diner. When had everyone cleared out?

"You must be hungry too."

Jesse glanced at her, not liking what he saw. He didn't have much experience with women. Zero, in fact, and he planned to keep it that way for the foreseeable future. Witnessing his brothers and his nephew Malachi go through different stages of grief during their relationships had only cemented his determination to stay out of the dating pool. But despite lacking knowledge of females and their ways, he could tell Norene was up to no good.

"I have to get back to the farm." His appetite had disappeared anyway.

"See you tonight?"

He'd already hurt one *maedel*'s feelings. What was one more? "*Nee*. Not tonight." Before she could stop him, he slid out of the booth and scurried out the door, glad that other than the diner staff, the only people around were an English couple eating in the dining room. The fewer people witnessing him turn tail and run, the better.

His work boots slid on the gravel as he skidded to a stop at the parking lot entrance. He glanced in the direction Charity had left. Even if he wanted to, he couldn't catch up with her. And what would he say anyway? His brother was the true culprit. She should direct her anger at Nelson, not him.

But there was something else keeping him from tracking Charity down. *I don't want to be alone with her.*

He'd intended to return to the horse farm after lunch, but he went straight home to deal with Nelson first. Jesse found him in the barn tossing hay bales to their younger brother Mahlon, who was stacking them against the opposite wall.

A huge grin broke across Nelson's face as he pitched another bale to Mahlon. "How was *lunch*?"

Jesse clenched his back teeth. "Mahlon, I need to talk to Nelson alone."

Mahlon looked from one brother to the other. "Do I need to get *Daed*?"

"*Nee*," they both said.

"Are you two gonna fight?"

"Probably," Jesse muttered.

After Mahlon hustled out of the barn, Jesse marched toward Nelson. "Why did you do that?"

"Do what?" Nelson held up his dusty hands in feigned innocence.

"Set me up with Charity Raber."

"Oh, she was there?"

"Don't play *dumm*. You caused both of us a lot of problems."

Nelson scoffed. "The way you did for everyone when you put that ad in the paper?"

He stilled. He hadn't said a peep to his brothers or anyone else about being behind the bride advertisement hoax. Only Cevilla Thompson knew what he'd done, having somehow figured it out on her own. She gave her word she wouldn't tell anyone, and he trusted she'd keep it. As for him . . . he'd planned to take his secret to the grave. "I—"

"Don't deny it."

He was tempted to do just that, but there would be no point in lying. "How did you find out?"

"I kept wondering who in Birch Creek would want to marry us off. Of course *Mamm* came to mind, but she would never stoop that low to find us *frau*. Neither would anyone else in the district. Then it came to me. *You* would. And you would think it was funny." He took a step toward Jesse, scowling. "Then I started paying attention. You sure like to tease everyone about their women problems, *ya*?"

Jesse held up his hands. "I was just having a little fun."

"There's *nix* funny about this."

He grasped for a defense. "It all turned out fine, didn't it? Some of our *bruders* even got married. It all worked out in the end."

"It worked out for some," Nelson muttered. "But not everyone."

"What?"

"Never mind." He waved his beefy hand. "What you did was wrong."

"And setting me up with Charity was right?"

"I was just having a little fun," he mocked. "No harm done, *ya*?" He shot him a bitter look. "You never admit you're wrong, do you?"

He slammed his shoulder into Jesse as he walked out of the barn, knocking him off balance.

Jesse regained his footing. Why was Nelson so angry with him? He was only fifteen when he put the ad in the paper on a whim. The thought of his brothers and friends floundering as man-hungry women chased after them was hilarious. And it had been . . . somewhat.

He wasn't laughing anymore.

He shook his head. Nelson's reaction was overblown. Good things had come from that ad. Even Cevilla admitted it, agreeing no harm had been done. *Yet.*

He thought about Charity. Surely she'd get over Nelson's prank and realize Jesse wasn't at fault. Maybe she'd even find a husband here someday. Or if not here, somewhere else. *No harm done.*

One thing for sure, though. This was his last practical joke. Ever.

One

> Getting a man isn't like throwing spaghetti
> against the wall and seeing what sticks. Getting
> a man requires patience and planning.
>
> *Getting a Man and Keeping Him, p. 14*

There's still time to change *yer* mind."

Jesse set the cardboard box of dishes *Mamm* had given him on the kitchen counter and turned to *Daed*. He and his younger brother Elam had helped move his things to Marigold this morning and had stuck around to help him unpack. Elam was getting Miss Peach settled in the small barn next to the house. "I don't plan on changing *mei* mind, *Daed*."

His father tugged at his long, gray beard. "Didn't think so, but it was worth a shot." He sighed.

Jesse walked over to him. "I'm just one town over. You'll barely know I'm gone."

"It will be a lot quieter, that's for sure." *Daed* smiled, the wrinkles in the corners of his eyes deepening.

Jesse rolled his eyes. "Ha ha."

"I guess me and *yer mamm* figured all our *kinner* would live in the same community." He sat down at the small round table in the middle of the kitchen.

"Devon spoiled that," Jesse said, referring to his eldest brother, who married Nettie, a woman from their hometown.

"*Ya*, but I figured he would probably leave and strike out on his own. I'd thought it would be because of his job as a roofer and not because of a *frau*, though. But it's different for you. We always figured you'd either stay on the farm or work for Zeb and Zeke."

"But this is a *gut* opportunity for me." Jesse sat down at the table, his excitement building. "Not only will I learn how to build buggies, but Micah's planning to machine some of the parts himself, and he wants to teach me how. I wouldn't get that experience in Birch Creek. Besides, you have plenty of farm hands. Owen, Perry, Nelson, Mahlon, Mose, Elam. And Mahlon's taken an interest in rehabbing horses, so he's a big help to Zeb and Zeke."

"True. God blessed us with plenty of *kinner*, that's for sure. And you're right, this is a *gut* opportunity for you." He gave Jesse a sly look. "So who are you gonna tease if you don't have *yer bruders* around?"

Jesse's smile faded a bit. "I'm pretty much past all that, *Daed*." *I hope.* He'd stuck to his vow not to play any more practical jokes—on his family or anyone else.

"Now don't turn too serious on me while *yer* living here in Marigold. I won't recognize you." They both chuckled as Elam entered the kitchen.

"Miss Peach is all settled down," he said.

"*Danki*, Elam. She turned out to be a *gut* horse, *ya*?"

"*Ya*. I guess." His youngest brother shrugged.

"Is there anything else we can help you with?" *Daed* asked.

"*Nee.* I just have that box and my clothes upstairs left to unpack."

"Guess we'll be heading home then." *Daed* stood behind Elam and put his hands on his shoulders. He was thirteen years old and still shorter than *Daed*, but at the rate he was growing he would end up taller than Ezra, their tallest brother. "Don't be a stranger, *sohn,*" *Daed* said.

Elam nodded in agreement, his expression somber. Was his youngest brother going to miss him too?

An unexpected lump formed in Jesse's throat. He wasn't that far from Birch Creek. A long buggy ride or shorter taxi trip was all he'd have to take to visit his family. He'd actually thought they would be happy to get rid of him, since they considered him a pest. Now that he was an adult, he realized they were right.

"And don't hesitate to let us know if you need anything." *Daed* smiled as he went to Jesse and clapped him on the back. "Time sure does fly," he murmured. "Faster than you expect." He turned to Elam. "How about you drive us home."

With a wide grin Elam nodded, and Jesse walked outside and watched them head to *Daed's* buggy.

Halfway there, Elam turned and jogged back to him. "Mind if I, uh, come visit you sometime?" He stared at the ground, the toe of his boot tracing a crooked circle in the flat gravel.

Jesse touched his shoulder. "Sure. Anytime."

Elam cracked a smile. He ran back to the buggy and hopped in. Jesse surprised himself by waiting outside until they were so far in the distance he couldn't see them anymore.

For the first time since he could remember, he was alone.

"Whoop!" he yelled, pumping his fist. He glanced around to see if anyone had heard him, other than Miss Peach, before going inside.

Oh, there were times when he'd been by himself before, but in a family as large as his, those were few and far between. Up until today he'd shared a room with Perry, and before his three oldest brothers had gotten married, he and Perry had bunked with Nelson. Often he would spend the night at his sister, Phoebe's, not only because he was best friends with his same-aged nephew Malachi, but also to get a break from the chaos.

Now he had his own room. His own house, even though he was renting it from his new boss, Micah Wagler. Still, he had his own place. He had to let that sink in a little.

He went back to the kitchen, tore the tape off the box on the kitchen counter, and peered inside. His mother had packed enough dishes for a family of four. He hoped that wasn't wishful thinking on her part. Then again, he'd had enough women after him lately that he wouldn't be surprised if she was already planning his wedding.

After Nelson had dressed him down that day a year ago, Jesse expected him to tell their brothers what he'd done. But none of them had said a word or let on that they knew, and he and Nelson never spoke about it again. When six months passed and no new women had shown up looking for husbands, he guessed the ad had finally run its course. *Thank God.* He was eager to put the hoax behind him.

His relief was short-lived when a dozen single women showed up last November, and now the women outnumbered the men. Worse, several of them were blatantly interested in Jesse. After what happened with Charity, he hadn't been as straightforward with them as he had with her, and he spent more time dodging women than he had working on both farms. He deserved the aggravation, he supposed.

When he saw the want ad for a full-time position at Wagler's Buggy Shop, he immediately applied. He wasn't just excited about a new opportunity, he'd also found a solution to his female problem. Two birds, one stone. He couldn't have asked for anything better.

As he made quick work putting away the dishes in the cabinet, Charity stayed in his mind. He hadn't thought about her in months, and that day at the diner was the last time he saw her. She had packed up and left Birch Creek without telling anyone goodbye, including the Stolls, and no one knew where she'd gone. Home, everyone had assumed, and then she wasn't mentioned again, not in his earshot anyway. Kind of sad now that he thought about it. If anyone in the community missed her, he hadn't heard them say.

There were two items left in the box—a flour sifter he'd never use and a small frying pan he would definitely put to work. Cooking wasn't his forte, but he was willing to learn. He was about to throw the box away when he saw a folded paper at the bottom. He picked it up and opened it, surprised to see his mother's even, delicate script on the page.

Dear Jesse,

It's hard to believe you're setting out on your own so soon. I say soon because to a mother, their kinners' childhoods are fleeting moments. I wanted to come with your daed and Elam today, but I couldn't. Not without tearing up, and you don't need to see that. I never thought you would do anything other than be a farmer, but you have always been the son that is full of surprises. What I do know is that you'll be successful at whatever you set your mind to.

Don't be shy about visiting. I miss you already.

Love,

Mamm

Jesse read the letter twice, then folded it carefully and put it in his pocket. Later he would find a special place for it. He wasn't sentimental, but his mother's words touched his heart. Between her, his father, and Elam, it was nice knowing his family would miss him. He would miss them too, but right now he was enjoying his freedom.

After he finished in the kitchen, he strode through the small, empty living room to his new bedroom. Micah had constructed the tiny dwelling at the same time he'd built his buggy business, and he'd lived here until he and Priscilla married and built their own house on the property on the other side of the shop. Other than a single bedroom and a small kitchen, there was a living area and a bathroom with a toilet, sink, and tub. No shower. He'd be surprised if the entire home was more than seven hundred square feet. But it was all he needed. He'd brought his twin bed, along with his dresser. He tucked his mother's letter underneath the mattress.

Dusky light entered through the windows by the time he made his way back to the kitchen to fix a bite of supper. His mother had sent a blue plastic crate filled with canned goods and a cooler full of meat, cheese, and a carton of milk. He was flipping open the top of the cooler when he heard a whining noise coming from outside. When he opened the door, a black and white dog stared up at him.

"Hey—"

The dog barged past him and sniffed the floor, making a circuit around the tiny kitchen before stopping at Jesse's feet. He sat on his haunches, his extra-long tongue lolling out of his mouth, his eyes a transparent blue. Those eyes locked on to Jesse.

Smiling, Jesse crouched down in front of the dog. "Who do you belong to, *bu*?" He glanced at the gold tag dangling from his collar. "Monroe." No address or phone number, but he appeared clean and well fed. He licked Jesse's chin.

"Definitely friendly." Jesse's fingertips rubbed the short fur behind Monroe's ears. His white fur looked like a mask covering his face, while the rest of his body was black, including his upright ears.

Stubby legs, wide body. Jesse had no idea what breed he was, other than a mutt.

"Mon-rooooo!" A high-pitched female voice sounded outside the kitchen door. "Come here, Mon-rooooo!"

Monroe froze. So did Jesse. *Where have I heard that voice before?*

"Monroe!" she snapped, sounding closer. "Come here right this instant!"

The dog turned his head, then looked back at Jesse. He didn't budge.

"Looks like you're in a little trouble, *bu*." Why did she sound so familiar?

"Micah, have you seen—there you are!"

A boyishly thin female with shocking red hair underneath a white *kapp* stood in the open doorway, glaring at Monroe. The dog moved closer to Jesse.

Jesse stilled. He'd seen that red hair before too. *It can't be . . .*

"Monroe—" The woman's eyes shifted to Jesse's, growing wider than teacup saucers. "Oh—"

"—*nee*," Jesse finished.

.⁓ৡৱৎ⁓.

Charity blinked. Her eyes were deceiving her, because that couldn't be Jesse Bontrager kneeling next to Monroe, professional canine escape artist. She loved the dog like crazy, but he had a bad habit of running out of the house to the buggy shop, and if Micah wasn't there, next door to where he lived with his wife, Priscilla. Probably due to Micah always keeping doggy snacks in his pockets after the first time Monroe had wandered there a little over two months ago.

"Jesse?" Her voice squeaked, holding on to the last shred of hope that this was his doppelganger and not the man she'd run away from twelve months, two weeks, and four days ago.

Shock covered his face as he rose to his feet. Monroe lay down next to them. "Charity?"

Yep. This was Jesse. Long-limbed, square-jawed, curly-headed Jesse. *Phooey.*

"What are you—" he asked.

"—doing here?" she finished.

He pointed his thumb at his chest. "*I* live here. And starting Monday, I'll work here. Well, not in the house obviously. At the shop."

"You know how to build buggies?"

"Um, *nee.* Not yet." He glanced at his feet before looking at her again. "Micah's going to train me."

"And you moved into his old house?"

"He's renting it to me."

She dug at the hangnail on her left index finger. Was God playing a joke on her? If he was, it wasn't funny.

"Any more questions?" The corner of his upper lip lifted into a quarter of a smile.

To her dismay, he was still ridiculously handsome, his curls still impossibly tempting. He wasn't wearing his hat, and his bangs were pushed to the side of his forehead. She took a step back, but couldn't speak. Of all the people Micah could have hired, it would have to be him. *Double phooey.*

Jesse tilted his head. "I'll take that as a *nee.* I've got one, though. Is Monroe your dog?"

"*Ya.* I mean, *nee.* I mean, *ya* and *nee.*" The hangnail stung as it gave way. "He belongs to Shirley."

"Shirley who?"

"Shirley Pearson."

Monroe laid his chin on the toe of Jesse's boot, sighed, and closed his eyes.

She glanced at the dog and frowned. Did Jesse have beef jerky in his boots? Monroe had never acted this calm around a stranger before. Even Micah had to ply him with cheese-flavored treats to get Monroe to trust him. But the dog was acting as if Jesse had been his best friend for years.

"And Shirley Pearson is?" Jesse asked, his feet unmoving.

"*Mei* boss. The *frau* I live with. And *mei* boss." *Here I go again.* Why couldn't she say a complete, or at least comprehensible, sentence? She drew in a deep breath. "We live next door." Finally.

His eyebrow raised. "You live next door? With Shirley?"

There was a decent-sized field between the two houses, but yes, technically they were neighbors. He didn't look too happy about the idea. "Well, I'm not happy about it either."

Jesse frowned. "I didn't say I was unhappy."

"You didn't?"

Buzz. Buzz.

"Your apron is buzzing," he said, still frowning.

She slipped the phone out of her waistband and glanced at the screen. "I have to get this." She tapped the On button. "Hi, Shirley." She didn't wait for her boss to respond. "I found him, and yes, he's at Micah's again. Yes, I'll tell Micah to stop feeding him, and I'll be home in a few minutes." She shut off the phone and tucked it back into her waistband. At Jesse's confused expression, she said, "I know what she's going to say, so I just give her the answers. Saves us both time. C'mon, Monroe. Time to *geh*. I've got supper cooking on the stove."

Monroe snored.

Jesse glanced at his feet. "He seems pretty content right here."

Charity moved closer. "Get a move on, Monroe."

He rolled on his side, opened his eyes, and yawned.

Phooey. She didn't think to bring his leash. He always followed her back once he'd finished snacking on a few of Micah's treats. Now what was she supposed to do? He wasn't a huge dog, but he was heavy. She should know—she was the one who had to bathe him once a month. Come to think of it, he ran away during his last bath too.

Jesse knelt down. "Hey, *bu*," he said, his voice low and gentle. "You gotta *geh* home now."

Monroe looked up at him with sad eyes.

Charity almost rolled hers. "Don't fall for it. He's not as innocent as he looks."

"How about a little chin scratch?"

"What? I'm not going to let you scratch my . . . oh." Her cheeks heated. "You meant Monroe."

The dog leaned into Jesse's fingers. If there was such a thing as doggy heaven, he seemed to be there right now. And if Jesse had heard her gaffe, he didn't say anything.

"Feels *gut*, huh, *bu*?" Jesse murmured.

Why did his voice have to be so deep and husky too? She didn't remember him sounding so relaxed the last time they talked. Then again, she made a point not to remember. After the way he'd treated her in Birch Creek, he was the last man on earth she'd be attracted to. Scratch that. The last man in the *universe.*

She also didn't have time to hang around while Monroe was getting a chin massage. "We're leaving, Monroe."

Both Jesse and Monroe looked at her, neither one of them moving.

"For goodness' sake, Shirley is waiting for me. Us."

Jesse put his finger over his lips and continued scratching Monroe. Slowly he stood, keeping his hands on the dog's chin, then moving to his back. Then he led Monroe over to Charity. "Do you have a leash?"

That was rather impressive. "I never needed one before. He usually follows me home."

"I'll walk with you then."

She fiddled with the hangnail again, ignored the sting, and walked next to Jesse and Monroe to the end of the large gravel driveway that doubled as a parking lot for the buggy shop.

"Where's *yer haus*?" he asked.

"This way." She turned right and started walking across the empty field that separated the two houses. She made sure not to walk in the street with Monroe, concerned he might get hit by a car. She didn't know how long she'd been walking when she realized neither of them had followed her.

"*This* way," she said, facing them. "Didn't you hear me?"

Jesse nodded. "I heard you. I was waiting to see if he'd follow you." He took a few steps forward, and with each one Monroe stayed by his side.

She'd never seen anything like this before. Then again, she'd never had a pet either. Her father worked in a plastics factory and the only animals they had were their horse, a few chickens, and a yearly pig. *Mamm*—Elaine, as Charity had started calling her when she left Cherry Springs for the second time and moved to Marigold—didn't like dogs. Or cats. Guinea pigs and birds were also out of the question. Too much fur, too much noise, too much trouble.

Monroe didn't shed and for the most part he was a quiet dog, but he did cause Charity trouble when he ran off like this. He was also sweet, affectionate, and totally worth it.

He and Jesse caught up with her, and they all walked to Shirley's together. The sun had dipped past the horizon, and twilight was breaking through. She hadn't thought to bring a flashlight either.

"When did you move to Marigold?" Jesse asked.

The tall grass brushed against her bare legs. Why was he asking her that? Did he really want to know? Was he making small talk, or was he only being polite and didn't care how she ended up at Shirley's? And did she owe him an answer? Or anything, for that matter?

She glanced at him. He was staring straight ahead as he walked, his hands casually placed in his pockets. He jerked his head a little so his curly bangs swept to the side again. "Why do you want to know?" she snapped.

"Fine. You don't have to tell me." He shrugged and continued walking.

She matched his stride, or at least tried to. Monroe was a few feet in front of them. "Fine. I won't then."

He glanced at her. "You haven't changed a bit, have you?"

That wasn't true. She had changed, or at least was trying to. "You don't know anything about me," she muttered, hugging her arms. Now that the sun was almost completely gone, the air had turned a little chilly, and of course she hadn't thought to bring a sweater. She hadn't thought she'd be gone this long.

He sighed. "*Yer* right, I don't."

Monroe suddenly sprinted away.

"I'll get him," Jesse said.

"You don't have to. He always does this. About halfway across the field he runs home." She pointed to Shirley's small house, the lights in the window faint at this distance but bright enough that she could see the dog's silhouette as he ran up the driveway, toward the front porch, where she'd find him patiently waiting like he hadn't just upended her life.

Jesse nodded. "Now that I know where he lives, if he comes over again I'll make sure he goes back."

She turned to him, waiting to see if he would say anything else now that Monroe was home. Would he mention what happened at the diner? The "date" that was a mistake? Or had he forgotten about it . . . about her?

"I, uh, guess I'll see you around. Since we're neighbors now." He turned and walked away.

Huh. Should she be upset that he hadn't said anything about the past, or grateful? She had no idea, and she didn't have time to dwell.

She hurried back to the house. Monroe was pacing in front of the door, wagging his tail. She opened the door and he dashed inside, going straight to Shirley, who was sitting by the fireplace reading one of the Christian romances that came in the mail every month.

"There's my boy." Shirley set the book down on the end table by her chair and cupped Monroe's white face. "Why are you so naughty?" She looked up at Charity. "How many treats did he eat this time?"

"None."

"Oh?" Shirley took off her reading glasses, her light-brown penciled-in brows lifting. "That doesn't sound like him."

"I need to finish up supper." Charity wasn't in the mood to talk about Jesse right now. Shirley would find out who he was eventually. Micah's wife, Priscilla, often stopped by to visit since their house was on the opposite side of the buggy shop and not that far from Shirley's. Charity usually made tea for the two of them before working on her daily chores. But Priscilla was pregnant with her and Micah's first child, and she was near her due date. She was also nesting, and she and Shirley had suspended their teatime until after the baby was born. Otherwise Shirley might have known that Micah had hired someone to help him in the buggy shop.

Oh well, she'd tell Shirley about Jesse later. It wasn't like he would ever come by here anyway. Except to bring Monroe home. *Phooey,* she'd have to keep a better eye on him when she took him outside. She didn't want him running over to Micah's or Jesse's anymore.

Charity stirred the pot of beef stew simmering on the stove and tapped the spoon against the side. She cut two slices of bread off the loaf she'd made this morning and set them on a small plate. *Jesse Bontrager lives next door.* Square-jawed, curly-headed, husky-voiced Jesse Bontrager.

"Is supper ready?" Shirley said as she pushed her seated walker into the kitchen and shuffled behind it, Monroe walking calmly at her side.

"Almost." Charity grabbed the bread and set it on the table, then she dished out stew into gray bowls, pushing Jesse out of her thoughts and focusing on supper. Since Shirley and her daughter, Wendy, had hired her a little over two months ago as a caretaker, Charity had taken the job seriously. She not only had to prove to Shirley that she was a responsible, capable employee, she also had to prove it to herself.

Initially she was nervous. She'd never worked for the English before. Actually, this was her first job ever. So far, so good, though. There had been a few mishaps, mostly due to her not knowing how to operate an appliance, like the time she set off the smoke alarm making s'mores for the two of them in the microwave, or putting liquid dish soap into the dishwasher. Thankfully Shirley had stopped her before she started the washer. It helped that Shirley was undemanding and easy to get along with. Also, she was patient, something Charity greatly appreciated.

Before each meal together, Charity said a silent prayer in accordance to Amish tradition, and Shirley followed with a second, spoken prayer. As they started eating, Jesse inched back into her thoughts. Or rather his voice did as she remembered how he'd mesmerized Monroe. She frowned and pushed at a chunk of potato in the stew.

"Something on your mind?" Shirley lifted her spoon, blew on the stew, and took a bite.

"No," she said quickly, dunking her spoon into the bowl and splashing the broth on the side of her hand. She grabbed a napkin and wiped it off.

"Are you sure?" Shirley gave her a pointed look, the wrinkles between her eyebrows deepening. "You seem preoccupied."

"Just glad Monroe is safe and sound."

"Me too." Shirley pinched off a piece of bread and gave it to Monroe. At Charity's lifted brow she said, "It's just a crumb."

Charity thought he was having too many crumbs, and between Shirley and Micah spoiling him, Monroe was getting fat. Not to mention a little entitled, considering he wouldn't listen to her when she called him to come home. But he was Shirley's dog, and it wasn't Charity's place to question his care. Besides, he was healthy and happy now, a far cry from how he was when Shirley had found him abandoned and starved in her driveway four months ago. Charity's heart cratered when Shirley had told her that story, and she was grateful her boss had rescued him.

"Delicious stew, Charity." Shirley smiled. "You keep saying you're not a good cook, and you keep proving yourself wrong."

Charity glanced at her half-eaten bowl. She wasn't a good cook, not compared to her grandmother. She held in a sigh. Shirley reminded her a little bit of *Grossmammi*. Short, on the stout side, with a soft smile and a backbone of steel. The hole she'd left in her life and her heart had never gone away.

Her stepmother was a good cook too, but hadn't imparted much instruction to Charity. Elaine wasn't stingy with her disapproval when Charity did cook, though, and by the time she was seventeen she'd given up on cooking altogether. But once she started making meals for

Shirley, Charity discovered that when her stepmother wasn't looking over her shoulder and criticizing her every move, preparing food was enjoyable. Fun, even.

"I guess I'll have to get a fence built for Monroe." Shirley wiped the bowl with the last piece of bread. "I'll make some calls and get some prices together."

"I can do that for you," Charity said.

Shirley shook her head. "I need something to do other than watch the news and read my books. Do you need some help with the dishes?"

"No, thank you. It won't take me long to clean up."

"I'll go to the living room then. C'mon, Monroe." Shirley grabbed the handles of her walker and stood, Monroe trotting behind her.

Charity set to work clearing the table, rinsing the dishes and stacking them in the dishwasher, and wiping down the counters. She preferred to hand wash the dishes, but Shirley had insisted Charity use the washer. "No sense having a fancy appliance and not using it," she'd said. Charity had to admit the conveniences did make chores go faster. But she was mindful not to get used to them. As much as she enjoyed working for Shirley, she wasn't going to be here for the rest of her life. She had no intention of leaving her faith. She also had other fish to fry, as her grandmother would say.

She still had a difficult time thinking about Birch Creek without a mix of hurt and humiliation. She also didn't understand why someone had advertised the need for brides when it wasn't true. She understood desperation, and if the men had been desperate to marry she would be hitched already. There had to have been a mix-up. The alternative—some jerk placing the ad knowing it wasn't true—was too awful to contemplate. She couldn't imagine anyone being that cruel. And after the fiasco with Jesse, there was no way she could continue to be snubbed by Birch Creek men.

Despite that awful time, she'd learned two lessons. First, she discovered it wasn't any easier fitting into a new community than it had been back home. She'd always struggled making friends, and having Elaine for a stepmother didn't help. She hadn't been accepted in Cherry Springs any more than she had in Birch Creek.

Second, and most importantly, finding a husband was serious business. And serious business needed serious planning. She had another chance at marriage now, and she had to succeed this time. She couldn't go back to Cherry Springs as a loser in love—twice. The first time had been hard enough, and she'd only gone back because of her father. At least he'd been glad to see her, although he was still as distant as ever. And Elaine? She was as eager to get rid of her as Charity was to leave again.

There was no alternative—she had to find a husband this time. If she didn't, she'd end up going back home for good. And she could never, *ever* do that.

Two

Don't give up hope. Your one true love is out
there in the world . . . you just have to find him.

Getting a Man and Keeping Him, p. 3

After Charity finished washing the supper dishes, Monroe sauntered into the kitchen looking for his nightly chew bone to
gnaw on. She gave it to him, picked up her notebook, pencil, and a
copy of *Getting a Man and Keeping Him* by Montague Persimmons,
and sat down at the table to work on her courtship plan.

Three weeks ago she'd gone to the library and perused the
shelves, looking for any book available about relationships, men,
and dating. There were four, including this one, and she snatched
them up. As she made her way to check out, she also blindly grabbed
three other books from two of the display tables near the front desk.

She separated the relationship books from the others. "Those are
for a friend," she said, not wanting the librarian to think she was un-
sophisticated. Or desperate. Even though she was both, no one else
had to know. She pointed to the other three books. "These are mine."

The librarian slipped on the black, round-framed glasses dangling
from a chain around her neck. "*Great Expectations.*" She scanned the
bar code underneath a bright-red light. *Beep.* "*French Cooking for*

Dummies." *Beep.* "And, *Learn Swahili in 90 Days or Less.*" She peered at Charity. *Beep.* "Those are yours?"

She winced. Swahili? She should have at least glanced at the titles before checking them out. "Um, yes. I have broad reading tastes."

The librarian nodded and finished the lending process without comment.

Since then Charity had devoured the relationship books, left *Great Expectations* in the bottom of her tote bag, copied six French recipes to make in the future, and read four pages of the Swahili book because she had no idea what Swahili was. She made a mental note to go back to the lessons later after she finished her courtship plan. Now that she was settled in her job, it was time to focus on her personal life.

She looked at her notes so far:

What do men like?

1. Youthfulness

She smiled. She was youthful.

2. Kindness

Hmm. She could work on that a little. She hadn't been all that kind when she lived in Birch Creek. Being Shirley's caregiver—or assistant, as her boss preferred to call her—had helped. When she was in Birch Creek she'd only thought of herself, completely focused on snagging an available man and marrying him. She also dealt with envy when she saw other women getting married and she couldn't even get a single date.

Then there was her life back home in Cherry Springs. If she didn't put herself first there, no one else would.

But being trusted with taking care of, er, *assisting* Shirley and Monroe had opened up a new world to her. At home she'd resented doing all the household chores, but in Marigold she enjoyed them, even doing the laundry. She was allowed to use the washer and dryer for Shirley's clothes, but she still hung her own clothing on a small clothesline in the backyard—only after she'd put away Shirley's, of course. Focusing on others instead of herself gave her a sense of satisfaction she'd never experienced before. Still, she could improve on being nice. That would be a lifelong pursuit.

She moved to the next item on her list.

3. Curves

Uh-oh. Frowning, she looked down. There was nothing she could do about her flat chest or her straight hips and scrawny legs. She'd had a boyish figure ever since she was a child, and when she finally started to develop, it was too subtle to notice. According to Elaine, she didn't have a pretty enough face to make up for her lack of shapeliness. She ignored the prick in her chest and picked up her pencil.

3. ~~Curves~~
3. Confidence

She'd been working on that too, although her fake date with Jesse had put a dent in her self-esteem, and that had plummeted the minute she went back home. Shirley and Monroe had given her a boost, but she still had a ways to go.

Jesse. Every time she tried not to think about him tonight, he popped up in her thoughts again.

"What's your type?"

"Not you."

Ouch. Even now that exchange still pained her, but she accepted some responsibility since she was dumb enough to ask the question. Still . . . *ouch.*

"Be confident," she said out loud, drowning out the memories of Cherry Springs, Birch Creek, and Jesse Bontrager.

"Confident about what?" Shirley said, pushing her walker into the kitchen.

Monroe sat up, looked adoringly at the old woman, then went back to chewing.

"Nothing." Charity placed her notebook on top of her advice book and smiled. So far she'd been able to hide her research from Shirley and she wanted to keep it that way. "Do you need something?"

"A glass of water." Shirley headed for the sink.

Charity jumped up from her chair. "I'll get it."

"Now, now." Shirley wagged a crooked finger at her. "Remember our new rule?"

She nodded. "I don't have to do everything for you."

"Right. I can get a glass of water myself." She continued to the sink and Charity returned to her chair. She folded her arms on top of the notebook.

"I just can't get over how delicious that stew was." Shirley leaned against the walker and took a cup from the cabinet. "Is that from your French cookbook?"

"No, it's one of my grandmother's recipes."

"Ah, I can see why it was so good." After filling the glass, she held it with one hand and turned her walker around with the other. "I wish I could have met her," she said. "From everything you've said about her, I imagine we would be friends."

Charity's heart squeezed. "I wish you could have too," she said softly. *And I wish she were still here.* If her *grossmammi* hadn't passed away when Charity was seven her life would have been different. Better. Happier, for sure.

Shirley sipped her water. "I'm going to turn in early tonight," she said.

"Are you feeling all right?"

"Yes, just tired. Do you mind letting Monroe out? I'll keep my bedroom door open for him when he comes back inside."

Charity nodded, and as Shirley left the kitchen, she got the leash from the kitchen drawer and clipped it to Monroe's collar. He got up and they both went to the backyard so he could do his business.

As she walked him around Shirley's lawn, she wondered what kind of fence Shirley would choose. She hoped it wasn't a privacy fence so Monroe could at least look at the field while he was outside. Maybe she could try to train him not to run off. He'd started dashing out the door last week. Before then he'd only run away when he was outside for more than a few minutes. But Shirley was right, a fence was necessary, not just for Monroe's safety, but also his waistline.

Charity took Monroe back inside, and he trotted off down the hall to Shirley's bedroom where he slept every night. She sat back down at the table and resumed her research. The other three books weren't as informative as *Getting a Man and Keeping Him,* and she found herself taking more notes out of this book than the other ones. Whoever Montague Persimmons was, he knew his stuff. She added a few more things to her list.

Men want:

1. Intelligence
2. Dependability
3. A Sense of Humor

She sighed. Three more things she would have to work on.

After filling two and a half pages with notes, she glanced at the clock. Almost nine o'clock. She'd been so engrossed in her research that time seemed to fly by. But she'd made a good dent in the plan. A few more evenings of thought and note-taking and she could put the pieces in place.

She gathered her things and went to her room at the back of the house. The bedroom was on the small side, but Charity didn't mind. It was private, and Shirley never came inside, so she didn't have to hide her collection of research books or her notebook. She put her books and notes on top of her dresser, eager to implement the first phase of her plan as soon as she could. Before the year was out, Charity would get a man . . . and she would definitely keep him.

The rest of the week flew by for Jesse. Micah had set him to work right away by teaching him how to build a buggy suspension. During the next few days Jesse learned how to attach the wheels, fasten the cover in place, and he received a tutorial on how the drum brakes worked.

"That's the main reason I hired you," Micah said, repeating what he'd told Jesse during their interview. "I need someone to machine and build the brakes. I purchased all the equipment needed. If you're successful, we can start taking orders from other buggy shops and shipping them out."

"Another revenue stream?" Jesse asked.

"You got it. Plus I have to wait on those parts sometimes, and if there's a problem with the supply chain, it puts me behind and the customers have to wait. This way we'll have the brakes at hand."

Jesse nodded, although he was a little overwhelmed with all the new information his boss had thrown at him since Monday. Just figuring out where everything was in the shop was a challenge, although Micah's supplies and equipment were well organized. He hadn't known there were so many different tasks to building a buggy, and when it came to mechanics, he had little experience. But he was open to learning, and he would take every aspect of the job seriously, something he didn't always do growing up on the family farm.

"Hope you're ready for a lunch break."

Jesse and Micah turned to see Priscilla enter the shop, carrying a picnic basket.

Micah hurried over to her. "You didn't have to do that," he said, taking the basket from her. "Or carry this."

"You haven't come home for lunch all week." She looked at Jesse and smiled. "And I'm sure you're ready for some home cooking by now."

"I've invited him to supper three times already." Micah gave him a stern look.

"I don't want to be a bother," Jesse said. Priscilla looked close to her delivery time, and when Bishop Fry dropped by the shop to introduce himself, he'd heard Micah tell him that Priscilla was supposed to be resting at home as much as possible due to her pregnancy being high risk.

"You wouldn't be a bother," she said, motioning for Micah to put the basket on the workbench. "I got used to cooking for a crowd when I married him."

"Very funny." But Micah was rubbing his hands together as she opened the basket lid. The scent of fried chicken filled the air, making Jesse's stomach growl. "*Mei* favorite. I hope you brought extra."

She smiled. "Always."

Micah was a huge man and as Jesse had seen from the size of the lunches he brought from home, he had a huge appetite. At Priscilla's urging, Jesse walked to the long bench and waited for her to fill his plate. "*Mei* husband better not be working you too hard," she said with a grin. "He can be a taskmaster."

"I heard that," Micah called out.

Jesse laughed. Micah was disciplined, but hardly a tyrant.

"You won't find a better boss, though." She looked at her husband, who was gazing adoringly back at her.

Jesse sat down on an old wooden chair near the bench and focused on his meal, ignoring the two of them making googly eyes at each other. Good thing he was hungry because the portions were big. In addition to fried chicken there was macaroni salad, pickles, homemade potato chips, and a plate of gingerbread cookies for dessert.

"Don't forget to bring the basket home," Priscilla said.

"I won't." Micah gave her a little salute and sat down on an identical wooden chair near Jesse's. He took off his straw hat and set it on the workbench behind him, his wheat-colored hair molded against his head.

As Priscilla walked out of the shop, she began to hum. Jesse paused. The sound was so sweet and pure he was compelled to listen until her humming faded away.

"Priscilla used to be a professional singer." Micah's eyes gleamed. "I know we're not supposed to be prideful, but when it comes to her, I can't help it. Her voice is straight from heaven."

Jesse nodded, not because he had to agree with his boss, but because it was true. After they said a silent prayer of thanks, he asked, "She was a professional singer?"

"*Ya.* Well, she tried to be." Micah chewed on a fluffy yeast roll. "Before she joined the church she lived in Nashville for ten years. She wanted to be a country star, but God had other plans."

"Does she miss singing?"

"*Nee*. She sings around the house, and in church, of course. She told me once that singing to the Lord was more satisfying than performing in front of a huge crowd of people." He took a drink from the thermos of water Priscilla had supplied. "I thank the Lord every day for bringing her into *mei* life. When you find the right woman, Jesse, *yer* world will change forever."

"That'll be a long ways off," he said, eyeing the golden-brown chicken leg on his plate.

"What about Charity?"

His head shot up, the chicken leg instantly forgotten. On Monday he'd mentioned Monroe's visit to Micah. "Charity?" His shoulders tensed.

"She's a nice *maedel*. Kinda offbeat, but *nix* wrong with that. Priscilla says she's been a huge help to Shirley."

"We didn't hit it off too well when we met." He was referring to the diner disaster in Birch Creek, but their second meeting hadn't been great either. She was her usual oddball self, and he'd kept conversation to a minimum to avoid saying the wrong thing again. It didn't work, because when he asked her why she'd moved to Marigold she turned testy, and he'd snapped right back at her. He hadn't meant to, but when it came to Charity Raber, he couldn't say anything right. "The two of us together . . . that's not gonna happen."

"You never know." Micah winked. "God's plans aren't our own."

Jesse nodded but didn't comment. Instead he finished his lunch, and Micah dropped the matchmaking. *Thank God.* He'd left that nonsense back in Birch Creek.

When they were done, Micah wiped his fingers on a blue cotton napkin and stood. "The supper invitation still stands. You need a little more meat on *yer* bones," he said in a teasing tone.

Jesse didn't take his words too much to heart even though his boss was right. He was thin, like Owen and Perry. His older brothers were average size, and his younger ones were strong and stout. Only Nelson, for some reason, was brawny.

It wasn't only genetics that formed Jesse's slight build. He'd been affected physically by the years he and his family had suffered malnourishment before moving to Birch Creek when he was six years old. No matter how much he ate, the food never stuck to him. He was healthy otherwise, thankfully. "*Mamm* sent plenty of food with me when I moved in," he said. "I've been eating well."

"That's *gut*. You should still come over. We'd like the company."

"*Yer* sure Priscilla won't be too tired?"

"If she is, she'll rest. And if I have to cook, I will."

"Then I'm definitely *not* coming over." Jesse grinned.

Micah laughed and scraped the last bits of macaroni salad from his plate. "If you need to buy anything, the Ebersol family runs a salvage store a few miles from here. Glen Burkholder has a dairy farm and his wife makes excellent farmer's cheese."

"*Gut* to know."

"Remember, we close at three on Saturdays. Priscilla's making breakfast for supper tomorrow. Waffles, pancakes, link sausage, gravy, biscuits, the works."

Although he'd eaten a big lunch, his mouth watered, and it would be nice to have another home-cooked meal. "I'll be there."

They spent the rest of the afternoon working on the buggy. When five o'clock hit, Micah called the day. "Used to work overtime a lot when I lived alone," he said, putting up his tools. "Now I don't work a minute past five unless there's a customer here. That reminds me, tomorrow morning I'll teach you how to take orders. You're catching on fast around here."

"Doesn't feel that way," Jesse admitted. "I haven't done much work with these kinds of tools or machines before. Farming and livestock mostly."

"Then I guess *yer* a natural." Micah opened a small drawer on one of the organizing units that housed nails and screws and pulled out a key. "Here. You can lock up tonight. See you in the morning."

"See ya." Jesse took the key and stared at it as Micah left the shop. Nice. He hadn't expected such a huge responsibility this soon.

He cleaned up around the shop, the task helping him cement in his mind where things were stored. About half an hour had passed when he saw Monroe trot into the shop. Jesse grinned. "Well, well. Look who's here."

Monroe hadn't been back since the day Jesse moved in. Micah had laughed when Jesse explained how the dog was searching for goodies. "*Ya*, he likes to come over for treats," he'd said. "That's *mei* fault. He's a little greedy, but I don't mind. You should have seen him before Shirley rescued him. Someone dropped him off in front of her house. He was skin and bones and shy with everyone except her. Knowing how he must have suffered, I can't resist giving him a little something when he visits."

Looking at Monroe now, with his plump belly and filled-out face, it was difficult to believe he'd ever been malnourished. But Jesse had seen enough mistreated horses to know that once they were cared for properly, their physical condition typically improved to the point that, as long as there wasn't noticeable deformity, they looked just like their well-treated counterparts.

Monroe sat at Jesse's feet and gazed up at him.

"Sorry, *bu*. I don't have anything for you." He crouched down and scratched behind Monroe's pointed ears, making a mental note to pick up dog treats when he went shopping.

When the dog rolled over and presented his belly, Jesse rubbed him there for a few minutes more. While it was good to know Monroe trusted him, he needed to go back home, and he was surprised Charity hadn't shown up yet.

Jesse rose and Monroe followed him as he locked up the shop. The dog continued padding right by his feet as he walked to the edge of the field separating Jesse's house and Shirley Pearson's. "*Geh* home, *bu*," he ordered, pointing at the field.

Monroe wagged his tail.

"Seriously." Jesse put a little more punch into his command. "*Geh.* Home."

Monroe sat down, his tongue lolling out of his mouth as he panted, mouth open and resembling a smile.

He couldn't bring himself to yell at the dog, especially now that he knew Monroe's history. Maybe Charity hadn't noticed he was on the lam yet. Or maybe she wasn't home. "C'mon," he said, motioning to Monroe and heading to Shirley's. "Let's get you back where you belong."

As he crossed the field, Monroe tagging along behind him, he thought about Charity again. She looked the same—millions of freckles, ginger hair, skinny as a string bean. She was still odd too. But not in a desperate way, like she'd been at the diner. Had she found a boyfriend in Marigold?

Where did that thought come from?

Micah. He'd brought up Charity and marriage. That had to be the reason.

When he and Monroe reached the halfway point, he expected Monroe to take off across the field. Instead the dog remained his loyal companion all the way to Shirley's house.

He paused near the front stoop, then wondered why he was hesitating. He was delivering their dog. No big deal.

Jesse knocked on the door and waited, Monroe sitting obediently next to him. He was about to knock again when the door finally opened. An older woman with steel-gray hair bordering on blue answered the door. "Hang on a sec," she said, fussing with a silver walker with an attached seat. "This blasted thing. There." She finally looked at Jesse. "Hello, young man."

Monroe barked.

"You stinker!" But her singsong voice held little censure. "Get in here." The dog ducked under the walker and went inside. "Thank you . . ."

"Jesse Bontrager. I'm working for Micah at the buggy shop."

"Oh. I didn't know he'd hired someone new."

Charity hadn't mentioned him to Shirley?

"Charity is out looking for this beast." Shirley motioned for Jesse to come inside. "She left her phone here so I can't tell her he's home. Why don't you come in for a drink and we can visit for a while until she gets back."

He hesitated again. He usually didn't spend time with English senior citizens. Actually, this would be a first.

"Isn't that what you Amish like to do? Visit?" She peered at him over her rimless eyeglasses, a genial gleam in her eyes.

She had him there. "Sure. I'd be happy to." He took off his hat and followed her inside.

They passed through a modestly furnished living room. Two brown leather recliners faced the square front window, the white plastic blinds open to the late-afternoon sunshine. Beside the window was a short cabinet with a TV on top. A loveseat was off to the side of the recliners, and in front of that was an empty oval coffee table. A few landscape pictures covered the walls, and he detected a scent of wintergreen in the air. Or was that arthritis cream?

"Come in the kitchen." Shirley waved to the doorway in front of her. "You can set your hat in one of the chairs if you'd like."

Jesse entered a serviceable kitchen. There was nothing fancy about Shirley's house, and it was extremely tidy. Unlike his own home, where the dishes were piled in the sink and he needed to take out the trash. His housekeeping skills could use some work.

"Hopefully you can help me with an issue that's cropped up."

He sat down and placed his hat on the empty chair next to him, wondering what he'd walked into. Even though he didn't know Shirley, if she needed help, he'd do what he could. "I can try."

Her light-pink lips formed a smile that didn't quite reach her eyes. "I appreciate it." She pointed to a stack of books and a single notebook on the table. "You can start by taking a look at that while I get our drinks. Do you like soda pop?"

"Yes."

"Any particular flavor?"

"Whatever you have is good." He sat down and glanced at the materials. *My Courtship Plan* was written on the first page of the notebook. "What am I looking at?"

Shirley sighed and turned around. "A huge problem."

.ം๑๒๑.

Shirley's knees ached as she handed Jesse a can of soda. She tried to ease herself onto the chair across from Jesse, attempting to maintain the remnants of her dignity that hadn't surrendered to severe arthritis, diabetic neuropathy, and, because she didn't have enough ailments in her dotage, the ministroke that had struck earlier in the year. Fortunately she'd fully recovered from the stroke, but all she could do was manage the arthritis stiffness and the neuropathy pain and numbness.

Oh well, not that she needed to impress anyone, especially this young Amish man. Although she had to admit he was quite handsome. She'd never seen a man with such crazy curls before. Nothing compared to her Alan in his prime, but still, a nice-looking boy.

Ah, Alan. A day didn't go by when her heart didn't ache to see him again. Moving to Marigold and buying this small house had been their retirement dream. Five years ago they'd pursued that dream, leaving their only child, Wendy, and the bustle of New York City behind. Her daughter had been surprised and unhappy when they had returned from a church trip visiting the Holmes County area and announced they'd fallen in love and were moving there as soon as Alan retired from his loan officer job at a major bank. Wendy didn't think they'd go through with it . . . but they did.

A year ago he passed away. Wendy wanted her to move back to the city, but Shirley couldn't return to that busy lifestyle. Alan wouldn't want her to. The four years they lived here together had been wonderful, and she felt close to him here. *Lord, how I miss that man.*

She cleared her thoughts and focused on her current problem, pushing Charity's notebook forward. "Is this normal for you Amish?" she asked.

He glanced at the notebook, then back at her. "I don't exactly follow."

His confused expression gave her a little hope that not every young Amish woman prepared some ridiculous plan to snag a man. Although she'd lived around the Amish long enough now to understand some of their ways, and she and Priscilla had become good friends, she didn't know all the ins and outs of their rules. The *Ordnung*, Priscilla had called them, but she hadn't elaborated. Shirley respected her privacy.

She would respect Charity's if she wasn't so troubled about this cockamamie plan. When her assistant had run off to find Monroe again after Shirley had taken him out for a potty break, she left behind her books and notes on the kitchen table. Shirley had caught the words *Courtship Plan*, and investigated further. She shouldn't have snooped, but once she realized what Charity was up to, she was glad she did.

The whole thing was an invitation to mortification, and somehow Shirley had to put a stop to it. However, she'd never butted into an Amish person's business before, and she wasn't sure what to do. She thought about talking with Priscilla, but she was resting and nesting. So this young man was the lucky one—or unlucky, depending on how things turned out.

"Just know that I don't normally advocate reading someone else's private thoughts," Shirley said. "Once she realizes she can't find Monroe and she's forgotten her phone, she'll be back."

To his credit he hesitated, tugging at his earlobe twice. "Are you sure this is okay?"

Probably not, but there was no time to discuss ethics. "Sure. Now read, please."

He slowly picked up the notebook and the first page. He turned to the second one, then the third, his eyes widening as he read. When he reached the sixth and final page, he looked at Shirley, bewildered. "I've never heard of a courtship plan before." He paused. "But maybe I'm not the best person to ask. I've got one sister and ten brothers, and my sister is over a decade older than me."

"Wow. That's a large family."

"Yep."

As he set the notebook down, she regarded him for a moment. He was clean-shaven, so she knew he wasn't married. And he was new to town, so he likely didn't have a girlfriend, although she couldn't know for sure. Now she wondered if she had made a mistake by showing him this. "I realize you don't know Charity—"

"I do." He glanced at the notebook again before lifting his gaze. "Not real well, but she lived in Birch Creek for a while. That's where I'm from."

"Welcome to Marigold." Shirley smiled. At least she wasn't going to seem like a complete lunatic by asking someone Charity didn't know to help her. Although from her experience with Micah and Priscilla, and the other Amish people living around here, she had found them eager to give assistance when asked. "I'll cut to the chase, Jesse." She tapped on the table. "You need to convince her to give up this ridiculous plan."

"Wait . . . what?"

"It's extremely important she doesn't go through with this lunacy."

"Have you talked to her about it?" he asked.

"No. Like I said, I just found out. And I will absolutely express my concerns. I'm not sure she'll listen to me, though. I'm not familiar enough with your ways to have any influence."

"I doubt I'd have any either," he mumbled.

"But you know each other. She'd view you as a helpful friend instead of a meddling old woman."

"I doubt that." He pushed back a mass of curls from his forehead, his frown deepening as his gaze shifted to one of the books on the table. "*Getting a Man and Keeping Him*," he said. "By Montague Persimmons."

"That *cannot* be a real name." Shirley sniffed. "I refuse to believe a mother would name her child something so absurd." She heard the front door open and Monroe shot out of the kitchen.

"Monroe!" Charity squawked from the living room. "I've been looking all over for you! Where have you been?"

"Quick," Shirley said, shoving the notebook back to its original place. "Act natural."

"Uh . . ."

Charity entered the kitchen, Monroe at her heels, her freckles almost blending in with her red-hued face. She froze in the doorway, her gaze going to Jesse, then to Shirley, then to the notebook and relationship book. She dashed to the table and grabbed everything, including the small pile of paper napkins Shirley liked to keep close at hand, then pressed the load to her chest and gaped at Jesse. "What are you doing here?"

"He brought Monroe home." Shirley's cheeks ached from grinning. Slowly—she couldn't move any other way—she rose from her chair. "I'll let you two young people talk."

"But—" they both said in unison.

"Don't mind me. C'mon, Monroe." She waved to her darling pup who had brought her both joy and aggravation. Right now she was thankful he'd run off, or else she wouldn't have known about Montague Persimmons and Charity's courtship plan.

Monroe snuck under the table and laid at Jesse's feet.

Shirley arched a brow, feeling a tiny tug of jealousy. Monroe always came when she called—when they were in the house, that is—and he followed her everywhere. Now he was glued to Jesse's shoe. She had no idea he was so fickle. *Oh well.*

She made her way to the living room, blew out a breath, and plopped onto her recliner, sinking into the supple leather. *I hope I'm doing the right thing.* Since Charity had started working for her she'd taken a shine to the young girl. Shirley and her daughter had gone round and round about hiring a caregiver. She didn't need one, and she'd intended to prove it to Wendy. But it wasn't long before she realized—and it was a painful realization—that she did need help. Charity had been more than eager to offer it.

Over the past weeks she had gotten to know her fairly well, even though she was tight-lipped about her family life back in Cherry Springs. Except when she talked about her late grandmother. Obviously they had been very close.

Shirley suspected this unconventional Amish girl was hiding a lot of pain. She'd experienced plenty of pain of her own in her seventy-seven years. Who hadn't when they reached her age? Maybe she had a sixth sense when it came to emotional burdens, or she'd gained some wisdom over time. Perhaps both.

She closed her eyes and started to pray. She'd add Charity to her church prayer list. Anonymously, of course, referring to her only as a friend who needed praying over. Right now she would pray Jesse would get through to Charity and she would abandon her silly court-ship plan.

Three

You don't want to be with someone exactly
like you. Find a man who is the complete
opposite and watch the sparks fly!

Getting a Man and Keeping Him, p. 34

Charity rushed to the nearest kitchen drawer, shoved her book and notebook inside, and slammed it shut. Or tried to. When the drawer wouldn't completely close she leaned into it and shoved, crinkling the paper. Hopefully she'd crushed her notes and not the book, or she'd have some explaining to do at the library.

She spun around and tried to behave like she didn't have a bear chasing her down. "Hi . . ." Oh no! What was his name? How could she have forgotten his *name*? "Uh . . ."

"Jesse?" He arched his left eyebrow.

A perfect eyebrow, she noticed. *Stop noticing!*

When she didn't find Monroe at the buggy shop, she panicked, then calmed down and went to Micah's, thinking Monroe had gone there in search of treats. When Micah said he hadn't seen Monroe since last week, alarm bells rang in her head. She widened her search, and when she hadn't found him, she went back to the cottage, praying he was waiting on the front stoop like he usually did after putting her through her paces. She'd been on the verge of tears when she didn't see him, and those were replaced with joy when she saw he was already home.

Her pulse was still racing when she walked into the kitchen, expecting to see Shirley since she hadn't been in the living room. Never in a thousand—make that a million—years had she thought Jesse would be sitting at the table with her courtship plan right next to him.

Her heart hammered in her chest and her forehead started to sweat. Was she going to have a heart attack? She was positive she was close to one.

"Charity?"

His concerned tone brought her to attention. "I knew you were Jesse." She waved her hand, trying to ignore the heat consuming her face. Best to pretend everything was normal. Did she even know what normal was? *Hospitable.* She could be hospitable. "Can I get you a drink?"

"Already have one." He raised the can of pop.

She needed a drink, and for the first time in her life she considered something stronger than soda. Not that she would ever drink alcohol, but she was sorely tempted. Shirley was a teetotaler so the point was moot, but the fact that she'd even thought about an alcoholic drink proved how close to hysteria she was.

She opened the fridge, her search for the soft drinks taking longer than it should have. Finally she found them, right under her nose. *Get it together!* She closed the door and popped the pull tab, praying the drink wouldn't explode. Being drenched in sugary water and bubbles was the last thing she needed.

Jesse tilted his head and regarded her for a minute. She squirmed under his scrutiny. Why was he still here? Why wasn't he saying anything? Why did he have such an attractive jawline? *Stop. It!*

"Um . . ." He awkwardly gestured to Shirley's chair. "Can you sit down? Please?" he added.

"I'd rather stand." She brought the drink to her mouth, bumping her chin in the process. She wiped away the soda.

"All right." He sat up in the chair and shoved his bangs to the side. His gaze flicked to the kitchen drawer. A corner of notebook paper stuck out of the top.

She almost dropped her drink. He'd seen her plan. There was no doubt he had. Hopefully he'd only seen the top page and nothing else. But wait . . . Montague Persimmon's book had been right next to it! She wanted to sink straight through the beige kitchen linoleum, never to be seen again.

The best thing she could do was get him out of there. "I'm sure you need to get back home," she said, plopping the can on the counter and hurrying to him. "I know *yer* busy and all that."

He glanced up at her and shook his head. "Not until we talk."

"About what?" Her voice climbed to the next octave. "The weather? Monroe's bad habits?" *How handsome you are?* Good grief, she was hopeless. Who cared if he was handsome? He'd been a jerk to her. Good looks didn't cover that sin.

His mouth opened. Closed. Opened again. Finally he said, "About your courtship plan."

Egad. She wasn't sure why that word popped into her head, or where she'd heard it, but it summed up her indignity perfectly. She didn't want to talk about her courtship plan with him, or anyone else. Wait. He didn't know it was *her* plan. She hadn't put her name on any of her notes. "Oh that," she said, forcing a chuckle as she sat next to him. She sounded like a squawking chicken, but pressed on. "I'm helping a . . . friend."

"What's her name?"

"Brenda."

"Does she live in Marigold?" Jesse asked, not missing a beat.

"*Ya*, er, *nee*." *Phooey*. She was a terrible liar and she didn't like the acidic feeling in her stomach when she didn't tell the truth.

"There isn't a Brenda, is there?"

"Why are you being so nosy?" She jumped up from the chair and loomed over him. Anything to get a semblance of the upper hand. "You had *nee* right to snoop!"

"I wasn't snooping." He frowned. "Not on purpose, anyway. Shirley showed me the notebook."

She gasped. Betrayed! By someone she trusted. "Why?" she wailed. "Why would she do that?"

"She's concerned about you. And after reading your 'plan'"—he made quote signs in the air—"I am too. Frankly, it's terrible."

Now she was hurt *and* angry. She took a step forward and glared at him. "Who are you to judge *mei* idea?" Then she did something she'd never done to anyone before.

She poked him in the chest.

⋅⟞⟊⟸⋅

Jesse stared at Charity's fingertip pressed against his sternum. He'd laugh at her attempt at being tough if he didn't know it would make things worse. How did he get into this mess? All he did was bring Monroe home. "Hey!" he said, louder than he intended.

The dog, who had been snoring at his feet until now, jerked up and shot out from under the table, cutting Charity off at the knees and propelling her forward.

Right into Jesse's lap.

On instinct, he grabbed her around the waist as she landed, their noses almost touching. She looked like a wide-eyed, red-faced, slightly perspiring statue. Felt like one too. Except there was a softness to her hip he hadn't anticipated. Or maybe all women were soft there. He didn't know—this was the first time he'd ever been this close to, much less touched, one.

Without thinking, his hand settled, his gaze unmoving as he realized her eyes were a slightly darker shade of blue than he thought, her eyelashes longer, her hair a deep-copper color instead of the shade of shredded carrots.

"Egad!"

The strange word, not to mention the strangled way she said it, brought him out of his fog. "What?"

She scrambled off him and sat down hard in the chair. Pushed her feet against the floor and moved the chair backward, the legs scraping against the shiny linoleum.

Jesse blinked. For a minute there he'd been . . . what? Caught off guard? Obviously. Women didn't drop into his lap—ever. Confused? Definitely. Fascinated?

Oh yeah . . .

She crossed her arms and scowled. "You had *nee* right to invade *mei* privacy. And *nee* right to say I'm stupid." As she spoke, Monroe laid back down in front of Jesse again.

"I didn't say you were stupid. I said your plan was." Yikes. He had a habit of being blunt, and right now would have been the perfect time to break it.

"That's the same thing!" She glanced away, and he noticed a small patch of almost solid freckles at the base of her chin. "I wouldn't have to do this if . . ."

"If what?"

"Never mind!"

She was right, he had no business looking at something so private, regardless of whether her plan was stupid or not. But he kept thinking about the worry he'd seen in Shirley's eyes. And once he saw what Charity was up to, she had a right to be concerned. While he'd been a little aware of her reputation for being beyond desperate and had noticed it during their calamitous lunch "date," her plan somehow managed to eclipse desperation and plunge straight into absurdity.

Even more confusing was why he was bothering with this conversation. He didn't owe Shirley anything. He'd just met the woman. And when she'd asked for his help, he assumed she meant hanging a picture or tightening up the faucet. Not this. *Time to* geh . . . *get up and* geh . . .

"You can leave now. The door is that way." She jerked her thumb at the kitchen doorway.

Despite agreeing with her that he needed to abandon this conversation and Shirley's kitchen, he didn't move. Charity was spunky, he'd give her that. He also didn't need Shirley's confirmation to know she was making a big mistake. "I'll *geh*, but not until you promise to stop reading dumb books and tear up that plan."

"*Nee.*"

Jesse paused. "*Nee?*"

"I don't answer to you." She lifted her chin. "Or Shirley. When it comes to *mei* private life anyway."

"She cares about you."

Charity swallowed. "And you figured that out after spending five minutes with her?"

"Ten, actually." He stretched out his legs and crossed his ankles. "I didn't have to figure it out either. She told me."

Charity stilled, her defiant chin dipping slightly. "She did?"

"*Ya.*"

"Really?"

Jesse nodded. Wow. Her reaction seemed extreme, as if she'd never encountered anyone who did care about her. "Really."

She leaned forward, her eyes brightening. "And you? Do you care about me?"

"Whoa." He held up his hands. "I'm just helping out Shirley."

"Why?"

Now that he'd finally met someone more straightforward than he was, he could see how annoying that trait was. Growing up, he'd asked tons of questions to anyone who would listen. Each answer spun off another query until he received the tried-and-true adult response—*because I said so.* That didn't fly with him, and it wasn't going to fly with her. "I'm helping because she asked me to. Simple as that."

"Oh. Well, I don't need your help." Her chin returned to its defiant position. "I know exactly what I'm doing."

Clearly she didn't. His lack of experience with women didn't make him an expert like that Persimmons fella, but he wasn't clueless about what made a woman attractive. "I didn't see anything in that plan that said to be yourself. You don't need an elaborate blueprint or contradicting advice. Be yourself. That's all you need to do."

"Be myself," she repeated. "Be myself."

"Exactly." He pulled in his legs, ready to get up and head home, pleased he'd taken care of the matter. There had to be a man somewhere who would be smitten with her. She just hadn't found him yet.

Slowly her eyes narrowed into slits. "That's the most ridiculous thing I've ever heard. Be myself? Ha!"

"But—"

"How many girlfriends have you had?"

Jesse wriggled in the chair. "That's a personal question."

"This is a personal conversation. How many? Three? Eight? A gaggle?"

It was one thing to hint at his lack of experience to an old lady he didn't know, and a totally different thing to talk about it with Charity Raber. How many were in a gaggle anyway? And why did she bring up geese?

"Never mind." She sighed. "I'm sorry. I shouldn't have asked that."

Whew.

"But I'm going through with my plan. Montague Persimmons guarantees that having a well-thought-out strategy is the best way to get a husband."

"Is that a money-back guarantee?"

"I checked the book out of the library," she mumbled.

"You got what you paid for."

"Ooh." Charity rose and stood over him again. "My courtship plan will work. I'll prove it to you and Shirley."

He stood and leveled his gaze at her, which took a bit of doing since she was several inches shorter than him. "Oh? And how do you *plan* to do that?"

"There's a singing at the Masts' this Sunday." She straightened her shoulders, her obstinant eyes locking with his. "By the end of the night I'll have at least one man wanting to ask me out. Maybe two. Or three."

At least she didn't say a gaggle this time, although she was still being preposterous. "What if you don't?"

She took a step forward. "I will."

He moved closer. "Are you sure?"

She held her ground. "I'm so sure that I'll . . ." Her mouth angled into a slight frown.

"You'll what?"

"I'll bake you a pie. *Ya*, that's what I'll do."

He threw back his head and laughed. "A pie?"

"Fine, a cake."

"Pie's *gut*." He crossed his arms. "I pick the flavor, *ya*?"

"*Ya*."

"Homemade crust," he said, not bothering to hide his grin. "Not that store-bought stuff."

She rolled her eyes. "Homemade crust. But don't get your hopes up." Her confident air returned. "You're *not* getting a pie." She turned and stalked out of the kitchen. "Show yourself out," she said as she disappeared into the living room.

He was still grinning, only for it to fade as he realized he'd done the opposite of what Shirley requested. He'd goaded Charity on instead of stopping her. *Egad*.

Jesse stared at Monroe, who was looking up at him. Was that censure in his pale-blue eyes? "Okay. I messed up." He stroked the top of the dog's head. Had he truly snafued, though? Charity wasn't going to listen to him, and he'd told Shirley as much. At least he'd made an attempt. Not a very good one, but it was something.

Monroe sauntered to his silver water bowl and lapped. Jesse left the kitchen and entered the living room. As expected, Charity was gone, and based on Shirley's disappointed expression from her perch on the recliner, she was aware he hadn't gotten through to her. "I'm sorry. I did try." Guilt plucked his conscience. "I should have tried harder."

Shirley sighed. "No, it's my fault. I shouldn't have asked you to speak with her in the first place. Or read her plan."

"Where did she go?"

"For a walk. She does that sometimes when she's frustrated. This

61

is the first time I've seen her upset, though." She removed her glasses and set them on the end table between the two recliners. "I'll apologize to her when she gets back. She reminds me of myself at that age. The stubbornness, certainly."

Jesse nodded, unsure what else there was to say. The situation was now between her and Shirley. "Well, I better get back—"

"So you two knew each other when she lived in Birch Creek?"

Uh-oh. He didn't like that little glint of hope in her eyes. "Barely," he said. "Our paths didn't cross much."

"But they did cross." She leaned forward. "What do you think of her, young man?"

He moved closer to the door. He was *not* going to be a part of either woman's antics. "Like I said, I don't know her very well."

Shirley observed him for a moment. Then she relaxed in her chair. "I see. Well, thank you for your help. And for bringing Monroe home." She sighed and shook her head. "I'm in the process of getting bids for a fence. He's determined to run next door and I don't want him to get hit by a car. Our road isn't busy, fortunately. But I worry just the same."

As if Monroe knew she was talking about him, he walked to her and laid his chin on her knee.

"Take care, Jesse." Shirley rubbed Monroe's right ear.

He seized the opportunity to leave. "You too, Ms. Pearson."

"Please." She smiled, a full, genuine one. "Call me Shirley."

As Jesse walked back home through the tall grass, he remembered something Charity had said during their discussion—or more accurately, argument.

"I wouldn't have to do this if . . ."

What had she meant by that? She didn't answer him when he'd questioned her, so he had no idea. For some reason she believed she had to get a man and keep him, for lack of a better phrase—and there *had* to be a better phrase. Why? Who or what was putting the pressure on her?

Then there was her reaction to the news that Shirley cared for her. She'd been surprised . . . no, she'd been *shocked*. Surely she had family where she came from. Didn't they love her?

Despite spending his childhood grasping for his parents' attention, he'd always known they loved him. When he grew older, he was able to comprehend how difficult it was to give undivided attention to so many children. He'd never felt uncared for, even when they had lived in extreme poverty in Fredericktown. Although he and his brothers and sister had suffered, he knew now his parents had agonized much more from being unable to support their family. Things had changed drastically when they moved to Birch Creek, but that didn't alter the past.

He swallowed the lump in his throat and shoved those memories away, along with Charity and her plan. She wasn't his responsibility. His job kept him plenty busy, and he was determined not to get distracted from work. Getting involved was the last thing he needed or wanted to do.

She'd have to learn her lesson the hard way.

Four

Be mysterious and seductive. Channel your
inner femme fatale and he'll do your bidding.

Getting a Man and Keeping Him, p. 46

The next evening, Charity left Shirley's house and headed to the Masts' more than ninety minutes before the singing was scheduled to start. This was her first singing since she'd moved to Marigold, and she was eager to spend some time with people in her age group. Marigold was a small and fairly new Amish community, so there weren't many young folks. But there were some, including a few single men, and they were part of the reason she had moved here.

Another reason she'd left early was to escape more lecturing from Shirley about her courtship plan. No, that wasn't fair to Shirley—she wasn't lecturing. She was strongly persuading her to drop the idea.

"I won't," Charity said, putting on her black tennis shoes.

Shirley rubbed her forehead. "Can you at least tell me why you're so determined to go through with this?"

Charity paused, halfway in the middle of tying her left shoe. She hadn't told Shirley much about her life in Cherry Springs, and until now, her boss hadn't asked. Most of the time they'd spent over the past two months had been getting acclimated to each other. Charity didn't know much about Shirley either, other than talking to her daughter, Wendy, when she was first hired, and Shirley's infrequent mentions of her late husband, Alan.

But now wasn't the time to get into family drama. "I want to get married." She quickly finished tying her shoes and stood. "End of story."

"But—"

She rushed out of the house before Shirley could try to stop her. Although she wanted to, she couldn't be angry with her, even though Shirley had snooped and dragged Jesse into her private sphere. When he'd told her Shirley cared, her heart leapt. Someone cared about her. She soaked that in like a dried-up sponge sitting in a saucer of fresh water.

But even though she wasn't angry, she wasn't giving in either. Shirley didn't understand. Neither did Jesse. If he did, he wouldn't have told her to be herself. What a load of malarkey. That's what she'd been doing the entire time, and it netted her nothing. Not even a single date. Being herself was the exact wrong thing to do.

She was Charity Raber, and she wasn't like other women. She'd never been accepted for herself. Definitely not by her stepmother, and her father was so aloof she wasn't entirely sure he wanted to bother with her either.

Then there were the men. She could understand her romance problems back home. Moving to Cherry Springs right after *Grossmammi* died had been a nightmare. The community consisted of only five families, all related to Elaine, and they seemed to take their cue from her about how to treat Charity. Friends were hard to come by, never mind dates. It didn't help that the more stressed she was, the weirder she behaved. That had gotten her into plenty of trouble with Elaine, and her peers kept their distance.

When she also struggled in Birch Creek, she knew something had to change. *Me.*

She mulled over phase one of her plan in her mind as she continued to walk.

1. Channel your inner femme fatale.

She'd had to look up *femme fatale* in the pocket dictionary Shirley kept with her crossword puzzle book. There were two definitions. One had to do with being seductive, and she wasn't prepared to do that. She didn't think she could even if she wanted to. But the other meaning was more achievable.

A woman who attracts men by an aura of charm and mystery.

She could learn to be charming, and she had being mysterious down. No one in Marigold knew her background, and she aimed to keep it that way for the foreseeable future.

2. Always maintain eye contact.

Easy enough.

3. Wear sexy perfume.

That was too worldly, but her bath soap smelled really good.

4. Add subtle touch.

Her face reddened. She'd never touched a man before . . . except when that troublemaker Monroe tripped her and she fell into Jesse's lap. A tiny thrill had gone through her as she gazed at his handsome face, the soft-looking curls framing his features. Even better was the warmth of his chest against her side. That had felt good. And she wasn't sure, but she thought she sensed his hand on her hip. Then again, she was so tied up inside she probably imagined his palm resting there—

Stop, stop, stop! She gave her head a hard shake. Jesse was the last person on earth she wanted invading her thoughts.

She jerked her mind back to phase one. If she had to lightly touch a man's arm tonight to get his attention, she could do that.

5. Don't forget to smile.

Charity grinned, practicing her smile the rest of the way to the Masts'. By the time she arrived, her mouth was tired, but at least she was ready to put phase one into motion. Butterflies danced in her stomach as she knocked on the door.

Saloma Mast answered it. "Hi, Charity."

Her excitement dimmed. Like Norene Yoder back in Birch Creek, and Doreen Zook—another one of her peers who wasn't nice—in Cherry Springs, Saloma was beautiful. She even resembled Norene—pale-blond hair, sky-blue eyes, and a figure that wasn't pencil shaped. Beside her, Charity felt like a limp carrot. That insecurity had kept her from interacting with Saloma other than saying hi at church. In fact, she held back from talking to anyone, other than exchanging pleasantries. Experience had shown that the less she said, the better.

But keeping to herself wouldn't land her a husband, and smiles weren't just for men. "Hi," she said, lifting the corners of her mouth. *Ouch.* "Am I late?"

Saloma shook her head. "*Nee.* You're almost an hour early."

An hour before she could put her plan into action. *Phooey.* She must have walked faster than she thought.

"I guess we can hang out if you want." Saloma glanced away as she opened the door for Charity to come in.

After standing in front of the closed door for several seconds, she waited for Saloma to say something. Instead she clasped her fingers in front of her and stared at the floor. When Charity couldn't take the silence anymore, she asked, "Is there anything I can do to help set up?"

"*Nee. Mamm* and *Daed* are in the basement setting out food and chairs." After another inelegant pause, she added, "Do you, uh, want to *geh* to the living room?"

Charity nodded and followed her farther into the house. She sat in one of the chairs directly across from the couch.

Saloma stared at the floor, her petite feet close together, saying nothing.

Awkward. Since Charity was the queen of awkward situations, she mimicked Saloma. But after a few seconds, boredom hit and she glanced around the Masts' living room. It was neat as a pin and sparsely furnished, but there were three small watercolors on the wall depicting wildlife. "Those are pretty," she said.

"*Mamm* insisted on hanging them up."

"You don't like them?"

"I do." She looked at Charity again, her flawless cheeks rosy. "It's embarrassing when people compliment them. I don't paint because I want my art displayed."

Charity looked at the paintings again. They were lovely—more abstract than real life, but the subject matter was still easy to see. The first one was a dragonfly, the second a pond with a dock, and the third a snow-covered barn. "You did those?"

"*Ya*," Saloma said, a small smile on her face. "Do you do any crafts?"

"*Nee. Mamm* said—" She needed to stop calling her stepmother

her mother, even in her head. *Elaine* had always said crafts were a waste of time, that there were enough chores to keep a person busy. "*Nee.* I never had the chance."

"I can show you how to paint, if you like?"

She remembered Katharine Miller's offer to teach her how to make baskets last year. She'd scoffed in response, more out of wanting to hurt Katharine than anything else. Even then she could tell Ezra Bontrager had his eye on her, despite Katharine being overweight, having bad skin, and rarely talking to anyone. *And she managed to get Ezra.*

That wasn't completely fair. Katharine had started losing weight before she and Ezra dated, and she'd heard about Katharine's abusive fiancé after the man showed up and tried taking her back to Wyoming where they were from. But Charity had been too caught up in her jealousy to apologize to Katharine for all the hurtful remarks she'd made . . . and there were more than a few. Shame filled her. She'd never apologized to Norene for her snotty behavior either.

"It's okay if you don't want to." Saloma broke into her thoughts. "Painting isn't for everyone. *Mei bruder* and *vatter* don't have the patience for it, and *Mamm* prefers cross-stitch."

"Where is *yer bruder*, by the way?" Charity hoped she sounded nonchalant. Saloma's twin brother, Olin, was as handsome as Saloma was pretty. Being early could have an advantage. Executing phase one would be easier with fewer people around.

"He'll be here by five. He's over at Clarence's house this afternoon."

"Saloma!" her mother's voice came from downstairs. "Can you bring the plates of cookies and brownies?"

"*Ya, Mamm!*" She turned to Charity. "We can wait for everyone downstairs. *Daed* will answer the door."

Charity followed her to the kitchen, where they picked up the two large platters piled high with scrumptious-looking treats, and headed to the basement. She couldn't remember Saloma's parents' names, so she just said hi as she walked over to a long table set up with snacks and drinks.

"We'll be upstairs if you need anything," Saloma's mother said. She had the same blue eyes as Saloma and Olin, and they were sparkling as she turned to her husband. "Remember our singings, Aaron?"

"Painfully." At her harsh look he grinned. "Just kidding. We had a lot of fun."

After they left, Saloma gestured to the Ping-Pong table on the other side of the basement. "Do you play? I do a little. Olin enjoys it, though."

Charity didn't play but made a mental note to figure out a charming and mysterious way to ask Saloma's brother to teach her Ping-Pong.

Footfalls sounded upstairs, and it wasn't long before several young women and men arrived. The females congregated on one side of the room while the males hovered around the refreshment table.

Charity held back from both groups and turned her attention to the men—all six of them. At least two were too young for her. But Olin, his friend Clarence, and another young man whom she hadn't seen before were around her age. She grinned. After the singing portion of the evening ended, phase one would commence. She said a quick prayer: *Please, Lord, let my future husband be here tonight.*

When everyone was settled in their places and ready to start the hymns, the sound of hurried footsteps came down the stairs.

"Wait," Olin said. "Someone's coming."

They all looked to the basement entrance and saw Jesse bolt into the room.

·ᕯᕲᕲ·

There were several reasons Jesse should have stayed home tonight instead of going to the Masts'. He couldn't sing, for starters. And that didn't mean he was out of tune here and there. A cow giving birth sounded more melodic than him. Last night during supper at the Waglers', Micah had asked Priscilla to sing. Quickly he'd joined his wife, and fortunately they hadn't asked Jesse to participate. If they had, he might have lost his job. A bit of exaggeration, but they certainly wouldn't have invited him back to supper any time soon.

He also knew there would be at least one young woman here assuming he was available. Considering singings were a prime venue to find a date, that assumption was expected. He was stepping into the proverbial lion's den on purpose.

Then there was the main reason he absolutely, positively shouldn't be here. Charity. He vowed to let her sink or swim on her own tonight, but for some inexplicable reason, he decided twenty minutes ago to make a last-ditch effort to convince her to knock off her nonsense, even though a pie hung in the balance.

All eyes landed on him. Unsurprising, since he was ten minutes late and wasn't even supposed to be here. Olin Mast had invited him to the singing last Sunday morning, but he'd declined. He'd been to only one singing in his life and Malachi literally dragged him there, yanking on his arm as they walked into Andrew and Joanna Beiler's house. That was right after a new crop of single women had arrived in Birch Creek. Before he had slipped out the back basement door, three of them were flirting with him.

"Hi." Olin, a tall, lanky man with cornsilk-colored hair, walked over to him. "Glad you changed your mind. We were just getting ready to sing."

Sweat broke out on the back of Jesse's neck. "Great," he said weakly. Now he wished he'd taken his time coming here, although he'd been in a rush to stop Charity. Well, he'd faked singing in church almost all his life. What was one more night?

"Just join in wherever." Olin grinned, then went back to the group.

Chairs were lined up on either side of a long table, with girls on one side and boys on the other. He counted ten people, with him being the eleventh. He went to the men's side of the table and stood . . . directly across from Charity. Her face was turning crimson.

Clarence, a tall, heavyset young man with suspenders straining against the sides of his belly and an already receding hairline, sang out a rich, on-pitch note from a common hymn. The rest of the young women and men joined in.

Jesse not only pretended to sing. He tried to ignore the young woman standing next to Charity, staring at him. She looked like a counterpart to Olin, and Jesse assumed she was his sister, Saloma. Olin had mentioned her to him when he was pointing out his family members after the church service. He glanced down at the table. Could she tell he wasn't singing? He hoped not.

Then he heard a sweet, clear voice rise above the others. He looked up and realized that voice belonged to Charity.

Her eyes were closed, and she was seemingly enthralled with the music. He forgot to mouth the words as he listened to her honeyed voice. She wasn't Priscilla, but she was close.

When she opened her eyes, they locked on to him. Uh-oh, she'd caught him staring. Quickly his gaze darted around the room as he lip-synced again.

The song must have been the longest one in the hymnal, but finally it ended. One down, many more to go. He'd heard that some youth groups sang as long as two hours. *Oh boy.*

As everyone else discussed the next song, Charity leaned over the table. "You're supposed to be singing," she whispered.

He gulped. "I am."

"*Nee* you're not. You were mouthing the words." She leaned closer. "You're checking up on me, *ya*?"

Busted. "*Nee*."

"Well, you're not here to sing, that's for sure."

"I'm here to make friends." Not quite a lie. Eventually he wanted to have friends in Marigold.

"Oh." Her whisper disappeared. "All right, but you need to stay out of *mei* way. Because I'm going through with *mei* plan *nee* matter what you say."

Saloma leaned forward. "What plan?"

Charity stilled, wide-eyed. "Um, *mei* plan to suggest a hymn."

"Why do you need a plan to do that?"

Everyone was looking at her now. Charity's cheeks turned scarlet. "I plan everything."

"What song should we sing next?" Olin asked.

Her jaw twitched. She shot Jesse a glare, then said, "Ah, 'It Is Well with My Soul'?"

"We just sang that," Clarence pointed out.

"Oh. Right." Charity opened her mouth again. Zero sound came forth. She resembled a petrified log while everyone waited for her to make another suggestion.

Seeing her flounder was excruciating. "How about we sing 'The Whippoorwill Song'?" Jesse said.

"*Gut* choice." Clarence grinned. "Start us off."

Jesse gripped the edge of the table. "What?"

"Start the hymn."

Cold dread raced to his heels. Clarence had no idea he was asking for everyone's ears to bleed. *I definitely should have stayed home tonight.*

But then Charity's clear voice sang the first verse.

Everyone smiled and joined in.

Jesse mouthed the words and looked at Charity, expecting her to glare at him again. Instead she was closing her eyes and singing in that wonderful voice of hers. Thank the Lord she'd saved his bacon. Being a bad singer wasn't a crime. Well, maybe it was criminal to music, but he wouldn't be ostracized for being tone-deaf. Still, it wasn't the kind of impression he wanted to make during his second week in his new community.

He faked his way through the next hour or so, Charity's singing making the whole thing bearable. When they were finished, Olin led the way to the snack table. The rest of the guys followed him, except for Clarence.

The girls gathered around Charity, who appeared flummoxed that she was the center of attention. They didn't ply her with compliments, as was the Amish way. But it was obvious they appreciated her singing ability.

"Do you know her?"

He turned to Clarence, who stood by his side. The man was gesturing with his beefy hand toward Charity. Jesse nodded. "A little. We lived in Birch Creek at the same time."

Clarence inched a little closer, still looking at the girls. "What's her name?"

"Charity," he said, looking at her again. Her cheeks were pink with excitement that the girls were being so open and friendly. He tried to remember if he'd ever seen her with a group of friends in Birch Creek. He couldn't recall. Then again, he hadn't paid attention.

"She sure is pretty," Clarence murmured.

That wasn't a word he associated with Charity Raber, but in that moment, being surrounded by young women tacitly giving her approval, Jesse had to agree with him. *She does look pretty.*

Saloma broke away from the group and walked over to Jesse. "We have plenty of snacks," she said. "*Mamm* and *Daed* always *geh* a little overboard. Can I get you something?"

Jesse shook his head.

"I'd like some chips," Clarence piped up.

Saloma turned to him, giving him a vacant stare. "You know where they are." Her tone wasn't rude. More akin to a long-suffering sister. She put her back to him and focused on Jesse again. "I can bring you some cheese puffs if you'd like."

"Uh, sure."

Smiling, Saloma headed to the snack table.

"*Ya*," Clarence said, gazing at her as she walked away. "She sure is pretty."

Jesse's brow shot up. Five girls had been in the group including Saloma. Why had he assumed Clarence had been watching Charity?

Because I am.

Five

Act like you don't care. Don't make a big deal about
mistakes and things will smooth over quickly.

Getting a Man and Keeping Him, p. 48

*F*emme fatale . . . *eye contact* . . . *smell nice* . . . *subtle touch* . . . *smile.*
Charity repeated the phrases in her mind as she walked over
to Olin, who was filling a plate with chips, cookies, pretzels, and a
cupcake piled high with chocolate frosting. Where did he put all the
calories? He was thinner than she was. And oh so handsome. She
should pay attention more in church because she hadn't fully realized
that Olin Mast was so good-looking.

Femme fatale . . . *eye contact* . . .

By the time she reached him she was on subtle touch. He lifted
the cupcake to his mouth.

Subtle . . . *touch.* She batted his arm.

Bloop. The cupcake smashed against his forehead.

Phooey. She scrambled for the napkins on the nearby table and
knocked his other hand.

His plate flipped to the floor.

She dropped down and slapped the food back onto the plate. "I'm
sorry!"

"It's all right," he said, sounding a little dazed and a lot confused.

When she scraped up as much as she could, she stood to see him wiping icing off his forehead with his fingers.

Maybe she could salvage this. What was phase one again? *Eye contact*, right. She widened her eyes and stared at him.

He frowned, bits of icing dotting his blond eyebrows. "Are you okay?"

She leaned forward, still holding his gaze. Or trying to. Why was he looking away? *Subtle touch, eye contact . . .* good gravy, she couldn't remember the others. Wait—femme fatale! She batted her eyes and lowered her voice. "Do you know I'm *mysterious*?"

"Here, buddy." Jesse handed Olin several napkins.

"*Danki.*" Olin continued to gawk at her as he accepted them.

"Charity," Jesse said, calmly reaching for the plate. When she wouldn't release it, he tugged it out of her hand. "I need your help with something."

"Now?"

"*Ya.*" His eyes bolted onto hers.

"Help with what?"

"I'll tell you on the way home," he muttered, leaning closer to her.

She didn't have time for this. "Whatever it is, I'm sure it can wait."

"*Nee*, it can't." His teeth clenched.

"Jesse, I'm busy right now—"

Somehow he managed to place his hand on the back of her waist and gently direct her to the stairs. "See you later," he called out to everyone over his shoulder, then nudged her forward again.

"Bye, Jesse!" Saloma said.

"What do you think you're doing?" Charity growled as she ran up the stairs.

He didn't answer, and he left little room between them for her to turn back. He hurried her through the Masts' living room, barely giving her time to tell Saloma's parents goodbye before jostling her out the door. "Keep going," he muttered, still right behind her.

As soon as they were at the end of the driveway she whirled around, not caring if she knocked him over. "Explain yourself."

As cool as a late-autumn day, he said, "You're welcome."

Bewildered, she threw up her hands. "For what?"

"Rescuing you." He whistled as he moved past her and ambled down the road.

Whatever was coming through his pursed lips wasn't music. "You're off-key." She hurried to fall in step with him.

"I know." He kept moving, thankfully ceasing his whistling.

"You're the most confounding man I've ever met! I didn't need rescuing."

He stuck his hands in his pockets. "Pretty sure you did."

"I had the situation under control."

They walked underneath a streetlamp and she could see he was smirking. That did it. She jumped in front of him. "You don't need help with anything, do you?"

His smirk faded. "*Nee*. But you did. You were making a fool of yourself."

Ouch. Deep down she knew he was correct but that didn't give him the right to interfere, something she told him not to do. "For your information, I was employing phase one."

"You were scaring Olin."

"Was not."

"You were staring at him like this." Jesse's eyes bulged to the point she thought they'd pop out of his head. Then he blinked several times, frowning. "How did you do that without hurting yourself?"

"Stop it," she snapped.

"I haven't gotten to the best part." He tilted one shoulder forward and looked at her, batting his eyelashes. "Do you know I'm *mysterious*?"

Her palm covered her mouth. Had she looked like that? Acted like that? In front of Olin . . . in front of *everyone*?

I did. Oh nee *. . . I did.*

Tears burned in her eyes. *Never let anyone see you cry.* But she couldn't stop them from coming. She'd made an idiot out of herself. Just like Jesse and Shirley said she would. She spun on her heel and fled.

.∽⊛∾.

Jesse hadn't meant to upset Charity, but her insistence that the disaster at the Masts' wasn't a problem got under his skin, and his response was less than mature. He'd had a problem mocking others in the past, especially to exasperate his brothers. But over the past year he'd tried to curb the temptation. Why did bad habits have to die so hard?

At least he'd finally caught her attention. He had a hard time believing she had no idea how she'd behaved tonight. Awkward didn't begin to cover it and he'd had secondhand embarrassment watching her flail with Olin, who'd been a good sport about the situation. But that didn't excuse him making fun of her. To her face. He cringed and chased after her.

She was fast for a girl, but not fast enough, and it didn't take him long to catch up. "Hey. Slow down."

She sped up instead.

"Charity . . ." He put some power into his legs and overcame her, jumping in front of her, leaving her no choice but to stop. They were under another streetlamp, and he could see her face clearly.

"Move." Her chest heaved up and down.

"*Nee*. Not until we talk this out."

"I have *nix* to say to you. So move."

But he remained in place. "You're upset."

She wiped at her eyes with the backs of her hands. Gave him a cool look. Jutted out her chin. "I'm not bothered."

"*Ya*, you are."

Her chin dipped an inch. "How would you know? You're not a mind reader."

No, but he could read the pain on her face as if it were written with her freckles.

Without a word, she stepped to the side, her back ramrod straight, and walked past him.

Jesse stood under the yellow lamplight, wondering what he should do. Chase after her again? Try to apologize? No, not now. She wouldn't accept it anyway. He might not know her well, but one thing he knew was she didn't listen. Any attempt to talk to her, even to say he was sorry, would be wasted breath. He'd wait a little while and try again.

He headed back home, his pace slower than it had been when he rushed to the Masts'. Tonight played out as he'd expected, although her shoving a cupcake into Olin's face and acting like a lunatic hadn't crossed his mind. Again he questioned why he was bothering. All they did was argue, and she was determined to go her own way regardless of what he said.

But there was the niggling thought he'd had ever since Friday. *If I don't watch out for her, who will?* She wasn't his responsibility, but he still couldn't shake her reaction to Shirley's fondness for her. She'd even gone as far as to ask him if *he* cared about her.

His family had raised sheep for a few years, and when one of them became separated from the rest, it was defenseless and confused. Charity reminded him a little of those sheep. And while he didn't have any romantic feelings for her—he wasn't sure he even *liked* her—he didn't want her to get into trouble either.

He shoveled his hair from his forehead and sighed. Maybe by some miracle her plan would accidentally work and she would find a husband. Then she'd be that guy's obligation . . . and Jesse could forget about her.

.ৎ৩৩৩.

When she arrived at Shirley's front porch, Charity heaved a breath, wiped her wet eyes again, and tried to forget the most humiliating night of her life. Considering her existence was in some state of shambles most of the time, that was saying something. She still couldn't believe Jesse had sabotaged her tonight. True, her first encounter with Olin had been a disaster, and she'd looked like a fool, but maybe she could have fixed it. Jesse hadn't even given her the chance, and then he had the gall to say she owed him her thanks. *Never.*

After another inhale, she opened the door, hoping Shirley had decided to turn in early tonight. The last thing she wanted was her boss to see her in distress. But in line with how her evening had gone, Shirley was in her recliner reading, Monroe near her feet and sitting at attention.

Shirley set her book in her lap and took off her glasses. "How was your evening?"

"Great!" She sniffed. Her nose was still stuffy from trying to hide her tears from Jesse. That was the second time she'd almost cried in front of him. *Triple phooey.*

"You sound a little sniffly. Are you feeling well?"

"Yep! I had a great night, a great walk home, and I'm going to have a great sleep. 'Night." Before Shirley could say anything else she dashed off to her bedroom, shut the door, and plunked down on the edge of her bed.

She'd spent most of her life in her bedroom, especially after her grandmother died. Whenever Elaine was angry with her, which was often, she had escaped to her room. Her stepmother was more than fifteen years older than her father, and her three boys were already grown, so it was just the three of them in Elaine's old house in Cherry Springs. When her father had married Elaine right after *Grossmammi* died, Charity had hoped she would fill a tiny part of the huge hole in her heart, a hole that started with her mother's death and grew after her grandmother passed away.

Instead he wed a woman who resented everything about her.

A knock sounded at the door. "Charity?"

She sighed. She should have known Shirley would check on her. Even in her sorry state, she managed a small smile, glad that one person in the world cared. "Yes?"

"Are you really okay?" Shirley's tone sounded hesitant.

Nee. *I'm not okay.* The memory of Olin's face smeared with brown frosting wouldn't leave her mind. Neither would Jesse's mocking.

Her fists clenched. She had to regroup. Just because she'd made a few mistakes didn't mean her entire plan was bad. Jesse's arrival threw her off. She'd been so nervous approaching Olin that her touch had been as subtle as a freight train plowing through a snowbank. She would be more prepared next time she saw him. Calmer. *Confident!*

"Charity?"

"I'm all right. I had a busy night, and I'm a little tired. That's all."

A pause. "Okay." Shirley's voice sounded muffled through the door. "If you need to talk to anyone, I'm here."

Charity heard the roll of her walker and her shuffling feet as Shirley left. She stared down at her fists, still closed in two tight balls.

No, her plan was just fine. Jesse was the one who ruined it for her. He was a snafu she hadn't anticipated.

She relaxed her hands, remembering what she'd read a few days ago in *Getting a Man and Keeping Him*. She wouldn't make a big deal about tonight. If she ignored the situation, it would go away. She would rally and try phase one again. The next time she would be successful.

And the next time, Jesse Bontrager wouldn't ruin things for her. She refused to allow him to.

Ugh, why was she thinking about him again? She should be focusing on Olin and when she would see him next. Probably in a week at church service, so she'd have to wait until then to employ a second attempt of phase one. She wasn't about to ask Shirley for time off two months into her job to take care of personal business.

She pulled the clips out of her *kapp*, removed it, and started to unbraid her hair. She wouldn't have to worry about her personal business if it weren't for Jesse. What was with him mouthing the songs tonight? He didn't sing a single note, and the look of terror in his eyes when Clarence asked him to start off the song had stunned her. He had so much confidence, he didn't seem afraid of anything. Except singing, apparently.

Her fingers caught on a small knot in her hair. She grimaced. There she went, musing about Jesse again. *Olin . . . think of Olin.* She repeated his name as she readied for bed and turned out the light. "Olin," she whispered in the dark.

But when she closed her eyes, she saw Jesse's face. His mocking face.

"Ugh!" She turned over and punched her pillow. Twice.

·~⁂~·

Early Monday morning Jesse buttered a slice of bread, grabbed a cup of black coffee, and yawned as he sat down at his kitchen table. He had to be at work in two hours, and after his insomnia last night, he reckoned he should go back to bed and try to catch at least a little sleep. But although he was tired, he knew he would end up tossing and turning like he had last night.

He bit into the bread and chewed. He was still vacillating between his annoyance that Charity was mad at him for bailing her out at the Masts', his remorse over mocking her, and his frustration that he was still thinking about the situation. Teasing was an automatic response for him, and he usually gave better than he got. Last night was the first time he'd ever mocked a female, though.

"Women," he muttered, finishing off the bread and sipping the hot coffee. Now that he had a key to the shop he could go ahead and open it early. He was sure Micah wouldn't mind, and he was desperate for a distraction.

Already dressed, he took the coffee cup, grabbed the key off the hook on the wall where he'd hung it Saturday evening, and headed to work. Less than a minute later he was there. He was liking everything about his job so far, especially the commute.

Almost two hours later, Micah arrived. "*Gute morgen*."

"Morning." Jesse worked on the old drum brake Micah had given him to practice on last Friday.

Micah walked over and peered down. He was several inches taller and probably a hundred pounds heavier than Jesse. But he rarely raised his voice and he had tremendous patience showing Jesse how to take apart and put back together the brake. "Looks *gut*. How long have you been working on it?"

"About two hours."

He rubbed his blond beard. "What time did you come in?"

"Around four."

"I like the initiative." Micah walked to the other side of the shop. "But you don't have to come in that early."

Jesse started to tell him he'd had trouble sleeping last night, then changed his mind. He wouldn't have hesitated to say that if his brother or Malachi had asked. But Micah wasn't his family and he needed to gain the habit of keeping work separate from personal, something he wasn't used to, having worked in the family business basically his whole life. Besides, if he brought up Charity again, Micah might get the wrong idea. "Just wanted to get a jump start," he said, going back to work on the drum.

The morning flew by and Jesse gained more confidence using the tools. "I've got a delivery to make after lunch," Micah said. "I'll be gone until later this afternoon."

"I'll hold down the shop," Jesse said.

"*Danki.* Close up for lunch, though." He put his straw hat back on and left.

Jesse walked the few steps to his house and went into the kitchen. He pulled out the bread again, spread it with the last of the jelly *Mamm* had sent, and scooped a knife full of peanut butter out of the jar. He filled a plastic cup with water from the tap and took a long drink. If he'd been thinking, he would have packed his lunch this morning. Then again, he hadn't been thinking, not about lunch anyway.

He finished his sandwich and went back to the shop. Fatigue settled over him. He didn't want another sleepless night. Perhaps he should have mentioned his predicament to Micah. He wouldn't have to name names. He could simply ask, on behalf of a *friend*, what was the best way to forget about someone. Too late now that Micah was gone. He'd have to figure out how to brush her aside on his own. *I need to mind* mei *own business.*

He started taking the brake drum apart again, and by the time it was in pieces on the workbench, he'd made his decision. After work he would go to Shirley's and apologize to Charity. Then she was on her own. Lost sheep or not, he was done . . . this time for good.

.⟶⟵.

"Anything else to add to the list?" Charity glanced at the piece of paper filled with a column of grocery items.

"Snack cakes." Shirley winked and patted Monroe's head.

"No." Charity gave her a pointed look. "And don't sneak them into the cart this time either."

"You're worse than Wendy," she huffed.

"You know how mad she'd be if she found out you were eating that much sugar." When Wendy had initially hired her, she'd insisted Charity not put any undue pressure on her mother. "You're to keep the house spotless, the meals healthy, and be available to Mom at all times." Shirley had amended that to *most* times, but the message was clear, and one Charity took seriously.

Shirley rolled her eyes. "Sometimes I wonder who's more stubborn—you or her."

"You are." Charity added sugar-free lemon drops to the list. If she were a better baker, she'd make diabetic desserts for Shirley, but she had a hard enough time making regular ones. Chocolate chip cookies and cakes from a box were more in her baking repertoire, and the desserts in the French cookbook were so out of her league she didn't even bother to read more than one.

Oh *nee*. The pie. She'd forgotten all about the pie she promised Jesse if she didn't have a man—or three—in her pocket by the end of last night's singing. "Well, he's not getting one."

86

"Who's not getting what?"

She really needed to work on keeping her thoughts to herself. "Nothing," she said quickly. "And no one."

Shirley tilted her head. "You are an unusual young woman."

Charity glanced at her, steeling herself for her boss's condemnation. *At least she didn't call me weird.* But there was no censure in Shirley's eyes. Only kindness, and a little glint of humor. Charity couldn't help but smile.

The front doorbell rang and Monroe started barking. "I'll get it," Charity said as Monroe dashed out of the kitchen. He was already at the front entrance by the time she got to the living room. She grabbed his collar and cracked open the door, surprised to see Saloma standing on the porch. "Hi," she said.

"Hi, Charity." Her small smile was tentative. "I hope you don't mind me dropping by for a visit."

This was a first. Back in Cherry Springs she never had visitors, not unless they were there to see Elaine first. She nodded and gave Monroe a firm but gentle shove to the side. "You'll have to slip inside quickly." Saloma slid through the gap between the door and the frame. Charity shut the door.

"Sorry about that. He keeps escaping every time we open the door. He didn't used to do it so often until . . ." Until Jesse moved next door. Ugh, she vowed when she woke up this morning that she wasn't going to think about him and she had, twice, in the past five minutes. *Thanks, Monroe.* "Shirley and I are in the kitchen finishing up our grocery list."

"I can come back another time if you're busy," Saloma said.

"We're almost done." Charity motioned for her to follow her to the kitchen. When they walked inside, she said, "Shirley, this is Saloma."

"Hello." She held out her hand. "It's nice to meet one of Charity's friends."

Friends. As if she had more than one. *I don't even have one.* That was pitiful, now that she thought about it. "Um, she's not—"

"I'm concerned she's spending far too much time with an old lady when she should be mingling with young people." Shirley glanced at Charity and smiled.

"Nice to meet you." Saloma sat down on the chair Charity pulled out for her. "I was really glad Charity came to the singing last night."

Charity froze and glanced at Shirley. *Don't ask . . . don't ask.*

"There was a singing last night?" Shirley's eyes brightened.

"Does anyone want a drink?" Charity dashed to the fridge.

Saloma shook her head as Shirley said, "No thanks." She looked at Saloma again. "I've always wondered what went on at a singing. Other than singing, of course."

"We do other things too. Last night we all hung out in *mei* basement, but most of the time our group meets to play volleyball or baseball. We also get together and do charity projects around the community. Of course we eat too." She grinned. "There's always a lot to eat."

"That sounds marvelous. How many are in your group?"

"There're five women and six men, counting Charity and Jesse. He's new."

Shirley's eyebrow went up. "A coed singing?"

Charity tapped her forehead against the fridge door. This was exactly why she didn't tell Shirley about the singing last night. Not only would she be full of questions, she would have used the opportunity to deter her from her courtship plan.

"And Jesse was there?" Shirley continued.

"*Ya*," Saloma said. "Do you know him?"

"I met him last week. Nice young man. Has quite the head of curly hair, doesn't he?"

"He sure does," Saloma gushed. She put her hand over her mouth and glanced at her lap.

Charity pressed her lips together and sat back down, not bothering to get a drink. She didn't want to talk about Jesse's hair. Or Jesse at all.

"Last night was a lot of fun," Saloma continued, looking at Charity. "Why did you and Jesse leave early?"

"You left early?" Shirley's penciled-in eyebrows shot up as she looked at Charity. "With Jesse?"

Nuts. "Can I talk to you privately?" Charity said to Saloma.

"Say no more." Shirley slowly rose to her feet. "Come on, Monroe. Let's let the girls talk." As she walked out, she gave Charity a look that said *we'll discuss this later.*

Oh boy. She wasn't eager for that conversation.

"Funny you wanted to talk to me in private," Saloma said. "That's why I came over—I wanted to ask you something."

"Oh?"

"You first."

"Um . . ." She'd used privacy as an excuse to divert Shirley, but she had no idea how to follow up. During her teenage years she'd wanted a friend to talk to and confide in, but it never worked out. "I'm sorry about last night," she said, realizing she needed to acknowledge her odd behavior. "Olin's mad at me, isn't he?"

"He didn't mention it. After you left he washed his face and played Ping-Pong for the rest of the night." Saloma tilted her head. "Why did you and Jesse leave early?"

She couldn't tell her they were arguing over her courtship plan, and she for sure wasn't going to let anyone else know she had a courtship plan. *Think, think.* "He forgot to tell me Shirley needed something." She winced. There was no way Saloma would buy that excuse.

Saloma nodded. "I wish you could have stayed."

A tiny thread of warmth flowed through Charity. Shirley cared, and now Saloma wanted her around, or at the least didn't think she was *ab im kopp.* Then she remembered how good she'd felt when the other girls at the singing had gathered around her, asking her how she learned how to sing. Elaine had always complained her singing was too loud, so she mostly sang quietly in church. Every time the youth group had a singing, she'd always been grounded. Last night had been fun, before the catastrophe with Olin and Jesse spoiling her evening.

Saloma ran her finger across the edge of the table, not looking at her. "Can I ask you something personal?"

"*Ya.*" Hopefully the question wasn't *too* personal.

She looked at her. "How well do you know Jesse?"

That was an easy one. "Not well at all." She explained that they both had lived in Birch Creek, but didn't go into details about their encounters with each other, or her reason for living in Birch Creek in the first place.

"So you two aren't dating?"

She let out a bark of laughter. "Me and Jesse? Absolutely not."

"Is he seeing anyone else?"

"I don't know. I guess not, unless there's someone in Birch Creek."

Saloma's shoulders relaxed. "Could you find out for me?"

Charity frowned. That meant she'd have to interact with him, violating her pledge to avoid him. But she wanted to help Saloma too. "I could try."

She clasped her hands together. "And if he isn't, can you help me get his attention?"

Her frown deepened. That was the last thing she'd expected Saloma to ask. "What do you mean?"

Glancing at the table again, she said, "You know. Give him little hints that I like him."

"Wait . . . you *like* him?"

"*Ya.*" Her fingertip moved faster across the table surface. "He's so *schee*, isn't he?"

She couldn't exactly deny that, since she'd noticed his good looks herself . . . more than once. "*Ya*, but—"

"And he was so nice to you last night after you smooshed Olin's cupcake on his head."

Charity froze. Was that a dig? She searched Saloma's expression for any malice, but all she saw was empathy.

"I remember the time I accidentally poured half a pitcher of fruit punch in Julia Beiler's lap." She shook her head, blushing. "At her wedding, of all places."

"Oh *nee.*"

"*Ya.*" Her cheeks grew deep pink. "That was four years ago but I still cringe when I see her. She used to be *mei* teacher too. But like she said, mistakes happen, and anyone could have spilled punch in her lap." She looked at Charity and smiled. "I can't tell you how many times I've wanted to smash a cupcake in *mei bruder*'s face."

Charity couldn't help but chuckle a little. Then she sighed. "I'm sure everyone talked about it after I left."

"*Nee.*" She shrugged. "Although they were wondering if you and Jesse were a couple, since you were bickering with each other and then left together. I'm glad to know that you're not."

Charity's feelings were a mixed bag. Thankfully Olin wasn't mad, although he had a right to be. That gave her a little more courage to approach him again with phase one. On the other hand, everyone thought she and Jesse were an item. Not good. Not at all. How could she find a husband if the men thought she was attached to him? "Can you let everyone know that we're not together?" she asked Saloma.

"Of course." She set her hands in her lap, her pretty blue eyes twinkling. She might look like Norene, but she didn't act one bit like her. "Do you have a boyfriend?"

"Me?" Charity waved her hand at her. "*Nee*, but hopefully—" *Oops.* She was about to reveal her plan. She needed to be careful about disclosing too much when it came to her husband hunt. "*Nee.* I'm not seeing anyone."

"I have an idea." She leaned forward. "What if you and I went out on a double date with Clarence and Jesse?"

"Clarence? The bigger guy with the suspenders?"

"*Ya.* He's been Olin's best friend since forever."

She didn't want to sound mean, and spending time with Clarence was fine. But she had her sights set on Olin. "Why can't Olin *geh* instead?"

"Olin's secretly dating Anna Kurtz. He doesn't know I know, though, so mum's the word."

"Oh." *Phooey.* Well, last night was for nothing. Back to the drawing board.

"But Clarence is nice. I think you'd like him."

Charity thought about it. She'd barely paid attention to him other than noticing his wonderful singing voice. Unlike Olin, he wasn't handsome—in her opinion anyway. He had small eyes, a big nose, and a double chin. He wasn't quite as tall as Micah and a little larger than him, especially around the middle. Not attractive at all.

Wait. What was she doing? Hadn't she been judged by her appearance all her life? "Freckle face," "carrot top," and "string bean" were choice favorites for teasing kids . . . and she often retaliated with her own biting commentary. Out of jealousy, she'd even insulted Katharine Miller last year. Her heart filled with shame. She was the last person to malign anyone's physical form. *I have to do better.*

"So you'll talk to Jesse?" Saloma broke into her thoughts.

Wait. In her musings she'd forgotten he'd be there. Well, she'd just ignore him. He'd be busy with Saloma anyway. *And I'll be busy with phase one: Clarence.* "*Ya.* I'll talk to him." Only because Saloma was nice, and she was helping Charity out too. Otherwise, she still didn't want to speak to him again.

"*Danki!*" Excitement entered her eyes. "This will be so much fun."

Her enthusiasm was contagious. "Yay!"

Saloma looked around the kitchen. "How long have you been living here?"

"Two months, one week, and five days." She grinned, inwardly proud that she had kept a job this long. Before, she'd made a little pocket money whenever Elaine would allow her to help bake bread to sell at the local farmer's market. But those times were few and far between. She was never able to make a loaf that met her stepmother's expectations. Shirley hadn't complained a single time about her home-made bread. Just the opposite, actually.

"Do you use the microwave? The dishwasher?"

"*Ya.* Only because Shirley wants me to."

"How about the TV?" Saloma asked, seemingly fascinated with English conveniences. "Do you watch TV shows?"

"*Nee.* Shirley doesn't watch much TV. She says it's too indecent now. She'll watch the local news to get the weather report, then she turns it off."

"Do you watch it with her?"

"If I'm in the living room or passing through," she said.

"What does Bishop Fry say about that?"

Charity paused. Saloma was being awfully inquisitive, making her wonder if she was asking out of curiosity or wanting to tattle to the bishop. There were two gossips back in Cherry Springs who loved to blab about any little *Ordnung* infraction. To her credit, even Elaine disapproved of them.

"I shouldn't have asked you that," Saloma said. "I didn't mean to be snoopy." She met Charity's gaze. "It can be hard to make friends, *ya?*"

Charity blinked. Of course she'd struggled to make friends, but she hadn't expected Saloma to have the same problem. "Don't you have a lot of friends?"

She folded in her lips and shook her head. "Not really. I always liked staying inside for recess during school to draw, and *mei* teacher allowed it. I'm a homebody too. I'm also a little too nosy, according to *Mamm* and some of the girls *mei* age. I can't help it, though. I'm genuinely interested in people . . . I just don't know how to act around them. I feel awkward most of the time."

She blinked again, trying to decipher if Saloma was telling her the truth or not. Considering there were some uneasy moments when they were talking to each other in her parents' living room, she tended to believe her. Why would anyone confess to being a social blunder? "I feel awkward all of the time," she admitted.

Saloma smiled. "I knew I liked you for a reason."

Charity laughed. She was starting to like Saloma too. "I talked to Bishop Fry after I was hired and he said as long as I didn't fall into the temptation to watch TV or use the appliances regularly, it would be okay to do so since I'm living here. The English stuff makes chores go faster, but I'd rather do them the Amish way."

"I think I would too," Saloma said.

"Charity?" Shirley yelled from the front of the house. "Monroe's out again."

"Oh *nee*." She sprung up from the chair and dashed to the front room. "How did he get out this time?"

"It's my fault." Shirley rubbed her forehead with her fingertips as she stood by the open door. "He needed to go outside, and I thought I could handle him. He's been listening better lately."

He hadn't been, but Shirley was so blinded with Monroe-love she couldn't see the truth.

"Is everything okay?" Saloma said, moving to Charity's side.

"*Ya*. I just have to chase after Monroe again."

"I'm sure he went to Micah's shop," Shirley said. "He's taken such a shine to Jesse."

Saloma's brow lifted at that bit of news. "Can I go with you?"

"Sure." That would get the introductions with Jesse out of the way.

They hurried across the field, the early afternoon sun warming Charity's back, the tall grass tickling her legs. She wasn't thinking about Monroe, though, sure that he had gone straight to Jesse. Instead she thought about her upcoming double date. *A date. An actual date.* She wouldn't have to worry about phase one now. She could skip straight to phase two. Her plan wasn't a lost cause after all. That made it worth interacting with Jesse again.

Almost.

Six

He wants to be your hero. Let him.

Getting a Man and Keeping Him, p. 59

Jesse wasn't surprised when he saw Monroe bounding into the buggy shop, but he was glad to see him. "Hey, *bu*," he said.

Monroe sat down and looked up at him expectantly.

Micah hadn't returned from lunch yet and Jesse still didn't have any treats. He made a mental note to get to the store the first chance he got. He was running out of jelly too. "You'll have to make due with a belly rub."

As if he understood Jesse's words, Monroe flopped down and rolled over.

Jesse laughed and knelt beside him and rubbed the dog's rotund belly. "You're gonna be in big trouble for running off again, *bu*. I'm also reconsidering the treats. You look like you're getting plenty at home." After a few more rubs he got to his feet.

Monroe sat back on his haunches and gazed up at him, tongue hanging out of his mouth.

Jesse started to tell him to go back to Shirley's, but didn't bother. "You'll have to stick around here until Micah comes back. Then I'll take you home." If Charity didn't come get him, that is. If she did, he'd apologize to her for mocking her. He owed her that. And then he would be done with her and her shenanigans.

Monroe followed him to the back table and lay on his side as Jesse cleaned up his tools. He'd taken the brake apart and put it back together several times, and he was ready to move on to another project. He picked up a small wrench at the same moment Charity rushed into the shop.

"Monroe!" She marched over to him, Saloma Mast directly behind her. Saloma wasn't paying attention to the dog, though. *Why is she staring at me again?*

"Sorry." Charity's tone was curt and, unlike Saloma, she wasn't looking at him. "He got away from Shirley." She grabbed for Monroe's collar, but before she could get a grip on it he slipped away and dashed to the other side of the shop. "*Bu!* Get back here!"

Monroe ignored her and raced around the shop, Charity chasing and yelling at him to stop.

Jesse fought to contain his laughter. He admired her tenacity and Monroe's ability to keep evading her, and they were both hilarious.

"Hi." Saloma moved in front of him.

"Hello." He peeked over her shoulder and caught a glimpse of Charity reaching for Monroe, who skillfully dodged the attempt. Jesse wasn't sure who to root for at this point.

Saloma stepped to the side and blocked most of his view. She wasn't as short as Charity, and he could only see a few inches over her head. "*Danki* for coming to the singing last night."

"Uh, *ya.*" Monroe knocked over Micah's stool and Charity almost tripped over it.

"Hopefully I'll see you at youth group again."

"Um . . ." Now Monroe was underneath the buggy frame. Charity laid on her stomach and slithered to catch him.

Uh-oh. If the frame fell over, it might not only bend and ruin hours of work, but it could hurt Charity, Monroe, or both. He brushed past Saloma. "Monroe! Get away from there!"

Before Jesse reached the frame, Monroe blasted out of the shop like a fired cannonball.

Charity jumped to her feet and shot a glare at Jesse. "I almost had him!"

"You almost knocked over the frame. You could have dented it."

"Oh." To her credit, she looked contrite . . . for half a second. "Now I have to chase him down again." She glared at him before hurrying back outside. "Monroe! Monroe!"

Jesse paused. Charity was right—she'd almost coaxed him out from under the frame before he interfered. Oh well, the mutt probably went next door to find Micah, a snack, or both. Charity could handle him.

Maybe.

"Jesse, I was wondering—"

"Hey." He spun around. "Can you watch the shop while I *geh* get Monroe?"

Her eyes bulged. "I don't think I can do—"

"Micah will be here any minute." He might even encounter Monroe on his way back to the shop and save Jesse the trouble.

"But—"

"*Danki*!" Jesse ran out of the shop. Looked left. Looked right. Didn't see either Monroe or Charity. He rushed to the end of the parking lot and searched down the road in the direction of Micah's. Nothing.

He started for Micah's, then caught a glimpse of something in the distance. He skidded to a halt at the sight of Charity dashing past the Waglers' driveway, no Monroe in sight. She quickly disappeared behind a small hill.

He ran after her, assuming she was still chasing Monroe. When it came to Charity, he never knew what was going on in her head. Once he breached the hill, he saw her turn into a tall field of grass and weeds. Good grief, she was speedy. He'd experienced that last night when he pursued her, but she was running even faster now. Then he spied the top of Monroe's head as he bounded across the field like an enormous bunny rabbit.

Now that he had a lead on both of them, Jesse sprinted. He got to the field in time to see both dog and woman speed into the woods. His lungs burned as he picked up the pace and entered the trees, slowing down so he didn't trip over any logs or debris. Where did they go? They couldn't have disappeared that quickly.

He wandered around for a minute or two before spying Monroe perched on a short tree stump, his tongue dangling as he panted.

Braking to a halt, he gasped for breath and slowly approached the dog. He didn't need Monroe taking off again. "*Gut bu . . . gut bu . . .*"

Monroe wagged his tail against the bark on the side of the stump, and when Jesse reached him, he held out his paw.

"This isn't the time for pleasantries." But he gave Monroe's paw a quick shake. "Stay put, you troublemaker," he said in a soothing voice he usually reserved for Miss Peach when she was in a mood. He guided Monroe off the stump, and the dog plopped on his workboots, his chest heaving. Jesse was still winded too. He hadn't had this much of a workout in a long time.

He wiped the sweat off his forehead and looked around for Charity, tempted to call out her name but not willing to risk Monroe bolting again. Instead he crouched near the dog, continued to pet him, and once again spoke in his Miss Peach voice. "I've got him, Charity. Can you hear me?"

"*Ya.*"

He frowned. Stood and turned around. He didn't see her but she sounded close by. "Where are you?"

"Up . . . here."

He glanced at the tree in front of him. Looked up. And saw her clinging to a thick tree branch.

.ᴥᕤᴥ.

Charity wasn't afraid of too many things. She was worried about not getting married, of course, but that wasn't a fear. Her stepmother was frightening, but she'd learned to deal with her . . . somewhat. But there was one thing that absolutely, positively, one-hundred-percent terrified her to the core. Snakes.

She wasn't sure why, and right now that didn't matter. All that mattered was that when she'd tripped over a log in her pursuit of Monroe and saw a wiggly nest of baby snakes underneath, she did what any normal person would do. She scrambled up the nearest tree.

Now that she was up here, though, she was realizing she was afraid of heights too.

"What are you doing up there?" Jesse shielded his eyes as he looked up at her.

What a dumb question. "I'm baking pies, obviously. What do you think I'm doing?"

"Speaking of pies, you owe me one."

"I don't owe you anything."

He took a step toward her. Then another one. "You promised me a pie if you didn't get a husband last night, remember?"

"I can't believe you're bringing that up now—Stop!"

He stilled. "What?"

"Snakes! There's hundreds of them by that rotted log."

He looked to where she was pointing. "Hundreds, you say?" Slowly he walked to the log and peered over the other side. He bent down and reached around.

"Are you *ab im kopp*?" Charity gripped the scratchy limb. "You'll get bit!"

Jesse lifted a small, thin, brown-colored snake and turned around. "Are you talking about these vipers?"

"*Ya.*" She recoiled. And people called *her* weird?

The snake slithered across his hand.

"Jesse, stop it. Please!" She started to shake.

He glanced up at her, then set the horrible creature back under the log. "They're harmless brown snakes, Charity," he said in the same calm, soothing voice he'd just used to talk to Monroe.

That ornery mutt. He was the reason she was stuck up a tree and was on the verge of throwing up.

"There were only three baby ones there." He moved closer to the tree. "But I can see why you thought there were more. They were slithering around each other—"

She felt the color drain from her face. "Jesse!"

"Sorry." He stood at the base of the tree. "You can come down now. Monroe's not going anywhere and the snakes will stay under the log."

She glanced at him. Her stomach churned and the ground appeared wavy. "I can't." She hid her face in her arm. Not only was she terrified, but she was also embarrassed in front of him. Again. It was becoming a regular thing.

"Sure you can. You climbed up there, you can climb down."

If she wasn't so scared and already mad at him for a number of things, she would enjoy listening to him. Somehow he managed to sound both calm and in control. Not to mention the deep, husky quality of his voice. She shook her head.

"Charity—"

"I told you I *can't*." She also couldn't stop shaking. Oh, this was bad. So very, very bad. Would he have to call the fire department to rescue her? How would they get a truck in the woods? Wait, they'd have a ladder. But even the thought of climbing down a ladder right now made her stomach twist into a Bavarian pretzel.

"If you don't come down," he murmured, "I'll have to come up."

She peered over her arm. "Then we'll both be stuck."

"*Nee*, we won't." He glanced at Monroe, who was now, unbelievably, napping peacefully a few feet from the snakes. The dog was stranger than Jesse and that was saying a lot.

Before she knew it, Jesse shimmied up the tree and was standing on the branch directly below her. The tree was sturdy, but not overly thick, and his arm almost circled around it. "I'll help you climb down."

"How?"

"Just come down to this branch. I'll carry you the rest of the way."

She balked. "Nope nope nope. That branch won't hold the two of us."

"*Ya*, it will." He started bouncing.

"Don't do that!"

"Okay." He stopped and held up his free hand toward her. "Just take *mei* hand, Charity. I promise, you'll be safe."

But she wasn't looking at his hand. Her eyes were locked on his and she couldn't break the visual contact. She didn't want to. What she saw there made his words true. Genuine confidence. Yes, she would be safe with him.

Still holding his gaze, she reached out her trembling hand and searched for his. When he took hers, she grabbed it tight. Warm, strong, calloused, and . . . perfect.

"I've got you," he said softly. "Let go of the tree."

She did what he said. Then she stepped down to the branch. When she felt the wood give way, she threw her arms around his neck. "We're gonna fall!"

"I won't let you fall." His warm voice was low in her ear. "Trust me, Charity."

She didn't exactly have a choice. But even if she did, in her heart she somehow knew she could.

He put his arm around her waist. "Hang on tight."

Without thinking, she wrapped her legs around his belt line, hid her face in the side of his neck, and squeezed her eyes shut. He didn't protest, and slowly he made his way down the rest of the branches until there weren't any more, and then he quickly climbed down the rest of the tree.

"We're on the ground now."

Charity lifted her head, fully intending on jumping out of his arms and possibly—more like probably—kissing the firm dirt beneath her feet, germs and all. But when she moved her head, she stilled. Her face was barely a breath from his, and every single sense went into overdrive. She could feel the strength of his arm around her, smell the mix of soap and sweat on his skin, see the short, black whiskers on his chin and upper lip. And now she was staring at his mouth, noticing for the first time that his bottom lip was a little larger than the top.

"Are you okay now?"

His gentle question sent a warm, pleasant shiver down her spine. It also brought her back to reality. "Uh, yeah." She started to move.

"Are you sure?" He held on to her, his eyes holding hers again. "You're still shaking."

True, but she wasn't entirely sure if she was trembling out of fear . . . or because of him. "*Ya.*" She unhooked her legs from around his waist. "I'm fine." That was the biggest lie she'd ever told, but she had to get her feet underneath her, both figuratively and literally.

He let her go and turned to walk to Monroe. "He'll come back with us now," he said with the same confidence he'd had carrying her down the tree. On cue, Monroe got to his feet and followed Jesse in the same direction from which they'd all come.

But her legs were still jelly, and her heartbeat thundered in her chest. This time it definitely wasn't out of fear. A jolt of attraction harder than anything she'd ever experienced slammed into her, making her legs shake even more. She'd never, ever, *ever* felt this way about any man she'd met. Not even a fraction. Not even a minuscule fraction.

Jesse glanced over his shoulder. "I need to get back to the shop, Charity. I don't think Micah will take too kindly to me being gone for so long."

He was right, and somehow she remembered how to walk again. She followed him and Monroe out of the woods and through the field, still marveling at the incredible emotions running through her, still hoping it was adrenaline from being so terrified. But being up the tree was a blip in her mind. All she could think about was how she'd felt wrapped in his arms. Safe. Secure. When was the last time she'd felt that way? That she'd been able to trust another person so completely?

When they got to the shop, Monroe trotted off in the direction of Shirley's, and Charity hoped he was doing his usual habit of going home after making her chase him. She didn't have the energy to run after him again.

They stopped in front of the shop. "That was an adventure," he said.

"*Ya.*" She couldn't stop looking at him.

Strong . . . gorgeous . . . courageous . . . heroic.

And then it hit her. Although he'd hurt her feelings back in Birch Creek and had interfered with her business at the singing, there had to be something between her and Jesse. He had to like her a little bit because he wouldn't have helped her out of the tree. And he wouldn't have made sure she was okay before setting her down on the ground. He also wouldn't have "saved" her from the singing, even though she didn't need it.

Then she remembered something she read in one of her books.

"Does he make your spine tingle?" Check.

"Your toes curl?" She looked at her feet. She couldn't see them curling but inside her tennis shoes they were practically folded under.

"Your heart race?" She put her palm over her chest.

He glanced at her hand and frowned. "Are you sure you're okay?"

Her pulse was galloping faster than a runaway buggy. *Oh yes.*

"There you guys are." Micah approached them. "Saloma told me you had to go after Monroe again. That nutty dog." He turned to Jesse. "She said she had to *geh* back home, but she wanted me to tell you something."

Oh no. She'd forgotten about Saloma. And Clarence. And the double date.

Jesse's expression was unreadable. "What's that?"

"That she'll see *you* again soon." Micah gave him a knowing look. "She seems pretty smitten, in *mei* unprofessional opinion."

Double oh no.

"Time to get back to work." Micah turned and chuckled as he went back to the shop.

Jesse glanced at Charity, his expression unreadable, as if he were used to hearing women were smitten with him. And for all she knew, he was. Then he turned and followed Micah into the shop.

But Charity stayed put, her thoughts and emotions a confused mess. Okay, time to regroup—again. She was doing a lot of that lately. If Jesse could make her toes curl, certainly Clarence could too. She closed her eyes and thought of him. Tall, burly, untamed brown hair, incredible singing voice. Like a teddy bear in suspenders.

Curl, toes, curl!

Jesse's image intruded her thoughts, shoving Clarence to the side. In her imagination, he was smiling at her.

Even her pinky toe responded.

Her eyes widened and she rushed back to Shirley's house. Monroe wasn't on the stoop but she didn't care. She went inside, blew past Shirley, who was petting Monroe—thank goodness he was home—and ran to her room. She shut the door, went to her dresser, and found the book she wanted. *The Science of Love.*

She thumbed through the pages until she found the passage she remembered. "Tingling spine, curling toes, rapid heartbeat . . ." The words jumped out at her, one paragraph in particular.

"If you're experiencing these and similar physical reactions, congratulations! You have chemistry! According to the science, if you have chemistry with someone, then that someone is the one for you."

Cumbersome sentence aside, she couldn't deny science. She also couldn't deny how she felt, even when he wasn't around. *I feel wonderful.*

She tossed the book on the dresser, missing her target. As it hit the floor she plopped on her stomach on top of the bed. Jesse Bontrager. Who would have thought? But was it really out of the realm of possibility? Her grandmother had told her the story of how she'd met and married *Grossvatter. "He was the last man I'd ever thought I'd fall in love with. We were complete opposites, in almost every way."*

Charity had only been seven at the time, but even then she loved hearing stories about happy endings. "Then how did you fall in love?"

"He wore me down." *Grossmammi* smiled. "He didn't just tell me he loved me . . . he showed me, while we were courting and every single day of our marriage. And I kept falling deeper in love with him as time passed. He might not have been the man I would have chosen for myself, but God knew what he was doing when he put us together."

Her grandfather had died shortly after her *mamm* did, but from what Charity could remember of him, he was a jolly, kind man who chewed peppermint candies and was always smiling when *Grossmammi* was around.

Her chest ached. First her *mamm* died, then her *grossvatter* . . . then *Grossmammi* . . .

Charity flipped over. She didn't want to think about her losses. She never wanted to think about them. The past was the past, and she had to focus on her goal—finding a husband. Up until now, with the exception being their first nondate at the diner, she'd dismissed Jesse as a possibility. For good reason.

But what if he was? What if she was like her grandmother, and not seeing what was right in front of her? Could she dismiss what professional relationship authors said was true? After all, they knew more about love than she did. If they were wrong, they wouldn't be writing books about the subject.

She sat up. There were two big problems she had to solve first. Saloma, for one. There was no way Charity could go on a double date with Clarence now that she knew she had chemistry with Jesse. That wouldn't be fair to him. But what about Saloma's feelings? Technically Saloma liked him first, because until he'd rescued her out of the tree, Charity had been perfectly fine with the two of them being together.

Phooey. She was so confused. She stood, picked up the relationship books off the floor, and went back to her bed. Maybe there was something in one of the books that could tell her what to do about her new feelings for Jesse and how to handle the situation with Saloma. If only she had someone to talk to about this. *If only I wasn't so alone.*

Shirley. She paused, her fingertips touching the smooth cover of a book. She could talk to her. Or could she? This was something so personal, and Shirley was her boss. Could she cross that line to discuss her confusion about Jesse? More importantly, should she? And as much as she liked Shirley, she did betray her confidence by reading and showing Jesse her courtship plan without permission.

What should I do, Lord?

The question had barely blipped in her mind before she opened the book. She didn't need to talk to Shirley—she had professional help right at her fingertips. She lay down and started reading . . . not bothering to wait for God to answer.

Seven

Be assertive. Go after what you want,
and he'll respect you for it.

Getting a Man and Keeping Him, p. 62

For the rest of the week, Charity reworked her courtship plan with Jesse in mind. After reading through her books, she didn't find anything speaking specifically to her situation, but she did read plenty of affirmations that her strong feelings for Jesse were worth pursuing, and she edited her plan with renewed gusto.

But there was still her dilemma with Saloma. How was she going to tell her new friend about her new feelings for Jesse? How could she rationalize going back on her word? She even considered going through with the double date and then telling her afterward, but that was a dumb idea, borne out of her reluctance to disappoint Saloma.

She had to be honest with Saloma, even if it hurt her feelings. *Or ruins our new friendship.*

Then there was Monroe. She was keeping him on a short leash, literally. She hadn't overly minded him going to the buggy shop in the past, but running off into the woods where there were snakes—she shuddered—was too much. Currently Monroe was under the kitchen table, the end loop of his leash wrapped around her thin wrist. The loop had slipped off several times, but she made sure to quickly put it back on before he got any inkling he was free to run off.

"Don't you think you're being a little unreasonable?" Shirley brought over a mug of tea and sat in the seat next to her at the table. She patted the dog's head. "Poor Monroe."

"He needs to learn his lesson." Charity glanced at him as he thoroughly enjoyed Shirley's attention. "Besides, he's hardly suffering."

"Do you plan to keep him by your side indefinitely?"

"One more day should do it. But don't try to let him out again by yourself. If I have to leave, I'll make sure to take him outside first. He can wait to do his business until I get back."

Shirley smirked as she took a sip from the mug. "Good thing I happen to agree with you. *This* time."

Charity smiled and tapped the eraser end of her pencil against her chin. She'd finished her Saturday morning chores and two hours ago they had a light lunch. She decided to try another French recipe today—*cervelle de canut*. The book said the name translated to "silk worker's brain," which made zero sense to Charity but the picture looked delicious. Goat cheese, a few herbs, some olive oil and vinegar, and she had a delicious spread for the bread she'd made the other day. That, along with some fresh fruit and tuna fish salad, made for a nice meal. Shirley had given the dish her stamp of approval.

She glanced at her notebook. Something was missing from her plan. Ah, she needed to make a list of date ideas. That way when she put her new and improved strategy into action she would be able to suggest ways she and Jesse could spend time together. Romantic time. *Sigh.*

"Oh brother." Shirley peered at the stack of papers. "You're still working on that cockamamie plan, aren't you?"

She lifted her chin. "Maybe."

"That dreamy sigh said definitely."

Huh. She hadn't meant to sigh out loud. Oh well, Shirley could voice her disapproval all she wanted to. Criticism was an everyday occurrence back home, from Elaine at least. Although it did sting that Shirley disagreed with her. More than once this week she'd reevaluated talking with her about Jesse, but she didn't want to hear any more negativity, not when she was on the right track. She wasn't after just any man within a twelve-mile radius. She and Jesse were meant to be together.

Ah, Jesse. She imagined him hard at work in the buggy shop. His strong hands . . . his even stronger arms . . .

"You're sighing again."

Charity looked at her, but this time there was a twinkle in Shirley's eye.

"Well, since I can't convince you to change your mind, I can at least try to be supportive." Shirley sipped her tea.

She stilled. She hadn't expected that. "You support me?"

"To a certain extent." Her expression softened. "You can't plan love, Charity."

"The books say—"

"I don't care what the books say. You're going to find a husband in God's timing. No sooner or later than that." She set down her cup. "My concern is how doggedly determined you are to force the issue."

"I'm not forcing. I'm planning." She looked at her neatly written notes, honing in on the little heart she drew on the end of the *J* in Jesse's name. Deep down she knew Shirley was right. Everything happened in God's time. But did that mean she couldn't be proactive? That she shouldn't even try?

"How are things back home? Cherry Springs is where you're from, right?"

Charity's head popped up. "Why are you asking me that?"

"Oh, I'm sorry." Shirley frowned. "I didn't mean to pry."

"You're not prying," she said, glancing at the heart again before looking at Shirley. "I'm just surprised."

"About what?"

"That you want to know."

Shirley gave her a soft smile. "Of course I want to know. I'll admit I kept my distance when you were first hired, mostly because I was resistant to any kind of help. But I think it's okay if we get a little personal with each other from time to time. I'll start." Her smile widened. "Today's my fifty-second wedding anniversary."

"It is? That's . . . wonderful." She wanted to smack her forehead. Alan wasn't here to celebrate the milestone. There was nothing wonderful about that.

"It's okay, Charity." Shirley took off her glasses and rubbed one of the earpieces. "I'll admit I cried a little bit this morning, but I'm fine now. We had over fifty amazing years together. I'm thrilled to have had that much time with him."

"Oh, Shirley." She jumped up from her seat and gave her a hug. "Happy anniversary."

"Thank you." She hugged Charity back.

Charity sat back at the table. After that personal revelation, the least she could do was answer her initial question. "*Daed* called me the other day," she said. "First time I've heard from him since I left." She rarely heard from her father when she was in Birch Creek, and their phone calls had been short, almost obligatory. This one was no different.

"That's nice," Shirley said. "Anything interesting going on back home?"

"Not according to him."

"Do you miss your family?"

Charity stared unseeingly at her new and improved courtship plan. She always missed her dad, even when they were in the same house together. He was a quiet man, content to let Elaine do all the talking—and the bossing. Still, it was good, and surprising, to hear his voice the other day. He asked how she was, how she liked Marigold, and did she like her job. And that was it. They said goodbye, and she wondered how long it would be before she heard from him again. Weeks? Months? *I hope not.*

Shirley's cell phone on the table rang. She glanced at it, her face brightening. "It's Wendy. I hope you don't mind if I get this."

"Of course not."

She put the phone to her ear, her smile brighter than Charity had ever seen it. "Hi, Wendy. Give me a minute, I'm going to my bedroom."

Charity smiled, but it faded after Shirley left. Seeing her boss so excited to hear from her daughter tugged at her heart. Such a contrast from her dad and stepmother. At least her father had called. When she'd left for Cherry Springs, she made sure to give her address and phone number directly to him. When she had called him for the first time after she arrived in Birch Creek, he asked why she hadn't left contact information with Elaine . . . even though she had. That was the last straw when it came to trusting her stepmother.

She shoved down the lump in her throat and focused on the task in front of her. Where was she? Oh, right. A list of date ideas.

1. Card and board games
2. Singings
3. Twenty questions
4. A home-cooked meal
5. Buggy rides
6. Meal at a restaurant

There wasn't a diner or restaurant in Marigold, although they could hire a taxi to take them to Barton, the nearest large town, or to Diener's Diner in Birch Creek. A startover date. *Not a bad idea.*

What else did couples do together? She tapped her chin again before going through her stack of books until she found the one with dating suggestions. Most of them were for English couples, but there were a few she could adapt.

7. Picnic
8. Sit by a pond or lake and feed the ducks
9. Have a lunch-hour date
10. Plant a garden together
11. Go to the zoo

Akron had a nice zoo. She'd always wanted to go to one, but never had the opportunity. Whenever she asked her father to take her, he always made excuses for why he couldn't, and she never dared ask Elaine. To go there on a date sounded like fun.

The doorbell rang. Eleven date ideas were a start, and she could add to the list later. She rose from the table and walked to the door. Was Shirley expecting company and didn't mention it? Charity certainly wasn't, although she wouldn't be surprised if it was Saloma. Guilt pinched her. She needed to talk to her ASAP.

Knock, knock.

She hadn't realized she'd stopped in front of the door without opening it. *Oops.* "Sorry to keep you waiting—"

"Um, hi, Charity."

Jesse.

.·ﮩ·.

"I'm sorry, Mom. I wish I could get away from work. You know how much I want to see you."

Shirley gripped the cell phone in her hand. *If she wanted to see me, she would make time.* "I understand, dear." She strove for an even tone. "Do you have any idea when you might be free?"

"Maybe in a week. Or two. We're working on three big cases right now, and I can't leave the other partners in a lurch. One of them is about to wrap up, so hopefully it won't be much longer before I can get out there."

"All right." She held on to that shred of hope. Her daughter was a highly successful corporate attorney, and Shirley had always been proud of her. She and Alan had invested a lot of money in her schooling, and Wendy had always been grateful. She'd always been busy too. "I can't wait to see you."

"Me too, Mom. How are things with Charity? Is she treating you right?"

"Yes. She's a quirky young lady, but she's very conscientious." And caring. At first Shirley had only been concerned about her ability to be responsible, and she certainly was that. But it was nice to know Charity cared about her too. And of course, she loved Monroe. That reminded her. "What do you think about fencing in the backyard?" She bit the inside of her cheek. She should have never agreed to let her daughter help her take care of her finances. But after her ministroke last year, it had seemed sensible to turn them over to her. Other than some spending money, Wendy was in primary control of Shirley's bank account.

"For Monroe? How much would it cost?" When Shirley told her, Wendy said, "That's expensive, don't you think?"

"It is, but it will be worth it to keep Monroe from running away."

"Mom," she said, her words measured. "If the dog is too much for you to handle, you need to find him a new home."

Her heart squeezed. "I didn't say he was too much."

"If he keeps running off, he is."

"If he had a fenced-in yard, he wouldn't run off."

Wendy sighed. "All right. But let me do some research and see if I can find a cheaper company."

Well, that was something. "Thank you."

"I've got to go, Mom. Love you. Talk to you soon."

"Love you—"

Click.

Shirley looked at the screen. Ten minutes. The calls were getting shorter. *Wendy is busy. She'll have more time after her cases are finished.* She just wished she was closer to her daughter.

Then she realized Wendy hadn't mentioned her parents' anniversary. The vise that surrounded her heart the moment Alan died tightened. *Lord, how I wish he was still here.*

Monroe padded into her bedroom, his leash dragging behind. "Poor Monroe," she said, holding out her hand to him, welcoming the distraction. He, along with Charity, had been a balm to her heart over the past four months. She'd intended to live alone after Alan died, with her friends from church as her social outlet. But now she understood that having canine and human company with her every day was what she needed most, and the Lord had provided both.

She patted the empty spot on the mattress next to her. He jumped up and laid down, half of his paws dangling over the edge. She was tempted to take off the leash, but decided against it. Charity would put it back on again, and Monroe did need to learn his lesson. She wasn't sure being on a leash all the time would do it, but she was willing to let Charity have her little experiment. The young woman did have an odd way of doing things.

Shirley frowned. If Monroe was here, where was Charity? She

stood and pushed her walker partway down the hall. She heard Charity's voice, along with a man's. Was that Jesse? She peered around the corner to see the two of them talking but she couldn't clearly make out what they were saying. She grinned and went back to the bedroom where Monroe rested his chin on his paws.

There was no need to interrupt the two of them. Time for a nice nap with Monroe.

.ᴼᵍᵉᵖ.

"You want to build a fence for Monroe?"

Jesse rubbed the back of his neck, fatigue gliding over him. After the debacle with Monroe the other day, his insomnia had increased. He was concerned about him, though, and that's why he was offering to build the fence. But that wasn't what kept him up at night this week.

It was the unconventional redhead in front of him. *I have to see if she's all right.*

His brother Zeke used to be scared of water, although he finally learned how to swim to impress his wife, Darla. But his fear didn't compare to the stark terror Jesse saw in Charity's eyes, even from such a high distance. It was bad enough that the sight of a few baby snakes had her fleeing up a tree. Even worse that she was too afraid to get down. As a kid he climbed enough trees and caught and released plenty of nonpoisonous snakes that he couldn't relate to her fear. All he knew was she was in trouble, and he had to calm her down enough to carry her to the ground.

"Jesse?" Charity tilted her head at him.

"*Ya?*" She looked okay. Calm.

"You said something about a fence."

"Oh, *ya.*" Now that he'd seen for himself she was fine, time to get back on topic. "Shirley will need to purchase the materials, and I can pick them up for her. I've built *mei* fair share of fencing, so it won't take long to put one up around her small yard."

"That's a great idea!" She started to clasp her hands, stopping when she realized the leash was gone from her wrist. "Phooey. Monroe, come back here."

Jesse chuckled as he glimpsed Monroe peek down the hallway. The boy loved his freedom.

She sighed. "Oh well. Hopefully he learned his lesson. Wait, it won't matter. If we have a fence, we won't have to worry about him running off." She threw her arms around his neck. "Oh, Jesse. *Danki.*"

"Uh . . ." He shouldn't be surprised she was hugging him. One thing he was learning about Charity was that she wasn't like any Amish woman he'd ever met. And now that she'd accepted his offer and didn't have any residual effects from their tree adventure, he could talk to Shirley and firm up the details. All he had to do was step out of her arms. That's all he had . . . to . . . do . . .

"I'll *geh* tell Shirley." She jumped back and whirled around. Then she faced him again. "Stay here. I'll be right back." Then she dashed off in the same direction Monroe went earlier.

He shook his head, chuckling again. Then he thought about her being up in the tree. His chuckle faded. Because what bothered him the most wasn't that she was scared of snakes, or got stuck in a tree, or even that he had to get her down when he should have been working at his new job.

He enjoyed holding her . . . and that terrified him.

He still remembered how every single sense tingled when she buried her head in his neck and clung against him. He remembered how nice her hair had smelled, how she had more freckles on her face than would be possible to count in a lifetime, how he'd felt her pounding heartbeat against his shoulder. All of it had felt good . . . so good he'd had a hard time letting her go. Just like now in the hallway.

Nuts. He rubbed the back of his neck again, unable to figure out what all that meant. None of it made sense. He shouldn't be reacting to her this way. She was Charity Raber . . . rude, blunt, odd, and . . . cute?

A tiny tingle rushed down his spine.

"She thinks it's a great idea," Charity said, bursting back into the living room, Shirley and Monroe trailing behind her.

"I can speak for myself, Charity." Shirley faced Jesse. "I think it's a great idea."

"I just said that." Charity shrugged.

Shirley beamed. "Talk about an answer to prayer. I was just discussing the fence with my daughter a few minutes ago. She wasn't happy with the quoted prices and was going to do some research to find a lower offer." She paused. "What's your price for labor?"

"Nothing. It's not a big project."

"But it is a lot of work." She lifted her chin. "I won't take charity. Pardon the pun, Charity."

"Shirley." Her voice was soft. "It's not charity. Helping neighbors is important."

"There might be one day I'll need your help," Jesse added. He couldn't imagine that day ever coming, but hopefully it would convince Shirley to forego payment.

Shirley dipped her chin. "Can't imagine that ever happening," she mumbled. Then she looked at Jesse again. "All right. Just get whatever materials you need and I'll pay you back."

"Sounds good. I'll check with the building supply store in Barton, and if they have the materials, I can start next week after work."

Charity let out a tiny squeal.

He looked at her, but now she was glancing up at the ceiling, her hands behind her back as if she hadn't made a sound. But the skin underneath her freckled face was rosy pink. *Cute.*

He nearly groaned out loud. *I've gone* ab im kopp. "Uh, now that it's settled, I better get back home." He started to turn when he heard Monroe whimper. "Sorry, *bu.* Can't believe I almost forgot about you." He knelt down and the dog came up to him. Jesse scratched his ears. "Hey, I got you a little something." He dug into his pocket and pulled out a small treat. He couldn't resist getting them when he went to Ebersol's Store yesterday to resupply his pantry. They were training treats, a little larger than a kernel of corn.

"Oh boy." Shirley laughed. "Now he'll never leave your side."

Monroe gulped down the treat and Jesse stood. He'd miss this mutt's impromptu visits, but Monroe's safety was more important. "I'll let you know when I've got the fencing supplies. Until then, Monroe," he said, leveling his gaze at the dog, "you stay put." He looked at Shirley, then at Charity. "See you later—"

"Will you *geh* out with me?"

Eight

Keep him on his toes every once in a while. You
don't want to make things too easy for him.

Getting a Man and Keeping Him, p. 99

Oh dear. Shirley's gaze hopped to Jesse, his mouth frozen in an *O* shape, to Charity, who was looking up at him expectantly, the moon and stars in her eyes. Is this what she was learning from those books? To ask men out without preamble? Shirley had always been a little old-fashioned, but she'd also lived through the sixties. She knew women didn't wait anymore to ask men on dates. But she thought the Amish were different.

"I, uh . . ." Jesse sounded like he was strangling on the words, the front of his neck turning red.

Poor guy. He was completely blindsided. When he backed away, Charity moved closer to him. Shirley had to do something. Then it hit her. "Ow!"

Charity spun around and rushed to her. "What's wrong? What happened?"

"My knee went out." It did no such thing, but it had before and was extremely painful. She could fake it with fairly decent precision. "Ow . . . ow . . ."

"Don't move." Charity put Shirley's arm over her shoulder. "I'll help you to your chair."

"Thank you." While Charity was busy guiding Shirley to her recliner, Shirley looked at Jesse and tilted her head toward the door. "Go," she mouthed.

He frowned. "What?" he mouthed back.

"Go." She jerked her head at the front door.

"Is there something wrong with your neck too?" Charity said in a worried tone. "Did you sleep wrong during your nap?"

"I'm sure that's it." Shirley sat down in the recliner and Charity hovered over her knee. "I'll be okay, Jesse." Her eyes bounced from him to the door and back. "You don't have to stick around."

"Are you sure you're all right—oh . . ." He nodded, finally catching her drift. "I just remembered I forgot to leave a note for Micah about . . . about . . ."

"About one of your customer's orders?" she supplied.

"*Ya.* Uh, yeah. That's it. Bye." He dashed out the door.

Shirley slumped in the chair. For a second she thought she'd have to draw him a map.

Charity knelt in front of her. "Which knee is it?"

"The right. It's feeling better now that I'm off it."

"Do you need a heating pad? Some ice? I can bring you both."

Her heart squeezed, and she couldn't help but touch her chin. "You're such a kind woman, Charity."

Charity's face fell. "I wasn't always. Not all that recently even."

"You are now. That's what counts." And so she wouldn't suspect that Shirley had a hand in Jesse's escape, she added, "It still smarts a little. I think a heating pad will help."

"I'll be right back." She jumped to her feet and went to the kitchen.

"Whew." Shirley patted Monroe on the head, then reached over and unclipped his leash. If Charity wanted to keep it on him, she could clip it back. Hopefully her diversion made Charity forget she'd asked Jesse out on a date. Or at least she'd realize she shocked him. The question seemed like it popped into Charity's brain and flew out of her mouth with little thought, if any.

Charity returned and rested the heating pad on Shirley's knee. *Ah.* That actually felt good. Her arthritis had been acting up, although it had been background noise compared to her neuropathy lately. She settled back in the recliner and closed her eyes. Getting old was a drag.

"He didn't answer."

Her eyes flew open. Charity stood in front of her with a confused, hurt expression. "What?"

"Jesse didn't say he would go out with me." She threaded her fingers together in front of her apron.

"Sweetie, I think you caught him off guard—"

"But he didn't say he *wouldn't* go out with me." She brightened. "Right?"

Shirley had to remind herself that for one thing, Charity was a grown adult—despite being childlike in some ways—and secondly, this wasn't her business. But her maternal instinct kicked in, like it had when she first saw the courtship plan. She sat up and looked at her. Saw the hope in her eyes, the smile on her face at the thought of Jesse saying yes. And she didn't want to be the one to throw water on her excitement. "He would be foolish to say no," Shirley said, meaning the words.

"You really think so?"

Charity's expression became so soft and vulnerable that Shirley found herself praying he would say yes. And maybe he would. She didn't know the young man much at all, although she was getting a fine impression of him so far. "When did you become interested in Jesse?" she asked.

Charity sat down on the sofa and told her everything that had happened when Monroe ran away. Shirley was shocked. "You both could have been hurt."

"I was holding on to him tight." She clasped her hands together. "He's so strong." She let out a dreamy sigh.

Shirley tried not to giggle. Charity really was a romantic, and an innocent one. She didn't seem to have had much guidance in her life when it came to relationships, though. Hadn't her parents explained anything to her?

"I should go over to his house and ask him again." She got up from the couch.

"No. Don't do that."

"But shouldn't I go after what I want? Shouldn't I be assertive?"

"Where did you get that idea . . . ? Never mind." She shook her head. "I already know." If those books didn't belong to the library, Shirley would have burned them in the fireplace—if she had a fireplace—to save Charity from herself. "There's a difference between being assertive and blindsiding someone. Does Jesse know you like him?"

She thought for a moment. "No. Definitely not. Until very recently, I didn't. I couldn't stand him actually."

"So you haven't been sure about your feelings for very long. Are you sure about them now?" Hopefully her question would make Charity realize she was jumping into this.

Charity paused.

Good. She's finally listening to reason—

"Yes," she said with a firm nod. "I'm sure. I want to go out with Jesse."

Shirley held in a sigh. "And what if he doesn't want to go out with you?" she said as gently as she could.

Her face fell again before she perked up. "Then I'll have to convince him, won't I? I'm going to start supper, if you're sure your knee is okay. Do you need some aspirin?"

"No, thank you."

"Okay. I'll let you know when supper's ready."

Shirley watched her leave for the kitchen, more pep in her step than usual. Well, Charity obviously was sticking to her plan, and Shirley needed to give up on trying to change the young woman's mind. Jesse was proving to be a nice man. But was he romantically interested in Charity? *I guess we'll all find out.*

She prayed Charity wouldn't get hurt in the process.

.~⧯~.

Dazed, Jesse crossed the field between his house and Shirley's. *Charity asked me out.* He ran his hand over his face. Even in Birch Creek none of the women had been that bold. She had just been angry with him about the Mast singing. Now she wanted to go out with him. Talk about inconsistent.

Jesse slowed his steps. He was getting worked up over nothing. The best thing he could do was pretend she never said anything. And if she brought it up again, he would gently, thoughtfully let her down, unlike he'd done last year. He wasn't ready to date anyone, especially a woman as mercurial as Charity. And those tingles he felt when she was close? Exhaustion. Plain, simple exhaustion.

The tension eased from his shoulders, and he planned out the rest of the evening. He and Micah had closed up shop at five, right before he went to Shirley's. As soon as he arrived home he'd brush Miss Peach, clean out her stall, fix himself supper—he was really missing his mother's scrumptious meals—and relax for the rest of the evening.

Huh. Normally he didn't plan his activities like this. He shrugged, but continued to mentally outline the rest of the weekend. Tomorrow was church. He'd taken Micah up on his offer of a ride to the Beilers, who lived on the far side of Marigold. Jesse usually enjoyed walking to church, but he didn't mind riding with Micah either. After service he would stay for lunch and spend the rest of the afternoon taking a nap. By Monday his fatigue would be gone, and so would any annoying tingles.

He shoved back his bangs and tilted his head toward the late-evening sun for a second. The sweet scent of freshly mown hay coupled with the rich, earthy scent of tilled land from nearby farms made him a little homesick. He hadn't thought much about Birch Creek since he'd moved, mostly because his mind had been on work . . . and Charity.

Good grief. How could he ignore her if she kept intruding on his thoughts? "Women," he muttered. At least he only had to deal with one, although she was more complicated than a handful of them.

"Hi, Jesse!"

Saloma stood in front of the buggy shop, Clarence beside her. Close beside her, Jesse noticed, as if he were her bodyguard. "Sorry, the shop's closed for the day," he said, quickening his steps. "I can get Micah if you need to talk to him, though."

Clarence nodded. "My wheels could use a little aligning—"

"I didn't come to talk to Micah." She glanced at Clarence, her eyebrows flattening for a split second before she turned to Jesse again. "Did Charity talk to you?"

His guard went up. Had she told Saloma she was planning to ask him out? "Uh, *ya.*"

"Oh, *gut.*" Saloma grinned. "I was worried she'd forgotten since I didn't hear anything from her."

"Forgot what?" Clarence asked.

Saloma ignored him. "What would you like to do? Where would you like to *geh*?"

So Charity's date invite wasn't spontaneous like he thought. She'd *planned* to ask him. Then it hit him like a cement block to the head. *She's using her courtship plan . . . on me!* But instead of going through all the nonsense he'd read on the plan, she'd cut to the chase. He had to give her some credit for that.

Wait. No, he didn't. What was she thinking? *What am I thinking?*

"Where are you two going? What are you gonna do?" Clarence's eyes narrowed at Jesse.

Saloma glanced up at him, exasperated. "You're going out with Charity . . ." She smiled at Jesse. "And I'm going out with you. A double date. "

"What?" Clarence and Jesse said in unison.

"Be quiet, Clarence." She sounded like a teacher scolding a rowdy student. "Jesse and I need to discuss the particulars."

"Particulars?" Jesse said faintly.

"Where we're going and what we're doing on our date." She tapped her toe against the gravel.

His brain whirred. *Charity asked me out. But she's supposed to go out with Clarence and I'm supposed to go out with Saloma.* Then why didn't Charity mention a double date? His temple throbbed.

"I don't want to *geh* out with Charity." Clarence scowled.

"What's wrong with Charity?" Jesse blurted.

"*Nix*," Saloma faced Clarence. "That's why I set her up with you."

"But I don't like Charity. Not in that way. I don't even know her."

Saloma waved him off. "You need to give her a chance."

"But—"

"Why don't you *geh* back home so Jesse and I can work out our date details." She whirled around, her smile returning.

Clarence tugged on his left suspender. "How will you get back to your *haus*?"

"Would you mind taking me, Jesse?" She moved closer to him.

Oh boy. Saloma was reminding him of Norene back at the diner in Birch Creek. At least she didn't have the same predatory look Norene had, although she seemed very determined to ditch Clarence to be alone with him. And now Clarence was glaring at Jesse like the entire mess was his fault.

"I, uh, can't. I, uh . . ." Why couldn't he think on his feet anymore? He'd had the same problem at Shirley's after Charity had gobsmacked him.

"I don't live that far," Saloma said. "You won't be gone that long."

He moved back a step. "I'm working late tonight."

"You said the shop was closed."

Never mind Norene. Saloma was sounding like Charity now. *Great, there's two of them.* "I'm busy," he said lamely. "Sorry."

"I can take you home," Clarence said.

"Never mind," she grumbled. "I'll walk." She turned and left.

Clarence watched her go, and if his hangdog look hadn't clued Jesse in, his next words did the trick.

"You're new around here, so I can't get too sore at you for this," he said. "But I love Saloma. If anyone is going out with her, it's going to be me." He took a step forward. "Understand?"

Jesse gulped. Clarence wasn't just hefty, he was tall. A huge fellow all around, and Jesse would be foolish to cross him. "*Ya.*" Then he raised his hands. "I had *nee* idea about a double date with you and Charity. I promise. I don't have any intentions toward Saloma either."

He eyed Jesse for a moment, then nodded. "I believe you. But she's still off-limits."

"Gotcha."

His hard expression lessened. "Think you and Micah could take a look at *mei* wheels next week?"

"I can look at them now if you want." Anything to get the big guy on his good side.

"I thought you were closed."

"We are, but you're here now. No sense in coming back next week if I can take care of it today."

Clarence nodded, not looking quite as fierce. "Appreciate it."

Micah had shown Jesse how to align wheels yesterday, and this was an opportunity to practice, and to also get his mind off Charity and Saloma. Double-dating was out of the question, not that it had been a question in the first place. And as for Charity's invitation . . . he didn't relish the thought of turning her down again. But he had to. There was no possible way they would ever date. Not even once.

This was why he avoided women. The confusion and exasperation weren't worth it.

He held in a sigh as Clarence pulled his horse and buggy into the shop. A few minutes ago he didn't think his personal life could get more out of control.

Boy, was he wrong.

Nine

Men love affection. Don't be afraid
to show him some PDA.

Getting a Man and Keeping Him, p. 17

"Are you sure you'll be all right while I'm gone?" Charity laced up her right tennis shoe and looked at Shirley, who was sitting in the recliner, Monroe at her feet. "What if your knee goes out again?"

"Trust me, it won't." Shirley sipped her coffee. "Go on to church and enjoy the service. I plan to watch my church's service on TV this morning."

"But I'll be gone until this afternoon." The Beilers' house was a far walk and, while she didn't mind, it was over an hour away. She could call a taxi to drive her there, but that seemed silly when she was capable of going there on foot.

"I've got Monroe here to take care of me."

Charity gave the dog a side-eye. Last night she'd gotten the idea to rig up a tie-out for him with some rope and one of his leashes so Shirley could let him out while Charity was gone. Fortunately Shirley didn't have back problems, and all she had to do was put him on the tie-out in the house, let him do his business, tell him to come in, and take the leash off his collar after she shut the door. She should have thought about this a long time ago. But he was a master at breaking away, and she didn't completely trust he wouldn't figure out how to escape.

"Charity," Shirley said in a gentle, yet firm tone. "I'll be okay. Promise."

She drew in a deep breath and nodded. "All right," she said, heading for the door. "As long as you're sure."

"For goodness' sake, shoo." Shirley grinned.

"I'm going, I'm going." She smiled back.

Fluffy white clouds dotted the sky. Shirley had checked the weather this morning, as she tended to do several times a day, and thankfully there wasn't rain in the forecast. She didn't want to show up to church and have Jesse see her a sopping mess.

Ah, Jesse. Last night she did a little more brainstorming about what they could do on their date, and she decided on a picnic. There was a small plot of land that could barely be called a park within walking distance of Shirley's. One bench and a small pond near the asphalt parking lot, as if someone had given up making the spot into a full-fledged park. But that was fine. The date was about the company, not the setting.

Instead of preparing her mind for worship, she mulled over date activities. Other than eat, what else would they do? Should she bring a card game? A list of twenty questions? And once they finished whatever they ended up doing, then what? She had searched for the answer in her books, but unfortunately didn't find one. While they all gave plenty of specifics on how to get a man's attention, they weren't at all informative about what happened next.

She had so many questions. When should she and Jesse hold hands? Should she kiss him first, or did she have to wait for him to kiss her? And how long should they date before they got married?

A tiny part of her knew she was putting the cart before the horse.

But she liked where her imagination was taking her. She was used to living with her head in the clouds, because after her mother and grandmother died, life on earth hadn't been all that great. Her imagination had been her saving grace more often than not.

She shook off her somber thoughts as she heard horses' hooves clopping behind her. A few seconds later, Micah Wagler pulled up beside her.

"Hi, Charity." Micah tugged on the horse's reins, slowing down the buggy. "Want a ride?"

"That's okay, I don't mind walking—" She froze. Lo and behold, Jesse was sitting next to him, stupendously handsome in his crisp white shirt, black vest, and black pants. His black hat covered most of his curls, but some were still visible. *Sigh.* So *schee*.

Jesse glanced at her, then stared straight ahead, his expression impassive. She hadn't expected Priscilla to attend church since she was so close to her due date. Hmm. Maybe she could talk to Priscilla about dating. Then again, she didn't want to bother her either, not when she was on bed rest.

"Climb on in, Charity." Micah motioned with his beefy hand.

"*Ya*! Sure! I'd love a ride!" Did that sound too eager? Probably. Oh well.

"I'll get in the back." Jesse started to move.

"*Nee* need," Micah said. "Just scoot over. There's enough room up front."

He hesitated, then scooched closer to Micah. Charity attempted to hide her smile, but it was impossible. There she was, walking and thinking about Jesse and *poof*! He appeared. She was so excited to sit next to him her foot slipped on the step.

"Here." Jesse extended his hand.

She gazed at his palm. Perfect, even with the small, visible calluses on the base of his fingers. He saved her from the snakes, he was building her a fence, and now he was helping her into the buggy. Okay, technically he was building Monroe a fence, but still. He was so nice.

Cutting off her thoughts before he caught her staring at his hand, she slid her fingers across his palm. Warm and strong. When she sat down and he quickly pulled his hand from hers, she wasn't even disappointed.

Micah was a large man, and there really wasn't much room in the front seat. Of course that didn't bother Charity one bit. She was pressed right up against Jesse, and there wasn't any other place she'd rather be.

Micah started the buggy again. "I hear Jesse's putting a fence in for Monroe. I've got some spare lumber left over from building our *haus* that would make *gut* fencing. I can cut it to size and bring it over to Shirley's if you want."

Wow, life kept getting better and better. She leaned forward and looked at Micah. "That would be great. Just let us know how much you want for it." She knew Shirley would insist on paying for the wood.

"Don't want *nix*. It's extra, and it's going to a *gut* cause."

Charity nodded. She'd have to convince Shirley not to offer to pay Micah, but eventually her boss would agree. "I know she'll appreciate that."

"Glad to help."

Jesse remained quiet, his palms on his knees, staring straight ahead as if he'd turned to stone. Charity's smile dimmed. She didn't expect him to talk about their upcoming date in front of Micah—she was determined to be positive and confident that at some point he would say yes—but he could at least add a word or two to the conversation about the fence, since he was the one building it. "What do you think about Micah's idea, Jesse?"

"Sounds *gut*."

His deep voice was low and hard to hear. "What?"

He turned slightly to her. "Sounds *gut*."

Swoon. She could gaze at his blue eyes all day. "Shirley's knee is okay, by the way."

He frowned. "What?"

"Shirley's knee. It gave out after I . . . after you told us about building the fence." Goodness, she'd almost mentioned their date.

"Oh. I'm glad she's feeling better." He continued to stare straight ahead.

Silence filled the buggy as they made their way down the road. What should she do now? Channel her inner femme fatale? No, not in front of Micah. Be assertive? She'd tried that, and she didn't know if she was successful since Jesse hadn't given her an answer about their date either way. What else could she do? Or say? The centers of her palms grew damp. What was the next step in phase two? She couldn't remember.

Wait. She did remember something. She glanced at his hand. Men loved affection, at least that's what the books said. That tidbit of info had made her pause, though. She was too young to remember any affection between her mother and father, and while Elaine was always around *Daed*, she couldn't recall seeing any romantic gestures between them. She assumed they kept all that private, like most Amish couples did.

A sweet memory came to the fore. Once, when her grandfather was still alive, Charity walked into their living room. They hadn't heard her, and she witnessed her *grossvatter* taking *Grosmammi*'s hand, cradling it gently. She must have been only six or seven, but her heart warmed thinking about the two of them.

She glanced at Jesse's hands resting on his knees, his long fingers draping over his kneecaps.

Her hand twitched. She lifted her fingers. Quickly put them down. Confidence. Assertiveness. Remember the plan. *Men love affection.*

Before she lost her courage, she slipped her hand into his.

.୬৵৶৽.

Jesse wasn't surprised Micah had offered Charity a ride to church. It was the right thing to do, and if things weren't so squirrelly between he and Charity and he'd been in Micah's shoes, he would have done the same thing. He also wasn't surprised she was practically sitting in his lap thanks to Micah's size taking up a good chunk of the buggy seat. And that was fine. They would be at the Beilers' soon enough. He could sit statue-still for the next ten minutes or so.

Then she shocked his socks off. Again.

He tried not to gape at their clasped hands. What in the world was she thinking? And what was he supposed to do? If he yanked his hand from hers he would draw Micah's attention and more than likely embarrass her. Maybe that's why she did this, because she knew he wouldn't make a scene in the buggy.

His teeth clenched as she tightened her grip around his fingers. This was too much. Too far. She couldn't go around holding men's hands—*his* hand—in public like this. It was as if she had no idea how Amish social conventions worked.

He glanced at Micah. If his boss noticed they were holding hands, he didn't let on. But he hadn't forgotten Micah's matchmaking hints over a week ago, and this would spark that dead fire again. His temple throbbed, a daily occurrence lately.

Jesse stared straight ahead again, fighting—and failing—to ignore her hand in his. A muscle jerked in his jaw when he felt her lightly brush her thumb back and forth over his thumb joint. Her touch was light. Soft. His eyes dropped to their clasped hands, noting the freckles sprinkled over her skin. He didn't realize her hand had been tense until she relaxed it against his. And as if they had a will of their own, his fingers tightened around hers.

His brain finally kicked in. He couldn't possibly be enjoying holding hands with Charity Raber. The idea was absurd, ridiculous, harebrained . . .

And nice.

That's it. He had to put an end to this nonsense, even if she ended up embarrassed. He also needed to get his head checked.

The buggy went over a bump, and he seized the chance to extricate his hand. Quickly he turned to Micah, giving her the literal cold shoulder. "I didn't realize the Beilers lived this far out." How he managed to sound normal, he had no idea.

"*Ya.* They live the farthest out in the community. They moved here seven months ago, maybe eight. *Gut* family. Marigold's grown a lot this past year."

"Sounds like back home." He continued to ignore Charity, who hadn't said a word since he let go of her hand. "Birch Creek is so full now, we've got families leaving for nearby districts."

"Because of the bachelor advertisement?"

Jesse gulped. "How did you know about that?"

"Oh, everyone knows." Micah laughed. "We have three married couples living here because of that ad. Did they ever find out who put it in the paper?"

"Uh . . ."

"Whoever did was a big jerk."

Jesse looked at Charity. Arms crossed, scowling face, angry eyes. *Uh-oh.*

"Why do you say that?" Micah asked.

"Because they lied." She turned to Jesse, but her attention was on Micah. "There were a lot of single men there, all right. But hardly any of them wanted to get married."

"Several *did* get married," Jesse pointed out. A jackhammer pounded both sides of his head. "Some were my *bruders*. They wouldn't have met their *fraus* if it weren't for the ad."

"And that erases the fact that there were plenty of women who didn't marry and had to *geh* back home without a husband?" She glared at the buggy's floorboard "We—they—were duped."

He didn't miss her slipup, and he refused to acknowledge it. "I'm sure that wasn't the intent," he mumbled.

"Maybe it was. Maybe it was one big joke. Maybe they didn't realize that some of us take getting married seriously."

He squirmed in his seat and looked at her. "Or maybe they had *nee* idea the ad would cause anyone problems. *Maybe* they've learned their lesson by now."

Slowly she turned to him. "How would you know?" Her eyes narrowed until he could barely see the light-blue irises. Then she gasped. "You—"

"Oh look, we're at the Beilers'." Micah coughed and tapped the reins on the back of the horse's flanks. Immediately the buggy sped up.

Jesse's throat went dry under Charity's glare. Had he said too much, and she figured out his secret? He couldn't tell. There were so many reasons she could be angry—the advertisement in general, his letting go of her hand, or worst of all, she guessed he was responsible for the bachelor hoax. Might be all three. Dread filled his gut. "Charity—"

She shifted her body until her back was to him.

He reckoned he should be used to her being angry with him. But this was different. He could sense her fury. Felt it, somehow. In the front of his mind he knew he should be relieved she was ignoring him now. No way she was going to hold his hand again while they were in the buggy. Or possibly ever. That was a good thing. *Right?*

Micah turned into the driveway and parked in the first empty space several yards from the barn.

"I'll tie up your horse for you," Jesse offered, partly because he wanted to help his boss, and partly because he couldn't go into church without finding out what had Charity so riled up.

"*Danki.*" He halted the horse. "I wanted to talk to Glen for a few minutes before church anyway." He handed him the reins and climbed out.

Jesse stared at the reins in his hand, then glanced at Charity again. *Yikes.* Her face was blood-red, her lips pressed so tightly together they were ashen. What he could see of them, anyway. Now wasn't the time to talk. He'd have to find her after church and—

"*You.*"

The way she ground out the word was terrifying. Okay, time to settle her down. He mustered his Miss Peach voice. "Ch—"

"You made a fool out of me," she whispered in a thick voice, like a handful of hay was trapped in her throat. "A fool out of all of us."

Ten

Is he being a huge jerk? Seriously
consider he isn't the one.

Getting a Man and Keeping Him, p. 128

Charity sprang out of the buggy before she said something she'd
regret. When her feet hit the ground, she halted and closed her
eyes. For the first time in days—no, more like weeks—she prayed.
For calm, for God to help her hold her tongue, and for strength not
to cry in front of Jesse and everyone milling around outside the barn.
She couldn't sit through a three-hour church service when she was
ready to explode.

"Charity."

She heard Jesse's voice nearby and disregarded him. *I know I've
been ignoring you, Lord. Please forgive me. And although I don't deserve
it, please . . . help me.*

"Charity," he repeated.

"Shh!" She held up her hand, her eyes still closed. "I'm praying."

He didn't speak, but he didn't move either. *Phooey.* How was she
supposed to concentrate on praying when he was loitering about? Her
eyes flew open and she glared at him. "Leave me alone."

"Not until you tell me why you're so angry."

Ha! As if he didn't know. Well, maybe he didn't know. But she wasn't inclined to explain it to him either. Maybe if she went inside the barn early she could sit on one of the benches and pray for some equilibrium. She started toward the wood-slatted building. His hand touched her forearm, stopping her.

"Is this about me letting *geh* of *yer* hand?" he asked.

Wow. She'd forgotten all about holding his hand, how good his skin felt against hers, and the way her heart sang when he squeezed her fingers. Even through her fury at him, her toes curled.

He glowered. "What were you thinking, doing that in front of Micah?"

Her toes flattened. Once again she was an idiot for believing he liked holding her hand. She'd even thought at the time it was the buggy being jostled that had caused them to slip apart, not him letting her go. Now she knew better. For multiple reasons she never wanted to hold his hand again.

"Hi, Jesse."

Charity suppressed a groan. Saloma. She'd planned to talk to her about Jesse after church was over and explain her romantic feelings for him. Not anymore. Saloma could have him.

Actually, her new friend had great timing. She could walk inside the church with Saloma, cool off, and put Jesse out of her mind . . . and heart. An easy task, now that she knew what kind of person he really was. She pasted a smile on her face and turned around. "Hi, Saloma. And Clarence," she added when she saw him hovering behind her.

"Charity." But Clarence barely looked at her before he crossed his arms and eyeballed Jesse.

Saloma sidestepped Charity and moved close to Jesse. "Would you walk with me to the barn? Church is starting soon."

He paled and glanced at Clarence, who shook his head. "Sorry,"

Jesse said, stepping away from her. "I already planned to walk with Charity."

That both surprised and irritated her. "I don't want to walk with you—"

"C'mon," he said, taking her elbow. "We don't want to be late."

"But, Jesse," Saloma said.

"I'll walk with you, Saloma," Clarence offered.

Jesse hurried away from the two of them, practically dragging Charity with him.

"Let me *geh*," Charity snapped.

"Gladly." He dropped her arm and looked over his shoulder. Charity followed suit, seeing Saloma and Clarence walking toward them, Saloma several steps ahead of the big man.

Jesse leaned close to her ear. "You and I are going to talk after the service," he whispered.

"What if I don't want to?" She tilted her chin.

"Too bad." He marched into the barn.

Her fingers clamped together. She'd never seen him angry before. Or so forceful. Her pinky toe twitched. "Stop it!" she hissed.

Saloma and Clarence came up beside her. "*Geh* on inside," Saloma said to him. "I need to talk to Charity for a minute."

"But everyone's already in the barn," Clarence pointed out.

"I'll be there in a minute!"

Clarence's mouth contorted and he walked away.

Saloma scowled. As soon as he was out of earshot she fussed, "I thought you said you and Jesse weren't together."

"We're not." And she could say that honestly. Not now, not ever.

"Then why did you leave with him just now? I said I wanted to go with him to church."

Charity rubbed her eyebrow. How had Saloma missed Jesse

dragging her away? Or maybe it only felt he was dragging since she didn't want to go with him. "That wasn't *mei* choice."

"You could have told him *nee*." Her scowl increased. "I thought you were *mei* friend, Charity. How could you do that to me?"

"I am your friend."

"You sure don't act like it."

Charity couldn't speak. She was Saloma's friend. And she thought Saloma was hers. A thought hit her. *Is she only being nice to me because of Jesse?*

A deep ache appeared in her heart. Was Saloma just using her? All that talk about being awkward and not having friends . . . was it all a lie? Charity had a moment of doubt at the time, and she should have gone with her gut.

Doris Zook had done the same thing to her, only not over a boy. Charity had brought a small bag of peppermints to school, ones she'd bought with the five dollars her father had unexpectedly given her the week before. He'd handed her the bill, gave her a small smile, and walked away. He did that from time to time, and she'd always wondered why but didn't have the nerve to ask him. Doris, who had never said more than two words to her before, stuck like glue beside her the whole day until Charity offered her a peppermint. "Can I have four?" Doris brazenly asked with a smile. Charity gave them to her, happy to have the girl's attention.

Doris didn't speak to her for the rest of the school year.

The ache bubbled up to her throat, and she knew she couldn't stand here much longer without dissolving into tears. *Never let them see you cry—*

"Oh, shut up," Charity muttered.

"What?" Saloma said, her pretty eyes expanding to the size of dinner plates.

But she didn't bother to explain. She whirled around, unsure of where she was going, knowing she needed to get away from her memories, Saloma, Jesse . . . everything.

"Charity!" Saloma called out to her.

She ignored her and hurriedly left the Beilers', not paying attention to her surroundings. She kept going, the lump in her throat refusing to budge. She was so foolish, so stupid. She'd never fit in anywhere. Even when she was little and lived with her father and grandparents in Indiana, she felt like she didn't fully belong. She was the only child in the community whose mother had died. Her father was always sad, her teacher felt sorry for her, and her classmates were told to treat her as "special." That translated to them not including her. Only her grandmother had acted normally toward her, not only encouraging and loving her, but not being afraid to discipline her either. And then she passed away . . .

"Ugh!" Hot tears ran down her face. Why did she think things would be different in Marigold? Or that she'd be able to find a husband, even with a foolproof plan? Her choices were always questionable. She'd been rejected by so many men in Birch Creek, and had latched on to Olin without even finding out if he was available. And then there was Jesse. Her books told her he was the one and she believed it, all because he had done a couple of nice things for her. Now that she thought about it, he would have done them for anyone. Turned out he was the worst of them all.

Charity rubbed her eyes until the tears stopped. By the time she calmed down, she had no idea where she was. A barrage of emotions slammed into her. Frustration that she was so witless. Anger that she'd let down her guard and believed Saloma was sincere. Fury that Jesse wasn't the nice guy he seemed to be. And, worst of all, shame, because she'd done something she'd never done before—skipped out on church.

She stopped in her tracks. Turned around and looked for something familiar. Nothing. She was lost.

Would anyone notice she was? Or even care?

Enough!

Charity was a master when it came to making mistakes and foolish decisions, and there were times she sank into self-pity. But not often, and she needed to stop her current spiral. She'd learned that feeling sorry for herself didn't change anything, and she wouldn't be able to find her way back to Shirley's if she kept sulking about the past and kicking herself for her current predicament. But there was something she needed to do first.

She sank down into the grass on the side of the road, not caring if anyone saw her. She folded her hands and bowed her head. "I'm sorry, Lord," she whispered. "Please forgive me for running off and leaving church." She prayed more, acknowledging that she'd been ignoring him for so long because she was consumed with finding a husband. She asked him to help her not feel sorry for herself so much. Finally, she asked for direction—literally. "Help me find *mei* way back," she whispered, before saying amen.

She stood, still unsure which way to go, yet knowing if she didn't move in some direction, she'd stay lost.

She turned to the left and started walking.

.⨀⨀.

During the service, Jesse's foot bounced up and down as he craned his neck and searched for Charity inside the Beilers' barn. When Saloma came in alone, he was surprised to see how pale she looked. Did she and Charity have a fight? At this point he wasn't ruling out anything, and he'd expected Charity to be right behind Saloma. With a voice like hers, she wouldn't want to miss the hymn singing that opened the service.

The singing came and went. No Charity. He looked to Saloma, who was sitting next to her mother, her gaze on the minister, Enos Shetler, as he stood in front of the congregation to deliver the sermon. If she was worried about Charity not being in church, she didn't show it.

His thoughts ping-ponged in his head. Should he go look for her? No. Better to let her cool off. She was probably outside of the barn doing just that.

But now it was hour three and she still hadn't come inside.

Micah nudged him with his elbow and arched a brow at his fidgeting.

Jesse stopped. But by the end of the sermon he had no idea what Enos had said. *Where is she?*

When church was over, he dashed out of the barn and searched around the Beilers' property. No sign of her. As he turned to do another quick check of the backyard, he saw Saloma, Clarence right behind her like a lovestruck puppy.

Any other time he would have walked in the opposite direction of those two, but Saloma was possibly the last person to see Charity. He met them by the long row of parked buggies on the side of the Beilers' driveway. "Have you seen Charity?"

"She left."

He pushed his black hat from his forehead, as if the motion would help the situation. "Where did she *geh*?"

"I don't know." Her bottom lip quivered. "I think I hurt her feelings."

Well, that made two of them. She'd already been hopping mad at him before Saloma had shown up. He glanced at Clarence, and for once Clarence didn't look like he wanted to throttle him. Her faithful companion lifted his hand and brought it to Saloma's shoulder, ready to comfort her, only to withdraw and put both hands behind him.

"We've been looking for her ever since the service ended," she said, her voiced strained.

"I'm sure she went back to Shirley's." Now that he had confirmation that she and Saloma had argued, it made sense that she went back home. *I hope.*

"That's what I was thinking too."

Clarence motioned to his buggy nearby. "We should *geh* check on her."

Jesse agreed. "I'll let Micah know."

He found his boss talking with the bishop, waiting for lunch to start. "Can I talk to you for a minute?"

"Sure." Micah followed him to a wooden play set a few feet from the house.

"I'm catching a ride with Clarence."

"You and Charity?"

Jesse inwardly groaned at the knowing look in his eye. Obviously he'd seen them holding hands in the buggy, but he would set him straight later. "She found another way home."

"All right." Micah grinned. "Glad to see you're making friends."

He sounded more like one of his older brothers, or even his father, than his boss, something he would appreciate if he wasn't so out of sorts. "See you tomorrow morning."

A few minutes later they were on their way to Shirley's. Clarence's buggy was a single seater, and Saloma sat between him and Jesse. He perched on the right edge of the seat, as far from her as he could get. He didn't need Clarence mad at him on top of everything else.

Silence stretched between the three of them as Clarence drove and Jesse observed the landscape as the horse trotted along. They passed by a mix of English and Amish houses, two large farm fields, and a small Amish school, yet the sights barely registered above the din in his brain. He was almost positive Charity was at Shirley's right now, so he wasn't worried about her whereabouts. Something else disturbed him, and it had simmered below his concern over her not showing up for the service. He slid his clammy palms over his black pants.

"I didn't mean to hurt her feelings." Saloma tapped his shoulder. "When I saw you two walk away together, I thought she'd lied to me about not liking you."

He gripped his knees. She was outright admitting to liking him in front of the man who was in love with her. *Oh boy.* Jesse glanced at Clarence, spotting a nerve jump in his jaw. He was more concerned about upsetting him than he was about Saloma's confession. *Tread carefully.* "I'm the one Charity's mad at."

"Why? What did you do?"

What was it with him and blunt women? "I'm not sure," he mumbled. A half-truth. Probably more like three-fourths of a lie, because the more he thought about it, the surer he was that she'd figured out he was the reason she came to Birch Creek.

He expected Saloma to bring up their impending double date. Thankfully, she didn't. Both she and Clarence were quiet as Charity's words echoed in his head. *"You made a fool out of me. A fool out of all of us."* Her words were bad enough but her wounded eyes had stabbed his soul. Nelson had pointed out how his prank negatively affected other people besides his brothers and friends, but to see how he had hurt Charity . . . *I should have never put that ad in the paper.* The advertisement hadn't been for naught, but that didn't mean he should have done it.

Just because God used his mischief for good didn't mean it wasn't mischief.

"Are those flashing lights?" Saloma said, pointing straight ahead.

"I think they are." Clarence tapped the reins, urging the horse to hurry.

Jesse looked up to see red lights flashing through lush green tree branches on the right side of the road. They were coming up on Micah and Priscilla's house.

"Oh *nee!*" Saloma cried out as an ambulance appeared in the Waglers' driveway. "Something's happened to Priscilla!"

Clarence spurred his horse to ride faster. As soon as they reached the driveway, Jesse leaped from the buggy and ran to the already opened front door. When he entered the house he saw Priscilla on a stretcher, ghostly pale . . . and Charity standing beside her.

Eleven

If he can't handle you at your worst,
he doesn't deserve your best.

Getting a Man and Keeping Him, p. 152

Charity held on to Priscilla's hand as the paramedics lifted the stretcher and the wheels locked into place. "You and the *boppli* are going to be okay," she said, squeezing her fingers. She had no idea if that was true, but she was sure Priscilla needed the encouragement. Charity would if she were in the same position—going into early labor with a high-risk pregnancy.

Priscilla gave her a small smile, closed her eyes, and started humming, her pitch perfect.

"Ma'am," one of the paramedics said to Charity. "We need to get her into the ambulance."

Priscilla's eyes flew open and she clung to Charity's hand. "Can she come with me?"

The paramedic exchanged a look with his partner, and the woman nodded. "Sure."

"Thank you."

Jesse suddenly appeared on the opposite side of the stretcher. "What's going on?"

"Micah's here?" Priscilla said, hope in her bleary eyes.

Jesse shook his head. "*Nee.* He's still at the Beilers'."

"Sir." The heavyset paramedic continued to move the stretcher. "We have to get her to the hospital. You'll need to get out of the way."

Jesse nodded and stepped back, then looked at Charity, fear in his eyes.

She ignored him. Priscilla was her focus now.

She followed the paramedics to the ambulance. Out of the corner of her eye she saw Clarence and Saloma standing in the grass near the driveway, a buggy behind them. "*Geh* get Micah and tell him to meet us at the hospital," Charity called out to them.

"Tell him I'm okay." Priscilla gave a thumbs-up as they loaded her into the ambulance. Charity climbed in, and they shut the doors behind her.

As Priscilla closed her eyes and hummed again, a sweet but unrecognizable tune, Charity fought to catch her breath.

After she'd meandered for a while trying to find her way back to Shirley's, she decided to knock on the door of a small English house, praying someone would answer. Ashley, a woman in her late thirties, offered to give her a ride. She accepted, but when she neared Priscilla's house, she decided to check on her since she'd been alone all morning, and asked Ashley to drop her off at the Waglers'. Thank the Lord she did, because when she went inside, Priscilla was on the floor, doubled over with a contraction. "I'm in labor!" she cried. "Call 9–1–1." She started to pant, pointing to the cell phone next to the couch. "I'm high risk."

Charity spurred into action, calling the emergency number as Priscilla's contraction seemed to subside. She hurried to the kitchen and brought her a glass of water. Wide-eyed, Priscilla was humming when Charity handed it to her.

"I'm not supposed to be in labor." She took a sip of the water and handed it back to Charity, then wiped the sweat from her forehead with her forearm. "I'm scheduled for a C-section at the hospital in three weeks. Oh *nee*, not another one!"

Priscilla gripped her hand and waited for the contraction to come. When it didn't, she relaxed a little. "Maybe I'm having Braxton Hicks."

Charity frowned. "What are those?"

"False labor. Although if this is false labor, how bad is the real thing?" She blew out a breath, a sheepish look crossing her face. "Don't tell Micah, but I've been nervous about the delivery. I was hoping we could have the baby naturally, but my doctor said a scheduled C-section would be necessary since I'm high risk due to *mei* age."

She had no idea how old Priscilla was, and she wasn't going to ask. She handed the glass of water to her again, glad she wasn't in pain for the moment. Up until now she didn't realize how little she knew about pregnancy. Being an only child, she didn't have a relationship with her older stepbrothers, who all moved to their wives' communities. She always wondered if they did so to get away from Elaine. "What song were you humming earlier?"

Priscilla smiled. "'Crazy' by Patsy Cline. She was *mei* go-to any time I felt down when I was living in Nashville."

"You used to live in Nashville?"

"Honey," Priscilla said, switching to English and a soft Southern drawl. "I was gonna be famous. A big country singin' star."

Charity's eyes grew wide. "Really? How did you become Amish?"

"I grew up Amish." She went back to *Deitsch*. "But I didn't join the church until I was in *mei* midthirties and realized God had a different plan than I did. I moved here, took a teaching job, met Micah, and stole him from the cradle." She grinned.

"Stole him from what?"

"He's ten years younger than me." She rested her hand on her swollen belly. "And here we are."

Charity let the new information sink in as Priscilla finished off the glass of water. The age difference between her and Micah didn't matter, but she'd never met anyone who wanted to be famous.

"Whew," Priscilla said, starting to sit up on the sofa. "I guess I made too big a deal about one measly contraction. How embarrassing. Now I'll have to tell the medics it was a false alarm—Ohhhh!"

Grabbing her hand, Charity held it while the contraction came and went.

Priscilla turned pale. "*Mei* water broke."

Charity glanced down at Priscilla's dress and saw the fluid mixed with blood.

"Oh *nee!*" Her nails dug into Charity's palm. "*Nee nee nee.*"

"It's gonna be okay. The ambulance will be here soon." Charity pushed back her own panic and gently removed her hand from Priscilla's. "Where are your towels?"

"In the hall closet near the bathroom."

"I'll be right back." She found the towels and cleaned up Priscilla the best she could. She was humming a new song now, but the notes were off-key.

"What tune is that?" Charity asked, setting the towels on the floor.

"'What a Friend We Have in Jesus.'" Priscilla grimaced in pain. "Here's another one!"

Charity's brain switched to the present as she held Priscilla's hand until her fingers ached.

"I'm sorry," Priscilla gasped as the contraction subsided. "I didn't hurt you too much, did I?"

"*Nee.*" She didn't dare shake the pain from her hand.

"I hope Micah can get to the hospital soon." She was drenched in sweat now.

"I'm sure he will." Charity glanced at the female paramedic who was seated on the other side of the ambulance, filling out paperwork. She didn't seem bothered by Priscilla's contractions or her pallor.

Priscilla closed her eyes, not humming this time. She seemed to be asleep.

The paramedic glanced at a group of monitors by Priscilla and scribbled something on her chart. Then she looked at Charity and smiled. "She'll be okay," she said. "Her blood pressure is a little high but it's not in the danger zone."

Thank God. She was also thankful Priscilla dozed until they arrived at the ER. She followed her and the paramedics inside until they told her to stay in the waiting room. She was pacing when Micah showed up.

"Where is she?" he asked, dashing into the waiting room carrying a small, light-pink duffel bag. If the situation weren't so serious, he would have looked a little silly.

"In the back." Charity went to him.

"Is she okay?" The stark terror in his eyes was alarming. She'd never seen him anything but calm and good-natured.

"She was fine in the ambulance," she said. "I haven't heard anything since they sent her back."

"*Danki* for being there for her, Charity. It means everything to me that she didn't have to *geh* through this alone."

She nodded and led him to the receptionist, who immediately let him back to see his wife.

Charity went back to the waiting room, flopped onto a chair, and glanced at the clock on the wall. Almost three o'clock. She leaned forward and covered her face with her hands, praying that Priscilla and the baby were okay.

The ER's sliding doors opened and she sat up. Bishop Fry, his wife, Verna, and an English woman she didn't know walked into the waiting room. The English woman sat down on a nearby chair while Charity went to the Frys and explained what had happened to Priscilla. "Micah is with her now, and the paramedics said she would be okay."

"If it's the Lord's will," the bishop said, his expression somber.

He was right. God's will always reigned. She said another quick, silent prayer for the Waglers.

"This is Susan," Verna said, motioning to the woman who had walked in with them. "She drove us and Micah to the hospital."

"Nice to meet you," Charity said as Susan walked over to them, her silver hair cropped short.

"I'll see if the receptionist has any new information." The bishop and his wife went to the front desk.

"Charity." Susan regarded her. "Are you the sweet girl who lives with Shirley?"

"*Ya.*"

"We go to church together, although I've been gone for the past two months. My husband and I took a European cruise, and then we visited our children. One lives in Florida, and the other in Nebraska. But we've been chatting on the phone." She smiled. "Shirley's been singing your praises, young lady."

That was nice to hear. Then she realized Shirley had no idea where she was.

"Can I borrow your phone? I need to call her and let her know what happened."

"Of course." She pulled her cell out of the pocket of her pale-blue ankle-length pants and tapped on the screen a few times. "I brought her number up for you. You've been the best thing to happen to her since she had her stroke. I'm glad she has someone looking out for her."

Charity didn't know how to respond to so many compliments. And Shirley had mentioned her to her friends? Her face heated as she took the phone. "Thank you," she whispered. She touched the Call button and Shirley immediately picked up.

"Hi, Susan," she said. "I can't talk right now, I'm waiting for a call—"

"Shirley, it's me. Charity."

"Oh, thank goodness. How is Priscilla? Jesse told me you went with her in the ambulance to the hospital."

Jesse was there? "She was okay on the way here, and Micah's with her now. We haven't heard anything yet."

"I guess Susan drove him since you have her phone."

"Bishop Fry and his wife are here too." Which meant that she could probably leave now, since Priscilla had her husband and friends for support, not to mention the medical team, and Susan could probably take her to Shirley's. But she didn't want to leave until she found out for sure Priscilla and the baby were okay.

"How are you holding up, Charity?"

She closed her eyes at Shirley's caring tone. *Phooey*, they were burning again, and she was so tired her limbs felt like soggy noodles. She swallowed and opened her eyes. "Is it okay if I stay here for a while longer? Hopefully the doctor will tell us what's going on soon. If they don't in an hour, I'll find a ride to your house."

"You stay as long as you need to. I'm just fine. Jesse and I have been playing gin. He's pretty good. Almost beat me once."

A smile twitched on her lips. Shirley was quite the card sharp. "I'll let you know about Priscilla as soon we hear something." She hung up and handed the phone back to Susan.

"I can take you home when you're ready." Susan slipped her cell back in her pocket. "I have my van, so there's plenty of room for you and the Frys."

Overwhelmed, she nodded her thanks.

A few seconds later, the Frys returned to the waiting room. "They transferred Priscilla to labor and delivery, so she's in good hands," Bishop Fry said. "Micah will stay with her until the baby is born."

Charity's knees nearly buckled with relief.

Susan's phone rang. "It's Micah," she said, glancing at the screen before she answered. "Hi, I hear you're going to have a baby soon. Congratulations." She smiled as Micah talked. "Sure, I can take them home. Do you have everything you need? Yes, it's a good thing Priscilla likes to be prepared. Okay, call me if you need anything. Tell her we're praying for a safe delivery." She turned off her phone. "Priscilla packed an emergency bag last week, so she and Micah have everything they need for tonight. They're prepping her for a C-section right now, so he said there's no need for all of us to stay." She looked at the bishop. "He'll let you know when Priscilla has the baby."

The bishop nodded, Verna smiled, and Charity wanted to cry— happy tears this time. Also tired ones. She'd never felt so drained.

A short while later she sat in the far back seat of Susan's fifteen-passenger van. Bishop Fry chatted with Susan from the front seat, and his wife sat directly behind him. Charity leaned her head back and sighed, grateful Priscilla and the baby were all right and pleased she'd been able to help. Before working for Shirley she might not have thought about checking on Priscilla, or even going with her to the hospital. She didn't know the Waglers very well, and although her Amish faith and culture required her to rally around her community, she hadn't done much of that in her life. She could blame Elaine, or her father, or the people in Cherry Springs for that.

Or she could be honest and place the blame where it belonged— squarely on herself.

"Charity?" Verna was smiling, her plump cheeks touching the bottom of her glasses.

"*Ya?*"

"*Danki* for taking care of Priscilla."

The thanks wasn't necessary, but it felt good. She nodded and Verna turned back around. Something warm and wonderful was blossoming within her. She hadn't felt useful or needed in a very long time. In fact, she couldn't remember if she ever had. Her grandmother had made her feel wanted, and Charity was realizing that useful, needed, and wanted were all interrelated.

But once she lost *Grossmammi*, she lost her way.

Susan pulled up in front of Shirley's house. "Tell her I'll stop by this week for a visit," she said. "It's been too long since we last got together."

"I will." Charity exited the van and waved goodbye as Susan pulled out of the driveway. She turned and faced the house, Jesse coming to mind. *Is he still here?* Most likely not. Susan had called Shirley and told her Priscilla was going to be okay. Once Jesse knew that, there was no reason for him to hang around. Shirley would encourage him to leave anyway since Charity was on her way back.

Jesse. She balled her fists, anger cutting through her fatigue. It was easy not to think about him when she had concentrated on finding her way back to Shirley's, even more so when she was focused on Priscilla. But now she was mad all over again. *Thank God I don't have to see him tonight.*

As soon as her mind finished the thought, the front door opened. Jesse stepped outside.

Phooey. No, phooey was too silly a descriptor for how she was feeling, seeing him standing on Shirley's front porch. Harsher words came to mind, and she pushed them away as she marched up the porch steps.

"I'm glad Priscilla's okay—"

She shoved past him, her foot hovering over the threshold.

"Charity."

His pleading tone stopped her. She straddled the doorway, unsure what to do. She didn't want to talk to him, or even look at him. Shame and anger wrapped her heart. She'd hoped and believed she would find a husband in Birch Creek. It had all been a lie. *His* lie.

She started back inside. She needed to change into her work dress, make supper for Shirley, and collapse into bed. For some unfathomable reason, she turned to face him instead. "What?"

"We still need to talk."

⸎

Charity's exhausted, furious expression almost caused Jesse to backtrack his request. Now was probably the wrong time to discuss anything, including the weather. But he needed to clear the air as best he could. He'd waited for her to come back from the hospital. Playing cards with Shirley had passed the time, yet he couldn't shake his worry about Priscilla, the baby . . . and Charity.

"I don't want to talk, Jesse." Her thin arms crisscrossed over her slim waist, and she turned to the door.

He grasped her arm before she could flee from him again. "Please, Charity. This won't take long."

Her eyes snapped to his hand. She shook him off. "Make it quick."

He had her attention but no clue where to start. He still owed her an apology for mocking her the night of the singing. And he wanted to know the truth about this double-date business with Saloma. Then there was the topic of her holding his hand in Micah's buggy.

It all flew out of his head. "I put the bride ad in the paper." There. He couldn't be any quicker than that.

"I know."

His gaze dropped to his feet. "How did you figure it out?"

"You tried to justify it. The only person who would defend something so awful would be the person who did it."

"It wasn't all bad," he blurted.

"You're still doing it! Rationalizing something so horrible. It doesn't matter if it worked out for some people. It was wrong. And *mean*." Her chin trembled. "I thought I'd find a husband because of that advertisement," she whispered.

"You could have," he pointed out. Even as the words left his mouth, he knew they were unfair, but he couldn't stop himself. "You're the one who left last year."

She dropped her arms to her sides. "I see. It's *mei* fault I didn't stick around to be rejected over and over."

"That's not what I meant." But it sounded like he did.

"You really are an awful, *awful* man, Jesse Bontrager." She dashed inside the house.

"Charity—"

Door shut. Lock clicked. Conversation over.

He stared open-mouthed at Shirley's front door. How did he manage to blow this so badly? Why hadn't he just apologized to her, instead of refusing to accept the blame he deserved? All he'd had to do was say he was sorry, that he'd been immature and hadn't meant for anyone to get hurt. Instead, he'd thrown her pain back in her face.

She was right. He was awful. He hadn't had any idea how awful until now.

He headed back home. The sun was setting, painting the semi-clouded sky with strokes of lavender and peach. His stomach soured with each step across the grassy field. He didn't glance at the buggy shop as he opened his door, walked inside, and turned on the gas lamp in the kitchen.

The silence slammed into him.

How many times had he longed for peace and quiet growing up in a loud, boisterous household? Sure he added plenty to the fracas, but there were times he wanted to be alone, to have a place to hear nothing but his own thoughts. Now that's all he heard. They roared in his head, as if he were in a dank cavern. They sounded a lot like his brothers, shouting at him in anger.

"You can never admit you're wrong, Jesse. Ever."

Nelson wasn't the first one to tell him that. Or to be mad at him for riling them up and walking away, laughing. And Charity was right. It didn't matter how many times he pointed out that marriages happened because of his foolishness. He'd gone too far this time. And he'd hurt Charity. More than once.

He was wrong. Oh so very, *very* wrong.

Twelve

D id you get a good night's sleep, Charity?" Shirley set her mug of coffee onto the seat of her walker and pushed it to the table. The delicious scents of eggs scrambling, crisp bacon sizzling, and fluffy biscuits baking in the oven filled the kitchen. She sure did love Charity's breakfasts. "You had an exciting day yesterday."

"*Ya.*" Charity laid several pieces of bacon on a paper towel–lined plate. "The biscuits should be done soon."

"Thank you. Everything smells delicious."

"You're welcome."

Shirley frowned and sat down at the table. Yesterday when Jesse came over and said Priscilla was in labor and Charity was going with her to the hospital, she tried not to fret. Several weeks ago Priscilla had confided she was worried about the baby. Not for any specific reason, just that the doctor had told her from the beginning she might have a difficult pregnancy because she was older than thirty-five. When the pregnancy progressed without any issues, he stressed the delivery could be a problem. Shirley thought Priscilla needed a new physician, one that wasn't such a worrywart.

Fortunately everything had turned out fine, and at ten o'clock, Susan texted her and said Priscilla had delivered a healthy baby girl. Shirley thought about telling Charity the news in the morning. The poor girl looked wrung out when she'd come inside last night. But she couldn't wait that long and had gone to her room. Charity was awake and said she was relieved. But the conversation ended there, and Shirley went to bed.

As she watched Charity pull the biscuits out of the oven, her concern grew. She'd never been this quiet before.

After Charity brought the rest of the food to the table, she sat down in the chair opposite Shirley's, closed her eyes, and bowed her head for prayer. Normally Shirley added an extra verbal prayer asking the Lord to bless the food, but she skipped it this morning.

"What are your plans for today?" Shirley selected a piping hot biscuit.

"I'm going to Barton." Charity put one piece of bacon beside the biscuit on her plate.

"Oh? Do you have some errands to run?"

"Just one. I'm taking my books back to the library. Then I'm coming home and I'm tearing up my courtship plan."

Shirley fell against the back of her chair. "Why would you do that?"

"I don't need it."

Finally, the young woman was seeing the light. After spending an afternoon with Jesse, Shirley was starting to see what Charity saw in him. He was polite, competitive at cards without being obnoxious, and didn't seem to mind spending his afternoon with an old woman he barely knew, although she suspected early on he was waiting for Charity to return. She learned plenty about his large family back in Birch Creek and his job at the buggy shop, and she told him about Alan and Wendy, and shared a few snippets of her life in New York. But on the subject of Charity, he stayed mute.

"That's good to hear," Shirley said with a nod. "Like I said, you don't need a plan to find a date, or a husband."

"Oh, I'm not looking for a husband anymore."

"Really?" Shirley smiled. "So you and Jesse . . . ?"

Charity stabbed the bacon with her fork. "There is no me and Jesse. There never will be."

"But—"

"I don't need a husband," she said, puncturing the bacon a second time. Then she lifted her head, looking past Shirley. "Wait, that's not what I mean. I don't *want* a husband."

Shirley tilted her head. She'd never met anyone who seesawed so quickly with her decisions. "Are you sure?" When it came to men, Charity didn't seem sure of anything.

"Positive." She crammed the bacon in her mouth.

Shirley thought about letting the subject drop. Wasn't this what she'd prayed for? That Charity would set her courtship plan to the side?

She glanced at her assistant, who was attacking her biscuit with a knife and fork, shredding it into crumbs. Something must have happened between her and Jesse last night. Going against her policy not to pry, she asked, "Why don't you want a husband anymore?"

Her fork and knife clattered against the plate. "Because a husband isn't the answer."

"The answer to what?"

She lifted her gaze, her eyes filled with pain. "The answer to fixing me."

Shirley's heart ached. My goodness, what had this child gone through in her life to believe she was broken? She reached for Charity's hand. "You don't need fixing," she said.

But Charity moved her hand away. "Yes, I do. There's something wrong with me." Her voice trembled. "There's always been something wrong with me." She stood. "Monroe needs to go outside."

Normally Charity ate every bit of her breakfast and cleaned the kitchen before starting anything new. And Monroe had gone out less than an hour ago. "All right," Shirley said gently.

After Charity left, she looked at the uneaten food on the table. The young woman was right about one thing—getting married wasn't the answer to whatever was going on with her, and Shirley was grateful Charity realized that. She was deeply wounded inside, and finding a man, even the right one, wasn't going to restore her.

She folded her hands and leaned her forehead against her knuckles. "Please Lord," she prayed, "heal Charity's broken heart. You're the only one who can."

.⊸ঙ৶৹.

For the next week, Jesse had no choice but to focus on work. Priscilla was in the hospital for three days after the birth, and Micah stayed with her and the baby, Emma Lynn, leaving Jesse to man the shop. Everyone in Marigold knew Micah was at the hospital, so he wasn't inundated with customers. Jesse did keep busy, though, reading through the manuals and instruction books Micah kept in the shop, familiarizing himself with as much as he could before his boss returned.

When Micah came back to work, it was obvious his mind was with his wife and daughter, and Jesse pointed that out. "I've got everything handled here," he said. "And if there's a problem, I'll let you know."

Micah was relieved, and he spent the rest of Thursday and Friday at home, happy as a clam. Or was it an oyster? Didn't matter. Jesse was happy for him and his family.

But that's where his happiness ended.

His days were consumed with work, but his nights were spent trying not to think about Charity. Impossible due to the way they had left things, or more accurately, how she'd left them. How were they supposed to work things out if she didn't talk to him? How could he apologize if she wouldn't hear what he had to say? He hadn't seen Monroe either, and he missed the mischievous mutt. Shirley had shown him the tie-out Charity rigged up, and it must be doing the job.

Friday afternoon the fence materials were delivered from the hardware store in Barton. He'd ordered them earlier in the week, and he planned to pick up the rest of the wood from Micah's tomorrow afternoon after he closed the buggy shop. Then he would go to Shirley's and start building.

Maybe Charity would listen to him then.

At five o'clock sharp he locked up the shop and went to his barn to feed Miss Peach. Other than letting her go to the pasture behind the shop to graze and a quick trip to Eberol's store, he hadn't taken her for a ride since he'd moved to Marigold. He patted her nose, and she whinnied softly before chomping on the hay he put in her trough. She was so gentle now, but she still had her stubborn moments. Still, she'd come a long way from the runaway horse that kicked mud on him a year ago.

His stomach growled. His mother would be serving dinner right now, his brothers and father gathering at the huge table in their spacious kitchen. More often than not his married siblings would come over too, bringing extra food. *Mamm* was probably serving one of her mouthwatering meals, like meatloaf smothered in brown gravy and mashed potatoes whipped so perfectly there wasn't a single lump. There would be corn, or maybe sweet buttered carrots, or possibly both. A fresh salad or sliced tomatoes, and without a doubt, plenty of buttered bread. Of course there would also be nonstop talking and laughter.

His stomach was howling now. "Miss Peach," he said, patting her flank. "You up for a ride?"

She bobbed her head, as if she understood his words. Knowing how smart she was, she probably did.

He waited for her to finish her supper, then hitched her to his buggy. He hadn't used the vehicle since he'd moved to Marigold. His parents' house was about an hour away, and while it would be quicker to take a taxi, his horse needed the work. No doubt he'd be back late tonight, but it would be worth it.

His heart was already halfway home.

.·๑๑๑.

"I'm sorry I upset you," Saloma said.

Charity's paintbrush hovered near a small, blank canvas. Saloma had arrived at Shirley's thirty minutes ago with paints, two canvases, and plenty of brushes. "You said you'd like to learn how to paint, remember?"

She remembered, all right. But did Saloma think she could pretend nothing had happened between them on Sunday? For a second she considered slamming the door in her face.

But she held back. More like God held her back, because a tiny murmur in her heart prodded her to at least see what Saloma wanted. Turned out, she wanted to paint, and to apologize. *Thank God I listened, for once.* "You don't need to keep saying sorry."

"But I feel awful about what happened." Saloma brushed her hand over the three layers of newspaper Charity had spread out on the kitchen table. Shirley still had a subscription, and each week a stack collected near her recliner. Right now her boss was in the living room chatting on the phone with Susan. "I don't blame you for being mad at me," she said.

"I'm not mad anymore. I just thought . . ." Cobalt-blue watercolor paint dripped from her brush, sprinkling colored water spots on the newspaper. "I thought you were using me to get to Jesse."

"I would never do that." Saloma's shoulders sagged. "I can see why you thought so, though." She paused, then looked at Charity. "We're still friends, *ya?*"

"*Ya.*" Charity smiled, a second load lifting from her shoulders. The first one disappeared when she returned her useless relationship books to the library—and renewed the French cookbook—then ripped up her courtship plan and tossed it in the trash. Montague Persimmons and his fruitless advice was permanently out of her life, and not having to plot and plan anymore was a huge relief. She dabbed at the left corner of the canvas.

"Have you seen Emma Lynn yet?" Saloma asked.

"*Ya.* She's so sweet. I'm so glad she and Priscilla are okay."

"Me too." She glanced at Charity's work. "Don't be afraid to put paint on the brush."

"What if it's too much? I don't want to ruin the painting."

"You won't. Experimenting is how we learn. Try sweeping the brush across the canvas instead of dabbing."

Charity dipped her brush into the square of watercolor paint and ran lightly across like Saloma instructed. "This is fun," she said, skimming her brush back and forth.

"Relaxing too." Saloma had already painted her sky, and was moving on to the grass portion. They were copying a magazine photo of a lush green field similar to the one between Shirley's and the Wagler buggy shop.

Charity didn't know how much time had passed while she and Saloma painted. Giving her undivided attention to her project, she focused on keeping the thin paint from forming too many blobs on the canvas.

Saloma broke the silence. "Do you mind if I ask you a question?"

"*Nee.*" Charity rinsed off the brush in the small glass from Shirley's cabinet, the water turning pale green.

"Are you still okay going on the double date?" she asked, her tone tentative. "Or are you and Jesse still on the outs?"

"On the outs," she said without hesitation. Obviously Saloma had seen her and Jesse arguing before church. How many other people had? *Egad.* Well, it didn't matter. She was never speaking to him again. "I don't want to *geh* out with Clarence either."

Saloma frowned. "Why not? He's a very nice *mann.*"

"Oh, I can tell he is. But I'm not interested in dating anyone." Not now, and possibly never. She was content helping Shirley, as long as Shirley wanted her to, and when that job ended—she didn't want to think about that—she would find another job, hopefully where she would be both needed and wanted.

"But you seemed so eager to *geh* out with him before," Saloma said.

"I changed *mei* mind." She moved to pick up the brush. "I should warn you about Jesse."

"Warn me?"

"He's not a nice *mann.*"

Saloma looked confused. "But he insisted on staying with Shirley until you came home, knowing she was worried about you and Priscilla. He told me and Clarence he didn't want her being alone."

That was a nice thing to do, she had to admit. He had done other nice things too—helping her out of the tree and offering to build a fence for Monroe for free. And of course Monroe adored him, and he usually had good taste in people. When he whined on his tie-out—something that pained both her and Shirley—he was always looking in the direction of the buggy shop.

But his thoughtful gestures paled to the pain he had inflicted.

He'd hurt her feelings in Birch Creek, mocked her behavior at the singing, and the worst affront of all, put a bald-faced lie in the paper. Her fingers tightened around the paintbrush.

"You should relax your grip."

Charity blinked and looked at her hand. "Oh. *Ya.*" She eased her fingers.

Saloma sighed. "Oh well, maybe it's for the best."

"What do you mean?"

She twirled her brush in orange paint, then laid it down. "Clarence isn't speaking to me."

"Oh?"

"*Ya.*" Saloma fiddled with the ribbon of her *kapp.* "I think he's mad at me for some reason. He's never been mad at me before."

"Why don't you ask him about it?"

"I tried. He didn't speak a single word when he dropped me off after we left Shirley's. Usually he comes over on Wednesdays for supper with our *familye.* He didn't this week. He hasn't missed a Wednesday evening meal in years, since he and Olin became best friends in fifth grade. I don't understand what I did."

"Maybe he's jealous." Charity twirled her brush in brown paint.

"Of what?"

"Of you and Jesse going on a date."

She scoffed. "That's ridiculous."

"Why?" She didn't have any inside information that Clarence liked her. Just a hunch. Now that she thought about it, he was usually either by her side or hovering close to her. Maybe she'd accidentally hit the nail on the head.

"I've known him almost all *mei* life, even before he and Olin became *gut* friends." She returned to her painting. "He's like a *bruder* to me."

"Could you see him differently?"

"Like in a romantic way?" Saloma swiped pale-purple paint on the horizon, making a nice effect. "I . . . don't think so. *Nee.* I definitely couldn't."

Both of them dropped the subject, although discussing someone else's love life instead of obsessing about her own was a welcome change. They didn't talk about Clarence or Jesse or dating for the rest of the evening, and by the time Saloma had to go home, Charity had a finished piece.

"Nice work," Saloma said with a smile.

"*Nee.*" Charity lowered her gaze, deflecting the praise. "It's *nix* compared to yours."

"I've been painting for years, though. I think you have some talent. Would you like to paint again sometime?"

Happiness flowed through her. Jesse was out of the picture, and Saloma still wanted to be her friend. "*Ya.* I'd like that."

Charity stood on the front porch and waved at Saloma as she headed back home. The sun was setting, and she wished she had her own set of paints and a canvas. She couldn't capture the brilliance of the gold, coral, and lavender light tinting the high clouds, but she wanted to try. Next time she went to Barton she'd stop by Walmart and see if they had any art supplies.

She needed to go back inside and make supper for her and Shirley, but she wanted to savor the sunset a little longer. Despite her earlier heartbreak over Jesse, she was happy—for the Waglers and their new daughter, that her friendship with Saloma was intact, and most of all, that her courtship plan was in the trash where it belonged. Shirley was right. So was Jesse. *Ugh.*

She had moved to Marigold to find a husband. Instead she found so much more. Purpose, friendship, and hopefully some needed wisdom, because tomorrow Jesse was starting on Monroe's fence. She sighed, some of her cheer slipping away. Then again, what was the problem? He would be busy, she'd make sure she was busy, and their paths wouldn't cross. That was a good plan . . . and one she would stick to.

.ᴄᴠⱺ₈ᴓ.

"Are you gonna stew on your problem the whole time you're here or are you gonna talk about it?"

Jesse patted the flank of Nelson's horse, Pickles. He'd volunteered to do the chores tonight for his younger brothers, and Nelson joined him. He gave him the side-eye. "Never said I had a problem."

"You didn't have to. You were downright silent during supper."

"Supper was almost over by the time I got here. Besides, I wasn't silent." His family had peppered him with questions about his job and Marigold, and Jesse was glad to answer them. He omitted anything about Charity.

"You haven't cracked a joke or a smile since you arrived," Nelson said. "Obviously, there's a problem."

Jesse stroked the shy horse's nose. Like Miss Peach, Pickles was a graduate of Zeb and Zeke's rehab program, but he was still reserved, even around Nelson. Jesse never understood how anyone could treat animals poorly. That made him think about Monroe. Tomorrow he would lavish that mutt with belly rubs until he was in doggy heaven.

"Stew it is." Nelson shut the stall of his father's new horse, Pleasant, who had also spent some time with Zeb and Zeke. The gelding was the exact opposite of his name, and Jesse didn't blame him for being onery based on that fact alone. Other than being given that horrendous moniker, he hadn't been abused or neglected. He did have an abscessed tooth that was healing nicely, however.

"I'm not stewing." Jesse gave Pickles another piece of carrot, then closed the stall door. "Just thinking."

"About what?"

He paused. Normally when someone pried into his business, he deflected with a joke or came up with a story well away from the truth. He wasn't one to confide in his brothers—or anyone, come to think of it. And now that he was thinking, he realized he'd fibbed more often than not when it came to revealing anything that bothered him. What was the word Charity used? Egad?

He drew in a breath. Now was as good a time as any to change a bad habit. "Charity Raber lives in Marigold."

Nelson's jaw dropped. "She does? When did she move there?"

"Two months or so before I did." He stared at the hay-strewn floor. "And, um . . . she knows I put the ad in the paper."

"Oh boy." Nelson rubbed his chin. "Is she mad?"

"That's an understatement."

Nelson leaned against one of the barn poles and crossed his ankles. "How did she find out?"

He told his brother about the ride in Micah's buggy, minus the hand-holding. Just admitting to Nelson she was angry at him was difficult enough, and he wasn't about to be a leaky faucet when it came to personal stuff. "She's not speaking to me."

"Can't say I blame her. I was hopping mad when I found out."

"Why didn't you tell anyone?"

"Because you need to fess up to what you did." He straightened and blew out a breath. "And I need to apologize to Charity. I'm *nee* better than you."

His remark hit Jesse in the gut, and he opened his mouth to parry.

He clamped his lips together. Nelson was right, and he needed to stop making excuses for himself.

"I'll stop by next week sometime and explain what I did," Nelson said. "I just need her address."

"She lives next door."

Nelson's right eyebrow raised. "She's that close to you, huh? Must have been awkward when you reunited."

"We didn't reunite," he grumbled. "That implies we were together in the first place."

"Wrong word choice. Got it. So what are you going to do about your *neighbor*?"

Jesse sighed. "I'll try to apologize again."

"This really bothers you, doesn't it?"

"Of course it does. I didn't mean to hurt anyone."

"*Ya*, you said that before." He tilted his head. "Up 'til now it hasn't bothered you enough to admit and apologize to the community. But when it comes to *Charity*—"

"Don't," Jesse warned.

"You're sweet on her." Nelson laughed. "You and Charity Raber. Never in a million, trillion, quadrillion—"

"I get your point," Jesse mumbled.

"—years did I see that coming."

"Why?" Jesse walked toward Nelson. "Because she's *seltsam*? Because she isn't pretty? Because she's desperate to find a husband?"

Nelson turned serious. "She is *seltsam*, and she is desperate, which makes her hard to be around. But I never said she wasn't pretty. Those are your words. I was talking more about you, by the way. Mr. I'm-Never-Getting-Married."

Something shifted inside Jesse as his brother spoke. "She is pretty," Jesse murmured.

"What?"

He looked at his brother. "She is pretty. Not in a typical way. In her own way."

Nelson frowned. "I can't tell if that's a compliment or an insult."

Definitely a compliment. She was also kind and caring. That was obvious in how she helped Shirley. The woman couldn't stop complimenting her while she demolished him at gin. Then there was the way she stayed by Priscilla's side when she went into labor, not leaving until she was sure Priscilla and the baby would be all right.

Those were all facts. But stating the truth, to Nelson and himself, didn't mean he liked her. He respected her, enough to make things right. They had to live in the same town, after all. And they were neighbors—

"There you *geh* again. Lost in *yer* thoughts." Nelson shrugged. "Look, if you like her, ask her out."

"But—"

"And if you don't, then there's *nee* reason for you to be thinking about her so much. I'm going to get some blueberry cobbler before it's all gone." He walked out of the barn.

Dessert never lasted long at the Bontrager house, but blueberry cobbler was the last thing on his mind. Nelson's words repeated in his head, giving him pause. He respected a lot of people—his family, Freemont Yoder, who was the Birch Creek bishop, Micah, Priscilla, Shirley . . . the list was endless.

But he didn't think about them as much as he thought about Charity.

He stilled. Pickles shifted around in his stall. Cicadas chirped outside. He could even hear his own breathing. If he didn't like Charity, why was she never far from his mind?

And if he did . . . what was he going to do about it?

Thirteen

Late Saturday afternoon, Charity stared out the kitchen door window, watching Monroe follow Jesse around the backyard as he marked off the fence postholes. Susan had picked up Shirley earlier that day for a salon and shopping trip. They invited Charity to go with them, but she declined, not wanting to intrude on their day together since they hadn't seen each other in over two months.

Now she was having second thoughts. Like her courtship plan, her plan to ignore Jesse had ended up in pieces.

As soon as he arrived with the posthole diggers balanced on one shoulder and a tool belt slung around his slim waist, he stopped at the front door and asked her if Monroe could be off his tie-out. "I'll get him if he runs off," he said.

A storm of emotions slammed through her. She thought she'd released most of her anger over the advertisement. She also thought she'd lost every shred of attraction she had for him. Wrong on both counts.

Monroe leaned against Jesse's legs, looking up at him with hearts and flowers in his eyes. She had no choice but to relent. Since then, the dog had stayed by Jesse's side.

But she didn't trust him not to get distracted and speed off, so she kept looking out the window at the two of them. It certainly wasn't because she liked watching Jesse work. No sirree, it wasn't that.

Phooey. She turned from the window and considered supper for herself. Susan and Shirley were dining at their favorite Chinese restaurant in Akron. She looked at the stove. Maybe she'd fix a sandwich or a snack later. Right now her nerves were too strung for her to eat.

She glanced around for something to do. Laundry, dusting, and vacuuming were done, the kitchen spotless. Modern conveniences cut down on the time she needed to do chores, and her goal to be too busy to acknowledge Jesse had sailed out the window. Shirley had a service that mowed the lawn, trimmed the bushes, and mulched the flower beds, and they were due to come next week, so yard work was out. Then she thought of her French cookbook. She could copy some recipes after she checked the mail.

She walked down the driveway, keeping a side-eye out for Monroe in case he heard her leave the house and decided to follow her to the mailbox. Typically the mail arrived at four o'clock or after, so it should be there by now.

Monroe stayed in the backyard, and the door squeaked as she opened the box. She made a mental note to oil the hinges. A thick, white envelope was crammed inside. She pulled it out, along with three junk mail letters, and headed back to the house. She glanced at the address on the package, positive it was for Shirley, who was the only one who received mail. When she saw her name, she halted in the middle of the driveway.

To: Charity Raber

She glanced at the return address.

From: Delbert Raber

Her father had sent her mail! She practically skipped to the house and went inside, plopped on the couch, and carefully opened the package. There was a smaller package wrapped in brown paper and tied with twine, along with a folded sheet of stationery. She opened the page and read her father's sloppy script, as if he'd scribbled the words down.

Dear Charity,

I found these letters last week. They're from your mamm.

Charity gripped the note. Which *mamm*—Elaine or her real mother?

They're made out to you, so I didn't read them. I don't think I could have even if they were for me.

Daed

She set down the paper and looked at the letters. Touched her name written in neat script on the brown paper. *Mamm.* A lump formed in her throat as she slowly untied the twine and opened the package. On top of six envelopes was another note, and she recognized the handwriting right away.

Dear Charity,

Before you were born, yer mamm planned to write a letter to you each year on your birthday. She kept that promise, and here they are. I'm saving them for when you are old enough to read them. I can't wait to give them to you.

Love,

Grossmammi

So many questions flowed through her mind. Why hadn't her grandmother given these to her before she passed away? She had been old enough to read them. And why were they hidden in the closet? Was her *daed* glad he found them? *Does he miss me?* His note was so terse she couldn't tell.

She looked at the first letter, sealed in a brown envelope, her name written gracefully across it. She ran her finger over her *mutter*'s handwriting. She opened the letter and read the first sentence.

And started to cry.

. məɡ.

Jesse thought he'd brought everything he needed to dig the postholes, but he'd forgotten one thing—something to drink. By the time he had half the holes dug, he was thirsty. He glanced at Monroe. "Don't guess you can fetch me some water, huh, *bu*?"

Monroe sat down, his wagging tail rustling against grass that could use some mowing. Maybe he'd stop off during the week and give it a quick mow before he put up the fencing. Unfortunately, right now he had to bother Charity for a drink.

He set down the posthole diggers, wiped his dirty palms on his pants, and headed for the house. He knocked on the back door and waited for her, figuring he'd see the same scowl on her face she'd had when he arrived an hour or so ago. On his way to Shirley's, he'd wondered if Charity was still furiuous with him. He had his answer.

He knocked again. Waited. No Charity. Monroe poked his nose at the door. Jesse turned the knob and opened it. He could sneak into the kitchen and grab his drink, avoiding her altogether. He still planned to apologize, but when she simmered down some. If she ever did.

He entered the kitchen . . . and stopped.

Charity was crying in the living room.

At a loss, he stared at the sink as if the faucet would tell him what to do. Should he check on her? Leave her alone? He'd never had to deal with female tears before. His mother was soft-hearted but stoic when she was upset. His sister, Phoebe, was so much older than him he barely remembered her crying.

Even if he did go to Charity, what would he say?

But he couldn't just walk away.

He moved to the living room. She was holding something to her chest, outright sobbing. Crinkled, brown wrapping paper was in her lap. "Charity?"

"*Geh* away." She turned from him.

He sat down next to her on the sofa. "What's wrong?"

"Jesse, please . . ."

He should do as she asked and leave. But he couldn't. There was something wrong, really wrong. This went beyond her being mad at him. This was *anguish*. He spoke in the gentlest tone he could muster. "Tell me what happened."

She sniffed and turned to him, tears trailing her freckled cheeks and sliding off her jaw. "*Mei mamm . . .*" She started crying again.

He looked at the paper in her hand. A letter. Several unopened ones were on her lap.

"I . . . can't . . . stop . . . crying . . ." She dropped the letter and put her hands over her face. "I . . . can't . . ."

He moved closer to her. Put his arm around her shoulders and guided her cheek to his chest. "Then don't."

.❧.

Charity couldn't remember the last time she'd cried like this. *Grossmammi's* funeral probably, although that event had been a blur. Her father had married Elaine two weeks later and they moved to Cherry Springs, leaving behind everyone she knew. The first night in her new stepmother's home, Elaine had proclaimed her edict: *"Don't let anyone see you cry."*

Tucked in Jesse's strong arms and sobbing against his chest, she couldn't obey those words. He stroked her back in silence, allowing her to spill all the pent-up emotion she'd held inside for so many years, the grief she hadn't been allowed to feel.

She sniffed and lifted her head. The first thing she saw was Jesse's eyes. The compassion and kindness in them. He had a smudge of dirt underneath his left eye, and a hank of curls touched his cheek. She couldn't tell if his shirt was wet because of his sweat or her tears.

Reality came into view. Quickly she sat up. "Sorry," she said, sniffing.

He moved his arm away, grabbed a few tissues from the box on the coffee table, and handed them to her.

She took them, wiped her eyes, and blew her nose so hard it sounded like a goose call. She glanced at him, expecting a smile. Or worse, a laugh. Double worse, him mocking her.

All he did was gaze at her intently.

She inhaled, her chest shuddering. She might as well explain herself after she'd sogged his shirt. "These are from *mei mamm.*"

"Is she all right?"

Charity realized he had no idea her mother was gone. She hadn't even told Shirley. She'd didn't want Cherry Springs intruding on her life in Marigold. Now she had no choice. "She died when I was five."

"I'm so sorry."

"*Mei grossmammi* passed away when I was eight. *Mei daed* married

Elaine and we moved to Cherry Springs. He sent me these today. When I tried to read the first one I—" *Phooey.* The lump that appeared in her throat right before she started crying had returned. Or was it a boulder? Sure felt like one.

His eyes filled with compassion. Or was that pity? She lifted her chin. "I don't want you to feel sorry for me. Everyone has loss in their lives."

"I don't feel sorry for you," he said. "I know how it feels to lose someone you love. I was young when *mei* grandfather died. I barely remember the funeral but I do remember *Mamm's* grief. She was sad for a long time. I also understand how hard it is to move to a new town. We left Fredericktown and moved to Birch Creek."

"Why?"

He glanced at his lap and didn't say anything. His jaw convulsed.

"You don't have to say—"

"We were starving."

Her mouth dropped open. "You were?"

He nodded, sliding his palms down the legs of his broadfall pants, his eyes fixed on the coffee table. "*Mei* younger *bruders* don't remember, but the rest of us do. We were poor, we were hungry, and according to the bishop, we didn't have enough faith. He said we got what we deserved."

She could hardly believe what he was saying. The Bontragers were one of the most well-off families in Birch Creek.

"I'm not sure why I told you that." His voice was almost impossible to hear. "I've never mentioned it to anyone before." He shrugged. "Guess I'm a leaky faucet after all."

"What?"

He finally looked at her, half smiling. "Never mind."

For some reason, knowing that Jesse experienced hardship in his childhood made her feel less alone. "I don't talk about *Mamm*," she admitted. "I haven't in a long time."

"What was she like?"

Charity shook her head. "I don't know. I was five when she died, and I don't have too many memories of her. I never understood why. I was old enough to remember, *ya*?" Her mouth trembled again. She'd never admitted that either. She didn't have a picture of her mother, in keeping with Amish tradition. She knew she resembled her, and sometimes she could hear her voice. Always faint, and not all the time. How could she not remember her mother?

Monroe set his muzzle on Jesse's lap. The dog had been quiet the entire time, as if he were offering his support too.

Jesse stroked the top of Monroe's head, not saying anything. "Good *bu*," he finally murmured, then looked at her. "I just came inside to get a drink. I'll leave you to read your letters."

But when he started to get up, she put her hand on his arm. "Can I ask a favor?"

He nodded.

She picked up her mother's letters. "I don't want to read these alone."

Fourteen

Jesse hesitated. Charity wasn't on the verge of crying. Instead her eyes were dry and hopeful. He didn't understand why she wanted him with her when she read the letters, but he couldn't tell her no. "Sure," he said, striving for a light tone. "Let me get that drink first."

He hurried to the kitchen, filled two glasses with water, and sat down next to her again. "Here." He handed her the glass.

"*Danki.*" She took a sip, set the glass on the table, and blew out a breath. "This shouldn't take long. The first letter looked pretty short."

"Don't worry about the time."

"But the fence—"

"Will get built. This is more important."

She nodded and started to read.

Dear Charity,

Today is your first day of life. Oh, how your father and I prayed for your arrival! I fell in love with you the second I saw you. I'll apologize right now for your red hair, but eventually you'll like yours the same way I like mine. Bright-red hair makes us unique.

And your father has always loved my red hair. He was so happy when he saw yours was red too.

You're not even a day old, and I love you so much, more than I ever thought was possible. God has given us an incredible gift.

Love,
Mamm

Her bottom lip quivered as she opened the next letter.

Dear Charity,

Today is your first birthday, and how adorable you were when you blew out the single candle on your tiny cake. I was shocked when you picked up a fistful of icing and tried to eat it! For the first time in my life, I wished I'd been able to take a picture of that moment. But I'll always have it in my heart, along with all the other memories from this year. It's been a joy to watch you grow from a tiny baby to a walking—and yes, talking!—toddler. I can already tell you're not only going to have my red hair and fair skin, but also my freckles. I caught your father counting them the other day. I think he's keeping a running tally, but if you do take after me and have so many, he won't be able to keep track of them all. It's sweet to see him try. He loves you so much, Charity. I know you're too young to have memories of this first year, but just know that he rocks you to sleep every night, and places a tiny kiss on your forehead before he puts you in your cradle.

Happy birthday, sweetheart! I can't wait to see what the next year brings.

Love,
Mamm

Tears rolled down her cheeks as she moved on to the third.

Dear Charity,

Today is your second birthday, and this time you didn't try to eat your entire birthday cake by yourself! You did chatter the whole time you ate your piece of cake, and of course you asked for seconds, which I gladly gave you. Now that you're two, you've already decided on some favorite foods—sweet potatoes, macaroni and cheese, and surprisingly, celery sticks. You like to sleep with the baby quilt your grossmammi made, and you cry whenever we try to put shoes on your feet. You're a lively, talkative little girl, and our love for you still grows each day.

Happy birthday, my darling girl! I pray this year is as wonderful for you as last year's was.

Love,
Mamm

"I still like celery," she whispered.

Jesse swallowed and handed Charity a tissue. She wiped at her eyes and moved on to the next three letters. He couldn't fathom her grief, and she was soldiering on without pause.

Dear Charity,

Today is your third birthday, and what a fun birthday it was! You wanted strawberry cake, and your father insisted on making it for you. The frosting was lopsided and he put a little too much salt in the batter, but you didn't notice. All you wanted was to sit in his lap while you ate your birthday piece.

Over the past year, you and your daed have grown very close.

We had hoped the Lord would have blessed us with a sibling for you by now, but his ways aren't our own. You and your father are inseparable. I'd be dishonest if I didn't say I was a little envious, but that feeling doesn't last long. And you do come to me when you have a bump or bruise, and you enjoy when I brush your pretty hair. Your daed is still trying to count your freckles!

Happy birthday, dear one.

Love,
Mamm

Dear Charity,

Today is your fourth birthday, and what an exciting day it was! Your daed insisted we take you to the Akron zoo, and you had so much fun! Your favorite animals were the elephants and the polar bear. You also liked the tigers, but when we tried to take you to where they kept the reptiles, you started to cry when you saw the snakes. Your daed scooped you up in his arms and told you he would never let any snakes or anything else hurt you. Then he put you on his shoulders and we finished looking at all the animals. You fell asleep on the ride home, and you were too tired for your birthday cake, so we will have it tomorrow. Strawberry, just like you asked. And yes, your father made this year's cake for you too.

Happy birthday, my sunshine girl!

Mamm

"I went to the zoo?" she whispered. "I always wanted to go to the zoo."

"But not to see the snakes," he joked.

She chuckled and brushed away a stray tear. "Never." She stared at the letter in her lap. "This is the last one."

"Do you want to save it for another time?" Although the letters were short, the contents were a lot to take in at once.

"*Nee*. I need to read all of them now. While I have the courage."

Dear Charity,

Today is your fifth birthday. I'm sorry we weren't able to celebrate the way we wanted to. You've been a strong girl while I've been sick, and as soon as I feel better we will have your party. The doctor says that after I finish this round of strong medicine I should be all well and we can go to the zoo again.

You've had lots of questions about cancer, and Daed and I have tried to answer them the best we know how. I won't be sick for much longer, and our lives can go back to the way they were. I'm glad you enjoyed the cake your daed made. He's getting better at spreading the frosting, isn't he?

I love you so much, Charity. Happy birthday! I can't wait to see what this year has in store for you!

Mamm

Charity set the letter down. Jesse was poised to grab more tissues. In fact, he might need one himself. He cleared his throat.

She smiled, her eyes clear. "*Mei mamm* did love me."

He frowned. "Did you ever doubt it?"

She touched the corner of the letter. "*Grossmammi* told me she did. But when my *mamm* died, she rarely talked about her. *Daed* never talked about her." She began putting the letters back in their envelopes.

He watched, taking in what she'd told him. Her family was complicated, and in many ways tragic. She didn't say much about her stepmother, and he wondered if there were issues with her too.

Monroe barked, making him and Charity jump. He leapt from the floor and yapped at the window.

"Shirley must be back." Charity put the letters in a larger white envelope and disappeared to the other side of the house.

Jesse rose from the sofa and went to Monroe. More time had passed than he thought, and there wasn't much daylight left to finish digging the posts. Not a problem. He'd work faster next week. He glanced out the big picture window and recognized Susan's van in the driveway. When Shirley slowly eased out of the passenger side, he said, "Stay, Monroe."

The dog followed him to the door but didn't try to slip out. Jesse met Shirley at the van. Another woman—Jesse assumed Susan—had opened one of the back doors and was pulling out Shirley's walker. "I'll get that." He took it from her, along with three hefty shopping bags.

"Susan, this is Jesse," Shirley said as he set the walker in front of her. "One of Charity's . . . friends."

Had Charity told her about their fight? About the newspaper ad?

"Hi, Jesse. Nice to meet you." She turned to Shirley. "That was great fun. We need to do it again soon."

"Agreed."

After Shirley hugged Susan, the woman went to the other side of the van and hopped in the driver's seat.

They made their way to the front door as Susan drove off. Jesse slowed his pace to match Shirley's. "What do you think of my new 'do?" She patted one side of her short hair.

"It looks nice." It didn't look all that different to him.

Shirley chuckled. "You sound like Alan. 'Nice, dear. If you like it, I like it, dear.' The man always knew the right thing to say."

Jesse was nothing like Alan.

"How's the fence building going?" she asked.

"Got some postholes dug today. I'll come back after work on Monday and finish digging the rest." No need to mention the letters.

"I don't like you overworking yourself, young man." Shirley gave him a sidelong look.

"Hard work is good for the body and soul."

"That's a wise saying."

Jesse grinned. "Straight from *mei daed*."

"Then he's a wise man. Well, as long as you don't mind working, who am I to tell you what to do?"

The porch light came on and Charity walked outside. "Did you and Susan have a nice day?" she asked, meeting them on the stoop. She reached to take the packages from Jesse. He waved her off.

"We certainly did." Shirley lifted her walker up onto the cement stoop. "You both were right, I need to get out more."

"Can I help you with the walker, Shirley?"

"No, I've got it. Just takes me longer to do things these days."

He waited as she made her way inside, wondering if she needed a short ramp to help her with the stoop. She wasn't having much trouble now, but she might in the future. He'd bring up building her one after he finished the fence.

Jesse set the bags near the couch as Shirley went straight to her chair and plopped down. "I'm beat."

Charity frowned. "You do look tired. Do you need—"

"Charity." She held up her hand. "I'm fine. This is a good kind of tired. I just need to rest a few minutes before I go to bed."

"Okay. Your hair looks pretty."

"Thank you." She touched the back edge this time. "Short and sassy, Susan calls it."

"She's right."

Shirley appeared pleased. "Did you have supper?"

Jesse glanced at Charity. He hadn't thought about food, although it was past suppertime.

"Uh, no. I wasn't hungry."

"Me either."

"Well, you two need to eat something. Don't worry about me, I'm full of egg foo yong. I think I'll do a little reading before I retire for the night." She glanced in the direction of the kitchen, then at Jesse.

He got her message quickly this time, and he wouldn't mind a bite to eat. But did Charity want him to stay? "I should get going," he said.

"I'll walk you out."

Now he knew.

She opened the door and he followed her to the porch. "*Nee, bu*," he said when Monroe tried to follow. The dog ducked back inside.

When he got to the bottom of the steps he turned to her. This wasn't the moment to bring up the list of his transgressions and beg her pardon. Not after what she'd gone through. "Will you be okay?"

"I think so." She moved closer to him. Her words contradicted the vulnerability in her eyes.

"You're sure? I can stick around if you need me to."

She smiled softly. "I'm sure."

He was a little disappointed. "Okay." He moved to leave.

"I tore up *mei* courtship plan."

He spun around. "Really?"

"*Ya.* I returned the books back to the library. I'm not looking for a husband anymore."

That was shocking. He was glad to know she wasn't going to be throwing herself at any more men in Marigold, though.

"*Danki*, Jesse," she said, surprising him further.

"For what?"

She closed the remaining space between them, stood on her

tiptoes, and pressed a light kiss against his cheek. "For caring. You're not the horrible man I thought you were." She went back inside.

His cheek tingled where her lips had touched. *She thought I was horrible?* Good thing he proved her wrong, but it didn't sit well that she ever thought that.

He walked across the field, twilight guiding his way, inclined to dismiss her poor opinion of him. Then he served himself some truth. He'd given her ample reason to think badly of him.

What would everybody else think if he confessed his prank? Would they think he was horrible too? Would his sisters-in-law think he was an awful person, even though they got their happy endings?

If they did, how could he live with everyone despising him?

His upper lip broke out in a cold sweat. Only Charity, Nelson, and Cevilla knew his secret. Was there a need to tell anyone else? Would dumping over the apple cart be worth it?

Fifteen

On Sunday morning, Charity walked outside with Monroe and looked at the backyard. Since they had church last week there was no service today, although she had the option to go visit another community and attend their church. She opted to stay home. She had managed to get some sleep, but she was still drained.

She clipped Monroe to his tie-out. Jesse had only dug six holes, and that was her fault. She'd taken up his time when he should have been working on the postholes. If it wasn't the Lord's day, she would have dug a couple of them herself. She had no idea how to use a posthole digger but she could figure it out.

She sat down on a patio chair as Monroe sniffed the grass. Shirley was so exhausted from yesterday's outing that she was still in bed, and Charity didn't have the heart to wake her. She made a batch of low-sugar apple cinnamon muffins and a pot of coffee for when she was ready to eat.

A small bird with mottled brown, white, and gray feathers bounced on the edge of the grass around the patio. She'd never seen feathers that resembled tree bark. She watched the bird peck at the grass a few times.

Whip-poor-will.

Monroe was rolling over one of the holes, and Jesse comforting her came to mind again. When she kissed him on impulse last night, there were no curled toes or slamming heartbeat. Just appreciation for helping her get through reading her mother's letters. The chemistry she'd believed was between them was solely in her imagination, and thankfully she'd given up on him and all men before she did anything else stupid.

She reread the letters before she went to bed, surprised she had a few more tears to shed, and again this morning, grateful to have a tangible piece of her mother after all this time. If only she had known about them before, and why they were hidden.

Only one way to find out.

She left Monroe on the tie-out and went inside to her bedroom. She pulled out her cell phone and laid it on her bed, staring at it for a good five minutes before she had the fortitude to pick it back up and dial her home number. There was a fifty-fifty chance her father would pick up. Wait, more like twenty-eighty that Elaine would answer. Oh well, her stepmother wouldn't want to talk to her anyway.

Ring, ring, ring.

She sat on the edge of the bed, her palms clammy. It took a while to get from the house to the phone shanty. Then she remembered it was Sunday. Were he and Elaine at church? She couldn't recall if they had service today.

"Hello?"

Her shoulders slumped with relief when she heard her father's voice. "Hi, *Daed.*"

"Hi." A pause. "Um, how are you?"

"Fine." Her pulse roared in her ears.

"*Gut.*" Another pause, this one longer. "I guess you got the letters."

"*Ya.*" Oh no, she was crying again. She sniffed. "*Danki* for sending them." She waited for him to say something. Anything. Why was he still silent? Her nose kept running and she wiped her upper lip.

"You're okay. Right?"

If she hadn't read the words herself, she wouldn't have believed she and her father were ever close. "*Ya*," she muttered, wishing she hadn't called. "I'm fine. Just wanted to let you know I got them. Bye." She moved to hit the Off button on the phone.

"Charity?"

She barely heard his voice. She brought the phone back to her ear. "*Ya?*"

"I . . . I hope they helped you."

She smiled. "They did. I think you should read them, *Daed*."

"*Nee—*"

"Please? I can bring them to you—"

"*Nee—*"

"But they're about—"

"I said *nee!*" He cleared his throat. "I'm sorry. I can't."

The toes of her shoes rested on top of each other. "Can you come for a visit then? I miss you."

No response. He hadn't hung up either. Monroe barked outside.

"I'll see what I can do."

She brought her fingertips to her mouth. That was more than she expected when she asked the impromptu question. "See you soon," she whispered.

"Bye, Charity."

"I love you—"

Click.

She stared at her phone, stunned that she risked him rejecting her, and even more shocked he hadn't outright said no. "*I'll see what I can do*" could be construed as a yes even. She would never have invited him to visit her in Birch Creek, not until she'd found a husband.

"Charity!" Shirley's voice rang out.

194

She dropped the phone on her bed and hurried to the front of the house. "What? Are you okay? What happened?"

"I'm fine but Monroe's gone." She pointed out the front window.

Charity moved to Shirley's side, then face-palmed as she saw him trotting down the driveway. He made a sharp left and disappeared into the field. "How did he get off his tie-out?"

"No idea. He's a wily fellow." Shirley shook her head. "I guess we know where he went."

"Jesse's," they both said at the same time.

"I'll get him." Charity left the house to chase after Monroe, this time not thinking about her mother or her father, but about Jesse and the kiss. Had he taken it the way she intended? She hadn't waited to see his reaction. Now she wondered if he was annoyed with her for being bold. Oh, why hadn't she kept her lips to herself?

She twiddled her fingers as she neared his house and the buggy shop. Should she apologize for kissing him? Pretend it never happened? *Focus on Monroe.* She'd get the dog and head back to Shirley's. Minimal contact—wait, no contact—was best.

But when she got to Jesse's, his buggy wasn't there, and Monroe was trotting in the direction of Micah and Priscilla's. "Monroe! Come back here!"

He ignored her and turned down the Waglers' driveway.

Phooey. It was only a little past nine and she didn't want him disturbing Priscilla and the baby. She ran to the Waglers in time to see Micah standing on his front porch, feeding Monroe a treat.

He waved her over. "I see he's up to his usual tricks."

"*Ya.*" She fought to catch her breath. "Sorry. Jesse wasn't home so he decided to come here. I hope he's not bothering you."

"He's never a bother. To me, anyway. To you and Shirley, I imagine that's a different story." He grinned, the end of his blond beard brushing against the top of his blue short-sleeved shirt. "C'mon inside. Emma Lynn just finished breakfast."

A short while later, Charity was sitting on the Waglers' couch looking down at Emma Lynn's adorable blue eyes. The last time she saw the baby was when Priscilla had just arrived home. She and Micah had called her to come over so they could thank her for helping them with the delivery. When Priscilla offered to let Charity hold her, she said no. She'd never held a baby before.

But this time both Priscilla and Micah insisted.

"What if I drop her?" She eyed the infant dubiously.

Priscilla chuckled as she gently placed Emma Lynn in Charity's arms. "You won't."

Her chest squeezed as Emma Lynn's tiny lips pursed together. In all her dreams about finding a husband, having a child barely entered her mind. The idea of having a family did, but snagging a spouse took precedence. Not pondering motherhood was another dumb decision. What did she know about being a *mamm*? *Nothing*.

She thought about her mother's letters. How she'd written the first one when Charity was younger than Emma Lynn was now.

Priscilla settled on the arm of Micah's chair and he slipped his hand around her shoulders. "You're a natural," she said.

Holding Emma Lynn didn't feel natural. She did enjoy watching her eyes open and close, then fully close as she fell asleep. "She's so dainty."

"Hard to believe she's mine." Micah's belly laugh woke his daughter, and Charity thought for a moment the baby was going to start crying. But her eyes fluttered closed again.

Monroe started pawing at the door to go out. Charity carefully stood and handed Emma Lynn back to her mother. "I guess he's ready to go back to Shirley's."

"Jesse needs to get a move on with that fence." Micah touched his beard. "Tell you what, I'll give him a hand this week. Then you don't have to worry about Monroe getting out. I just have one request."

"What's that?" Charity asked.

"That you bring him over from time to time. I'm going to miss giving him treats."

She laughed. "Done."

She attached Monroe's leash to his collar and headed back to Shirley's. As she passed Jesse's house, she wondered if he was in Birch Creek to visit his family, or if he had gone somewhere else. She shrugged, reminding herself he wasn't her concern anymore. "C'mon, Monroe," she said, starting to jog. "Time for lunch."

Jesse squirmed in his chair. After vascillating between keeping his mouth shut and copping to the bachelor advertisement, he hitched Miss Peach to his buggy and went to Zeb and Zeke's. Like Marigold, they didn't have church this morning. Now he was in Amanda's kitchen, seated across the table from Amanda and Darla, withering from their stunned glares. Egad, indeed.

"I'm so sorry," he said after explaining what he'd done.

"The whole thing was a *joke*?" Darla's gaze narrowed.

Amanda's expression mirrored her identical twin. "You were laughing at us?"

He sucked in a breath, fighting the urge to deflect, fib, and just plain flee. If he did any of those, he'd have to add cowardice to his list of appalling behaviors. "*Ya.* I'm sorry for that too. I was stupid and immature."

"That's for sure," Darla muttered.

Amanda shot her a reproving look. "What Darla means is, we're glad you recognize you need to grow up."

Ouch. That hurt, even though it was accurate.

Darla slid down in her chair. "I'm so embarrassed."

He winced. "Why?"

"I truly believed the single men in Birch Creek were looking for wives." She crossed her arms, not looking at him. "I'm the butt of a joke."

A smack upside his head would have hurt less. "I wasn't laughing at you, Darla. Or any of the women. Just *mei bruders* and friends."

"Oh, that's so much better."

Neither of his sisters-in-law were prone to sarcasm, and her comment drove home how hurt she was. He scrubbed his hands over his face. While he knew this would be hard, he hadn't anticipated how much.

Amanda reached for Darla's hand. "We found our husbands, didn't we?"

"That's not the point," she said.

"You're right, it's not." He dipped his chin. "All I can do is ask your forgiveness and promise I'll never do something that cruel again. I've learned *mei* lesson, a hundred times over."

Amanda and Darla exchanged a look.

Jesse squirmed again as he watched the sisters. With two sets of identical twins in his family, he knew those visual exchanges spoke more than words. Zeb and Zeke, and Mahlon and Mose—they all had their own language with each other. He could only imagine what Amanda and Darla were talking about right in front of him.

"Okay." Amanda smiled. "We forgive you."

"*Ya.*" Darla also grinned.

Uh-oh. He was happy they absolved him, but their sudden cheerful mood made him uneasy.

"And it's a start." Amanda leaned back in her chair. "But . . ."

"But what?"

Darla grinned. "It's your turn."

His stomach churned. "*Mei* turn for what?"

"To find a *frau*!" They dissolved into giggles.

"Oh *nee*." He held up his hands. "That's not going to happen."

"*Ya* it is," Darla said.

"For sure and certain," Amanda added, laughing again.

"What's so funny?" Zeke entered the kitchen, Zeb on his heels.

"Jesse's getting married."

He popped up from his chair. "Now wait just one minute—"

"Congratulations, little *bruder*." Zeke clapped him on the back.

"Who's the lucky—or unlucky—*maedel*?" Zeb said, grinning.

He deserved their ribbing. After all the years he'd made snide comments, played pranks on his brothers and friends, and ultimately engaged in the worst practical joke of all, he couldn't expect to get off totally free. But marriage? Out of the question. "I'm *not* getting married."

"There are plenty of available women here." Darla moved near Zeke.

"And we're more than happy to introduce you to *all* of them." Zeb stood behind Amanda.

He sagged onto his chair. "You don't have to do that."

"Oh, but we *want* to," all four of them said at the same time.

I'm doomed.

"All right," Zeb said. "Enough with the teasing. We're just joking, anyway."

"We are?" Zeke and Darla said.

"*Ya.*" He gestured to Jesse. "Look at the poor guy."

Amanda nodded. "He does look scared."

"More like terrified," Zeke said with a grin.

Darla huffed. "I still think we should—"

Zeke put his hand on her shoulder, quieting her. "Pretty sure he's had enough. If we push anymore he'll never come back to visit."

Jesse glanced down, stunned to see his slightly shaky hands. He shoved them under the table.

"Don't worry, we're not going to play matchmaker," Amanda said, her tone kind. "And we do forgive you."

"Forgive him for what?" Zeb asked.

She glanced at her husband. "I'll explain later."

He stayed for breakfast—he never could resist pancakes and sausage—and endured some more teasing. When he went back to his buggy he was more confident about confessing to Ezra and Katharine. Talking to them should be easy after what he'd just endured.

Who was he kidding? Asking for forgiveness wasn't easy at all when he was one-hundred-percent in the wrong. And he had more confessing to do next Sunday, when he would admit his sins to the entire community.

He was being humbled, and it should have happened long before now.

Sixteen

On Monday evening after the buggy shop closed, Jesse and Micah showed up to work on the fence. Charity and Shirley stood on the back patio watching the men work as Monroe, who was off his tie-out, stayed close by. Micah had brought his posthole diggers and they were finishing up the last two holes.

"I feel bad." Shirley was perched on the seat of her walker. "They worked all day and now they're working all evening. I'm sure Micah would rather be with Priscilla and the baby."

Charity agreed, even though Jesse and Micah were glad to help out and Priscilla understood. It was the Amish way. She tucked her legs underneath her dress on one of the wrought iron chairs that matched the rest of Shirley's set.

"You're quiet tonight." Shirley took a sip of the lemonade Charity made earlier. The pitcher and two empty glasses were on the table, waiting for Jesse and Micah to fill them when they were thirsty. "That usually means you're thinking about something . . . or plotting something." She winked.

"No more plotting," Charity said with a firm nod. But she was thinking. She'd hoped to hear from *Daed* today and wasn't surprised when she didn't. They'd only spoken less than twenty-four hours ago, and she was trying to be patient. But was he sincere about visiting her, or did he use that as an excuse to end their call?

Then there were *Mamm*'s letters. A part of her wanted to tell Shirley about them, but then she'd have to go into detail about her family life, a topic she didn't want to discuss. Eventually she would talk to her boss about her father and stepmother, and she'd have to if—or when—her father visited. But it was all too much right now.

"Are you having second thoughts about abandoning your courtship plan?"

Charity started to put her finger to her lips to shush Shirley, in case Jesse and Micah could hear her. But there was no need for that now. Jesse already knew she'd ripped up her plan, and at this point she didn't care if Micah found out about her folly. "Absolutely not." Jesse pulled out a plug of dirt from the hole closest to Shirley's house. "I'm done with men."

"For now." Shirley took a smug sip of her lemonade.

"For a long, long, *long* time."

Micah walked to the patio, carrying his posthole digger over his broad shoulder. Charity jumped up from her chair, poured him a glass of lemonade, and brought it to him.

He set the digger down, took the cup from her and drained it in seconds. "As long as it's not raining, we'll be back on Wednesday with the concrete and get the posts set."

"There's clear skies all week, according to the forecast." Shirley smiled as Charity sat back down. "I can't thank you enough for helping Jesse."

"Glad to do it. I need to head home now. I don't want to miss giving Emma Lynn her evening bottle."

How sweet.

As Micah left, Shirley shook her head, chuckling. "He'll have his hands full soon."

"What do you mean?"

"I've seen that twinkle in his eye before. Alan felt the same way about Wendy. She had him wrapped around her pinky finger. That man had a hard time telling her no. Fortunately I didn't."

Charity pulled her knees to her chest and thought about *Daed* again. How different would their relationship be if her mother hadn't died and he hadn't married Elaine? From the letters it seemed like she was the apple of her father's eye until then. She closed her eyes, her throat scratchy. How blessed Emma Lynn and Wendy were to have, and have had, a father who loved them so deeply.

"Wendy turned out great." Shirley slowly got up from her seat as Charity opened her eyes. "I wish she'd visit more often, but it's hard with how busy she is." She yawned. "I'm going inside to read for a little bit before bed. This romantic suspense novel I'm reading has me on the edge of my seat. Or my walker, I should say." She whistled for Monroe, who of course ignored her as he stuck his nose in the hole Jesse had finished digging. "Oh well."

"I'll bring him inside after Jesse leaves."

"Thanks." She pushed her walker toward the back door. "I think I'm a little jealous of Jesse, to be honest. I thought I was the love of Monroe's life." She shoved open the sliding door, then lifted her walker over the track and went inside.

Charity faced the yard as Jesse was heading toward her, the digger on his shoulder the same way Micah had carried his. Monroe trotted beside him.

She got up and poured him a glass of lemonade.

"*Danki*." He took a drink. "You okay?"

"Sure." She frowned a little. "Why?"

"Well, the last time I saw you, uh, you were . . . um . . ."

Touched by his concern, she nodded. "I'm okay."

"*Gut*." He finished the lemonade, and she expected him to leave like Micah had. He set the glass down, but he didn't move.

"Micah said you were coming back Wednesday."

He nodded and looked out in the yard. Monroe had sprinted to the far side and was sniffing about. After a few seconds, he faced her again.

"Can I talk to you for a minute?"

"Sure." She gestured to the chair across the table from her. "Have a seat."

He brought the chair closer to her and sat. Rubbed his palms over his pants. Stared at the yard again.

"Jesse," she said. "What did you want to talk about?"

He turned to her the same time Shirley's patio light turned on, and she saw the strain at the downturned corners of his mouth. "I, um—" He blew out a breath. "I told *mei familye* about the advertisement. I apologized and asked them to forgive me."

"Did they?"

"*Ya*." His expression relaxed. "They did. Gave me a hard time about it, as they should have."

Charity nodded. "I'm glad you talked to them."

"Me too." He tapped his toe against the flagstones beneath his feet. "Next Sunday I'm confessing to the congregation."

"*Gut*." It would be a hard thing to do. Getting up in front of people Jesse lived, worked, and worshipped with and admitting what he did took courage. "You're doing the right thing."

"I know. And there's one more thing I need to do." He turned to her. "I'm sorry, Charity. I'm sorry about the ad, about hurting your feelings last year at Diener's, about making fun of you after the singing . . ." He tapped his finger on his chin. "I'm sure there's more."

If there was, she couldn't remember either. "I forgive you. For all of it." She smiled, glad she'd been wrong about him. He wasn't a bad guy. And the more she got to know him, the more she was realizing he was a pretty good one.

He leaned back in the chair, full on grinning. "*Danki*, Charity. I gotta say, it feels *gut* to get all that off *mei* chest." He looked at her, the relief in his eyes changing to concern. "I'm glad you're okay. I know Saturday was tough for you."

"*Ya*, it was. But I got to know *mei mamm* a little bit more, so it was worth it." She tugged on the side edge of her apron. "*Daed* might come for a visit." She told Jesse about their phone call.

"That's terrific."

A squirrel streaked by them, and Monroe scampered after it. Before he could make a break for the front yard, Jesse sprang from his chair and caught him by the collar. The dog started barking. "Whoa, *bu*." He held on to him as he strained against his grip, continuing to bark.

Charity got up from the chair. The squirrel was long gone. What had him so excited now? She turned around, stunned to see Nelson Bontrager walking toward them.

"Hi, Charity," he said, then looked at his brother, his eyebrow raised. "Hi, Jesse."

⁂

Jesse patted Monroe's head as he kept his gaze on Nelson. Charity was in the house getting another glass for the lemonade as his brother settled onto a patio chair.

A sly grin spread over Nelson's face. "Didn't expect to see you here."

"Ditto." Although he was surprised to see him, he also guessed Nelson was here to apologize to Charity, per their discussion Friday night. And that was fine. Great, actually. But he didn't like his brother's current slippery expression. "I'm building a fence for Monroe." He unnecessarily pointed at the dog. "That's why I'm here. It's the *only* reason I'm here." Other than to apologize to Charity, and he'd finally done that. What a relief. Only one more hurdle to go—confession next Sunday—and he could put everything behind him.

Nelson locked his hands behind his head. "I see."

"Look at the yard." He gestured to the holes.

"So you've been digging in the dark?"

He had him there. "I finished a while ago."

"I see."

Jesse glanced at the patio door. Why was it taking Charity so long to get a glass? He'd get up to leave but he didn't want to risk Monroe following him, and he detested the idea of tying him up, even though it was unavoidable.

The sliding door opened. "Sorry. Shirley wanted some fruit cocktail." She picked up the pitcher and poured lemonade into the glass, then handed it to Nelson.

He unclasped his hands and took it. "*Danki*." The smug grin disappeared. He held the glass without taking a sip. Unusual, since Nelson loved lemonade.

Charity sat back down. Silence stretched between the three of them. A moth fluttered over her head and landed on the patio light. Monroe, who was lying over Jesse's feet, started to snore. After another long minute, she gave Jesse a questioning look. He turned to Nelson, who was still staring at the lemonade in his glass. They'd be here all night if he didn't act now.

"Nelson has something to say." He leveled his gaze at him. "*Ya?*"

After a moment's hesitation, his brother nodded. "Charity . . . I . . . uh . . ." He gulped down half the lemonade. "I owe you an apology. I lied to you last year about Jesse, uh . . . liking you. He didn't then, he doesn't now, and I shouldn't have told you he ever did." Nelson turned to him. "I'm sorry I lied to you too, Jesse. That was wrong, and I hope you can both forgive me."

"You're forgiven." Her words flew out in a rush. Jesse caught the flash of pain on her face before she dipped her head and stared at the ground.

Whoa. And Jesse thought he was bad at apologizing. Nelson's explanation didn't have to be so harsh . . . even though it was the truth. "It wasn't exactly like that," he blurted.

"What wasn't?" Nelson's eyebrow arched again as Charity's head shot up.

He froze. Even Monroe was staring at him now. "I, uh, mean, uh . . ."

His brother's smug expression returned.

He glanced at Charity. It had been exactly like that. He didn't like Charity . . . back then. And as for now . . .

"Tell you what," Nelson said, setting the lemonade on the table. "Just so you know I'm really sorry, I'd like to make it up to you."

Jesse shook his head. "You don't have to—"

"I'm talking to Charity." Nelson smirked and turned to her. "Come by for supper."

"*What?*" Jesse barked, catching Monroe's attention.

Nelson rose from the chair. "*Mamm* always makes plenty of extras on Saturday nights. I owe you a meal."

She blinked. Several times. "Uh . . . okay?"

He smiled. "Great. I'll pick you up—"

"I'll bring her." Wait. What was he doing? He could use some duct tape on his mouth right about now. But considering his normally angelic sisters-in-law weighed the option of throwing him under a bus full of single ladies as revenge, he didn't trust them. Or his brothers—especially Nelson.

"I didn't say which Saturday," Nelson pointed out.

Jesse stood. "This Saturday. We'll be over this Saturday."

"*Nee.* We're going to Phoebe's for supper that night."

"Next Saturday?" He looked at Charity. "If that's okay with you."

She nodded.

"Then it's a *date*." Nelson beamed.

He hurried to his brother. "Let's *geh*," he muttered, almost shoving him in the direction of the front yard.

"Bye, Nelson," Charity said.

"Bye, Charity." He grinned and waved at her.

When they were out of her sight, Jesse pushed him. "What was that about?"

"Be specific." Nelson snickered.

"The supper invitation?"

"Like I said, I owe her a meal."

"You owe her lunch," Jesse ground out. "Not dinner with our *familye*. And what about that crummy apology?"

Nelson looked insulted. "What was wrong with it?"

"You told her I didn't like her."

Holding out his hands, he said, "Isn't that the truth?"

"It's . . ."

Nelson moved away, shaking his head. "You got some figuring out to do, *bruder*." He turned and called out over his shoulder, "Supper's at six."

Jesse gaped as Nelson climbed into the buggy. What just happened?

"Jesse?"

He turned to see Charity behind him, Monroe trotting next to her. *Oh boy.* Had she heard their conversation?

She stopped, folding her hands in front of her. "We don't have to *geh*."

He was so discombobulated that for a second he had no idea what she was talking about. *Supper. Right. At* mei *house, er,* mei familye's. "You don't want to?"

Her teeth pressed against her bottom lip. "I wouldn't mind."

"Then we're going." He glanced back. Nelson's buggy was halfway down the driveway, the reins jingling in the distance. "I hope he didn't upset you."

"I wasn't upset." She paused. "All right. A little. It's hard to hear that someone doesn't like you." Before he could respond she said, "What should I bring?"

He scratched his arm. "Where?"

"To supper? Are you even listening?"

"*Ya.*" What he wasn't doing was comprehending. "You can bring whatever." Should he address her comment about him not liking her? But what should he say? He didn't want to give her the wrong idea.

"I'll bake a pie," she said. "I owe you, after all."

"You do?"

Her eyebrows furrowed. "Don't you remember? I said I'd bake you one if I didn't get a husband at the singing. I didn't get one, so you get a pie."

"Ah. Right." He'd forgotten about the pie.

She turned around and signaled to Monroe. "'Night, Jesse."

"'Night." As she headed to the house, he thought about calling her back, then changed his mind. Anything he said at this point would make him sound dotty. He *was* feeling a little dotty, actually.

Jesse walked back to his house, ticking off on his fingers everything that had happened in the last ten minutes. He was taking Charity to supper at his parents' because Nelson owed her lunch. And she owed him a pie because she didn't get a husband, and now she no longer was looking for one. Oh, and his brother was a lousy apologizer and made him look bad in front of Charity . . . which bothered him. A lot. *Makes sense.*

None of it made sense at all.

.ംഃ.

By Saturday, Jesse and Micah had finished Monroe's fence, perfectly straight and evenly placed slats of wood that not only kept Monroe safe, but also improved the backyard's appearance. It was freeing to be able to open the back door and let him outside without worrying about him taking off. She thought she saw tears in Shirley's eyes when her boss saw the completed project.

On Sunday morning, Charity watched Monroe bound about, sniffing the fresh wood around the perimeter of the fence and pressing his nose between some of the slats. He paused at the left back corner and hiked his leg. *Guess he likes it.*

She'd put a few new toys in the backyard, and Monroe chewed on a twisted length of rope with a ball attached at one end. She watched him play, her mind on Jesse. Again. Although almost a week had passed since Nelson's apology and invitation to the Bontragers', they hadn't talked and she still hadn't baked his pie. She and Shirley had left him and Micah alone to finish their work so they wouldn't keep Micah away from his family any longer than necessary.

She did spend part of the week wondering why he'd offered to take her to his parents' house instead of letting Nelson pick her up, only to drop the subject. It didn't matter how she got to the Bontragers'. It was the fact she was going. There was something she hadn't admitted to anyone—Jesse and Nelson weren't the only ones who had to apologize for their past behavior. She had some apologizing to do of her own, to Ezra and Katharine. She'd put that off long enough.

The patio door opened and Shirley poked her head outside. "What a delightful day. No rain in the forecast, but tomorrow everyone will need umbrellas."

Charity smiled. She could always depend on Shirley for a weather report.

"Susan will be here in a few minutes to pick me up for church." She touched the pearl earring on her left earlobe. "When are you leaving?"

"Not long after." Church was at the Kings' today, and they lived about a twenty-minute walk away.

"See you this afternoon."

She continued to watch Monroe play, giving him the maximum time outside before locking him in the house for the next several hours. She put thoughts of Jesse aside, and as she made her way to the Kings' house, she prepared her mind for worship, asking the Lord for patience with her father, who still hadn't called her. If she didn't hear from him by next week, she was going to contact him again. She wouldn't mention the letters, though. It occurred to her a few days ago that maybe he hadn't followed up because of her insistence he read them. She still thought he should, but she wouldn't push him anymore.

When she arrived at the Kings', she waved to Saloma, who was standing by herself near the large elm tree in the front yard. Pink and coral begonias circled the trunk and the earthy scent of fresh mulch filled the air. "Hi," she said walking over to her. She frowned at her distressed expression. "Is something wrong?"

Saloma glanced at the large barn. Clarence and Olin were standing near the open doors, their backs to them. "He's still not speaking to me," she murmured.

The man could hold a grudge, whatever that grudge was. "Not at all?"

"*Nee.*" She looked at Charity with sorrowful eyes. "I miss him.

I don't understand why, because he hasn't gone anywhere. I just . . . miss him."

The men began to enter the barn, signaling the start of church. She wanted to hug Saloma, but that would draw undue attention. As they started for the barn, she racked her brain. There had to be a way for her and Clarence to reconcile. Wait, what if . . . ? She snapped her fingers. "I've got it."

"Got what?" Saloma asked, sidestepping some pebbles strewn on the asphalt driveway. A few of the families in Marigold had asphalt instead of gravel.

Oops. She hadn't meant to speak out loud. "I'll tell you after church."

"All right." Her thin shoulders slumped as she walked into the barn.

Charity hoped her last-minute plan would work. Of course, she had to talk to Jesse first before implementing anything. But if he agreed to her idea, Saloma's problem would be solved.

After the service was over, she searched for him. When she saw him talking to Micah and Glen, she waved him over. He excused himself from the two men and followed her behind the barn. The pungent aroma from a manure pile a few yards away hit her nose. Not the best location to talk, but it couldn't be helped. They needed some privacy.

"Hey," he said, glancing at the pile. "Interesting choice of venue."

"I need to ask you something."

"Can you ask me somewhere else—"

"Will you *geh* out with me?"

He froze.

Double oops. Maybe she should have given him some warning before making her request.

"You want me to what?" he finally asked.

If she wasn't in such a hurry she'd chuckle. There wasn't any chemistry between them anymore, but he was still handsome, and with his bewildered expression, he was downright cute. It also wasn't lost on her that this was the second time she'd asked him out. But this was different. This was an emergency. "*Geh* out on a date."

He pushed up his hat brim with one finger. "Here we *geh* again."

"I'm not talking about a real date . . . wait. What do you mean, 'Here we *geh* again'?"

"Never mind. Okay, I'll bite. What are you talking about?"

"I think Saloma likes Clarence."

He paused. "I thought she liked me."

Oh. How did he know that? Had she told him? Things had been so chaotic lately maybe she did. This was a snafu she hadn't anticipated. "Do you like her?" If he did, Saloma would have more than one complication on her hands.

He shook his head, animating his curls. "She's a nice *maedel* and all that, but *nee.* I don't."

Whew. Awkward conversational tangent avoided. "Remember when we were supposed to *geh* out on a double date?"

"Vaguely."

"Well, we should do that. To help Saloma and Clarence."

"If she likes him, why doesn't she tell him?"

"Because he's not talking to her. And I could be wrong, but I have a feeling he likes her too. That's why he's so upset with her."

Jesse nodded. "He doesn't just like her, Charity. He's in love with her."

She clasped her hands together. "Really? How exciting." It was much more fun helping others find love than chasing after it herself.

"I don't know if I would say that." He waved off a fly. "And I don't think we should get involved."

"We're not getting involved." At his dubious look she added, "Maybe a smidge. But it's for a *gut* cause."

"I don't understand how you and I going out will help them . . . Oh, I see. Those two pair up, and you and I, uh . . ."

"Watch the sparks ignite." She smiled. "It's a foolproof plan. Much better than my previous one." Her mirth faded. The courtship plan she'd thought was so clever and infallible was the exact opposite.

"Don't be too hard on yourself."

His pinpoint accuracy threw her off a bit. "I'm not. I'm being honest. I was desperate, Jesse. If I didn't find a husband in Marigold, I didn't know what I was going to do."

He canted his head, confused wrinkles above his brow.

"But I'm over that now," she quickly insisted, before she told him more than she should. "I'm officially content in *mei* circumstances."

"Like the Bible says to be."

Yes, and she had never been happier helping Shirley and taking care of Monroe. Now she had a chance to give her friend a love life assist, and she was taking it. "I'll talk to Saloma and think of a way to get Clarence to agree to the double date."

"Leave Clarence to me." His mouth tilted up into a smile.

Her little toe started to itch. She ran the side of her foot on the grass. "Sounds *gut*. I guess the only thing left to discuss is what we'll do while we're out."

He shrugged. "Don't look at me. I have *nee* idea."

"You don't?" That was a shocker. "You had to do something when you went out with a *maedel* before." A personal question, but she was genuinely curious.

"I, ah . . . well, I've never been on a date before."

"*Never?*"

"Nope." Instead of annoyance, his eyes were slightly amused. "Don't look so surprised."

"But I am. I thought . . ." Ooh, she shouldn't say what was going through her mind right now.

"You thought what?"

Her cheeks heated. Oh well, it's just Jesse. It's not like she'd held back her thoughts with him before, often to her detriment. What was one more moment of transparency? "I find it hard to believe that a handsome, smart, mostly kind man like you wouldn't have gone out on at least one date."

"*Mostly* kind?"

"You have your moments." She couldn't help but smile. "Oh, and you also have a great sense of humor, when you're not being a jerk."

He stared at her for a moment. Then two, and possibly three more. Her smile vanished. *Phooey.* Once again, she'd said too much.

The flies were buzzing, the manure pile stunk, and she needed a quick exit. "Saloma and I are painting tomorrow evening," she said quickly. A fly whizzed near her ear and she flicked it away. "I'll talk to her then and let you know what she says."

"Okay."

More flies gathered around. "Ugh. We need to get out of here." She started to leave.

"Charity."

She stopped. "*Ya?*"

"I've never been on a date because I haven't met anyone I'd want to ask out. And I wouldn't ever *geh* out with a *maedel* unless I was serious about her."

"I understand."

His gaze met hers. "I just wanted you to know."

Integrity. She mentally added that to the list of his virtues she hadn't realized she'd been keeping until now. "I'm glad you did."

Seventeen

I'm so nervous, Charity."

She touched Saloma's arm as they waited for Clarence and Jesse to pick them up for their Saturday evening date. They couldn't have asked for better weather—she'd spent the entire week watching the forecast with Shirley, something she'd never done before—and under any other circumstance she would have enjoyed the warm breezes and cloudless sky. But she couldn't, not when Saloma was so on edge.

When she'd discussed the idea of the double date with her on Monday, she'd been surprised at her friend's eagerness. *"If you think he'll talk to me again, I'll do it."* But now it looked like she was having second thoughts. "Don't worry. You and Clarence have known each other forever, remember?"

"But this is a date." Saloma tugged at the thin, white ribbon dangling from her *kapp*. "I don't want anything go *geh* wrong. If it does, he might ignore me forever. I don't think I could handle that."

"I'll be right beside you." Charity smiled.

"Won't you be busy with Jesse?"

"We're going as friends, remember?"

Saloma glanced around Shirley's front yard. "I still don't understand why a friend would want to *geh* on a double date."

Charity paused. This wasn't a date . . . not for them, anyway. "Jesse's that kind of friend."

She turned to her. "Or maybe he likes you."

Scoffing, she said, "*Nee*. He doesn't. And I don't like him, not that way." There was no reason for her to tell Saloma that she had liked him at one time. For nearly a week, actually. She didn't anymore, and that's what counted.

"You could change your mind."

Never. Which was what she said to Shirley when her boss told her the same thing as she explained this evening's festivities right before Saloma showed up. She didn't bother to invite her friend inside, not wanting to answer her boss's inevitable questions.

"I did with Clarence."

Well, that was true. But the situations were completely different. And Saloma was ready to date and get married. Charity wasn't. *How the tables have turned.* "Oh, look, Clarence is pulling into the driveway," she said, pointing to the buggy heading down Shirley's driveway, relieved that they had finally shown up.

"Do I look okay?" Saloma smoothed her lilac dress as Clarence brought the buggy to a stop.

Charity smiled. She doubted Saloma could ever look unattractive. "Better than okay."

She pulled on her ribbon again, and Charity took her hand and placed it at her side before she accidentally yanked her *kapp* off. Clarence and Jesse walked toward them. They were dressed in the same clothing they normally wore: short-sleeved shirts—pale yellow on Clarence, light blue on Jesse—navy broadfall pants, straw hats, and of course, Clarence had his suspenders on. But for some reason the men looked extra nice, Jesse in particular. Her breath hitched a little, but she chalked it up to excitement about Saloma and Clarence getting together. Still, it took a little effort to budge her gaze from Jesse.

"Uh. Hello." Clarence stopped at the foot of the front porch, his face damp with sweat. She glanced at Saloma, who was gawking at the sky.

Charity winced. So far, not so good. "Who wants to *geh* on a picnic? I sure do! I love picnics! Doesn't everybody!" A quick glance at Jesse, who was gesturing with a swipe at his neck, told her she needed to temper her enthusiasm. And her nerves. She grabbed the huge basket she'd borrowed from Priscilla yesterday and had filled with delicious food right before Saloma arrived—another reason she had to explain to Shirley why she was leaving with all the snacks she'd spent the day making. "Everyone ready?"

Clarence nodded, and without a word he walked back to the buggy.

Saloma glanced at Charity. "This is a bad idea," she whispered.

"Don't worry, it will be fine." But when she looked at Jesse, he seemed uncertain too. Having had lots of experience putting on a positive front, she walked down the porch steps and stood by him. "I don't know about you, but I'm hungry."

Jesse nodded, catching on quick. "Me too. C'mon, Saloma. I can't wait to see what Charity made."

The women walked to the buggy, Jesse a few feet behind them. Clarence was already in the front seat holding the reins and mopping his brow with a handkerchief. It wasn't even that hot today, poor guy. Charity climbed in the back seat, and after a moment's pause, Jesse sat next to her. Saloma sat by Clarence, who chirruped to his horse and they were on their way.

After a few minutes of absolute silence, save the rhythmic *clip-clop* of the horse's hooves against the pavement, Charity began to lose a little hope. Saloma stared out the window while Clarence gazed straight ahead. Maybe this was a bad idea.

Jesse spoke low in Charity's ear. "We should have stayed out of this."

His breath was feather light. She shivered.

He frowned. "You're cold?"

She wasn't and she had no idea why she had shivered, so she ignored the question and frantically tried to figure out how to salvage the situation with Saloma and Clarence. Suddenly her courtship plan activity list came to mind. At least all her work might be worth something. "Why don't we play twenty questions?"

"I've never played that before," Saloma said.

Clarence nodded. "Me either."

"It's easy. One person thinks of something, and it has to be an animal, vegetable, or mineral. Then we take turns asking twenty yes or no questions until one of us figures out the answer."

"*Mei familye* used to play this when we were *kinner*," Jesse said.

Oh good, she had an ally. Charity looked at him. "You start then."

He paused, in deep thought. "Okay, got it—"

"Why won't you tell me what's wrong?" Saloma turned and faced Clarence. "I apologized to you a dozen times, and I don't even know what I did to make you mad."

He glanced at her. "I'm not mad. And it was twice, not a dozen."

"See, you are angry with me. You don't come over anymore, you haven't talked to Olin in over a week, and you won't even look at me." She pressed her lips together.

"Oh, so now that you're being ignored, you decide to notice me?" The buggy slowed down as he glared at her. "How does it feel to be forgotten, Saloma?"

She moved a little closer to him. "You're upset because I don't pay enough attention to you?"

"Your words, not mine."

For the next ten minutes—or hours, it seemed like to Charity—Saloma and Clarence bickered like an old married couple. The horse had slowed to turtle speed, and at this rate they wouldn't reach Overlook Park until Christmas.

Jesse pressed the heel of his hand against his forehead as Clarence and Saloma continued to argue. "What do we do now?"

She sank down in her seat. "I don't know. Fighting wasn't part of the plan."

"I have *nee* idea what I ever saw in you," Clarence snapped. "You're so full of yourself. You might be pretty on the outside, but you sure aren't on the inside."

Charity and Jesse exchanged surprised looks. Yikes. That was a low blow.

Saloma's chin quaked.

Charity slid farther down in the seat. Jesse joined her.

Suddenly Saloma jumped out of the buggy.

"Saloma!" Clarence yelled.

Charity twisted around and saw her running in the direction they came from.

Clarence huffed. "Of all the stupid things to do. Whoa!" He pulled the reins. The buggy stopped. He launched off the seat faster than a man his size should have been able to and chased after her.

Charity looked at Jesse, who was staring at the stopped horse. A light breeze passed through the open sides of the vehicle as the buggy rocked back and forth.

"Okay," Jesse said, drawing out the word. Then he turned to Charity. "Now what?"

"I guess we wait." She looked behind her. Saloma was still running and Clarence, bless him, was trying to catch up. "I'm sure they'll be back once they realize they abandoned us."

"Oh well, we can't say this wasn't exciting." He started climbing over the seat to grab the reins.

She sighed. "This wasn't the excitement I expected—"

The horse took off.

⚬⚬⚬

Jesse tumbled over the seat, his back slamming against the buggy floor. The reins flapped as the horse ran at breakneck speed, dragging the buggy not only forward but also pitching it from side to side. He fought to seize the reins while trying to upright himself.

"Jesse!" Charity screamed behind him.

But he couldn't check on her right now. He had to get the horse under control before catastrophe struck. Somehow he managed to get on his knees and find the reins. He grabbed them and pulled as hard as he could. "Whoa! Whoa!"

The horse didn't slow.

"Whoa!" Jesse's knees dug into the floorboard, his muscles burning as he struggled to slow the horse down. "Whoa!"

Finally, the horse responded and slowed to a canter, then a walk, and finally he stopped, his flanks heaving as he gasped for air. Jesse's arms went limp. He let out a long breath—

Charity!

Holding on to the reins—he didn't dare let them go—he jerked around, and his stomach lurched. Food had splattered everywhere, the picnic basket was gone, and Charity was in a lump on the floorboard. "Oh *nee*, oh *nee*." He eased the reins as much as he dared as

221

he slowly got off his knees, not wanting to scare the horse again. "Charity?" He reached over and touched her shoulder.

She didn't move.

"Everyone all right?"

Jesse turned to see a bald English man appear beside the buggy. "She's hurt," he rasped. "I can't let go of the horse. He's still skittish."

"I'll check on her."

"*Danki.*"

The man carefully leaned over and peered into the back of the buggy. "I was driving the other way and saw what happened." He removed a brownie that had landed on Charity's cheek. "She's got a bump on her head," he said.

Jesse felt the horse move again, and he tugged to get him to stop. Cold fear traveled through him. His brother Owen had a concussion two years ago and had to go to the hospital. Was Charity's bump as bad . . . or worse?

"Jesse?" Charity said weakly.

She was conscious. "Thank you, Lord," he said, turning around to look at her. The man was helping her to the seat. "Are you okay?"

"I think so. My head hurts a little."

"That was quite a ride you had," he said. "My name is Tony." He peered at her. "Are you seeing one or two of me?"

"Just one." She shifted in the seat and looked around. "Where are we?"

"A few miles from Marigold. Are you hurting anywhere other than your head?"

"No."

"Bleeding?"

She glanced down at her dress, which had scraps of food on it. "Not that I know of."

Tony took a step back. "I think you'll be okay. I'm a nurse at Geauga Hospital."

Only now did Jesse realize Tony was wearing a blue hospital uniform.

"When you get home, you need to rest." He looked at Jesse. "You too. You're not hurting or bleeding anywhere, are you?"

He shook his head, although his shoulders and biceps ached and his knees smarted. Nothing he couldn't tolerate and nothing compared to Charity. "Thanks for stopping," he said.

"Good thing I was on my way home from work." He smiled, took off his glasses, and slipped them into the pocket of his shirt. "I'll give you my number in case either of you start having headaches or throwing up. You can call me anytime. I'll be right back."

As Tony jogged to a silver pickup truck, Jesse said, "I have to check on the horse, okay?"

She closed her eyes. "Okay."

He exited the buggy and carefully approached Clarence's horse, who thankfully had settled down. "*Gut, bu,*" he said, using his Miss Peach tone. "Everything's going to be just fine." He made sure the horse hadn't injured himself, and that the buggy was okay to drive back to Marigold. When he reached the other side of the vehicle, Tony was handing Charity a slip of paper.

"Don't hesitate to call. I mean that." Then he looked at Jesse. "Keep an eye on her tonight to make sure she doesn't lose consciousness. If she does, call 9-1-1."

Charity lifted one finger. "But—"

"Will do," Jesse said.

Tony grinned. "I'm just glad you're both okay. The horse too."

As Tony went back to his car and drove off, Jesse looked Charity over. "Are you sure you're all right?"

She pulled a large piece of lettuce off her *kapp*. "*Ya*. I'm fine. What a mess."

"We need to get back to Saloma and Clarence. Can you get in the front seat?"

"*Ya*." But when she got out of the buggy he noticed a red splotch on her left shoulder and started to panic. "You're bleeding."

"What? Where?"

"Here." He gingerly touched the spot. When she didn't flinch or cry out, he inspected it closely and laughed.

Her expression turned indignant. "Why are you laughing?"

"Did you pack strawberry jelly?"

"*Nee*," she said, looking confused. "No jelly . . . oh. I made a cherry Jell-O salad."

"You're wearing some on your shoulder." He leaned against the buggy, relieved. Then he saw the bump on her forehead, almost dead center. "We need to get you back to Shirley's."

Charity nodded, but before she could climb into the front seat, he scooped her up in his arms.

⚬✖⚬

The knot on Charity's head was starting to ache, she was horrified at the food explosion in the back seat of Clarence's buggy, and she was absolutely *not* going to tell Jesse the Jell-O salad wasn't just on her shoulder, but had also slithered into her brassiere. Actually, she couldn't tell him anything. She'd lost her ability to speak when he whisked her against his chest, set her gently on the buggy seat, kept his arm around her shoulder, and spoke to her in his low, husky voice.

"Are you sure you're okay?"

She was not okay. She was so far from okay right now.

"Charity?"

"*Ya*," she managed to say.

The strain on his face eased. "Thank God." Then he looked at her forehead and grinned. "There's macaroni and cheese on top of your *kapp*."

She rolled her eyes. Of course there was. She reached up to remove it.

"I'll get it." His arm still around her shoulders, he leaned forward. A lock of his corkscrew hair brushed against her cheek.

She swallowed. Unable to stop herself, she touched it. Wound one of the curls around her finger. It was as soft as she'd imagined it to be.

And she forgot how to breathe.

Suddenly his mouth brushed against hers. Once. Then twice. The third time, he lingered, and she closed her eyes. Soft, sweet, and so very tender, she couldn't help but respond. When he pulled away, all she could do was smile. Her heart fluttered when he smiled back.

Then he blinked and pulled away from her. Gave his head a shake. "Uh, *gut*. You're okay." He hurried to the other side of the buggy and climbed in. Tapped the reins, checked for traffic, and headed back to Marigold.

She tried to gather her senses, the smell of picnic food, mown grass, and car exhaust from the vehicle that just flew by hitting her all at once. Her mouth still tingled and she touched her bottom lip.

Silence stretched between them. She didn't dare look at him. If he was disappointed, she didn't want to know.

In the distance she saw Saloma and Clarence on the side of the road, waving for them to stop. Jesse pulled over the buggy.

"My goodness, are you two okay?" Saloma rushed to Charity's side of the buggy.

"We saw him take off." Clarence peeked on the driver's side, then checked his horse. Jesse got out and joined him.

"I'm so sorry," Saloma said, tears in her eyes. "This is *mei* fault. It was stupid of me to jump out like that." She spied the bump on Charity's forehead. "Oh *nee*! You're hurt."

"I'm all right," she reassured her. At least physically. Emotionally? That was another story.

"The horse is fine," she heard Jesse say to Clarence. "No damage to the buggy. You might have some food stains to tackle, though."

"I don't care about that. I'm glad you two are all right." He shook his head. "This is *mei* fault too. I wanted to hurt Saloma." He looked at her, his eyes turning soft.

"And I understand why you did."

Charity's gaze jumped back from Clarence to Saloma, who now seemed to forget about her and Jesse, the horse and buggy, and the pungent aroma of ranch dressing coming from the back seat. The jar she packed must have broken.

Jesse started to climb into the back seat. "I'll clean up some of this mess."

"I'll help," Charity offered.

"*Nee* you won't." Saloma said. "You're going to stay put. I'll do the cleaning."

"Me too." Clarence started picking up the spilled food on one side, Saloma on the other.

"You've got mac and cheese on your *kapp*," Saloma said.

She'd completely forgotten, and apparently Jesse had forgotten to remove it. *He was a little distracted.* She inwardly smiled as she felt for the glob and tossed it on the ground.

"Jesse," Clarence said. "Do you mind driving back? Saloma and I have a few more things to talk about." He didn't wait for a response and climbed into the back seat, his bulk taking up most of the room. Saloma scooted close to him.

But as they drove to Shirley's first to drop off Charity, whatever the two of them were doing, it wasn't talking. They weren't kissing, were they? Surely not in front of them, or more technically, behind them.

Her head was starting to throb even more as she thought about Jesse's kiss. Were all kisses that amazing, or did he have special skills? A little thrill passed through her as she realized she wouldn't mind him kissing her again.

Oh no. Not good. She had just come to terms with not wanting or needing romance, and now all she could think about was Jesse's mouth. That, and playing with his hair again.

No, this wasn't good at all.

He turned into Shirley's driveway. As he and Clarence got out of the buggy, Charity jumped to the ground, the impact jostling her entire body. She winced, but didn't say anything. All she wanted to do was go inside, take some aspirin, and lie down. *And stop thinking about kissing!*

She headed for the front door, not bothering to say goodbye to anyone, and went inside.

"Good grief." Shirley took off her reading glasses as Monroe went to Charity and started sniffing, well, everything. "What happened to you?"

She glanced down. The cherry Jell-O had seeped through her undergarment and was splotched across the left side of her chest. She could only imagine the orange stain the mac and cheese left on her cap, and Monroe's muzzle was currently poking at her dress. What a day. "I'm going to bed," she said, and marched right past Shirley to her room and shut the door.

Eighteen

"From the sound of it, that was quite an adventure."

Sitting on Shirley's couch, Jesse glanced in the direction of Charity's room for the dozenth time since he'd gotten out of Clarence's buggy and followed her in the house. The ride back to Marigold had been excruciating. Saloma and Clarence were so quiet he was positive they were making out behind him and Charity. He was proven wrong when he pulled the buggy to a stop and glanced back. Saloma's eyes were opening as she lifted her head off Clarence's shoulder. She, or both of them, had fallen asleep.

Apparently he was the only one with kissing on his mind.

"I don't think you're telling me everything, however." Shirley sat back in her chair, her smile growing.

She had no idea. Holding Charity in his arms, seeing the glow in her eyes as he gazed at her, and when she touched his hair . . . he couldn't stop himself from kissing her. More than once. Actually, he lost track of how many times.

"And that grin on your face makes me suspect you're leaving out the good parts."

His face flamed.

"Ah, youth." She motioned for Monroe to come to her, but he

remained by Jesse's feet. "Bah. Anyway, you don't have to tell me everything. It's none of my business." Her jovial expression faded. "Unless you hurt her."

Had he hurt her when he kissed her? From the way she responded to him, he didn't think so. He doubted she even realized she'd squeezed his arm while they were kissing. Yeah, it was definitely mutual. He didn't need experience to know that.

But the kiss came on the heels of him telling her he wouldn't ask a girl out unless he was serious about her. And then he leapfrogged over dating to kissing Charity, who he wasn't at all serious about. He didn't even like her that way. *Who's being fickle now?*

Shirley leveled her gaze at him. "I haven't known Charity all that long, but she's become very important to me. She needs people who care about her as unconditionally as possible. I don't think she's had much of that in her life."

Jesse knew she hadn't. He glanced at the hallway again, Nelson's words coming back to him. *You have some figuring out to do.*

Or had he already?

He got up from the couch. "Can I check on her?"

She nodded. As he walked to her room she called out, "Leave the door open."

He almost laughed. Of course he'd leave the door open . . . even if he was tempted not to.

Jesse lightly knocked. When he didn't get a response, he opened the door a crack, trying not to wake her. He'd peek in, make sure she was all right, then go back home.

She was lying on the bed, her knees curled to her chest, still wearing the stained *kapp* and dress. From what he could tell she seemed okay. He started to close the door.

"Shirley?"

He hesitated. "*Nee.* It's Jesse."

"Oh." She sat up and turned on the little lamp on her nightstand. "Are you okay? Is Shirley all right?"

He smiled. Naturally her first thought would be for others. "We're both fine. Just worried about you."

"I'm fine. That little nap helped. It also cleared my head."

"You don't have a headache?"

"Oh, I do. I'm talking about here." She tapped her temple. "*Mei* brain."

Intrigued, he walked a few steps into her room, keeping the door open like he promised. "Do you need some aspirin?"

"In a minute." She got up from the bed and walked to him, her chin tilted slightly upward. "I need to know one thing."

"What's that?"

"Why did you kiss me?"

⋯⋯⋯

Charity told Jesse the truth about being clearheaded. Right before her catnap she also remembered reading something in the third relationship book she checked out from the library, the one that had been a bit on the dry side and didn't have much practical advice—except for one statement: "*Don't play games.*" They might not have a romantic relationship, but that kiss meant something, and this wasn't the time to be coy or evasive. In her opinion, anyway.

But now that the question hung between them, she wondered if she should have waited until her headache was gone and she'd put on clean clothes. From his lack of response, she began to think she'd made a mistake. "Um, you did kiss me, right?"

He nodded, his gaze remaining on hers. "*Ya.* I did."

"Do you know why?"

"Maybe?"

She expected yes or no, not indecision. She crossed her arms over her chest. "Are you teasing me again?"

Jesse closed the space between them and touched her arms. Gently he nudged them down to her sides. "*Nee*. Definitely not."

"But you don't know why you kissed me."

He exhaled. "I kissed you because . . . because . . ."

Her phone rang and she glanced at the screen. She froze. *Daed*. She picked it up and turned her back to Jesse. "Hello?"

The rumble of him clearing his throat sounded in her ear. "Hi, Charity."

"Hi, *Daed*." She sat down on the bed, her heart racing. Was he finally coming to see her?

Long pause. "How have you been?"

"*Gut*."

"That's nice."

She waited for him to say something else. When he didn't, she spoke. "Did you decide when you're coming to visit?"

Another pause, this one longer than the first. "Not yet."

"Oh." A heaviness settled in her chest. Just when her hopes had started to lift, he struck them down.

"There's a lot going on here," he added. "Very busy."

Too busy for me. But wasn't that always the case? He always had something to do other than spend time with her.

"I should *geh*."

Already? They hadn't even talked for two minutes, or really even talked. It was a wasted phone call. Almost. At least he'd thought enough about her to dial her number. For some reason, that made her feel worse.

Daed cleared his throat again. "Goodbye, Charity."

"Bye." She didn't bother to tell him she loved him. He didn't care anyway. She turned off the phone and set it on her nightstand, her shoulders falling forward until her chest was caving in. He was never coming to visit. The sooner she accepted that fact, the better her heart would be.

Then she remembered Jesse was here, and he was about to tell her why he kissed her. But she couldn't dredge up a single smidgen of excitement. She couldn't ignore him either. She turned around to face him.

He was gone.

She exhaled and hung her head. He was probably glad for the escape. She shouldn't have cornered him anyway, just like she shouldn't have pressed her dad to read the letters. If she hadn't, he would visit her. *Maybe.*

Slowly she changed out of her dirty clothes and put on her nightgown. She replaced her *kapp* with a kerchief and tried to bolster her own spirits, like she always had. But she failed. She was tired, so tired of being her own cheerleader.

Charity dragged her feet as she went to the kitchen to get a glass of water. Shirley stood by the table, a plate with a sandwich, chips, and fruit cocktail on the seat of her walker. Monroe crouched by the back wheels, his head in its usual upright and locked position when he was near food, waiting for a morsel.

Guilt rammed into her. Shirley shouldn't have had to make her own supper. That was her job. "Sorry," she said, going to her. She gestured to the plate. "I'll fix you something more substantial."

"Oh, this isn't for me. " Shirley smiled. "I was bringing this to you."

Charity's hand went to her chest. "You made me supper?"

"Such as it is. I'm out of practice, as you can see." She looked at Charity's forehead. "That bump looks painful."

"It's not too bad." She didn't know whether to feel pleased or guilty about Shirley's thoughtfulness. Actually, she was experiencing both.

"Do you want to eat in your room or at the table?" Shirley asked.

"What about your supper?"

"I had a snack before you came home. Susan and I went out to lunch and I overindulged on chips and salsa. They are my weakness." She picked up the plate.

"I'll get it." She reached for the food.

Shirley shook her head. "Let me do this for you, Charity. You do so much for me."

She was about to mention that taking care of her was her job, but Shirley's expression brooked no argument. She nodded and sat at the table, Monroe nestling at her feet. Shirley set the plate in front of her, then poured her a glass of milk and brought it to her. "Mind if I join you?"

"Not at all." She silently gave thanks for the food, then picked up a sour cream and onion potato chip. She nibbled, her thoughts on her father again. Why did he call her if he had nothing to say? She tried to switch her thoughts to Jesse and their kiss, but it was futile. She couldn't even enjoy her first kiss, regardless of the motive behind it.

"Charity," Shirley said gently. "What's wrong?"

She didn't respond, keeping the pain over her father's neglect deep inside. *Never let them see you cry.*

Shirley's hand covered hers.

Tears slipped down Charity's cheeks. She couldn't hold them back—or her need to talk to someone, especially when that person was as kind and understanding as Shirley. "*Daed* called while I was talking to Jesse." She grabbed a napkin from the middle of the table and wiped her cheeks. "I asked him to visit, but I don't think he will. He says he's too busy."

Shirley nodded. "I know that excuse all too well."

"He doesn't want to see me," she whispered, staring at the half-eaten chip on the edge of her plate. "Or spend time with me. He never has." Through her pain, she knew that wasn't exactly true. When she was little he did. But that had changed after *Mamm* died, and she had no idea how to make him want to be with her. *Or to love me.*

"Oh, honey." Shirley squeezed her hand. "Family can be complicated."

"Mine sure is." She drew in a breath and sat up. "I'm sorry."

"For what?"

"Crying in front of you. Throwing a pity party." She tried to smile. It didn't work.

"For goodness' sake, why would you apologize?"

Charity slipped her hand away. "You're *mei* boss. You hired me to take care of you, and now you're comforting me."

"If you haven't figured it out by now," she said, "you're more than my assistant."

Charity hung her head, closing her eyes against more tears. "Thank you."

Shirley reached over for a chip. "Just one, if you don't mind."

Charity smiled. "Help yourself." Surprisingly she felt much better, and not only because she'd admitted her father didn't want to see her. It was Shirley's response that helped her. Elaine would have told her to stop crying, that other people's lives were worse than hers, and to stop feeling sorry for herself. Her boss didn't try to solve the problem or berate her feelings. She simply listened and commiserated.

Suddenly she was hungry and she took a big bite out of the sandwich. "PB&J," she said, her mouth sticky from the peanut butter.

"Nothing goes better with milk." She snuck another chip off the plate.

Nodding, Charity took a gulp of her drink and set down the glass. "Did Jesse tell you what happened today?"

"Yes. And like I told him, it sounded like an adventure."

"Oh, it was." She crunched a chip and told her everything that happened, including the kiss. Shirley now knew her deepest pain. There was no reason to keep anything else from her.

Her brow shot up. "You kissed?" She chuckled. "He sure did leave out the good part."

Charity didn't know what that meant, but she continued. "When we were talking in my bedroom, I asked him if he knew why he kissed me." At Shirley's second shocked look she said, "Was that a mistake?"

"It was certainly bold. I can't say if it was a mistake, though. What did he say?"

"He said 'maybe.'" Her shoulders hunched a little. "How can he not know for sure why he kissed me?"

"Do you know why you kissed him?"

She knew exactly why. She kissed him back because he made her feel good. Safe. *Wanted*. And that was just skimming the surface. "*Ya*," she said softly. "I do."

Shirley nodded. "Could you tell him if he asked?"

Her face heated. That seemed like a lot of intimate information, and even though they'd shared an intimate moment, she wasn't sure she could be that forward. "Maybe."

Shirley pointed a chip at her. When had she abducted that one? "There's your answer. You keep blindsiding that boy. Give him some time to breathe before you do it again."

She pushed around a cherry half in the fruit cocktail. Her boss was right. From asking him at Diener's who his type was, to asking him for a date, then to go on a double date . . . all that would keep anyone off-kilter. "Thanks, Shirley. That's good advice. I'll follow it this time." She paused. "Do you think he kissed me because he likes me?"

"Only he can answer that."

Charity ended up fixing a PB&J and a glass of milk for Shirley, and after they finished the meal, they were both tired. She let Monroe out, and when he came inside he headed straight for Shirley's bedroom. As she made her nightly round of the house—locking doors, a last-minute fluff of the recliner pillows, and turning off lights—she spied a piece of paper on the floor in front of the door, folded in thirds. Huh. How long had that been there? She picked it up and unfolded it, noticing it was a sheet torn off a slim notepad, the words Wagler's Buggy Shop printed on top with handwritten scrawl underneath.

I'll pick you up at four thirty Saturday.

Jesse

Huh, again. Why was he picking her up—oh! Supper at the Bontragers'. She'd forgotten about that. She was relieved he still wanted to go. Now that Shirley had pointed out her bad habit of knocking him off-kilter, she wouldn't blame him if he'd changed his mind. She read the note again.

Does he like me? Up until the kiss, he'd given every indication that he didn't.

Do I like him? That was an even harder question. Considering her track record when it came to romance, she didn't trust her feelings or decisions. All she knew was that she liked the kiss. *Very much.*

She folded the note, barely aware she was tapping it against her mouth. Whether she liked him romantically or not, she needed to turn over another leaf when it came to Jesse. No more impulsive questions or requests. She would be quiet. Demure. Keeping a rein on her mouth would be beneficial to them both, and not just her words.

Ah . . . that kiss. She smiled. She'd sleep well tonight.

·⤳⦚⤴·

Shirley couldn't stop chuckling as she readied for bed. Young love. So exciting, confusing, and at times, ridiculous. When Charity had come home covered in food, she was curious, but not all that surprised that something outrageous had happened to her. That seemed to be the norm for her assistant. When Jesse told her about the buggy accident, her curiosity transformed to concern. She could tell he was concerned too, more than a casual friend would be. Now that she knew he'd kissed her, she prayed he would straighten out his feelings and intentions, because she meant what she'd said—he better not hurt Charity. The poor girl had been hurt enough.

She put on her nightgown and sat down on the bed. Monroe trotted into the room and curled up on his large, dark-brown dog bed in the corner and sighed. She picked up her hand cream on her nightstand, and saw notifications on her cell phone screen. She'd left the phone in her room while she and Charity were having dinner. Her daughter had called three times.

Panicked, Shirley grabbed the phone and called her back. Wendy was a night owl and she would definitely still be up at nine thirty.

After one ring she answered. "Mom," she said, sounding worried. "Where have you been? Are you okay?"

"I'm fine. Is everything all right?"

"Why didn't you have your cell? You're supposed to keep it with you at all times."

Shirley flinched at her harsh tone. "It was by my bedside. Charity and I were having supper in the kitchen. I forgot to take it with me."

"She should have made sure you had it." Wendy huffed. "That's what I pay her for."

"Why are you so upset?"

"I'm not upset."

She counted to ten. Clearly her daughter was agitated, and she could be extreme at times when she was under stress. That had to be the reason she was being so contentious. A switch of topic was required. "How are things at work?"

"I didn't call to talk about work," she snapped. "Your neurologist contacted me today. You missed your six-month appointment."

Oh. And, oops. She'd forgotten she canceled the appointment a month ago. She also forgot to reschedule. "I'll call his office in the morning."

"I hired Charity to help you with these things."

"*You* hired Charity?"

Wendy paused. "I sign her check."

Shirley gripped the phone. "Charity didn't know I canceled the appointment. This isn't her fault."

"Mom, I know you like her, and that you like living in Marigold. But if I can't trust you to keep your doctor appointments, then you can't live independently."

Her words rankled. "I can live any way I want."

"You need to move in with me," she said. "That way I can make sure you're okay."

"You would see I'm just fine here if you visited every once in a while." She hadn't meant to say the words out loud, but the thought had been in her head since her talk with Charity. Her father wasn't the only one who used busyness as a pretext.

Silence.

She pinched the bridge of her nose. "Wendy, I'm sorry. I didn't mean to snap at you."

More silence. *Click.*

Shirley clamped her arthritic fingers over the phone. *How dare she hang up on me?*

She counted to ten again. Then twenty. By the time she hit thirty-five she was able to put the phone back on her nightstand. As irritated as she was with Wendy right now, she had given her daughter a reason to worry. Her neurological appointment was important, and she couldn't remember why she'd canceled it in the first place. She'd have to be more diligent in the future. The occupational therapist she worked with after her stroke told her to write things down and keep a calendar to help her remember details. Shirley had balked at that. She'd never used a calendar in her life and it hadn't been a problem. Until now.

She also promised Wendy she'd keep her cell phone with her. She'd forgotten that too. Then again, she was in her seventies and had experienced a mild stroke. A few memory lapses were normal.

Monroe snorted in his sleep. Shirley turned and looked at him. She couldn't move back to the city. Wendy's upscale apartment building in Manhattan wasn't suitable for him. He needed room to run and play. And there were times when she let him on Alan's recliner. Wendy wouldn't stand for a dog on her furniture.

Oh how she loved her daughter, whether she was kind and loving—and she often was—or snippy and demanding, like she'd been during the call. She missed her too. But more than ever, she believed Marigold was home. She didn't want to go back to the bustle of the city, and she certainly didn't want to live in a facility. The time might come for that, but not right now. And Charity had become the perfect companion—next to Monroe, of course.

A somber thought occurred to her. As much as she was coming to love Charity as a daughter, her employment would end eventually. Maybe sooner than anticipated if she and Jesse ended up together.

But she didn't need to borrow trouble. She'd let Wendy cool off and call her back in the morning. As far as her future in Marigold . . . well, she would trust God on that one. She'd trusted him with her life since she was ten years old, and she wasn't going to stop now.

Nineteen

Yep. She's mad at me.

Jesse glanced at Charity seated next to him in the buggy. As promised, he picked her up at four thirty after spending an entire week thinking about what he was going to say to her when he did. Her question was still on his mind. Why had he kissed her? He was so flummoxed when she asked him, he couldn't think straight. Fortunately her father had called, and he left to give them some privacy. He'd been wondering how that phone call went too.

He spent all day Saturday steeling himself for her to pick up where they left off Saturday night, trying to come up with an answer to her inevitable question about kissing her. At 4:27 p.m. when he turned into Shirley's driveway, he still didn't have an explanation. But all Charity had said was hi and climbed into the buggy. For nearly an hour she sat primly in the seat, holding a pie covered with foil, remaining silent. He couldn't believe she still remembered the pie. He'd forgotten all about it—again.

A few sprinkles splattered against the buggy. "Didn't know it was going to rain," he said, hoping to stir some conversation.

"*Ya.* Seventy-five percent chance."

"I have an umbrella in the back."

She nodded, still looking ahead.

After a few minutes, he couldn't stand her silence anymore. He pulled Miss Peach to the side of the road and halted the buggy.

Her head whipped around. "What's wrong?"

"Are you mad at me?"

She looked shocked. "Why would I be mad at you?"

Rain softly fell around them. He scooted closer to her so he wouldn't get wet. And even though she'd given him a gift by not bringing up his kissing her, for some bizarre reason he couldn't let it go. "The kiss?"

"You think I'm mad about the kiss?"

"You're not speaking to me. What else am I supposed to think?"

She glanced at the pie. "I'm not mad at you."

"Then why aren't you talking?"

Her chin lifted but she kept her eyes downward. "I'm trying to be *diffident*."

He'd never heard that English word before, and he was about to ask her what she was talking about . . . but he could only gaze at her, riveted. He'd never noticed how small her ears were—they were covered in freckles, of course—or the slender curve of her neck. She smelled nice too, like a mix of vanilla and peaches.

He reclined back from her. He didn't need to be thinking about how sweet she smelled or how cute her ears were. She was acting unnatural for some reason, and she didn't have to. "Charity."

She turned to him, her blue eyes guileless. "*Ya?*"

"Remember what I said you needed to do to get a husband?"

She rolled her eyes and glanced up at the buggy roof. "Why are you bringing that up?"

"Because I want to make a point."

"Fine." She stared at the buggy ceiling. "You told me not to be desperate."

"*Nee.* I never said that."

Her gaze met his. "That I don't need a plan?"

"Not that either." Somehow during this short conversation he'd leaned closer to her again. He had missed her this week. It was the longest he'd gone without seeing her since moving to Marigold. "I told you to be yourself."

"Oh, that's right. Now I remember." She blinked, her light-amber eyelashes fluttering. "Why are you bringing this up?"

"Because you don't have to be diffident, whatever that means."

"It means reserved, and I should be." She angled her body toward him, shifting the pie in her lap. "I've been informed that I blindside you too much."

He couldn't argue with that. She was sort of doing it right now. He also suspected that said informant was Shirley. But he couldn't imagine the woman would want Charity to change her personality. She was enchanting just the way she was.

Wait . . . enchanting? Did he actually think that, even though the word was so girly if his brothers ever found out he'd mentally used it in a sentence they'd never let him live it down? Ya . . . *and she was so much more.*

"So I decided to be quiet," she continued on, not knowing she was upending his world at the moment. "Diffident, which can also mean—"

"I kissed you because I like you," he blurted.

She stilled, her mouth still open. But no sound was coming out.

He was gobsmacked by his declaration too, and how easily the words had come to him. All that time he'd spent ruminating over his feelings, trying to comprehend where he stood with her, was a complete waste. All he had to do was admit the truth, to her and himself, and the confusion cleared. He smiled. "I like you, Charity Raber. The real you. The one who's full of surprises. The one who keeps me on *mei* toes."

She stared at the pie. At least her mouth was closed now.

He waited for her to say something. When she didn't, the tendons in his neck tightened. Now he knew what she felt like when she knocked him off center, and the feeling wasn't good. Especially when he'd revealed what was on his heart.

"Jesse?"

He almost fell against her with relief that she was talking again. "*Ya*?" he said, his heart hammering in his chest.

"Do you feel sorry for me?"

◦◦◦

Charity rubbed her thumb against the aluminum foil covering the peach pie she made this morning. So much for being diffident and not blindsiding him. She'd vowed to turn over a new leaf today, and had even looked up the definition of *demure* to make sure she understood it correctly. Then she saw Shirley's crossword puzzle thesaurus and found the word *diffident*. She liked that term better.

She was also quiet for a different reason, one she didn't plan to share with Jesse. She was sure Katharine and Ezra would be at supper tonight, and she had practiced her apologies to them all week, up to the moment Jesse had pulled over Miss Peach. Now they were gone from her thoughts as she tried to detect what he was up to.

He looked completely confused at her question. She was a little confused herself. He was so close to her—handsome, kind, and smelling amazing, like he'd just stepped out of the shower. She was so full of chemistry she thought she would explode.

He said he liked her. Jesse Bontrager liked her. She was his type after all.

Or was she? Was he telling her the truth, or did he have another motive? How could she be sure she wasn't falling for another trick?

"Charity, why in the world would I feel sorry for you?" he asked.

Did she have to spell it out for him? Apparently so. "You know about *mei mamm*. How messed up *mei familye* is." He knew more than Shirley, actually. Or anyone else. And more than anything she wanted to believe he liked her because of who she was. She wasn't sure why, though, since she was a skinny, weird, pitiable woman with too many freckles and a penchant for blabbing what was on her mind. "Are you just being nice to me? Do you feel guilty about the ad?" Her throat closed. Where were these questions coming from? "Is all this a *joke* to you?"

"You're going to cut yourself." He took her hand, and the pad of her thumb was red from rubbing the foil. He put his other hand over hers as Miss Peach shook her head, jostling the buggy. "I don't feel sorry for you, I don't feel guilty, and I promise, this isn't a joke."

She searched his eyes for any sign of deception. All she saw was unabashed sincerity.

"I haven't given you much reason to trust me," he said. "I'd like a chance to correct that. I want to take you on a date. A real one—just you and me."

"A date." She let that sink in. Jesse was asking her on a date. An actual, bona fide, one-hundred-percent authentic date. All ten of her toes wiggled.

"*Nee* pressure, though. I know Shirley is your priority."

"*Ya*. Shirley." A date. He wanted to date her.

He let go of her hand and picked up the reins. "Give it some thought, *ya*?"

She nodded, unable to speak. Jesse didn't say anything either, but when she glanced at him, she saw a hint of a smile, his shoulders relaxed as he guided the horse down the road.

Now that she had finally been asked out on her first date, she didn't know how to respond. She was still grasping the fact he'd said he liked her, and she believed he meant it. A miracle in itself, considering their history.

"*If* we did *geh* out on a date," she said, fiddling with the foil again, "what would we do? Neither of us has been on one before."

"I'm sure we'll figure out something."

She was surprised at his nonchalance. Didn't he know how important a first date was? But when she glanced at him, he was grinning. Which made her smile. Ah, chemistry.

When they arrived at the Bontragers', the gentle rainfall had transformed into a downpour. She clutched the pie as Jesse grabbed the umbrella, and as soon as they scrambled out of the buggy he popped it open and held it over them both. They hurried to the expansive front porch that wrapped around the front of the huge house. "Get ready," he said, shaking the rain droplets off the umbrella before leaning it against the white siding.

"For what?"

He smiled again and opened the door. "*Mei familye.*"

Immediately she was greeted by a passel of Bontragers, and from that point on there was no time to ponder that Jesse Bontrager, Birch Creek's most stubborn bachelor, wanted a date with her.

Everyone welcomed her, from Jesse's father to his youngest brother, Elam. Only two held back—Katharine and Ezra. They were standing close to each other near the woodstove on the other side of the living room. Her stomach twisted as she walked over to them. "Hi," she said, still gripping the pie. In the bustle of the introductions she hadn't had a chance to take the dessert to the kitchen.

"Hi, Charity," Ezra said. His tone was polite, but much less welcoming than the rest of his family.

Katharine's arms crossed over her waist. She'd slimmed down

some more since Charity had left Birch Creek last year—though she was still plump—and her acne scars weren't as prominent. "Hello."

"Can I talk to you for a minute?" she asked.

Katharine glanced at Ezra, who nodded. "Sure," she said, dropping her arms to her sides.

After Ezra left—Charity didn't miss the way he squeezed Katharine's fingers before he stepped away—she gathered her thoughts. There was an air of ease and openness to Katharine that hadn't been there when Charity knew her. Shame hit as she remembered calling her ugly and fat, for the sole reason she was upset about Ezra ignoring her and frustrated she couldn't get his, or any other man's, attention. "I'm so sorry for being so horrible to you," she said. There was no reason to dance around the truth. "I wasn't a *gut* person back then, and I'm trying to do better now. I hope you can forgive me someday."

A smile appeared on her round face. "I already have. A long time ago. And I can already tell you've changed for the better."

"How?"

She held up her hands. "You wouldn't apologize to me if you hadn't."

That was true. If she had stayed in Birch Creek, she would have ignored Katharine and pretended she hadn't hurt her feelings. She would have been more concerned about saving face than doing the right thing. "You've changed too," she said.

"*Ya.*" Katharine glanced at her emerald-green dress, the pleats resting against her full hips. "I've lost some more weight."

"I didn't mean that. You seem . . ." She didn't know how to put it in words.

"Happier?"

"*Ya,* that's it."

Her smile widened. "I'm definitely happy."

"Because of Ezra?"

"He's part of the reason," she said. "But I had to let God change me first, to shape me into the person he wants me to be so I can deal with my past. I'm a work in progress, that's for sure. But I'm finally at peace."

Charity nodded. Was God changing her too? She believed so. She hadn't been able to change herself, no matter how hard she'd tried.

"So . . ." Katharine's smile turned sly. "You and Jesse?"

"Um . . ." *Was* there a her and Jesse? They still had a lot to discuss and puzzle out before she could tell. How should she answer Katharine then? *With the truth.* "Nelson invited me for supper, and Jesse gave me a ride."

Confused, Katharine said, "So you and Nelson?"

Oh boy. "Nee. He owes me lunch."

She tilted her head. "Huh?"

"I should take this pie to the kitchen." If Charity took the time to explain the situation to Katharine they'd end up missing supper. "Do you think Miriam needs help?"

"Miriam never turns down help. I'll *geh* with you."

As soon as they entered the room, they were each given a job assisting Jesse's mother and the other women in the family as they prepared supper. The spacious kitchen allowed enough room for everyone to work without being on top of one another. Amanda, Zeb's wife, handed her a peeler and a bag of carrots.

As she sat at the massive table and worked on the carrots, the other women cooked, talked, and laughed. Phoebe, the oldest child and only Bontrager daughter. Identical twins Amanda and Darla, who were married to twins Zeb and Zeke. Margaret, Owen's spouse, and Katharine, who would be marrying Ezra in the fall. They were only missing Nettie and Devon, Jesse's eldest brother and his wife, who she learned from the conversation lived in Fredericktown, the Bontragers' hometown.

And then there's me. Other than Jesse, she didn't know the Bontragers very well. But after spending only a short time with them, she realized they were the family she always wanted. Not necessarily the size, but the closeness. It made her wish more than ever that things were different between her and her *daed*. She was close to losing hope they ever would be.

·⊲✧⊳·

"Well, everyone, a miracle has happened."

Jesse shot a look at Ezra, who was sitting on a hay bale in the barn. Zeke and Zeb were there, along with Owen, Nelson, and their nephew Malachi. Even without the youngest Bontragers' help they made quick work of the evening chores.

"It sure has." Owen grinned.

"Never thought it would, to be honest," Zeb said.

"Yep." Zeke nodded. Nelson chuckled. Malachi smirked. Perry, the quietest brother, nodded.

"All right," Jesse said. "What are you talking about?"

"You found someone who will actually put up with you!" Ezra laughed.

He held up his hands. "*Nee.* I just brought her over. Nelson's the one who invited her." He wanted to smack himself for sounding so defensive, even though his words were technically true. But there was more to them. What had he been thinking, telling Charity he liked her, and then asking her out on a date? He hadn't been thinking, that's what. He'd been feeling, and his feelings hadn't changed. He still wanted to go out with her. Actually, he couldn't wait to. But until she gave him an answer—and he prayed she'd say yes—he couldn't confirm Ezra's words.

"You sure did jump at the chance to bring her." Nelson shut the door to Pickles' stall.

"We live next door. It made sense." His neck ached. He didn't like pretending she didn't affect him. And he didn't appreciate the teasing.

"Suuuuure," Nelson said, chortling. His brothers joined in the laughter. "That's the real reason."

Jesse stalked over to him. "Enough."

"But—"

"I said"—he glared at his brother, driving his point home— "enough."

The rest of the men standing around grew silent. Jesse's eyes didn't leave Nelson's.

"I'm ready for dessert," Zeb piped up, motioning for everyone to leave. Zeke bolted without comment, Perry right on his heels.

Owen nodded, heading to the barn door. "That peach pie Charity brought looked *gut*."

"So did Phoebe's caramel corn," Ezra added as he scuttled behind Malachi.

Minutes later, only Jesse and Nelson remained.

"So when's the wedding?" Nelson asked, but his jibe lacked any punch.

Jesse's jaw hardened. "Charity isn't going to be the butt of your jokes anymore. Got it?"

"Hey, I was teasing you, not her." He held up his hands, partly in surrender and partly to ward off Jesse's anger. "But I'll stop. Promise." He paused, scrutinizing him.

"What?"

"I think you're finally growing up, little *bruder*."

No one was more surprised than him.

The rain had stopped during supper, and he and Nelson walked out of the barn into the damp night air. Neither man spoke. He wasn't in the mood to talk anyway. Nelson led the way, opening the sliding back door to the kitchen, and stepped inside, Jesse behind him.

Charity was at the large kitchen table, placing slices of spice cake on dessert plates, taking extra care to make sure each slice was even with the others. She brushed a few crumbs off the edge of one of the plates. A bowl of his sister's caramel popcorn was by the cake, and the peach pie was still covered in foil on a nearby counter.

She lifted her gaze. Tilted her head. And smiled at him.

His toes curled in his boots.

"I saved you one." She pointed to a piece a smidge bigger than the others. "Or would you rather have pie? I made it for you anyway."

The pie she promised to bake because her plan had failed. She hadn't snagged any of the men at the singing weeks ago . . . until now.

"Pie, for sure." How could he refuse? She'd baked it just for him.

She took the foil off the pie and cut him a large slice. Chunks of peaches and sweet cinnamon-flavored filling spilled out from underneath a perfectly brown crust. He couldn't wait to dive in.

"I'll join everyone in a few minutes," she said, handing him the dessert. "I want to finish up here."

He preferred to stay in the kitchen, even though she didn't need any help. All he wanted was to be near her.

Instead he went to the living room and sat on one of the many folding chairs his mother brought out when company came over. It was odd to think he was a visitor in the house he grew up in. Perry, Nelson, and the younger brothers were playing a game of dominoes on the coffee table, while the older ones sat with their wives and visited. Ezra and Katharine, who were already acting like a married couple, were seated close on one of the two sofas, whispering to each other. His parents were together on the other one, and Jesse doubted anyone but him noticed their hands were clasped together.

Charity entered the room and sat in the empty chair next to him. "*Yer familye* is amazing," she whispered.

"*Ya*. They are." Despite the fights, the hard times, and yes, the teasing he was mostly guilty of, he loved every single one of them. But he was already settled in the Marigold community, and less connected to Birch Creek. And that was okay.

He glanced at Charity. Saw her smile. And because he had this intense need to touch her, he linked his pinky finger with hers, not caring if anyone saw them.

Out of all the feelings he was experiencing tonight, what he felt for Charity right now outshone them all.

.◦◦◦◦.

Jesse was quiet on the way back to Marigold, but Charity didn't mind. She was still relaxed from spending time with the Bontragers, despite how boisterous they were. Everyone talking at once, laughing with one another, and at the end of the night no one was shy with their hugs. They welcomed her into the fold, and she hadn't felt the need to be anything but herself. Best of all, Katharine had forgiven her.

No, that wasn't the best thing that happened tonight, although it was a huge deal. That had been Jesse. She'd been shocked—and delighted—when she felt his little finger curve around hers. What a cute gesture, and not something she would have expected from him, especially in front of his family. But everyone was so busy she was sure they didn't notice. The big surprise was that he didn't seem to care if they did.

She glanced at him, unable to see his profile now that night had fallen. Battery-operated lights were in key places on his buggy to alert drivers, but the inside was dark. The rain had stopped more than two hours ago, and an orchestra of bullfrogs and cicadas serenaded them on their way to Shirley's. The empty pie dish sat on the seat between them. Again, she thought about him asking her out, and appreciated his willingness to wait for her answer.

But what if she didn't want to wait?

He pulled into Shirley's driveway, bringing Miss Peach and the buggy to a stop. Shirley had turned on the outside lights, and they shined faintly into the buggy. She tapped her fingers on the tops of her knees.

"Charity?"

"Jesse?" she said at the same time. They both laughed, and she enjoyed the sound of his husky chuckle.

He turned to her. "I guess this is good night then."

None of the books or talks with Shirley or even her own day-dreams about dating and romance had any influence on what she did next. All she could do was rely on her heart. She put the pie plate on her lap and moved closer to him. "Jesse?"

"*Y*—" He cleared his throat. "*Ya*?"

"Is it okay if we call tonight a date?"

He didn't say anything right away, and she thought she heard him breathing. Or she was hearing her own, her heartbeat was pounding so fast.

"*Ya*, Charity." His voice was huskier than she'd ever heard it. "I'd like that."

She smiled, her heart singing. "Guess what?"

He chuckled. "When it comes to you, I have no idea."

Leaning over, she kissed his cheek. "I can't wait for the next one."

Twenty

ONE MONTH LATER

T here." Charity fluffed a plain tan-colored pillow on Jesse's new love seat. "That's the last one." She plopped down on the couch and spread out her arms. "Your house is finally furnished!"

"Thanks to you." He sat down next to her. "I'd probably still be sitting in the kitchen all the time if you didn't take the initiative."

"Shirley helped a lot too. She enjoyed going furniture shopping with me." She gave him a sly grin. "It's easy when you're spending someone else's money."

He laughed, and she rested her head on his shoulder and sighed. Monroe walked twice in a circle on the braided rug in the center of the room and lay down.

The last month had been busy but satisfying, both personally and professionally. He'd learned so much from Micah that they were both confident they could start taking orders for buggy brakes next week, and he was in the process of building an entire buggy on his own without his boss's supervision. Charity kept busy assisting Shirley, and the two of them decided to learn how to knit. He remembered how Cevilla Thompson always had yarn and a hook thing with her.

Crochet, he thought she called it. They were hoping to make hats and scarves to donate to those in need.

"You've gone quiet," he said, picking up her hand and running his thumb over the freckles on the back. He tried counting them one time but gave up. "Or is it diffident?" He winked.

She lifted her head, frowning slightly. "Neither. I think Shirley's keeping something from me."

"That doesn't sound like her."

"I know." She let go of his hand and sat up, facing him. "She's been talking to Wendy a lot lately. She was upset after their last phone call, but when I asked her if anything was wrong, she said no. That wasn't the truth. I heard her tell Wendy she didn't want to move." She worried her bottom lip. "I think she wants Shirley to go back to New York."

"Oh." He could see why she was concerned. "Do you think she will?"

"I don't know. Maybe she thinks I'm not doing a *gut* enough job."

"I'm sure that's not it." He couldn't imagine anyone more devoted to Shirley than Charity.

She hopped up and started to pace. "If she moves in with Wendy, I'll have to find another job." She halted, anguish on her face. "I'll never see Monroe again!"

Jesse went to her and gathered her in his arms, partly to comfort her and partly because he enjoyed holding her. If he had his way, he'd hug her all the time. "Don't jump to any conclusions," he said, running his palm over her back.

"But what if she leaves?" She looked up at him. "I'll have to leave too."

"Leave Marigold?"

"Possibly."

He didn't want to think about that. He guided her over to the couch, still holding her hand. "Don't worry about it, Charity. Enos

255

was talking about that on Sunday, remember? Cast all your care on the Lord."

"You're right. It's hard sometimes, though."

He kissed her.

"What was that for?" she said, touching his hair. She wound a curl around her finger.

Oh, how he liked when she did that. "A distraction." Then he moved away from her, stifling a sigh. "Better not get too distracted," he mumbled.

"I need to get back to Shirley's. We're going to learn the seed stitch tonight."

"The what?"

She kissed his cheek. "Knitting stuff. See you later."

He watched her go, then went back inside and sat on his new couch. Although the house was filled with furniture, without her it seemed empty. He marveled at how much had changed since he and Charity had decided to "spend time together" as they liked to put it. Even more incredible was how much *he'd* changed.

It wasn't that long ago he was steadfast about staying single. Now he didn't want to be alone. Correction—he didn't want to be without Charity.

But if Shirley moved to New York, he might be.

Taking his own advice, he halted his thoughts. No need to worry about her leaving when there wasn't a reason to. But it wouldn't hurt to think a little more about his future—his and Charity's.

.ﻮﺤﻠ.

A week after she finished decorating Jesse's house, Charity spent the afternoon at Saloma's painting note cards. She was still unsure about her painting skills, but Saloma had picked a design that was basically several layers of color in the center of each card. They were pretty, simple, and very much Saloma.

"Can I ask you a question?" Saloma asked.

Charity laughed. Her friend always preprepped her questions, even if she was asking her to pass the ketchup. "Of course."

"Will you be an attendant at *mei* wedding?"

She whirled around, splattering paint on the card she was working on. She didn't care. "You and Clarence are getting married?"

Saloma beamed. "*Ya.*"

"When did he propose?"

"The day after our fight."

Charity gasped. "Really? You've been engaged that long?"

"*Ya.*"

"Congratulations!" She set down the brush and hugged her.

"*Danki.*" Saloma smiled, her eyes misty. "I still can't believe I didn't see what was right in front of me all this time. He said he's loved me for years, and I had *nee* idea. Once I realized I could lose him, my heart opened up. I'm thankful he's so understanding. I wasn't very nice to him for a long time."

"And now you love him."

She sighed. "More than anything."

They went back to working on the cards.

"Can I ask you a question?" Saloma said again.

Charity nodded, carefully adding a few more splatters of the pink paint she'd accidentally sploshed on her card.

"Do you love Jesse?"

Her paintbrush slipped from her hand, landing square in the middle of the card. Talk about a splosh.

"Sorry," Saloma said. "I didn't mean to surprise you."

"It's okay." She picked up the brush, trying to figure out how to answer such a serious question. Now that she was in an actual relationship, she could see how absolutely naïve she'd been when she was searching for a husband. She thought she would find a guy, fall in love, and—*poof!*—marriage. But it was far more complicated than that. And she and Jesse had kept their relationship to themselves for the most part. Other than Shirley, only the Waglers and Saloma knew they were dating. "I don't know if I love him," she said. "How did you know you loved Clarence?"

Saloma blew on the canvas, somehow making the green paint look like a tiny tree. "I'm not sure how to explain it. I just know. It's like our hearts are locked together."

She'd never heard of that before. Was her heart locked with Jesse's? She had no idea. She liked him, that was for sure. A lot. And the more time they spent together the more chemistry they had, so much so there were a couple of times they cut their dates short, for both their sakes. She missed him when he wasn't around, and he made her feel cared for when he was. Above all, he kept his promise. He proved to her that she could trust him.

But did it all equate to love?

Saloma patted her on the arm. "You'll know when it happens."

But what if it happened to her . . . and not to him?

Around four o'clock, Charity packed up her watercolors and paintbrush, ready to head to Shirley's to make supper. She'd returned the French cookbook to the library three weeks ago and checked out a cookbook with Southern dishes instead. Tonight was cornbread, turnip greens, and fried shrimp. Jesse was eating his weekly supper with the Waglers or he would join them. Her mouth started to water.

"Would you mind teaching me how to knit?" Saloma asked as they walked outside, enveloped by the warm summer air. "I'd like to make a scarf for Clarence."

"Sure. I can teach you the garter stitch. It's simple and once you get the hang of it, the project works up quickly." She gave Saloma another hug. "Thanks for asking me to be an attendant. I'm honored."

"*Danki* for saying yes."

She waved goodbye to Saloma and headed to Shirley's. For the first time in her life she was going to be a wedding attendant. How exciting!

When she neared the house, she saw an unfamiliar car parked in the driveway. Shirley hadn't mentioned she was expecting company. Charity frowned. She only had enough shrimp for the two of them. She could make tuna casserole instead, if the company wanted to stay for supper, in keeping with the seafood theme. As she walked by the red car, she was unable to resist glancing inside. There was a black suitcase in the back seat.

Her heart started to thump. A suitcase meant an overnight visitor. Had her father finally decided to visit? She rushed to the door. The suitcase could belong to anyone, and usually a taxi driver didn't stop and visit. They just dropped the Amish and their luggage off at their destination. But Shirley knew a lot of the English in Marigold and many of them drove for the Amish. And if she'd been expecting an out-of-town guest, she would have definitely mentioned it to Charity.

Her thoughts were racing and she forced herself to settle down before she opened the door. Monroe was there to greet her but she barely acknowledged him when she glimpsed someone sitting on the couch. It wasn't her father.

It was Wendy.

.⚬৯৹⚬.

Shirley stroked the top of Monroe's head, staring straight at the picture window. Since Wendy's unannounced arrival two hours ago, she'd said little to her daughter, who had caught a flight to Ohio early this morning to convince her in person to go back to NYC.

"The food smells good," Wendy said.

Charity had arrived almost an hour ago, and after greeting Wendy, she wisely went straight to the kitchen to start preparing the meal. Tuna casserole, one of Shirley's favorites. Charity's cooking had improved tremendously since she first moved in, but Shirley was positive Wendy would find something to criticize. She was shocked her daughter had even said something decent about the delicious aromas coming from the kitchen.

Wendy's list of complaints so far included Monroe, who smelled and needed a bath. She wasn't wrong but Charity had planned to bathe him tomorrow morning anyway. The windows were dirty (they weren't), the floors needed washing (they didn't), and the throw pillows needed fluffing (so what?).

"Is this how you're going to be, Mom? Giving me the silent treatment like a child?"

"You are a child." She continued to stare at the window.

"I'm talking about you. You're being childish."

"Because you're being ridiculous."

Wendy sighed and got up from the couch. The low-heeled pumps of her sensible shoes clicked on the clean hardwood floor as she paced in front of her. "I didn't fly all the way out here to get into a fight with you. We've done enough of that over the phone. We need to discuss the logistics of you moving back home."

"There's nothing to discuss. My home is here, in Marigold."

Monroe ducked out from underneath her hand and hurried to the kitchen, as if he sensed something was going to erupt. *He's probably right.*

Her daughter faced her, hands on her slim hips. Her navy-blue power suit with a crisp, white shirt underneath sharpened her strong features. Her hair was cut short, not in a cute pixie or updated bob, but a stick-straight, blunt style. No makeup or jewelry. She was nearly forty years old, and as far as Shirley knew, she'd never dated anyone. Wendy was married to her career. And for the first time, that saddened her.

"*Mother*," she said, using the arch term whenever she was at her wits' end, and that had been often lately. "It's time for you to be reasonable. You have multiple health issues. You're far away from quality health care."

"That's not true. There are plenty of fine hospitals in this area. The Cleveland Clinic is a little more than two hours away, and Akron is even closer. So is Geauga." She sighed. "You already know this."

Wendy pressed her fingertips against her temples. "Living in a rinky-dink town and depending on an Amish girl for your care . . . that's not acceptable to me."

Shirley was about to tell her that she didn't care what was acceptable. That this was her life, and after spending so many years scrimping and saving with her husband to give Wendy the finest of everything they could, including the education that had helped make her such a successful lawyer, it was time Shirley lived life on her own terms, the way she and Alan had planned.

But she said none of those things. She looked at her daughter, the epitome of an overworked woman. Her skin was so pale, she doubted Wendy spent more than ten minutes a day outside. She had no hobbies to speak of or interests other than the law. Her heart broke. "Wendy."

"What?"

She rose from her chair, making sure her feet were steady and she had her balance, went to her daughter, and gave her a hug.

Wendy stiffened in her arms. "What's this for?"

Shirley pulled away and brushed the blunt-cut bangs from her daughter's face, taking in the lines of tension around her eyes and mouth. "Because you need it."

Wendy's lower lip trembled. "Thank you," she said in a thick voice.

"Sit down." Shirley guided her to the couch, and then roosted in her walker chair across from her. "Tell me what is really upsetting you."

She lifted her chin, but only for a millisecond. "They passed me over for partner again," she said, her shoulders sinking. "After all the work I've done for the firm. The hours I spent, the sacrifices I've made. I've worked there for over ten years. The last lawyer they made partner had only been there for three." She shook her head. "I don't know what I'm doing wrong."

"Oh, sweetheart." Shirley took her hand, noticing Wendy's cold fingers. "I'm so sorry. Don't they give you a performance review or something? Any information so you know what they're thinking?"

"I get a review every year. And every year it comes back the same. I'm a hard worker. I'm extremely knowledgeable about the law." She looked at her mother. "And I need to learn how to relax."

That much was true, but Shirley kept that to herself.

"This year my review was different. It said the same things, but they also pointed out I've seemed distracted. I nearly bungled my last case because of a technicality that I should have noticed a mile off. Fortunately my paralegal caught my mistake."

"What's distracting you?"

"To be honest, I think it's you. I've been so worried about you being so far way after your stroke."

Guilt latched on the back of her throat. "But I'm fine. You can see that now."

"I know." She sighed and looked around. "And I know I was picking on your house when I got here."

"Well, Monroe does need a bath. That's on Charity's list of things to do tomorrow."

"I saw the list on the refrigerator when I got a drink of water. She seems very organized."

"She is." Shirley frowned and squeezed Wendy's hand. "I didn't realize I was causing you this much stress."

"To be honest . . . It's not only you." Wendy didn't say anything for a moment. "I . . . I met someone. A great guy. At least I thought he was. We broke up a month ago." Her lip quivered again. "I know I'm a grown woman, but I just wanted my mom around for a little while. I miss you."

Her heart broke. "I miss you too, sweetheart."

"Excuse me." Charity entered the room carrying a foil-covered bowl. "Supper's ready whenever you want to eat. No hurry. It's a big casserole. It will be warm for a while. I'll give Monroe his bath now."

"You can eat with us first," Shirley said.

Charity glanced at Wendy. "That's all right. I'll let you two spend some time together."

"I'll make sure she eats," Wendy said.

Shirley looked at her. "Trust me, eating's not a problem. I could probably stand to lose five pounds." Charity's delicious cooking contributed to her weight gain but she wasn't telling Wendy that.

Charity took Monroe outside and she and Wendy sat down for supper. They were both quiet throughout the meal, the silence peppered with Charity's occasional squeals and laughter as she bathed Monroe in the backyard.

Shirley drank her iced tea as Wendy picked at her food. Her daughter had revealed more in the last hour than she had in many years. She didn't want Wendy's life to be impacted negatively by her decision to stay in Marigold. She had assumed Wendy wanted the convenience of having her close by, not that her daughter *needed* her close by.

It was time to rethink some things.

Twenty-One

"What do you call these?" Jesse picked up one of the small, deep-fried discs Charity had brought over to his house after work.

"Fried green tomatoes." She pushed a small jar of orangish sauce toward him with her fingers. "You dip them in spicy ranch dressing."

He poked a third of the crusted tomato into the dressing and took a bite. "*Sehr gut*," he said. "*Mamm* fries up tomatoes sometimes but they don't look, or taste, like this."

"Mm-hmm." She let her chin fall into the curve of her hand.

He looked at her across the table. This was the second night in a row she'd brought him a snack, and he could get used to it. She was a great cook. But right now she wasn't here with him, at least not mentally. "Charity?"

"*Ya?*" She stared at the platter of tomatoes in the center of the table. She'd made enough for lunch tomorrow.

"Got something on your mind?"

She nodded. "Wendy's still here."

"Oh." Shirley's daughter had been visiting the whole week.

"She still wants her to go back to New York City."

He didn't like the sound of that. "What do you think Shirley will do?"

"I don't know." She looked at the cell phone she'd brought with her

264

and had set on the table in case Shirley needed her. "I probably should *geh* back over there."

"But you just got here."

"I know." She looked at the doorway.

"You want to be there for her," he said.

"*Ya.*"

But there was another reason, and while he doubted she realized it, he knew. She wanted to prove to Wendy that she was taking good care of Shirley. Anyone could see that, but if her daughter was insistent on Shirley moving to New York, there was nothing Charity could do to change her mind. But she had to try, and he expected nothing less.

She picked up the phone. "I'll be back tomorrow night, though. Ready for some stuffed peppers and mashed potatoes?"

"You bet." He stood and went to her, intending to give her a kiss. She put her hand on his chest, stopping him. "Are our hearts locked together?"

He blinked. "Can you repeat that?"

"Our hearts." She wiggled her fingers against his shirt. "Are they locked together?"

His first inclination was to say he didn't know, since he had no idea what she was talking about. He paused and thought instead. Was this some sort of relationship code he'd never heard of?

"Saloma and Clarence are getting married." She dropped her hand to her side and looked up at him. "I asked Saloma how she knew she was in love with him, and she said their hearts were locked together."

"Ah." He smiled. Picked up her hand. He'd been thinking about their future a lot lately, and he couldn't have asked for a better opening to tell her how how he felt. "I—"

The phone buzzed in her other hand. "Hang on a minute."

Really?

She glanced at the screen and then at him, shock in her eyes. "It's *mei daed*."

Jesse groaned inwardly. The man had the worst timing. Despite wanting to tell her to let him leave a message, he let go of her hand. Her father's few and far between phone calls were important to her. "You should answer it."

She stared at the screen. "I'm not sure I want to," she whispered. "I don't think I can take him telling me again that he won't be coming here."

"How about I talk to him?" Jesse slipped the phone out of her hand, giving her a reassuring smile. He pressed the Answer button. "Hello?"

Silence from the other end. Then, "Who is this?"

He frowned at the sharp female voice. "Jesse Bontrager."

"Why are you answering Charity's phone?" she snapped. "Where is she?"

Charity moved closer to him, her face near the phone. "Elaine?"

"That's Charity, isn't it? I recognize her voice from a mile away. Why do you have her phone?"

Jesse grimaced. He didn't appreciate this woman's tone.

"Give it back to her. Now."

He was glad his parents had drilled good manners into him—not an easy task—or he would have said something he might regret. "May I ask who's calling?" he asked, forcing a noncommittal tone.

"I am Charity's mother."

·⚬✦⚬·

At the sound of Elaine's pinched voice, Charity took the phone from Jesse. The volume was up high on the speaker and she'd heard everything Elaine had said. That woman was not her mother. "Hello, Elaine."

"Who was that?"

Her stomach swirled, like it always did when she and her stepmother interacted. "Is *Daed* all right?"

"Of course he's all right. Why would you think he wasn't?"

"Because you never call me."

A second's pause. "I'm only calling to inform you that Delbert and I will be in Marigold tomorrow afternoon."

Daed was coming to visit? Yay! Oh wait, so was Elaine. *Phooey.*

"Now pay attention. The bus arrives at two p.m. We already have a taxi arranged to pick us up and drop us off at your address. We will visit for an hour, no longer than two, then the taxi will pick us back up and take us to the hotel in Barton. The next morning we will stop by, say goodbye, and catch the nine a.m. bus back to Ashtabula. Are you clear on our itinerary, or do I have to repeat it to you?"

"I'm clear." Her jaw started to ache. "You don't have to stay at a hotel."

"We will see you tomorrow afternoon. Goodbye, Charity." She hung up.

Charity stared at her phone.

"Wow," Jesse said. "She's, ah, something."

"You heard all that?"

"Hard not to." He gave her a half smile. "So . . . your parents are coming to visit."

Then it hit her. Her father would be here tomorrow. A tiny flame of anticipation sparked. Obviously Elaine had every minute of their short trip planned out, but at least she would see him. Wait. Did her stepmother know about the letters? And why had she called instead of *Daed*? *Probably to drive me* ab im kopp. She nodded, hardly believing it was finally happening.

"That's *gut, ya*?"

"*Ya*." She thought so, anyway. Somehow she'd figure out a way to

267

get her dad away from Elaine so they could talk. This wasn't the trip she hoped for, but she was grateful he was coming after all. "I have to tell Shirley and Wendy," she said, heading for the door.

"I'll walk you over," he said.

"*Nee.* Your tomatoes are growing cold."

"I don't mind."

But she was almost out the door, thinking about everything she had to do before they arrived. Clean the house, first off. Elaine would probably run her finger over the furniture the moment she arrived. She might bathe Monroe again. She didn't want to give her stepmother an excuse to insult him. Then she had to—

"Do you want me to be there when they arrive?"

She stopped. She was already in the field, Jesse behind her. She didn't realize she'd walked that far. She turned around, shaking her head. "You'll be working."

"Micah won't mind if I take a day off." He moved closer to her. "I want to be there for you."

Her heart warmed. How wonderful it would be to introduce Jesse to her father. Even better, Jesse wanted to meet him. Then reality hit. Elaine would badger him with so many insignificant questions and insulting comments he'd run for the hills, if there were any nearby. No, she didn't want to drag him into her dysfunctional family. Bad enough he'd gotten a taste of Elaine's personality. "*Nee.* This is something I have to do by myself."

Confusion flashed across his face. "Are you sure?"

"*Ya,*" she said, wishing she had a normal family like his. Then there wouldn't be a problem with him meeting them.

"Okay." He put his arms around her waist. "If you change your mind and want me to come over, call the shop. I'll be there faster than Monroe chasing a squirrel." He leaned toward her.

"Now *that* I'd like to see." She moved out of his arms.

When she was a few steps away, he said, "Charity?"

She looked at him, her mind halfway to Shirley's. "*Ya?*"

"Our hearts . . ."

"What about them?"

He paused, long enough that she started to lose patience. She had so much to do before tomorrow morning. "What about them?"

"Just . . . let me know if you need anything tomorrow."

"I will." She hurried across the field, eager to get started on her chores. Would *Daed* and Elaine be able to tell she'd changed? Hopefully her father would. She didn't care if Elaine did or not. But if he could see she was a better person, maybe their relationship would change too. Maybe he would want to spend time with her . . . at least for a little while.

·~∾∾~·

Jesse closed the door behind Charity and shook his head. He should have insisted on walking her home. He didn't mind eating cold food. Then he could have reminded her that she was the one who asked if their hearts were locked together—and he wanted to give her his answer.

There was no point in doing so now, though. Clearly she was consumed with her parents' impromptu visit, and he couldn't blame her. They hadn't talked about her father since his last phone call, and she never brought up more about her family or her life in Cherry Springs. He hadn't talked much about Birch Creek either. Eventually they would discuss their pasts. That was natural as people got to know each other better. There was plenty of time for that.

But there was also the real possibility of Shirley moving to her daughter's. Charity had that worry to deal with too. He just wished she'd let him help her.

He walked to the table and covered the green tomatoes with foil, screwed the lid back on the jar, and put them in his large ice cooler. Why was she insisting on shutting him out of her problems? Weren't couples supposed to share things in a relationship? That's what his family and all the Amish families he knew did. They shared their burdens.

Charity wasn't his family. *But I want her to be.* He'd been about to tell her that their hearts were locked together, now that he understood what that meant. But she'd been in such a hurry to go home, he knew it wasn't the right time, even though she'd posed the question.

He sat on his sofa, a new, thrilling sensation flowing over him. For once he wasn't bewildered, flummoxed, or mystified. As sure as the sunrise, and against all odds and his own obliviousness, he loved Charity. Right now he was sorely tempted to run across that field, take her in his arms, and tell her just how much.

But he wouldn't, not until after her parents' visit. He hoped it would go well for her and them. But once they went back to Cherry Springs and he had her to himself, he would ask Charity Raber to marry him.

.·ↄ৶৹.·

Charity paced in front of Shirley's house as she waited for her father and Elaine to arrive. Thankfully Wendy decided to take her mother shopping for the day. While Charity had told Shirley about *Mamm's* letters more than a month ago, she didn't want her and Wendy to be there if things went downhill with her parents, as they usually did. She had learned to temper her hope with reality.

She heard Monroe whining inside the house, wanting to come out and join her. Poor pup. She waited a few more minutes. When the taxi still hadn't arrived, she decided to let him out in the backyard and enjoy his freedom. She started for the door when a car turned into the driveway. Her nerves jounced. *He's finally here.*

As Charity hurried to greet them, Elaine got out of the front seat. Her stepmother looked the same as she always did—slim build, gray hair slicked back under her white kapp, and silver glasses, her posture upright. She wore a black bonnet over her *kapp,* as was the custom for married women when they traveled, and a navy-blue dress with black stockings and sensible black shoes. As soon as her foot hit the ground she was barking orders at the driver to get their luggage out of the trunk.

Then the back passenger door opened, and her father stepped out. Like Elaine, he was thin, and several inches taller than her. Even from here she could see the frayed band of the yellow hat he'd worn for years, and his graying beard hit the collar of his yellow short-sleeved shirt. He looked at her, his puffy eye bags as pronounced as ever. But he didn't move toward her.

She found her feet and walked to him, ignoring Monroe's pawing at the front door. "Hi."

He scrubbed the back of his neck. "Hi."

"Take this inside, Charity." Elaine handed her the small suitcase. "Delbert, pay the driver."

The pain in her jaw pulsed. Ordering her around already. Nothing had changed in that department. She took the suitcase and started for the house. Her parents followed and they walked inside. Monroe immediately pounced in greeting.

"Do something with this dog, Charity." Elaine stepped back, frowning as Monroe sniffed the hem of her dress.

She set the suitcase near the door. "That's how he says hi. He's really friendly—"

"Charity." She scowled.

"C'mon, Monroe."

After one more sniff of her father's boots, the dog followed her to the back patio door and bounded outside. In the kitchen Charity had already set up a tray with three mugs, a small plate of zucchini bread, and several tea bags since Elaine didn't drink coffee. She put the small kettle of hot water on the tray and carried it to the living room.

Elaine was sitting in Shirley's chair while her father was on the couch. She set the tray on the coffee table. "Would you like some tea?"

Both her parents looked surprised, and she realized this was the first time they'd witnessed her hospitality. "*Ya*," her father said. "That bread looks *gut* too."

"Made it fresh this morning." The tension at the back of her head loosened as she opened a tea bag and hung it in one of the cups. "Elaine, would you like some?"

"*Nee*." She folded her hands in her lap and took in the surroundings while Charity made the tea. "There's a TV here."

"*Ya*."

"Have you been watching it?" She gave Charity a disapproving look.

"Only the weather, and only on occasion." She wasn't going to let Elaine spoil this short visit. "Bishop Fry gave me permission."

"He sounds too permissive."

"Here, *Daed*." She handed him the tea, then held out the bread for him. He took a slice. Then she offered some to Elaine, who refused. She set the plate down, then sat on the opposite end of the couch.

Silence.

She fiddled with the hem of her apron, anxiety welling within her.

The only sound in the room was her father slurping the tea. This was going to be a long two hours.

"Delbert." Elaine's shrill voice cracked the stillness. "Tell Charity why we're here."

Her father nearly choked on his tea. He pulled out his handkerchief and wiped his mouth.

She looked at *Daed*, then back at Elaine's imperious expression. Then suddenly her stepmother's face softened. "Delbert," she repeated, her voice milder than Charity had ever heard it. "Tell her."

Elaine being kind—or at least less like a bossy hen—had never happened before. Not that Charity could remember, anyway. She wasn't sure if she should be worried or relieved. "Tell me what?"

He paled. Took another gulp of tea.

Elaine turned to her. "He wants to read the letters, Charity."

"*Nee*. I don't," he bellowed. "And I told you I don't want anything to do with them. I didn't even want to co—" He averted his gaze.

A chill sheathed Charity's heart. "You didn't want to come," she finished for him.

"That's not what I meant." But he wasn't looking at her.

"It's okay." She stood, her body going numb. "You don't have to stay." *Never let them see you cry.* She didn't have to worry about that now. There were no tears left to shed. "I'll call the taxi to pick you up."

"Charity, don't." Her father stood and walked over to her. "I didn't want to come here, that much is true. But it's not because of you. I . . . I can't read those letters. I didn't even know they existed until I found them in the closet." He rubbed his palm over his wrinkled forehead. "I don't even know how they got there."

"I put them there."

They both gaped at Elaine. Her chin quavered as she stared at her lap, her fingers clutched together. "I saw the box among Rose's things after she passed away." She drew in a breath and faced them. "I took it with us to Cherry Springs and hid it in the closet."

"Why?" Charity fisted her hands. "Why would you keep them from us?"

"I did what I thought was best . . . at the time."

Daed turned to her, stunned. "I don't understand."

"You never got over her, Delbert. Even after we married, she came first." She put her fist to her mouth, hesitating, then recomposed. "I knew when we were courting that you were still grieving. I also knew you needed a mother for Charity. I wasn't under any illusion that either of you loved me, but I hoped . . . I prayed that would change. I didn't want you to have any more reminders of her to grieve over."

Her father went to Alan's chair and sat down. "Why didn't you tell me this before?"

"Would it have done any *gut*?" Her voice caught. "Would it have changed how you felt about me?"

He hung his head.

Charity couldn't believe what she was hearing. All this time she thought Elaine hated her. "You wanted me to love you?"

"I wanted to be your *mother*. You were so young, had lost so much. I understood that pain. I'd lost *mei* husband. But you were so hard to reach. So . . ."

"*Seltsam*," she muttered.

Elaine nodded. "You were odd. You were feisty and your *gross-mammi* indulged you too much. You needed rules and boundaries, and you chafed against all of it."

"You were always criticizing me," she said.

Her chin lifted. "I was trying to parent you."

"Because I failed to," *Daed* uttered.

Charity looked at her father. He seemed to age a decade during their conversation, the bags under his eyes saggier than before. "I'm sorry," he said. "I should have been a better *vatter* to you, Charity. And I should have been the husband you needed, Elaine. I neglected both of you, and let *mei* pain cause so many problems." He turned to his wife. "Why did you change your mind about me reading them?"

Her hands were shaking, but the rest of her body was unflappable. "Years ago I realized I was wrong. I had *nee* right to keep them from you, but I was afraid to tell you what I did. When you found them, I knew I had to confess. I was going to—after you read them. I never considered you would refuse to read them, or send them to Charity." She dabbed her finger at the corner of her left eye. "I couldn't live with myself any longer, and that's why I arranged this trip. Please . . ." Her shoulders trembled. "Forgive me."

Her *daed* stood and knelt in front of Elaine. He took her into his arms as she sobbed.

Numb for a different reason, Charity quietly slipped to her room to allow them some privacy. She sank onto her bed. Elaine had wanted her? Mind-boggling. Even more stupendous was that she'd lied about the letters all those years. Was she lying about wanting to be a caring mother to Charity to save face now?

She just saw her emotionless stepmother break down into heart-wrenching sobs. *Never let them see you cry.* That was Elaine's motto. She had to be telling the truth.

Memories washed over her, although they were different from the usual ones. Elaine showing her how to bake bread, and Charity purposefully adding too much salt. That had been shortly after they moved to Cherry Springs. The time she had made Charity a dress, and Charity refused to wear it. There were other instances where she'd been insolent, most of them when she was still angry about *Grossmammi* dying and having to leave the only home she'd ever known. By the time she was a teenager, her adversarial relationship with Elaine was cemented. The more Charity rebelled, the tighter the boundaries became.

Her mouth dropped open. This whole time she'd blamed Elaine for everything . . . and took responsibility for nothing.

A knock sounded on her door. "Charity?"

Daed. She got up and opened the door. "Is she all right?"

He nodded, his eyes red rimmed, his old straw hat in his hand. "She wanted some time to collect herself. Can I come in?"

"*Ya.* Please do." She gestured for him to sit on the bed.

He eased down on the mattress. "Nice bed."

"It's comfy." She sat next to him, and neither of them spoke for a long time. She had no idea how to apologize to Elaine for being a brat, and she'd have to figure that out before their two hours were up. Her stepmother liked to stick to her schedules.

Daed sighed. "I've made a mess of things, *ya?*"

The feeling in her limbs and soul started to return. "We all have, *Daed.* Now we have to decide how to fix it."

He looked at her with a small smile. "You're the spitting image of her."

"*Mamm?*"

"*Ya.*" He stared at the closed door. "You even sound like her. I think that's why I've kept *mei* distance from you all these years. Every time I looked at you, heard your voice, she was there . . . and that always reminded me that she was gone. I realize now that wasn't fair to you."

"*Daed*—"

"Did your *grossmammi* ever tell you how me and your *mamm* met?" When she shook her head, he said, "We were six years old. Her family had moved to Indiana, and I saw her after church, and then on the first day of school." He smiled, a faraway look in his eyes. "I

276

was fascinated by her freckles and bright-red hair. I fell in love with her that day."

Her heart squeezed in her chest. "When did she fall in love with you?"

"Oh, it took her a lot longer to come around. Almost fourteen years. But when she finally agreed to *geh* out on a date, that was it for her too. We married two months later." His voice caught. "I thought we'd spend the rest of our lives together. With you, and any other *kinner* God saw fit to bless us with. Then she got cancer . . . and I fell apart."

"Oh, *Daed*." She started to reach for his hand but held back. He'd never been this open with her before and she didn't want to do something to make him retreat again.

"I made a lot of mistakes after she died. Do you remember Bishop Renno?"

"Vaguely."

"He kept wanting to pray with me about Leona's death and talk to me about grief. I couldn't do either, so I kept sending him away. That's when your *grossmammi* Rose moved in. But I didn't want to talk about Leona with her either, even though she'd lost her daughter. And I couldn't even look at you . . ." His head drooped. "The daughter I loved so much. It was too painful. And I was too selfish. When Rose died, Elaine stepped in and I married her, thinking she would give you the love and care I couldn't. I didn't realize I had to be a part of that process too." He lifted his head. "Can you forgive me?"

"Of course I can." She put her arms around him, and closed her eyes, the gray hairs of his beard tickling her cheek. "I love you, *Daed*. I always have."

"How can you? I haven't been any kind of a decent *vatter* to you."

She moved away and smiled. "Because you're *mei daed*."

"And you're *mei maedel*. All grown up now, and a lot different from when you left. Marigold has been *gut* for you. I can see you have more confidence, but there's also a softness that was missing."

That was a lot of insight after a short period of time. "How can you tell?"

"I kept *mei* distance when you were growing up, but I also paid attention. You know what I loved most about your *mamm*?"

"Freckles? Red hair?"

He shook his head. "Her spirit. Her joy. Her ability to make me laugh. She used to say the oddest things and keep me off-balance. You're exactly like her."

It sure sounded like it.

"Most of all, she was determined. More than anything she wanted to be a *gut frau* and a *gut mamm*. She was both." He smiled. "She fought until the very end, Charity. And she loved you, probably more than she loved me."

Charity didn't try to fight her tears as she stood and went to her dresser, opened the bottom drawer, and brought out the packet of letters. She had rewrapped them in the paper and tied them together with the same twine. She sat down next to him and set them on her lap. Neither of them said anything for a long time.

Then her father picked up the packet, his hands trembling.

"Ready to read them?" Charity asked gently, a lump forming in her throat.

He nodded, touching the rough string holding the treasured letters together. "It's past time I did."

.~∾⊷∾~.

That evening after work, Jesse was halfway to Shirley's when he saw Charity and Monroe hurrying toward him. The dog was on his leash, and he trotted by her side as she picked up her pace. More than once he almost asked Micah for the rest of the day off so he could check on her and make sure her meeting with her parents was going well. But he had to respect her decision to meet with them alone, and as soon as he closed up the shop, he headed for the field.

"Jesse!" She skidded to a halt in front of him. "I have so much to tell you!" She paused, excitement lighting up her eyes. "Were you going to Shirley's?"

He nodded. "I wanted to make sure you're okay."

"I'm more than okay." She took his hand and headed for his house, both he and Monroe in tow. "C'mon! I want to tell you everything."

He laughed and allowed himself to be partially dragged to his own home. Her day must have gone well. He'd prayed for exactly that last night, and this morning. Oh, and at lunch too. *Thank you, Lord.*

When they were seated on his couch, Monroe lay on the rug chewing a dog toy, and she breathlessly explained what had happened.

"*Daed* read the letters," she began. "It was hard for him, and I had to leave him alone in *mei* room for a while so he could gain his composure. But we had a talk before he read them, and he explained why he's been so distant all *mei* life." She took Jesse's hand. "He loves me, Jesse. I didn't think he did, but he was too caught up in grief over *Mamm.* He says I'm exactly like her. And you won't believe this—I couldn't believe it either—but Elaine apologized to me."

He listened as Charity took responsibility for her part in their broken relationship, and admitted she hadn't given Elaine a chance. "You won't believe what happened next."

"There's more?" He couldn't resist touching the tip of her cute nose.

"*Ya.* Wendy's moving in with Shirley." She grinned.

"Wait a minute." He let go of her hand. "You're happy about that?"

"I am, because Shirley is. After spending a week here, Wendy realized she needed to take a break from her job for a few months or so. She's taking a sabbatical and subletting her apartment." She frowned. "I'm not sure what that means, but the end result is that Wendy and Shirley will be together. Shirley is overjoyed."

Charity seemed to be too, which didn't make sense. "But you'll be out of a job."

"That's okay, because *Daed* and Elaine asked me to *geh* back to Cherry Springs with them."

He stilled. "They did?"

"I need to give them a second chance, Jesse, especially Elaine. I was so unfair to her. And *Daed* said he wants to do things together. Like go to the Akron zoo again. I've always wanted to *geh* to the zoo."

He knew that, and he'd planned to surprise her with a trip there next month. "That's . . . *gut*." And it was. This is what she'd always wanted, a reciprocal relationship with her father. If things worked out, she'd have a new one with her stepmother too.

"Wendy's flying out tomorrow to take care of things back in the city, and when she returns she'll move in."

This was all going so fast, his head was spinning. "And then?"

She met his gaze. "I'll *geh* home to Cherry Springs."

Home. A mix of dread and awareness consumed him. He'd never seen her as happy as she was right now, and not once had he heard her call Shirley's house her home. It was always "Shirley's" or "Shirley's house." He was realizing that even through all the time she'd spent wanting a husband—or believing she wanted one—her heart wasn't in Marigold any more than it had been in Birch Creek. Her heart had always been with her family. Or it had yearned to be.

That left one question unanswered. He swallowed the knot in his throat. "What about us?"

"Oh, I have that all figured out too." She knelt in front of him and took his hand, a confident grin on her face. "Jesse Bontrager . . . will you marry me?"

·⁓⧉⧉⁓·

Charity held her breath as she waited for Jesse's answer. Admittedly her asking him to marry her was a last-minute thought she'd come up with when he asked about their relationship, but it was perfect. All he had to do was say yes, and her life, which had been in a miserable, awkward shambles until recently, would finally be normal. At long last, she would finally be happy.

But he was staring at her, not saying a word. And the longer he remained silent, the more his expression shuttered, until it was completely unreadable.

"Jesse?" Her confidence wilted. She gulped. "Say something."

"You want to get married." A statement, not a question.

"*Ya*. We would get married in Birch Creek, of course, since your *familye* is there and they wouldn't have to travel. Then we can move to Cherry Springs. I can't wait for you to meet . . ." Come to think of it, other than her parents, there really wasn't anyone she was all that eager to introduce him to. But wouldn't Doris Zook be a smidge jealous when she saw Charity's handsome husband?

"Or you could stay here," he said flatly.

Well, that wasn't the answer she wanted. "I can't do that." She let go of his hand, which had gone limp in hers right after her proposal. "*Mei familye* needs me. Especially now." She'd explained all that to him already. Wasn't he listening?

"And *mei familye* is here. So is *mei* job."

"You wouldn't leave Marigold? Even for me?"

His throat bobbed. "You won't stay here? To be with me?"

She jumped up from the floor. "I thought you understood. *Mei daed needs* me. So does Elaine."

"They said that?"

"Not in those words." Why was he puncturing holes in her happiness? "But I know they do. They wouldn't want me back home with them if they didn't." She put her hands on her hips. "Do you need me, Jesse? Do you?"

He glanced away.

She waited for him to say something. To at least look at her. She even whistled for Monroe and clipped his leash on his collar. "Let's *geh*," she said, louder than necessary, as if Jesse had lost his hearing. But she didn't move, knowing that any minute he would do the sensible thing and tell her she was right and their hearts were locked and they would get married and move to Cherry Springs and her life would be perfect. Their life, she meant.

He didn't look at her. Didn't ask her to stay. Didn't . . . say . . . a . . . word.

Oh.

Pain tore at her. She had her answer. He didn't need her, which meant he didn't love her either. Their hearts weren't locked together after all. At this point, she was starting to think he didn't even want her. If he did, wouldn't he stop her from leaving?

She started for the front door. Monroe, the traitor, refused to move. He whimpered and stared at Jesse. "C'mon," she said, yanking harder on his leash than she ever had before. He resisted, and whined again.

Jesse didn't respond.

Finally Monroe got up, his tail sagging, and padded to the door. As soon as they were outside and her feet touched the grassy field, she ran. Monroe kept pace, and by the time she arrived at Shirley's she was gasping for air. She stayed in the front yard, out of sight from the front window, and let go of Monroe's leash. He dutifully sat on the front stoop.

Bending over, she pressed her hands against her chest, as if that would stop the pieces of her heart from crumbling. Her whole life she had suppressed her pain. She could do it now too. She just needed a few minutes. She needed to . . . breathe.

When she was able to stand, still gulping for air, she turned to see if Jesse had come to his senses and followed her.

Grass swayed in the field. No Jesse.

Her body went cold, every molecule of love she'd felt for him draining away. All the affectionate words they'd exchanged, all the kisses—and there were many—all the fun times they had together, and the not-so-fun ones . . . all of it was for nothing. She should have expected as much. She'd been wrong about him, time and time again. When would she ever learn?

She welcomed the dullness veiling her emotions. Jesse Bontrager didn't need her, and she certainly didn't need him. She would start her life over again in Cherry Springs, where she had belonged all along. Going forward, she wouldn't be so foolish. She would protect herself. That was the only way she could survive, because she was never, *ever* going through this agony again.

She collected Monroe, went inside, and shut the door. On Marigold, on Jesse Bontrager . . . and on her heart.

Twenty-Two

FOUR MONTHS LATER

Along with two other attendants, Charity helped Saloma get dressed for her wedding to Clarence. It was strange being in Marigold after all this time. She'd arrived here two days ago, and Wendy had picked her up at the bus station. The entire way to Shirley's she'd talked about how great it was to live in Amish Country, how fun Monroe was, and how she and her mother were closer than they'd ever been. She didn't mention moving back to New York City, and Charity wasn't surprised. According to the letters she had exchanged with Shirley, her former employer expected her daughter to stay with her permanently. "Or at least until she gets married, Lord willing," she'd written, more than once.

Charity was glad to see Wendy and Shirley so happy. She missed her former boss so much. And the Waglers, but she didn't keep in touch with them. Only Saloma, who had been confused and upset when she told her she wasn't coming back to Marigold except to be her bridesmaid.

"What about you and Jesse?" she'd asked, tears filling her eyes when it was time for Charity to board the bus to Ashtabula.

"It wasn't meant to be." And since then, neither her boss nor her friend mentioned him again.

Once she was back in Cherry Springs, it was easy to keep her mind busy with other things. After an adjustment period, she and her parents were growing closer. Her father was making an effort to spend time with her, and they often spent evenings working on jigsaw puzzles, something they both enjoyed. Elaine could still be critical, and her father still wasn't overly demonstrative. It hadn't been as easy as she thought it would be to fit into the community either, and she wasn't any more adept at making friends in Cherry Springs than she'd been in Birch Creek or Marigold. Which was why she treasured her friendship with Saloma and wouldn't miss being here for her wedding.

When Saloma was ready and the ceremony was about to start, she went to Charity, who was standing near Saloma's dresser. "I'm so glad you're here," she said. "I wouldn't want to get married without you."

She smiled, happy for her friend, ignoring the ache in her heart that appeared the moment she got off the bus. "Are you ready to be Mrs. Clarence Hostetler?"

"*Ya*. More than ready."

The ceremony was beautiful, and she wasn't the only one who saw the love in the couple's eyes as they looked at each other. Jesse wasn't in attendance, and she didn't see him at the reception. At least her friends had gotten their happy ending.

Would she ever have hers?

She hadn't given love a single thought since her return to Cherry Springs, but now that she was back in Marigold, and around Saloma and Clarence, she couldn't stop thinking about love . . . or about Jesse. *Phooey*. She missed him, and she couldn't deny that, as much as she tried. When she left Marigold, she thought the deadness inside would last forever. But he still had a part of her heart—okay, most of it—and she had to figure out how to let him go. He certainly had let her leave, without a single protest. And if she could just remember that, and hang on to the memory of how that pain had pierced her soul, she might be able to make it through her visit with her emotions unscathed.

During the reception, she sat at the corner table and looked at the place card, hand-painted in pale purple, blue, and green watercolors by Saloma. She couldn't imagine anyone painting a card as pretty as this one. Then she looked at the name in the center.

"*Charity Bontrager.*"

She peered at it. Yes, that's what it said. Bontrager. What in the world? She rose and took the card to Saloma, who was seated at the table, whispering something to Clarence. Should she say anything? Maybe she should let the mistake pass, surreal as it was. She was going to do just that when she locked eyes with Saloma. Her friend's gaze went to the card, and she blanched.

"Oh *nee.*" She hurried to her. "This is the wrong one. I made these cards in June, before you and Jesse broke up. I was so sure you were going to get married. It must have been mixed up in the pack. I'm so sorry."

Charity gave her a hug. She didn't want her to be upset on her wedding day over a silly error. "Don't worry about it." She smiled. Or at least she tried to.

Saloma thanked her and sat next to Clarence again.

Whew. Whatever expression Charity had on her face, Saloma bought it.

As the wedding supper was served, she put the card in her lap and looked at it again. *Charity Bontrager.* A sharp pain pricked her chest. She picked it up and folded it in half, then in fourths. As soon as she could, she'd throw it into the trash. And somehow, someway, she was going to enjoy the rest of this day. *Lord help me.*

·‿◦❧◦‿·

The day of Saloma and Clarence's wedding, Jesse worked in the buggy shop. Micah, Priscilla, and Emma Lynn had gone to the wedding and had offered to give him a ride to the Masts' since he'd been invited. Micah even pointed out that he always closed shop on wedding days, somewhat axing Jesse's excuse that someone needed to mind the place. He declined anyway. The last thing he wanted was to celebrate someone else's successful relationship after his disintegrated.

He was about to turn the Open sign to Closed when the phone rang. He could take one last call. Wasn't like he had anything better to do tonight, anyway. "Hello?"

"Hi, Jesse, it's Shirley. Monroe's feeling a little lonely, so I thought if you had some free time you could come over and play fetch with him. Wendy went to the movies and she won't be back until late tonight."

"Sure." He had all the free time in the world when he wasn't working. "I'll be there after I finish closing up."

"Splendid. I'll order some pizza too. It's been a while since we've talked."

Hmm. Jesse hung up the phone. He should have known right off the bat that Shirley was up to something. Monroe didn't get lonely, not with Shirley as his owner, and her daughter enjoyed taking him for walks in the evening. No, Monroe was a ruse.

He was tempted to call her back and tell her he was busy, but that would be a lie. And he did miss seeing Monroe. Now that Charity had moved away, he hadn't seen the dog other than when Wendy walked him by his house, although Shirley had given him an open invitation to stop by anytime, and this wasn't the first time she'd called and asked him to come over. He always refused. It was too painful. Even now it was painful, but he couldn't keep hiding from Shirley. Pizza sounded good too.

He locked up the shop and walked across the field, trying not to remember all the times he and Charity had strolled through the grass together. He'd have to stop thinking about her someday . . . right?

Shirley must have been right by the door because it opened as soon as he stepped on the stoop, and Monroe came bounding out. "Hey, *bu*," he said, as the dog wagged his tail, panted, ran around him, then leaned on his legs so hard Jesse almost lost his balance.

"He misses you," Shirley said, smiling at them both.

He patted Monroe's head. "Let's *geh* inside before you knock me over."

Shirley grinned as the dog dashed into the house. Jesse waited for her to turn around, and he followed her inside. He realized how much he'd missed seeing her too, and made a mental note to visit her more often. "The pizza will be here soon," she said, pointing to the couch. Monroe was sprawled across it. "Have a seat. Monroe, scoot."

Monroe shot up, and when Jesse sat down, the dog plopped into his lap. "Whoa, there." He leaned down and said in a low voice, "I missed you too."

"He was like that when Charity came back yesterday . . . oops."

Jesse lifted his head, catching Shirley's wide eyes and less than stellar acting chops. The woman didn't look the least bit contrite. "What do you mean *oops*?"

"We're not talking about her anymore, are we?"

So Charity had returned for the wedding. He figured she would, since Saloma mentioned she was an attendant, and Charity wasn't someone who would go back on her word. He'd kept his distance from most of the young people in the community since she'd left, other than occasionally hanging out with Clarence and Olin, but only because they insisted. He was single now, but he absolutely wasn't looking. Back to status quo.

Shirley sat back in her chair, her silver hair curling around her ears. She'd let it grow out since her last short haircut. "Catch me up on your life," she said. "I feel like we're almost strangers now."

This was embarrassing. How could he tell her that his life consisted of work, and anything outside of that was him trying to forget about Charity?

Over the past four months he'd run through the gamut of emotions—anger that she expected him to give up everything and move without even discussing it, irritation that he'd let his pride get in the way of working things out with her before she left, and heartache because he missed her. *Ach*, he missed her, every part of him aching when he thought about her. The only recourse he had from the pain was to remind himself that she left him when she didn't get what she wanted, without a second thought.

"Too many things to list?" Shirley broke into his thoughts, thankfully.

"*Ya*, that's it." But he could tell from her skeptical expression that she didn't believe him.

Monroe calmed down and rested his muzzle on Jesse's lap. He petted the dog, his heart squeezing, remembering how dejected Monroe had been when he wouldn't respond to Charity, as if the mutt understood *Dietsch*. The moment those two walked out of his house had been the hardest of his life.

"You need a haircut, Jesse."

His head jerked up. He couldn't argue. His mop was out of control. His curls always put up a fight on a good day, and lately he just shoved a hat on them and gave up. His house was a mess, too, and he hadn't been back to Birch Creek since Charity left. Nelson, Elam, and Malachi came over for a visit last month, and God bless them for not asking questions or making snide remarks—something he would have done when he was younger. Not only did he have a broken heart, but he also felt like a lowlife for ever finding humor in someone else's misery. Lesson learned, among many.

"I'll get it cut," he mumbled. He'd ask Priscilla if she wouldn't mind giving him a trim.

"Good. You also need something else."

"What's that?"

"A sharp kick in the pants."

He sulked. So this is what she was up to. A lecture. Probably about Charity. "You think you're the one to give it to me?"

She leaned forward. "If necessary. But I'm hoping a little pep talk will do the trick."

"Shirley . . ." He shook his head. "It won't. Trust me." He gently shoved Monroe off his lap and started to get up, his appetite gone.

"Where are you going?"

"Home. Thanks for inviting me over, but this wasn't a good idea." Being in her house, around her and Monroe, was too much to take right now.

She lifted her index finger. "Wait—"

The doorbell rang.

"Oh praise the Lord, that must be the pizza," Shirley said. "You can't go now. I can't eat a whole pizza by myself, and Wendy's gluten free." Her bottom lip extended out. "Help an old lady out, will you?"

Her bogus plea made him chuckle. She had a perfectly good refrigerator in her kitchen to keep the leftovers. "All right," he said, finally able to smile. The doorbell rang again. "I'll get it."

"Thanks for being such a dear."

When he opened the door, he froze. Charity stood there, a pizza box in her hands.

His heart skipped a beat. Then two, three, until he wondered if it had gone completely off track. He took in the beauty he'd missed so much, her freckles, red hair, and light-blue eyes stirring him inside.

She left you. Remember that.

His walls went up.

"Oh, Charity, you're back already," Shirley said, not sounding a bit surprised. "I thought you would return after supper."

"I left a little early." She shut the door, sidestepping Jesse and looking only at Shirley, as if he weren't even there. "I ran into the pizza delivery man in the driveway." She held up the box. "This is your supper?"

"It's mine and Jesse's, yes."

She still wouldn't look at him. Fine, she could be that way. He crossed his arms over his chest, keeping his gaze on Monroe.

"What do you want me to do with it?" she asked her.

Shirley's eyes bounced between the two of them. She sighed. "Put it on the coffee table." After Charity complied, she said, "Have a seat. Right there. On the sofa."

"What's all this about?" But she did what Shirley told her to do.

"Jesse, sit next to her."

Knowing by now it was useless to argue, he sat on the couch. Monroe parked himself in the middle between them.

Shirley got up and rolled her walker in front of them, then sat down in the seat. "I'm thoroughly disappointed in the two of you." She pointed at Jesse, then at Charity.

"What?" Charity said.

"Why?" Jesse asked, surprised at her anger.

"For being so foolish." She took off her glasses, her eyes narrowing. "I have never met two more stubborn people before in my life. Or more thickheaded."

Jesse's face burned as he glanced at Charity, who sat stock-still. Nothing like being a grown man and getting scolded like a schoolboy in front of the former love of his life.

Monroe yawned.

"You will both sit here and talk to each other, understand?" Shirley continued. "If you don't work things out, so be it. But you'll at least do the mature thing and have some closure." She put her glasses back on and stood.

"You're leaving?" Charity said.

"Of course." Shirley smiled, her cranky schoolteacher routine over. "This is between you two. I don't butt into other people's business."

If Jesse hadn't been so floored he would have burst out laughing.

She turned around and pushed the walker. Halfway out of the living room she snapped her fingers without turning around. "Monroe."

He jumped off the couch, gave Jesse one last look, and followed his master.

Jesse stared at the empty doorway. Then at his lap. What was his next step?

"Now what do we do?" Charity asked, echoing his thoughts.

He looked at her. Without Monroe between them and free of Shirley's orchestrations, his pulse started to gallop. A different ache appeared. He missed her. No, he *yearned* for her. Naturally he'd known that, but now that he was close to her again he fully realized how much.

Shirley was right. Both of them were at fault for how they left things. And there was only one thing left to do. "We talk."

·❧·

A shiver traveled down Charity's spine as she met Jesse's gaze. *Phooey.* One look at him and the chemistry was back, with a vengeance. If her toes didn't stop curling she'd get a cramp. And his hair was so long now, the curls so springy. If only she could touch one of them again.

Wait. *Stop!* What was she doing? Chemistry or not, she wasn't interested in talking to him, not now or any other time. "What if I don't want to?"

His thick eyebrows flattened into a line. "Too bad. I'm going to say *mei* piece."

"Fine." She crossed her arms. "Say what you have to."

"I love you."

She almost fell off the couch. *Now* he was telling her he loved her? With as much fanfare as Shirley giving a weather report? Still, the words made her skin tingle. *Stop it!* "You have a funny way of showing it," she mustered, putting as much bite as she could in her tone.

"I know." He stood, and for a minute she thought he was going to leave. Instead he sat right next to her, his eyes never leaving hers. "Do you love me?"

She didn't hesitate to answer. "*Ya.* I do."

The corner of his lips lifted. "You also have a *seltsam* way of showing it."

Charity scoffed. "I said funny, not weird."

"Same thing."

Ugh. She'd spent so much time and effort trying to forget how much she missed him, she'd forgotten how irritating he could be. "If you love me, why did you reject *mei* proposal?"

"Because you wanted me to give up everything and *geh* with you." He inched closer until there was hardly any space between them. "Don't you think that's a little selfish?"

Oh. Now that he put it that way, she had been selfish, and more than a little. But that also led her to another question. "If you loved me, wouldn't you want to?"

He rubbed his chin, a five o'clock shadow evident on his jaw. "I didn't have a chance to think at the time. You did spring the proposal on me, remember?"

"Um, yeah." How could she forget? She also didn't forget that she hadn't thought it through.

"You were so eager to leave . . ." He glanced down. "I seemed like an afterthought."

She drew in a sharp breath, shame consuming her. "You weren't—"

"Wasn't I?"

She blinked. He was right. All she'd thought about from the moment her parents had asked her to come back with them was how she finally felt needed. Wanted. What mattered were her feelings, not his. "I'm sorry," she whispered. "I didn't mean to treat you that way. But . . . you didn't need me."

"Oh, Charity." He closed the last bit of distance between them and cradled her face. "I do need you. So much. But my stupid pride wouldn't let me admit it. And because of that, I lost you."

Tears filled her eyes. *Never let them—*

"Oh shut up," she said.

His eyes widened and he dropped his hands. "Excuse me?"

"*Nee*, not you." She picked up his hands and put them back where they were, tenderly holding her face. "There. Forget I said anything. I was talking to Elaine anyway."

He grinned. "Oh, have I missed you."

"Enough to kiss me?" She laughed.

"Definitely." He drew her into his arms and let chemistry take over.

"You're supposed to be talking," Shirley yelled from the kitchen.

They jumped apart, but he held on to her hand as he cleared his throat. "She's quite the chaperone."

"*Ya*. Poor Wendy."

Jesse snickered. "Before she scolds us again, we should keep talking. Besides, I never did answer your question."

"I asked you a question?"

"*Ya*. Before you left. The one about our hearts being locked."

"Oh. That one."

"In case me telling you I love you, not to mention my kisses, haven't convinced you yet, maybe this will. Our hearts are locked, Charity. Forever. And I'll *geh* wherever you want to *geh*, even Cherry Springs. Fool that I am, I should have said that the first time you asked."

Over the last year she'd been wrong about Jesse on several occasions—and one more, if she counted the Diener Diner debacle. But this time she was absolutely, positively sure he not only needed her, and wanted her, but that he loved her. And she was so very grateful. "*Danki*," she said, unable to stop touching one of his curls, only to draw back her hand in case Shirley suddenly appeared. "I'm sorry I was so selfish. You got a glimpse of the old me. Only thinking about myself."

"We were both selfish." He took her hand.

"What if Shirley catches us?" she whispered.

"She only has herself to blame. Now, let's get down to business. Do you still want to get married?"

"*Ya*," she said, nodding emphatically.

His smile widened. "*Gut*. I also happen to want to get married. And we can live in Cherry Springs, or Marigold, or Timbuktu if you want."

"Where's Timbuktu?"

"I have *nee* idea. Read the word in a book somewhere. Did I mention how much I missed you?" He kissed her again.

She really, *really* appreciated Jesse Bontrager's love of affection.

"Well?" he said, breaking the kiss and sounding as breathless as she felt. "Will you marry me?"

"On one condition."

He touched his forehead to hers. "Anything."

"Can we live in Marigold?"

He pulled back, his eyes filled with shock. "You want to live here?"

"*Ya*. Mei parents can visit whenever they want, and we can visit them. But here is where my heart belongs. With you."

"I love you, Charity Raber."

She wound a curl over her finger, her heart full. It was her turn to kiss him, again and again . . . and Shirley didn't say a word.

Epilogue

Love never fails.

1 Corinthians 13:8

I have to say, I'm glad that's over."

Charity looked up as Jesse plopped down next to her on the love seat. Their love seat, now that they were married, a month after he'd proposed. No one seemed surprised that they had wanted to marry so soon, and Saloma, along with Charity's future mother-in-law and sisters-in-law, were eager to help her, and the big ceremony had gone off without a hitch. Elaine even pitched in. "Are you talking about the wedding, or the visiting?" she asked her new husband.

"Both." He drew her into his lap and started to hum.

Oh boy. She tried not to cringe. She loved her husband, and that meant listening to his humming and not giving a single critique—*ooh!* She winced.

"Sorry. Bad note."

They were all bad but she didn't care. She nestled her head on his shoulder.

He tilted her face to him. "It was fun to visit everyone in Birch Creek, Cherry Springs, and Marigold but . . ."

She shivered as he planted a kiss on her neck. His beard was already growing in, and the whiskers brushed against her skin. "But what?"

"I like having you all to myself."

Knock, knock.

Jesse leaned his forehead against hers and groaned. "Almost. I almost had you to myself."

She climbed out of his lap and went to the door. When she opened it, Micah was standing there holding Emma Lynn, while Priscilla carried the big basket Charity had replaced after the buggy accident. "Welcome home! We brought you a little after-wedding gift."

"Oh *gut*, I'm starving." Jesse got up to take the basket from Priscilla. "Please tell me you made fried chicken."

Micah laughed, making Emma Lynn giggle. "Open it up and see."

He lifted the lid and Charity peered inside. "Oh my stars." She lifted a puppy out of the basket. He was all black with a patch of white on his chest.

"A puppy?" Jesse looked at Micah.

"It was Priscilla's idea."

She scoffed. "Don't throw me under the bus." They both turned serious. "Two puppies were left on our doorstep. I have *nee* idea where they came from."

"So we kept one," Micah said.

"And you get the other. We put a small bag of puppy food in the basket."

Charity snuggled the pup under her neck. "Oh, it's adorable."

"She," Priscilla said. "We thought you could introduce her to Monroe. He needs a playmate."

"He'll meet our *bu* too." Micah nodded.

"What did you name him?" Jesse asked.

"River," Priscilla said, exchanging a glance with Micah.

"Okay, gotta *geh*." He cradled Emma Lynn in one beefy arm and opened the door with the other. "Enjoy."

"Bye!" Priscilla grinned as she closed the door behind them.

Charity looked up at Jesse, who was frowning at the closed door. "Hmm. That was kind of sneaky—"

The door opened again and Micah poked his head inside. "By the way, take Monday off."

"Micah!" Priscilla yelled from outside.

He gave Jesse a small salute, and disappeared.

"—not to mention intrusive," Jesse finished. But he was smiling now.

"Look how adorable she is." She handed him the puppy.

"They could have waited until tomorrow," he muttered. He cuddled her in his arms. "She is cute. Not as cute as you, but cute."

"Stop it." She blushed. "What should we name her?"

"You can decide. Uh-oh, she's wiggling. Let me take her out before she christens our floor." He held her up in the air as he rushed to the back door.

Charity followed him to the backyard. He set the puppy on the ground and talked to her softly while she sniffed the grass, neither of them seeming to mind the sharp winter wind, even though Jesse was only wearing a pullover. She drew her navy-blue sweater close around her and thought about all that had happened over the past year. Moving to Marigold. Meeting Jesse again. Making new friends that now included Wendy, who had grown close to Priscilla. Her relationship with her parents, which was better than it had ever been, even though they lived in separate towns. Shirley thought of her as another daughter, and Charity loved her like a second mother.

And then there was her stupid courtship plan. She still felt a bit embarrassed about that, even though Jesse told her not to. "You snagged me, after all," he'd said. Her plan hadn't worked out as expected. But God's plan did.

She smiled as her husband scooped up their new puppy off the ground and cradled her like a baby. *He'll be a* gut daed.

Jesse slipped his arm around her waist as the puppy closed her eyes. "Did you come up with something?"

She touched her tiny nose. "*Ya.* How about Brook? Her *bruder* is River, so it fits."

"I like it." He handed Brook to her. "I'll *geh* to the shop and find a box for her to sleep in until we can get her a proper dog bed."

A short time later, they were both sitting on the edge of their bed, gazing at the sleeping puppy. "Have you ever had one before?" Jesse asked.

"A puppy? *Nee.* I never had a dog until I lived with Shirley."

"Well, we Bontragers have had many animals over the years. And I'm here to tell you"—he met her eyes—"they're just like a *boppli.* So which one of us is taking her out in a few hours?"

"I'll do it."

"That's *mei maedel.*" He drew her into his lap again. "Now where were we before we were unceremoniously interrupted? Oh, that's right." He kissed her. "Can I have you to myself now?"

She played with the curls lying against his cheek. "For the rest of your life."

He grinned. "I wouldn't have it any other way."

Acknowledgments

*T*he Courtship Plan is filled with twists and turns, more than in any other book I've written. While it was lots of fun to write, it was also a challenge to keep everything straight. Thanks to my editors, Becky Monds and Karli Jackson, I was able to. They always give great insight and keep me on track! As always, my agent Natasha Kern is in my corner, cheering me on as I work. And a big thanks to you, Dear Reader. I hope you enjoyed Charity and Jesse's story—as I was writing it, I wanted to give Charity a big hug! Thank you so much for your support.

Discussion Questions

1. Shirley asked for Jesse's help when she found Charity's courtship plan. What would you have done if you had found the plan? What advice would you have given Charity?
2. Charity thought that leaving home and getting married was the only way to escape her unhappy home life. Has there ever been a time in your life when you've wanted to escape? How did you handle the situation?
3. What does the statement "everything happens in God's time" mean to you?
4. Jesse struggled with admitting he was wrong. What keeps us from taking responsibility for our actions when we make mistakes?
5. Charity thought finding a husband would "fix her." What did she really need?
6. After she abandons her courtship plan, Charity finds she's content in her circumstances. Do you find it difficult to live out this biblical teaching? Why or why not?
7. Charity has difficulty trusting others. Sometimes she even

distrusts herself. What advice would you give her to help her learn to trust?

8. Charity had put her faith in her plan instead of turning to God. Discuss a time when your faith was misplaced, and what made you change and turn to the Lord?

About the Author

With over a million copies sold, Kathleen Fuller is the *USA TODAY* bestselling author of several novels, including the Hearts of Middlefield novels, the Middlefield Family novels, the Amish of Birch Creek series, and the Amish Letters series, as well as a middle-grade Amish series, the Mysteries of Middlefield.

·⊷⟡⟿·

Visit her online at KathleenFuller.com
Instagram: @kf_booksandhooks
Facebook: @WriterKathleenFuller